JOY WILLIAMS is the author of four novels – the most recent, *The Quick and the Dead*, was a runner-up for the Pulitzer Prize in 2001 – and four collections of stories, including *99 Stories of God* (Tuskar Rock, 2017), as well as *Ill Nature*, a book of essays that was a finalist for the National Book Critics Circle Award. Among her many honours are the Rea Award for the Short Story and the Strauss Living Award from the American Academy of Arts and Letters. She lives in Tucson, Arizona, and Laramie, Wyoming.

Praise for Joy Williams

"*The Visiting Privilege* cements Williams' position not merely as one of the great writers of her generation, but as our pre-eminent bard of humanity's insignificance" *New York Times Magazine*

"One of the most fearless, abyss-embracing literary projects our literature has seen … ruthless, hilarious work that holds our human folly to the fire … you can't much pin Joy Williams down with any obvious dark masters. She is American and contemporary and strange, comfortable in the skin of domestic realism, even if that mode is a kind of misleading costume for a far more sinister project not often seen in American, or any, short fiction" Ben Marcus, *New York Times Book Review*

"Our first real opportunity to stand back from Williams' particular accomplishments and to see her genius whole … Her extravagantly original artistic gifts aside, Williams has never seemed more in accord with the needs of her time" Jonathan Dee, *Harper's*

"Williams is a flawless writer, and *The Visiting Privilege* is a perfect book … the rare collection that doesn't have a single story, even a single paragraph, that's less than brilliant" *NPR*

"Powerful, important, compassionate, and full of dark humor. This is a book that will be reread with admiration and love many times over" *Vanity Fair*

"This volume traces Joy Williams' journey to *sui generis* master. Her nearest cousin among American writers is Don DeLillo, but only because, as with him, nobody writes sentences like she does … Though she treats common states – parenthood, pet ownership, alcoholism – Williams eschews the realist story writer's bromide that in the ordinary we find the extraordinary, because there's nothing ordinary about her work" *New York*

"This career-spanning collection solidifies Ms Williams' position as a thorny American writer of this first rank. Dire circumstances blend with offbeat wit … plump with soul and real feeling" The Top Books of 2015, *New York Times*

"Joy Williams has long been one of America's greatest living writers, and *The Visiting Privilege* might have been the best book of the year. Her sentences are as sharp and precise as scalpel incisions, and her ability to turn the real beautifully surreal is second to none … If you have yet to read Williams' work, there is no better place to start than this book, which collects stories from across her decades of groundbreaking work alongside several new stories" *Electric Literature*

"Her books have been finalists for major prizes, including the National Book Award and the Pulitzer Prize, because she is a fiery writer with a sharp humor and a dark energy and her sentences are weird, funny, and full of emotion … Williams writes about the enormous, inconvenient human capacity for love, the weighty responsibility of it, the loneliness of it" *Bookforum*

"She has often been anointed as the literary heir to Anton Chekhov and Flannery O'Connor, but Williams' voice is most emphatically her own. Her stories begin realistically enough, then permute into hallucinatory fairy tales, as grim as anything in Grimm, but also grimly funny. Some adjective, as proprietary as 'Kafkaesque,' is needed for stories in which murder, addiction and madness are discussed so dispassionately. The pieces are chilling, but never smug about their own seriousness. There is a deep pleasure to be had, and a kind of explosive surprise, in Williams' unflinching alchemy" *Washington Post*

"Jolting, tonic, and valiant in their embrace of the ludicrous and the tragic, Williams' masterful stories belong in every fiction collection" *Booklist*

Also by Joy Williams

NOVELS

State of Grace

The Changeling

Breaking and Entering

The Quick and the Dead

STORIES

Taking Care

Escapes

Honored Guest

99 Stories of God

NONFICTION

Ill Nature

The Florida Keys: A History and Guide

The
Visiting
Privilege

The Visiting Privilege

Joy Williams

First published in this edition in 2017 by Serpent's Tail

First published in Great Britain in 2016 by Tuskar Rock Press,
an imprint of Profile Books Ltd
3 Holford Yard
Bevin Way
London
WC1X 9HD

First published in 2015 in the USA as a Borzoi Book by Alfred A. Knopf, New York

Copyright © 2015, 2017 by Joy Williams

Page 493 constitutes an extension of the copyright page.

1 3 5 7 9 10 8 6 4 2

Printed and bound in Great Britain by CPI Group (UK) Ltd, Croydon CR0 4YY

A CIP record for this book can be obtained from the British Library

ISBN 978 1 78125 747 0
eISBN 978 1 78283 307 9

Mixed Sources
Product group from well-managed
forests and other controlled sources
www.fsc.org Cert no. TT-COC-002227
© 1996 Forest Stewardship Council
FSC

For Rust,
and to Caitlin and Cole

Behold, I tell you a mystery; We shall not all sleep, but we shall all be changed,

In a moment, in the twinkling of an eye . . .

I CORINTHIANS 15:51–52

Contents

COLLECTED STORIES

Taking Care

JONES, THE PREACHER, HAS BEEN IN LOVE ALL HIS LIFE. HE IS baffled by this because as far as he can see, it has never helped anyone, even when they have acknowledged it, which is not often. Jones's love is much too apparent and arouses neglect. He is like an animal in a traveling show who, through some aberration, wears a vital organ outside the skin, awkward and unfortunate, something that shouldn't be seen, certainly something that shouldn't be watched working. Now he sits on a bed beside his wife in the self-care unit of a hospital fifteen miles from their home. She has been committed here for tests. She is so weak, so tired. There is something wrong with her blood. Her arms are covered with bruises where they have gone into the veins. Her hip, too, is blue and swollen where they have drawn out samples of bone marrow. All of this is frightening. The doctors are severe and wise, answering Jones's questions in a way that makes him feel hopelessly deaf. They have told him that there really is no such thing as a disease of the blood, for the blood is not a living tissue but a passive vehicle for the transportation of food, oxygen and waste. They have told him that abnormalities in the blood corpuscles, which his wife seems to have, must be regarded as symptoms of disease elsewhere in the body. They have shown him, upon request, slides and charts of normal and pathological blood cells that look to Jones like canapés. They speak (for he insists) of leukocytosis, myelocytes and megaloblasts. None of this takes into account the love he has for his wife! Jones sits beside her in this dim pleasant room, wearing a gray suit and his clerical collar, for when he leaves her he must visit other parishioners who are patients here. This part of the hospital is like a motel. Patients can wear their regular clothes. The rooms have desks, rugs and colorful bedspreads. How he wishes that they were traveling and staying overnight, this night, in a motel. A nurse comes in with a tiny paper cup full of pills.

There are three pills, or rather, capsules, and they are not for his wife but for her blood. The cup is the smallest of its type that Jones has ever seen. All perspective, all sense of time and scale seem abandoned in this hospital. For example, when Jones turns to kiss his wife's hair, he nicks the air instead.

JONES AND HIS WIFE HAVE ONE CHILD, A DAUGHTER, WHO, IN turn, has a single child, a girl born six months ago. Jones's daughter has fallen in with the stars and is using the heavens, as Jones would be the first to admit, more than he ever has. It has, however, brought her only grief and confusion. She has left her husband and brought the baby to Jones. She has also given him her dog. She is going to Mexico, where soon, in the mountains, she will have a nervous breakdown. Jones does not know this, but his daughter has seen it in the stars and is going out to meet it. Jones quickly agrees to care for both the baby and the dog, as this seems to be the only thing his daughter needs from him. The day of the baby's birth is secondary to the positions of the planets and the terms of houses, quadrants and gradients. Her symbol is a bareback rider. To Jones, this is a graceful thought. It signifies audacity. It also means luck. Jones slips some money in the pocket of his daughter's suitcase and drives her to the airport. The plane taxis down the runway and Jones waves, holding all their luck in his arms.

ONE AFTERNOON, JONES HAD COME HOME AND FOUND HIS WIFE sitting in the garden, weeping. She had been transplanting flowers, putting them in pots before the first frost came. There was dirt on her forehead and around her mouth. Her light clothes felt so heavy. Their weight made her body ache. Each breath was a stone she had to swallow. She cried and cried in the weak autumn sunshine. Jones could see the veins throbbing in her neck. "I'm dying," she said. "It's going to take me months to die." But after he had brought her inside, she insisted that she felt better and made them both a cup of tea while Jones potted the rest of the plants and carried them down cellar. She lay on the sofa and Jones sat beside her. They talked quietly with each other. Indeed, they were almost whispering, as though they were in a public place surrounded by strangers instead of in their own house with no one present but themselves. "Let's go for a ride," Jones said. His wife agreed.

Together they ride, through the towns, for miles and miles, even into the next state. She does not want to stop driving. They buy sandwiches and milk shakes and eat in the car. Jones drives. They have to buy more gasoline. His wife sits close to him, her eyes closed, her head tipped back against the seat. He can see the veins beating on in her neck. Somewhere there is a dreadful sound, almost audible. Jones presses her cold hand to his lips. He thinks of some madness, running out of control, deeply in the darkness of his wife. "Just don't make me go to the hospital," she pleads. Of course she will go there. The moment had already occurred.

Jones is writing to his daughter. He received a brief letter from her this morning, telling him where she could be reached. The foreign postmark was so large that it almost obliterated Jones's address. She did not mention either her mother or the baby, which makes Jones feel peculiar. His life seems as increate as his God's life, perhaps even imaginary. His daughter told him about the town in which she lives. She does not plan to stay there long. She wants to travel. She will find out exactly what she wants to do and then she will come home again. The town is poor but interesting and there are many Americans there her own age. There is a zoo right on the beach. Almost all the towns, no matter how small, have little zoos. There are primarily eagles and hawks in the cages. And what can Jones reply to that? He writes, *Everything is fine here. We are burning wood from the old apple tree in the fireplace and it smells wonderful. Is the baby up to date on her polio shots? Take care.* Jones uses this expression constantly, usually in totally unwarranted situations, as when he purchases pipe cleaners or drives through tollbooths. Distracted, Jones writes off the edge of the paper and onto the blotter. He must begin again. He will mail this on the way to the hospital. They have been taking X-rays for three days now but the pictures are cloudy. They cannot read them. His wife is now in a real sickbed with high metal sides. He sits with her while she eats her dinner. She asks him to take her good nightgown home and wash it with a bar of Ivory. They won't let her do anything now, not even wash out a few things. *You must take care.*

JONES IS DRIVING DOWN A COUNTRY ROAD. IT IS THE FIRST SNOW-fall of the season and he wants to show it to the baby, who rides beside him in a small cushioned car seat all her own. Her head is almost on a level with his and she looks earnestly at the landscape, sometimes smiling. They follow the road that winds tightly between fields and deep pinewoods. Everything is white and clean. It has been snowing all afternoon and is doing so still, but very very lightly. Fat snowflakes fall solitary against the windshield. Sometimes the baby reaches out for them. Sometimes she gives a brief kick and cry of joy. They have done their errands. Jones has bought milk and groceries and two yellow roses that are wrapped in tissue and newspaper in the trunk, in the cold. He must buy two on Saturday as the florist is closed on Sunday. He does not like to do this but there is no alternative. The roses do not keep well. Tonight he will give one to his wife. The other he will pack in sugar water and store in the refrigerator. He can only hope that the bud will remain tight until Sunday, when he brings it into the terrible heat of the hospital. The baby rocks against the straps of her small carrier. Her lips are pursed as she intently watches the fields, the trees. She is warmly dressed and wearing a knitted orange cap that is twenty-three years old, the age of her mother. Jones found it just the other day. It has faded almost to pink on one side. At one time, it must have been stored in the sun. Jones, driving, feels almost gay. The snow is so beautiful. Everything is white. Jones is an educated man. He has read Melville, who says that white is the colorless all-color of atheism from which we shrink. Jones does not believe this. He sees a holiness in snow, a promise. He hopes that his wife will know it is snowing even though she is separated from the window by a curtain. Jones sees something moving across the snow, a part of the snow itself, running. Although he is going slowly, he takes his foot completely off the accelerator. "Look, darling, a snowshoe rabbit." At the sound of his voice, the baby stretches open her mouth and narrows her eyes in soundless glee. The hare is splendid. So fast! It flows around invisible obstructions, something out of a kind dream. It flies across the ditch, its paws like paddles, faintly yellow, the color of raw wood. "Look, sweet," cries Jones, "how big he is!" But suddenly the hare is curved and falling, round as a ball, its feet and head tucked closely against its body. It strikes the road and skids upside down for several yards. The car passes around and avoids it. Jones brakes and stops, amazed. He opens the door and trots back to the animal. The baby twists about in her seat as well as she can and peers after him. It is as though the animal had never been alive at all. Its head is broken in several places. Jones bends to touch its fur, but straightens again without doing so. A man emerges from the woods, swinging a shotgun. He nods at Jones and picks the hare up by the ears. As he walks away, the hare's legs rub across the ground. There are small crystal stains on the snow. Jones returns to the car. He wants to apologize but does not know for what. His life has been devoted to apologetics. It is his profession. He is concerned with both justification and remorse. He has always acted rightly, but nothing has ever come of it. "Oh, sweet," he says to the baby. She smiles at him, exposing her tooth. At home that night, after the baby's supper, Jones reads a story to her. She is asleep, panting in her sleep, but Jones tells her the story of al-Boraq, the milk-white steed of Mohammed who could stride out of the sight of mankind with a single step.

JONES SORTS THROUGH A COLLECTION OF RECORDS, NONE OF which have been opened. They are still wrapped in cellophane. The jacket designs are subdued, epic. Names, instruments and orchestras are mentioned confidently. He would like to agree with their importance, for he knows that they have worth, but he is not familiar with the references. His daughter brought these records with her. They had been given to her by an older man, a professor she had been having an affair with. Naturally, this pains Jones. His daughter speaks about the men she has been involved with but no longer cares about. Where did these men come from? Where were they waiting and why have they gone? Jones remembers his daughter when she was a little girl, helping him rake leaves. For years, on April Fools' Day she would take tobacco out of his humidor and fill it with cornflakes. Jones is full of remorse and astonishment. When he saw his daughter only a few weeks ago, she was thin and nervous. She had plucked out almost all her eyebrows with her fingers from this nervousness. And her lashes. The lids of her eyes were swollen and white, like the bulbs of flowers. Her fingernails were crudely bitten, some bleeding below the quick. She was tough and remote, wanting only to go on a trip for which she had a ticket. What can he do? He seeks her in the face of the baby but she is not there. All is being both continued and resumed, but the dream is different. The dream cannot be revived. Jones breaks into one of the albums, blows the dust from the needle and plays a record. Outside it is dark. The parsonage is remote and the only buildings nearby are barns. The river cannot be seen. The music is Bruckner's *Te Deum*. Very nice. Dedicated to God. He plays the other side. A woman, Kathleen Ferrier, is singing in German. The music stuns him. *Kindertotenlieder*. He makes no attempt to seek the words' translation. The music is enough.

IN THE HOSPITAL, HIS WIFE WAITS TO BE TRANSLATED, NO LONGER a woman, the woman whom he loves, but a situation. Her blood moves as mysteriously as the constellations. She is under scrutiny and attack and she has abandoned Jones. She is a swimmer waiting to get on with the drowning. Jones is on the shore. In Mexico, his daughter walks along the beach with two men. She is acting out a play that has become her life. Jones is on the mountaintop. The baby cries and Jones takes her from the crib to change her. The dog paws the door. Jones lets him out. He settles down with the baby and listens to the record. The baby wiggles restlessly on his lap. Her eyes are a foal's eyes, navy blue. She has grown in a few weeks to expect everything from Jones. He props her on one edge of the couch and goes to her small toy box, where he keeps a bear, a few rattles and balls. He opens the door again and the dog immediately enters. His heavy coat is cold, fragrant with ice. He noses the baby and she squeals.

> *Oft denk' ich, sie sind nur ausgegangen*
> *Bald werden sie wieder nach Hause gelangen*

Jones selects a bright ball and pushes it gently in her direction.

·   ·   ·

IT IS SUNDAY MORNING AND JONES IS IN THE PULPIT. THE CHURCH
is very old, the adjacent cemetery even older. It has become a historic
landmark and no one has been buried there since World War I. There
is a new place, not far away, which the families now use. Plots are
marked not with stones but with small tablets, and immediately after
any burial, workmen roll grassed sod over the new graves so there is no
blemish on the grounds, not even for a little while. Present for today's
service are seventy-eight adults, eleven children and the junior choir.
Jones counts them as the offertory is received. The church rolls say
that there are 350 members but as far as Jones can see, everyone is here
today. This is the day he baptizes the baby. He has made arrangements
with one of the ladies to hold her and bring her up to the font at the
end of the first hymn. The baby looks charming in a lacy white dress.
Jones has combed her fine hair carefully, slicking it in a curl with water,
but now it has dried and sticks up awkwardly like the crest of a king-
fisher. Jones bought the dress in Mammoth Mart, an enormous store
that has a large metal elephant dressed in overalls dancing on the roof.
He feels foolish at buying it there but he had gone to several stores and
that is where he saw the prettiest dress. He blesses the baby with water
from the silver bowl. He says, *We are saved not because we are worthy. We
are saved because we are loved.* It is a brief ceremony. The baby, looking
curiously at Jones, is taken out to the nursery. Jones begins his sermon.
He can't remember when he wrote it, but here it is, typed, in front of
him. *There is nothing wrong in what one does but there is something wrong in
what one becomes.* He finds this questionable but goes on speaking. He
has been preaching for thirty-four years. He is gaunt with belief. But
his wife has a red cell count of only 2.3 million. It is not enough! She is
not getting enough oxygen! Jones is giving his sermon. Somewhere he
has lost what he was looking for. He must have known once, surely. The
congregation sways, like the wings of a ray in water. It is Sunday and
for patients it is a holiday. The doctors don't visit. There are no tests
or diagnoses. Jones would like to leave, to walk down the aisle and out
into the winter, where he would read his words into the ground. Why
can't he remember his life! He finishes, sits down, stands up to present

communion. Tiny cubes of bread rest in a slumped pyramid. They are offered and received. Jones takes his morsel, hacked earlier from a sliced enriched loaf with his own hand. It is so dry, almost wicked. The very thought now sickens him. He chews it over and over again, but it lies unconsumed like a muscle in his mouth.

JONES IS WAITING IN THE LOBBY FOR THE RESULTS OF HIS WIFE'S operation. Has there ever been a time before dread? He would be grateful even to have dread back, but it has been lost, for a long time, in rapid possibility, probability and fact. The baby sits on his knees and plays with his tie. She woke very early this morning for her orange juice and then gravely, immediately, spit it all up. She seems fine now, however, her fingers exploring Jones's tie. Whenever he looks at her, she gives him a dazzling smile. He has spent most of the day fiercely cleaning the house, changing the bedsheets and the pages of the many calendars that hang in the rooms, things he should have done a week ago. He has dusted and vacuumed and pressed all his shirts. He has laundered all the baby's clothes, soft small sacks and gowns and sleepers that froze in his hands the moment he stepped outside. And now he is waiting and watching his wristwatch. The tumor is precisely this size, they tell him, the size of his watch's face.

JONES HAS THE BABY ON HIS LAP AND IS FEEDING HER. THE EVE-ning meal is lengthy and complex. First he must give her vitamins, then, because she has a cold, a dropper of liquid aspirin. This is followed by a bottle of milk, eight ounces, and a portion of strained vegetables. He gives her a rest now so the food can settle. On his hip, she rides through the rooms of the huge house as Jones turns lights off and on. He comes back to the table and gives her a little more milk, a half jar of strained chicken and a few spoonfuls of dessert, usually cobbler, buckle or pudding. The baby enjoys all equally. She is good. She eats rapidly and neatly. Sometimes she grasps the spoon, turns it around and thrusts the wrong end into her mouth. Of course there is nothing that cannot be done incorrectly. Jones adores the baby. He sniffs her warm head. Her birth is a deep error, an abstraction. Born in wedlock but out of love. He puts her in the playpen and tends to the dog. He fills one dish with water and another with kibbled biscuit. The dog eats with great civility. He eats a little kibble and then takes some water, then kibble, then water. When the dog has finished, the dishes are as clean as though they'd been washed. Jones now thinks about his own dinner. He opens the refrigerator. The ladies of the church have brought brownies, venison, cheese and applesauce. There are turkey pies, pork chops, steak, haddock and sausage patties. A brilliant light exposes all this food. There is so much of it. It must be used. A crust has formed around the punctures in a can of Pet. There is a clear bag of chicken livers stapled shut. Jones stares unhappily at the beads of moisture on cartons and bottles, at the pearls of fat on the cold cooked stew. He sits down. The room is full of lamps and cords. He thinks of his wife, her breathing body deranged in tubes, and begins to shake. All objects here are perplexed by such grief.

Now it is almost Christmas and Jones is walking down by the river, around an abandoned house. The dog wades heavily through the snow, biting it. There are petals of ice on the tree limbs and when Jones lingers under them, the baby puts out her hand and her mouth starts working because she would like to have it, the ice, the branch, everything. His wife will be coming home in a few days, in time for Christmas. Jones has already put up the tree and brought the ornaments down from the attic. He will not trim it until she comes home. He wants very much to make a fine occasion out of opening the boxes of old decorations. The two of them have always enjoyed this greatly in the past. Jones will doubtlessly drop and smash a bauble, for he does this every year. He tramps through the snow with his small voyager. She dangles in a shoulder sling, her legs wedged around his hip. They regard the rotting house seriously. Once it was a doctor's home and offices but long before Jones's time, the doctor, who was highly respected, had been driven away because a town girl accused him of fathering her child. The story goes that all the doctor said was, "Is that so?" This incensed the town and the girl's parents, who insisted that he take the child as soon as it was born. He did and he cared for the child very meticulously even though his practice was ruined and no one had anything more to do with him. A year later the girl told the truth—that the actual father was a young college boy whom she was now going to marry. They wanted the child back, and the doctor willingly returned the infant to them. Of course this is an old, important story. Jones has always appreciated it, but now he is annoyed at the man's passivity. His wife's sickness has changed everything for Jones. He will continue to accept but he will no longer surrender. Surely things are different for Jones now.

FOR INSURANCE PURPOSES, JONES'S WIFE IS BROUGHT OUT TO the car in a wheelchair. She is thin and beautiful. Jones is grateful and confused. He has a mad wish to tip the orderly. Have so many years really passed? Is this not his wife, his love, fresh from giving birth? Isn't everything about to begin? In Mexico, his daughter wanders disinterestedly through a jewelry shop where she picks up a small silver egg. It opens on a hinge and inside are two figures, a bride and groom. Jones puts the baby in his wife's arms. At first the baby is alarmed because she cannot remember this person and she reaches for Jones, whimpering. But soon she is soothed by his wife's soft voice and falls asleep in her arms as they drive. Jones has readied everything carefully for his wife's homecoming. The house is clean and orderly. For days he has restricted himself to only one part of the house to ensure that his clutter will be minimal. Jones helps his wife up the steps to the door. Together they enter the shining rooms.

The Lover

THE GIRL IS TWENTY-FIVE. IT HAS NOT BEEN VERY LONG SINCE her divorce but she cannot remember the man who used to be her husband. He was probably nice. She will tell the child this, at any rate. Once he lost a fifty-dollar pair of sunglasses while surf casting off Gay Head and felt badly about it for days. He did like kidneys, that was one thing. He loved kidneys for weekend lunch. She would voyage through the supermarkets, her stomach sweetly sloped, her hair in a twist, searching for fresh kidneys for this young man, her husband. When he kissed her, his kisses, or so she imagined, would have the faint odor of urine. Understandably, she did not want to think about this. It hardly seemed that the same problem would arise again, that is, with another man. Nothing could possibly be gained from such an experience! The child cannot remember him, this man, this daddy, and she cannot remember him. He had been with her when she gave birth to the child. Not beside her, but close by, in the corridor. He had left his work and come to the hospital. As they wheeled her by, he said, "Now you are going to have to learn how to love something, you wicked woman." It is difficult for her to believe he said such a thing.

The girl does not sleep well and recently has acquired the habit of listening all night to the radio. It is an old, not very good radio and at night she can only get one station. From midnight until four she listens to *Action Line*. People call the station and make comments on the world and their community and they ask questions. Music is played and a brand of beef and beans is advertised. A woman calls up and says, "Could you tell me why the filling in my lemon meringue pie is runny?" These people have obscene materials in their mailboxes. They want to know where they can purchase small flags suitable for waving on Armed Forces Day. There is a man on the air who answers these questions right away. Another woman calls. She says, "Can you get us a report on the progress of the collection of Betty Crocker coupons for the lung machine?" The man can and does. He answers the woman's question. Astonishingly, he complies with her request. The girl thinks such a talent is bleak and wonderful. She thinks this man can help her.

The girl wants to be in love. Her face is thin with the thinness of a failed lover. It is so difficult! Love is concentration, she feels, but she can remember nothing. She tries to recollect two things a day. In the morning with her coffee, she tries to remember, and in the evening, with her first bourbon and water, she tries to remember as well. She has been trying to remember the birth of her child now for several days. Nothing returns to her. Life is so intrusive! Everyone was talking. There was too much conversation! The doctor was above her, waiting for the pains. "No, I still can't play tennis," the doctor said. "I haven't been able to play for two months. I have spurs on both heels and it's just about wrecked our marriage. Air-conditioning and concrete floors is what does it. Murder on your feet." A few minutes later, the nurse had said, "Isn't it wonderful to work with Teflon? I mean for those arterial repairs? I just love it." The girl wished that they would stop talking. She wished that they would turn the radio on instead and be still. The baby inside her was hard and glossy as an ear of corn. She wanted to say something witty or charming so that they would know she was fine and would stop talking. While she was thinking of something perfectly balanced and amusing to say, the baby was born. They fastened plastic identification bracelets around her wrist and the baby's wrist. Three days later, after they had come home, her husband sawed off the bracelets with a grapefruit knife. The girl had wanted to make it an occasion. She yelled, "I have a lovely pair of tiny silver scissors that belonged to my grandmother and you have used a grapefruit knife!" Her husband was flushed and nervous but he smiled at her as he always did. "You are insecure," she said tearfully. "You are insecure because you had mumps when you were eight." Their divorce was one year and two months away. "It was not mumps," he said carefully. "Once I broke my arm while swimming is all."

The girl becomes a lover to a man she met at a dinner party. He calls her up in the morning. He drives over to her apartment. He drives a white convertible that is all rusted out along the rocker panels. He asks her to go sailing. They drop the child off at a nursery school on the way to the pier. She is two years old now, almost three. Her hair is braided and pinned up under a big hat with mouse ears that she got on a visit to Disney World. She is wearing a striped jersey stuffed into striped shorts. She kisses the girl and she kisses the man and goes into the nursery carrying her lunch in a Wonder Bread bag. In the afternoon, when they return, the girl has difficulty recognizing the child. There are so many children, after all, standing in the rooms, all the same size, all small, quizzical creatures, holding pieces of wooden puzzles in their hands.

It is late at night and the girl is listening to the child sleep. The child lies in her varnished crib, clutching a bear. The bear has no tongue. Where there should be a small piece of red felt there is nothing. Apparently, the child had eaten it by accident. The crib sheet is in a design of tiny yellow circus animals. The girl enjoys looking at her child but cannot stand the sheet. There is so much going on in the crib, so many colors and patterns. It is so busy in there! The girl goes into the kitchen. On the counter, four palmetto bugs are exploring a pan of coffee cake. The girl goes back to her own bedroom and turns on the radio. There is a great deal of static. The Answer Man on *Action Line* sounds annoyed. An old gentleman is asking something but the transmission is terrible because the old man refuses to turn off his rock tumbler. He is polishing stones in his rock tumbler like all old men do and he refuses to turn it off while speaking. Finally, the Answer Man hangs up on him. "Good for you," the girl says. The Answer Man clears his throat and says in a singsong way, "The wine of this world has caused only satiety. Our homes suffer from female sadness, embarrassment and confusion. Absence, sterility, mourning, privation and separation abound throughout the land." The girl puts her arms around her knees and begins to rock back and forth on the bed. The child murmurs in sleep. More palmetto bugs skate across the Formica and into the cake. The girl can hear them. A woman's voice comes on the radio now. The girl is shocked. It seems to be her mother's voice. The girl leans toward the radio. There is a terrible weight on her chest. She can scarcely breathe. The voice says, "I put a little pan under the air conditioner outside my window and it catches the condensation from the machine and I use that water to water my ivy. I think anything like that makes one a better person."

The girl has made love to nine men at one time or another. It does not seem like many but at the same time it seems more than necessary. She does not know what to think about them. They were all nice. She thinks it is wonderful that a woman can make love to a man. When lovemaking, she feels she is behaving reasonably. She is well. The man often shares her bed now. He lies sleeping, on his stomach, his brown arm across her breasts. Sometimes, when the child is restless, the girl brings her into bed with them. The man shifts position, turns on his back. The child lies between them. The three lie, silent and rigid, earnestly conscious. On the radio, the Answer Man is conducting a quiz. He says, "The answer is: the time taken for the fall of the dashpot to clear the piston is four seconds, and what is the question? The answer is: when the end of the pin is five-sixteenths of an inch below the face of the block, and what is the question?"

She and the man travel all over the South in his white convertible. The girl brings dolls and sandals and sugar animals back to the child. Sometimes the child travels with them. She sits beside them, pretending to do something gruesome to her eyes. She pretends to dig out her eyes. The girl ignores this. The child is tanned and sturdy and affectionate although sometimes, when she is being kissed, she goes limp and even cold, as though she has suddenly, foolishly died. In the restaurants they stop at, the child is well behaved although she takes only butter and ice water. The girl and the man order carefully but do not eat much either. They move the food around on their plates. They take a bite now and then. In less than a month the man has spent many hundreds of dollars on food that they do not eat. *Action Line* says that an adult female consumes seven hundred pounds of dry food in a single year. The girl believes this of course but it has nothing to do with her. Sometimes, she greedily shares a bag of Fig Newtons with the child but she seldom eats with the man. Her stomach is hard, flat, empty. She feels hungry always, dangerous to herself, and in love. They leave large tips on the tables of restaurants and then they reenter the car. The seats are hot from the sun. The child sits on the girl's lap while they travel, while the leather cools. She seems to want nothing. She makes clucking, sympathetic sounds when she sees animals smashed flat on the side of the road. When the child is not with them, they travel with the man's friends.

The man has many friends whom he is devoted to. They are clever and well off; good-natured, generous people, confident in their pro-longed affairs. They have known one another for years. This is discomforting to the girl, who has known no one for years. The girl fears that each has loved the others at one time or another. These relationships are so complex, the girl cannot understand them! There is such flux, such constancy among them. They are so intimate and so calm. She tries to imagine their embraces. She feels that theirs differ from her own. One afternoon, just before dusk, the girl and man drive a short way into the Everglades. It is very dull. There is no scenery, no prospect. It is not a swamp at all. It is a river, only inches deep! Another couple rides in the back of the car. They have very dark tans and have pale yellow hair. They look almost like brother and sister. He is a lawyer and she is a lawyer. They are drinking gin and tonics, as are the girl and the man. The girl has not met these people before. The woman leans over the backseat and drops another ice cube from the cooler into the girl's drink. She says, "I hear that you have a little daughter." The girl nods. She feels funny, a little frightened. "The child is very *sortable*," the girl's lover says. He is driving the big car very fast and well but there seems to be a knocking in the engine. He wears a long-sleeved shirt buttoned at the wrists. His thick hair needs cutting. The girl loves to look at him. They drive, and on either side of them, across the slim canals or over the damp saw grass, speed airboats. The sound of them is deafening. The tourists aboard wear huge earmuffs. The man turns his head toward her for a moment. "I love you," she says. "Ditto," he says loudly, above the clatter of the airboats. "Double-ditto." She begins to giggle. Then she sobs. She has not cried for many months. Everyone is astounded. The man drives a few more miles and then pulls into a gas station. The girl feels desperate about this man. She would do the unspeakable for him, the unforgivable, anything. She is lost but not in him. She wants herself lost and never found, in him. "I'll do anything for you," she cries. "Take an aspirin," he says. "Put your head on my shoulder."

The girl is sleeping alone in her apartment. The man has gone on a business trip. He assures her he will come back. He'll always come back, he says. When the girl is alone she measures her drink out carefully. Carefully, she drinks twelve ounces of bourbon in two and a half hours. When she is not with the man, she resumes her habit of listening to the radio. Frequently, she hears only the replies of *Action Line*. "Yes," the Answer Man says, "in answer to your question, the difference between rising every morning at six or at eight in the course of forty years amounts to twenty-nine thousand two hundred and twenty hours or three years, two hundred twenty-one days and sixteen hours, which are equal to eight hours a day for ten years. So that rising at six will be the equivalent of adding ten years to your life." The girl feels, by the Answer Man's tone, that he is a little repulsed by this. She washes her whiskey glass out in the sink. Balloons are drifting around the kitchen. They float out of the kitchen and drift onto the balcony. They float down the hall and bump against the closed door of the child's room. Some of the balloons don't float but slump in the corners of the kitchen like mounds of jelly. These are filled with water. The girl buys many balloons and is always blowing them up for the child. They play a great deal with the balloons, breaking them over the stove or smashing the water-filled ones against the walls of the bathroom. The girl turns off the radio and falls asleep.

The girl touches her lover's face. She runs her fingers across the bones. "Of course I love you," he says. "I want us to have a life together." She is so restless. She moves her hand across his mouth. There is something she doesn't understand, something she doesn't know how to do. She makes them a drink. She asks for a piece of gum. He hands her a small crumpled stick, still in the wrapper. She is sure that it is not the real thing. The Answer Man has said that Lewis Carroll once invented a substitute for gum. She fears that is what this is. She doesn't want this! She swallows it without chewing. "Please," she says. "Please what?" the man replies, a bit impatiently.

Her former husband calls her up. It is autumn and the heat is unusually oppressive. He wants to see the child. He wants to take her away for a week to his lakeside house in the middle of the state. The girl agrees to this. He arrives at the apartment and picks up the child and nuzzles her. He is a little heavier than before. He makes a little more money. He has a different watch, wallet and key ring. "What are you doing these days?" the child's father asks. "I am in love," she says.

The man does not visit the girl for a week. She doesn't leave the apartment. She loses four pounds. She and the child make Jell-O and they eat it for days. The girl remembers that after the baby was born, the only food the hospital gave her was Jell-O. She thinks of all the water boiling in hospitals everywhere for new mothers' Jell-O. The girl sits on the floor and plays endlessly with the child. The child is bored. She dresses and undresses herself. She goes through everything in her small bureau drawer and tries everything on. The girl thinks about the man constantly but without much exactitude. She does not even have a photograph of him! She looks through old magazines. He must resemble someone! Sometimes, late at night, when she thinks he might come to her, she feels that the Answer Man arrives instead. He is like a moving light, never still. He has the high temperature and metabolism of a bird. On *Action Line*, someone is saying, "And I live by the airport, what is this that hits my house, that showers my roof on takeoff? We can hear it. What is this, I demand to know! My lawn is healthy, my television reception is fine but something is going on without my consent and I am not well, my wife's had a stroke and someone stole my stamp collection and took the orchids off my trees." The girl sips her bourbon and shakes her head. The greediness and wickedness of people, she thinks, their rudeness and lust. "Well," the Answer Man says, "each piece of earth is bad for something. Something is going to suffer eventually on it and the land itself is no longer safe. It's weakening. If you dig deep enough to dip your seed, beneath the crust you'll find an emptiness like the sky. No, nothing's compatible to living in the long run. Next caller, please." The girl goes to the telephone and dials hurriedly. It is very late. She whispers, not wanting to wake the child. There is static and humming. "I can't make you out," the Answer Man shouts. The girl says more firmly, "I want to know my hour." "Your hour came, dear," he says. "It went when you were sleeping. It came and saw you dreaming and it went back to where it was."

The girl's lover comes to the apartment. She throws herself into his arms. He looks wonderful. She would do anything for him! The child grabs the pocket of his jacket and swings on it with her full weight. "My friend," the child says to him. "Why yes," the man says with surprise. They drive the child to the nursery and then go out for a wonderful lunch. The girl begins to cry and spills the roll basket on the floor.

"What is it," he asks. "What's wrong?" He wearies of her, really. Her moods and palpitations. The girl's face is pale. Death is not so far, she thinks. It is easily arrived at. Love is further than death. She kisses him.

She cannot stop. She clings to him, trying to kiss him. "Be calm," he says.

The girl no longer sees the man. She doesn't know anything about him. She is a gaunt, passive girl, living alone with her child. "I love you," she says to the child. "Mommy loves me," the child murmurs, "and Daddy loves me and Grandma loves me and Granddaddy loves me and my friend loves me." The girl corrects her. "Mommy loves you," she says. The child is growing. In not too long the child will be grown. When is this happening! She wakes the child in the middle of the night. She gives her a glass of juice and together they listen to the radio. A woman is speaking on the radio. She says, "I hope you will not think me vulgar." "Not at all," the Answer Man replies. "He is never at a loss," the girl whispers to the child. The woman says, "My husband can only become excited if he feels that some part of his body is missing." "Yes," the Answer Man says. The girl shakes the sleepy child. "Listen to this," she says. "I want you to know about these things." The unknown woman's voice continues, dimly. "A finger or an eye or a leg. I have to pretend it's not there."

"Yes," the Answer Man says.

Summer

CONSTANCE AND BEN AND THEIR DAUGHTERS BY PREVIOUS marriages, Charlotte and Jill, were sharing a summerhouse for a month with their friend Steven. There were five weekends that August, and for each one of them Steven invited a different woman up—Tracy, India, Yvette, Aster and Bronwyn. The women made a great deal of fuss over Charlotte and Jill, who were both ten. They made the girls nachos and root-beer floats, and bought them latch-hook sets and took them out to the moors to identify flowers. They took them to the cemeteries, from which the children would return with rubbings which Constance found depressing—

> This beautiful bud to us was given
> To unfold here but bloom in heaven

or worse!

> Here lies Aimira Rawson
> Daughter Wife Mother
> She has done what she could

The children affixed the rubbings to the side of the refrigerator with magnets in the shape of broccoli.

The women would arrange the children's hair in various elaborate styles that Constance hated. They knew no taboos; they discussed everything with the children—love, death, Japanese whaling methods. Each woman had habits and theories and stories to tell, and each brought a house present and stayed seventy-two hours. They all spent so much time with the children because they could not spend it with Steven, who appeared after 5:00 p.m. only. Steven was writing a book that summer; he was, in his words, "writing an aesthetically complex response to hermetic currents in modern life." This took time.

Ben was recovering from a heart attack he had suffered in the spring. He and Constance had been in a restaurant, and he had had a heart attack. She remembered the look of absolute attentiveness that had crossed his face. At the time, she had thought he was looking at a beautiful woman behind her and on the other side of the room. The memory, which she recalled frequently, mortified her.

Things appeared different now to Constance: objects seemed to have more presence, people seemed more vivid, the sky seemed brighter. Her nightmares' messages were far less veiled. Constance was embarrassed at having these feelings, for it had been Ben's heart attack, after all, not hers. He had always accused her of taking things too personally.

Constance and Ben had been married for five years. Charlotte was Constance's child from her marriage with Paul, and Jill was Ben's from his marriage with Susan. The children weren't crazy about each other, but they got along. It was all right, really, with them. Here in the summerhouse they slept in the attic; in Constance's opinion, the nicest room in the house. It had two iron beds, white beaverboard walls and a small window, from which one could see three streets converging. Sometimes Constance would take a gin and tonic up to the attic and lie on one of the beds and watch people place their postcards in the mailbox at the intersection. Constance didn't send postcards herself. She really didn't want to get in touch with anybody but Ben, and Ben lived in the same house with her, as he had in whatever house they'd been in ever since they'd gotten married. She couldn't very well send a postcard to Ben.

August was hot and splendid for the most part, but those who stayed for the entire season claimed it was not as nice as July. The gardens were blown. Pedestrians irritably swatted bicyclists who used the sidewalks. There was more weeping in bars, and more jellyfish in the sea.

On the afternoon of the first Friday in August, Constance was in the attic room observing an elderly couple place their postcards in the mailbox with great deliberation. She watched a woman about her own age drop a card in the box and go off with a mean, satisfied look upon her face. She watched an older woman throw in at least a dozen cards with no emotion whatever.

Charlotte came upstairs and told her mother, "A person drowning imagines there's a ladder rising vertically from the water, and he tries to climb that ladder. Did you know that? If he would only imagine that the ladder was horizontal he wouldn't drown."

Charlotte left. Constance sat on a bed and looked around the room. On the bureau mirror were photographs of two little boys, Charlotte's and Jill's boyfriends. Their names were Zack and Pete. They were just little boys but there they were. It worried Constance that the children should already have boyfriends. Another photograph, which Constance had not seen before, showed a large dog in front of a potted evergreen. Constance was not acquainted with either him or his name. She got up and began picking up candy wrappers that were scattered around the room and putting them in her empty glass. She was thirty-seven years old. She thought of F. Scott Fitzgerald's line that American lives have no second act.

Constance went downstairs to the kitchen, where Tracy was drinking some champagne she had brought, and waiting for Steven to appear at five o'clock.

"I just love it here," Tracy said. "I love it, love it, love it."

Her eyes were shining. She was a good sport but she had rather bad skin. She was a vegetarian; for three days after she left, the children demanded bean curd. She was Steven's typist in the city, where she and her epileptic lab, Scooter, lived in the same apartment building as Jill's aunt.

"You were in my apartment a long, long time ago," Tracy told Jill, "when you were a little tiny girl, and you pulled Scooter's tail and he growled at you and you said, 'Stop that at once,' and he did."

"I can't remember that," Jill said.

"It's a small world," Tracy said, pouring herself more champagne. She sighed. "Scooter's getting along now."

Charlotte and Jill were sitting on either side of Tracy at the kitchen table, making lists of the names they wanted to call their children. Charlotte had Victoria, Grover and Christopher; Jill had Beatrice, Travis and Cone.

"Cone," Tracy asked. "How can you name a child Cone?"

Constance looked at the ornately lettered names. The future yawned ahead, filled with individuals, each expecting to be found.

"Do you swim," Constance asked Tracy.

"I do," Tracy said solemnly."I just gave the girls a few pointers about panic in the water."

"Would you like to go swimming," Constance asked.

"It's almost five," Tracy said. "Steven will be coming down any moment."

"Cone is both a nice shape *and* a nice name," Jill said.

"Would you like to go swimming?" Constance asked the girls.

"No thanks," they said.

Ben came in the kitchen door, chewing gum. Since his heart attack, he had given up smoking and chewed a great deal of gum. He was tanned and smiling, but he moved a little oddly, as though he were carrying something awkward. Constance got a little rush every time she saw Ben.

"Would you like to go swimming with me," Constance asked.

"Sure," Ben said.

They drove out to the beach and went swimming. On the bluff above the beach was the white silo of a loran station, which sent out signals that enabled navigators to determine their position by time displacement. Constance and Ben swam without touching or talking. Then they went home.

INDIA CAME THE NEXT WEEKEND. TRACY'S CHAMPAGNE BOTTLE held a browning mum. India was secretive and feminine. She brought two guests of her own, Fred and Miriam. They all lived on a farm in South Woodstock, Vermont, not far from the huge quartz testicle stones there. "There are megalithic erections all over our farm," India told Constance.

A terrible thing had happened to Fred—his wife had just died. A mole on her waist had turned blue and in six weeks she was dead.

Fred told Constance,"The last words she said to me were 'Life goes on long enough. Not too long, but long enough.'" Fred's eyes would glass up but he did not cry. He had brought a tape of Blind Willie Johnson singing "Dark Was the Night," which he frequently played.

On Saturday they had a large lunch of several dozen ears of fresh corn and a gallon of white wine. Miriam said to Constance, "It wasn't

Rose that died, it was Lu-Ellen. Doesn't Fred just wish it was Rose! Lu-Ellen was just a girl in the office he was crazy for."

Miriam whispered this so Fred would not hear. She had corn kernels in her teeth, but apart from that she was the very picture of an exasperated woman. Was she in love with Fred? Constance wondered. Or Steven? Actually, it was Edward she spoke to constantly on the phone. Miriam would say things to India like "Edward said he got in touch with Jimmy and everything's all right now."

After lunch, there was a long moment of silence while they all listened to the sound of Steven's typewriter. Steven did not eat lunch; he was bringing together the cosmic and the personal, the poetic and the expository. During working hours, he was fueled by grapefruit juice only.

India had brought four quarts of Vermont raspberries to Constance and Ben. The berries had been bruised a little during their passage across the sound. She had brought Steven a leather-bound book with thick creamy blank pages upon which to record his thoughts.

"Nothing gets past Steven, not a single thing," India said.

"I've never known a cooler intelligence," Miriam said.

"You know," Fred said, "Vermont really has somewhat of a problem. A lot of things that people think are ancient writings on stones are actually just marks left by plows, or the roots of trees. Some of these marks get translated anyway, even though they're not genuine."

India lowered her eyes and giggled.

Later, India and Miriam and Fred took Charlotte and Jill to the cliff that was considered the highest point on the island, and they all jumped off. This was one of the girls' favorite amusements. They loved jumping off the cliff and springing in long leaps down the rosy sand to the beach below, but they hated the climb back up.

The next day it rained. In the afternoon, the girls went with the houseguests to a movie, and Constance went up to their room. The rain had blown in the open window and an acrostic puzzle was sopping on the sill. Constance shut the window and mopped up. She sat on one of the beds and thought of two pet rabbits Charlotte and Jill had had the summer they were eight. Ben would throw his voice into the rabbits and have them speak of the verities in a pompous and irascible tone.

Constance had always thought it hilarious. Then the rabbits had died, and the children hadn't wanted another pair. Constance stared out the window. The rain pounded the dark street silver. There was no one out there.

That night, the house was quiet. Constance lay behind Ben on their bed and nuzzled his hair. "Talk to me," Constance said.

"William Gass said that lovers are alike as lightbulbs," Ben said.

"That's just alliteration," Constance said. "Talk to me some more." But Ben didn't say much more.

YVETTE ARRIVED. SHE HAD FINE FEATURES AND LARGE EYES, BUT she looked anxious, and her hair was always damp "from visions and insomnia" she told Constance. She entertained Charlotte and Jill by telling them the entire plot line from *General Hospital*. She read the palms of their grubby hands.

"Constitutionally, I am more or less doomed to suffer," Yvette said, pointing to deep lines running down from the ball of her own thumb. But she assured the girls that they would be happy, that they would each have three husbands and be happy with them all. The girls made another list. Jill had William, Daniel and Jean-Paul. Charlotte had Eric, Franklin and Duke.

Constance regarded the lists. She did not want to think of her little girls as wives in love.

"Do you think Yvette is beautiful," Constance asked Ben.

"I don't understand what she's talking about," Ben said.

"You don't have to understand what she's talking about to think she's beautiful," Constance said.

"I don't think she's beautiful," Ben said.

"She told me that Steven said that the meanings of her words were telepathic and cumulative."

"Let's go downtown and get some gum," Ben said.

The two of them walked down to Main Street. Hundreds of people thronged the small town. "Jerry!" a woman screamed from the doorway of a shop. "I need money!" There was slanted parking on the one-way street, the spaces filled with cars that were either extremely rusted or highly waxed and occupied by young men and women playing loud radios.

"What a lot of people," Constance said.

"There's a sphere of radio transmissions about thirty light-years thick expanding outward at the speed of light, informing every star it touches that the world is full of people," Ben said.

Constance stared at him. "I'll be glad when the summer's over," she said.

"I can't remember very many Augusts," Ben said. "I'm really going to remember my Augusts from now on."

Constance started to cry.

"I can't talk to you," Ben said. They were walking back home. A group of girls wearing monogrammed knapsacks pedaled past on bicycles.

"That's not talking," Constance said. "That's shorthand, just a miserable shorthand."

In the kitchen, Yvette was making the girls popcorn as she waited for Steven. She chattered away. The girls gazed at her raptly. Yvette said, "I love talking to strangers. As you grow older, you'll find that you enjoy talking to strangers far more than to your friends."

Late that night, Constance woke to hear music from Steven's tape deck in the next room. The night was very hot. Beyond the thin curtains was a fat bluish moon.

"That's the saddest piece of music I've ever heard," Constance said. "What is that music?"

Ben said, "It's pretty sad all right."

The children came into the room and shook Constance's shoulder. "Mummy," Jill said, "we can't sleep. Yvette told us that last year she tried to kill herself with a pair of scissors."

"Oh!" cried Constance, disgusted. She took the girls back to their room. They all sat on a bed and looked out the window at the moon.

"Yvette said that if the astronaut Gus Grissom hadn't died on the ground in the Apollo fire, he would probably have died on the moon of a heart attack," Charlotte told Constance. "Yvette said that Gus Grissom's arteries were clogged with fatty deposits, and that he carried within himself all the prerequisites for tragedy. Yvette said that if Gus

Grissom had had a heart attack on the moon, nobody in the whole world would be able to look up into the sky with the same awe and wonder as before."

Jill said, "Yvette said all things happen because they must happen."

"I'd like to sock Yvette in the teeth," Constance said.

CONSTANCE HAD NOT SEEN STEVEN FOR DAYS. SHE HAD ONLY heard the sound of his typewriter, and sometimes there was a glass in the sink that might have been his. Constance had an image in her mind of the Coke bottle caught in the venetian-blind cord tapping out incoherent messages at the end of *On the Beach*. She finally went up to his room and knocked on the door.

"Yo!" Steven yelled.

Constance was embarrassed about disturbing him, and slipped away without saying anything. She went upstairs to the girls' room and looked out the window. A man stood by the mailbox, scrutinizing the pickup hours posted on the front and shaking his head.

ASTER CAME WITH HER CHILD, NORA. NORA WAS PRECOCIOUS. She was eight, wore a bra, had red hair down to her kneecaps and knew the genuine and incomprehensible lyrics to most of the New Wave tunes. She sang in a rasping, wasted voice and shook her little body back and forth like a mop. Aster looked at Nora as she danced. It was an irritated look, such as a wife might give a husband. Constance thought of Paul. She had been so bored with Paul, but now she wondered what it had been, exactly, that was so boring. It was difficult to remember boring things. Paul had hated mayonnaise. The first thing he had told Constance's mother when they met was that he had owned twenty cars in his life, which was true.

"Do you ever think about Susan," Constance asked Ben.

"She's on television now," Ben said. "It's a Pepsi-Cola commercial but Susan is waving a piece of fried chicken."

"I've never seen that commercial," Constance said sincerely, wishing she had never asked about Susan.

Aster was an older woman. She seemed more impatient than the others for Steven to knock off and get on with it.

"He's making a miraculous synthesis up there, is he?" she said wryly. "Passion, time? Inside, outside?"

"Are you in love with Steven," Constance asked.

Aster shrugged.

Constance thought about this. Perhaps love was neither the goal nor the answer. Constance loved Ben and what good did that do him? He had just almost died from her absorption in him. Perhaps understanding was more important than Love, and perhaps the highest form of understanding was the understanding of oneself, one's motives and desires and capabilities. Constance thought about this but the idea didn't appeal to her much. She dismissed it.

Aster and Nora were highly skilled at a little parlor game in which vowels, numbers and first letters of names would be used by one person, in a dizzying polygamous travelogue, to clue the other as to whispered identities.

"I went," Aster would say, "to Switzerland with Tim for four days and then I went to Nome with Ernest."

"Mick Jagger!" Nora would yell.

Jill, glaring at Nora, whispered in Aster's ear.

"I went," Aster said, "to India with Ralph for a day before I met Ned."

"The Ayatollah Khomeini!" Nora screamed.

Charlotte and Jill looked at her, offended.

That evening, everyone went out except Constance, who stayed home with Nora.

"You know," Nora told her, "you shouldn't drink quinine. They won't let airline pilots drink quinine in their gin. It affects their judgment."

That afternoon, downtown with Aster, Nora had bought a lot of small candles. Now she placed them all around the house in little saucers and lit them. She and Constance turned off all the lights and walked from room to room enjoying the candles.

"Aren't they pretty!" Nora said. She had large white feet and wore a man's shirt as a nightie. "I think they're so pretty. I don't like electrical lighting. Electrical lighting just lights the whole place up at once. Everything looks so *dead*, do you know what I mean?"

Constance peered at Nora without answering. Nora said, "It's as though nothing can *happen* when it's all lit up like that. It's as though everything *is*."

Constance looked at the wavering pools of light cast by the little candles. She had never known a mystic before.

"I enjoy things best that I don't have to think about," Nora said. "I mean, I get awfully sick of using my brain, don't you? When you think of the world or of God, you don't think of this gigantic brain, do you?"

"Certainly not," Constance replied.

"Of course you don't," Nora said nicely.

The candles had different aromas. Finally, more or less in order, one after another, they went out. On Sunday, after Nora left with her mother, Constance missed her.

CONSTANCE WAS HAVING DIFFICULTY SLEEPING. SHE WOULD GO to bed far earlier than anyone else, sometimes right after supper, and lie there and not sleep. Once she slept for a little while and had a dream in which the cart she was wheeling through the aisles of the A & P was a crash cart, a complete mobile cardiopulmonary resuscitation unit, of the kind she had seen in the corridors of the intensive-care wing at the hospital. In the dream, she bit her nails as she pushed the cart down the endless aisles, agonizing over her selections. She reached for a box of Triscuits and placed it in the cart between a box of automatic rotating cuffs and a defibrillator. Constance woke up, her own heart pounding. She listened to Ben's quiet breathing for a moment; then she rolled out of bed, dressed and walked downtown. It was just before dawn and the streets were cool and quiet and empty, but someone, during the night, had pulled all the flowers out of the window boxes in front of the shops. Clumps of earth and broken petals made a ragged trail before her. The wreckage rounded a corner. Constance wished Ben were with her. They could just walk along, they wouldn't have to say anything.

THE WEEKEND THAT BRONWYN ARRIVED WAS EXTREMELY FOGGY. Bronwyn was from the South. She was unsmiling and honest, a Baptist who had just left her husband for good. She had been in love with Steven since she was thirteen years old.

"My parents are Baptists," Constance told her.

Fog slid through the screens. A voice from the street said, "I can't believe she served bluefish again!"

Bronwyn had little calling cards that showed Jesus knocking on the door of your heart. Jesus wore white robes and he had a neatly trimmed beard. He was rapping thoughtfully at the heavy wooden doors of a snug little vine-covered bungalow.

"I remember that picture!" Constance said. "When I was little, that picture just seemed to be everywhere."

"Have one," Bronwyn said.

The heart did not appear mean, it simply seemed closed. Constance wondered how long the artist had intended Jesus to have been standing there.

Bronwyn took Charlotte and Jill out to collect money to save marine mammals. They stood on the street and collected over thirty dollars in a Brim coffee can.

"Our salvation lies in learning to communicate with alien intelligences," Bronwyn said.

Constance wrote a check.

"Whales and dolphins are highly articulate," Bronwyn told Constance. "They know fidelity, play and sorrow."

Constance wrote another check, made herself a gin and tonic and went upstairs. That night, from Steven's room, she heard murmurs and moans in repetitive sequence.

The following day, Bronwyn asked, "Have you enjoyed sharing a house with Steven?"

"I haven't seen much of him," Constance said, "actually, at all."

"Summer can be a difficult time," Bronwyn said.

ON THE LAST DAY OF AUGUST, BEN RENTED A BRIGHT RED JEEP with neither top nor sides. Ben and Constance and Charlotte and Jill bounced around in it all morning, and at noon they drove on the beach to the very tip of the island, where the lighthouse was. Approaching the lighthouse, Constance was filled with an odd excitement. She wanted to climb to the top. The steel door had been chained shut, but about four feet up from the base was a large hole knocked through the cement, and inside, beer cans, a considerable amount of broken glass and a lacy black wrought-iron staircase winding upward could be seen. Charlotte and Jill did not go in because they hadn't brought their shoes, but Constance climbed through the hole and went up the staircase. There was a wonderful expectancy to the tight climb upward through the whitewashed gyre. She was a little breathless when she reached the top. Powering the light, in a maze of cables and connectors, were eighteen black, heavy-duty truck batteries. For a moment, Constance's disappointment concealed her surprise. She saw the Atlantic fanning out without a speck on it, and her little family on the beach below, sitting on a striped blanket. Constance inched out onto the catwalk encircling the light. "I love you!" she shouted. Ben looked up and waved. She went back inside and began her descent. She did not know, exactly, what it was she had expected, but it had certainly not been eighteen black, heavy-duty truck batteries.

IN BED THAT NIGHT, CONSTANCE DREAMED OF PEOPLE LAUGHING. She opened her eyes. "Ben," she whispered.

"Hi." He was wide awake.

"I dreamed of laughing," Constance said. "I want to laugh."

"We'll laugh tomorrow," Ben said. He turned her away from him and held her. She felt his mouth smiling against her ear.

Preparation for a Collie

THERE IS JANE AND THERE IS JACKSON AND THERE IS DAVID. There is the dog.

David is burying a bird. He has a box that once held tea and he is digging a hole beneath the kitchen window. He mutters and cries a little. He is spending Sunday morning doing this. He is five.

Jackson comes outside and says, "That hole is far too big."

Jackson is going to be an architect. He goes to school all day and he works as a bartender at night. He sees Jane and David on weekends. He is too tired in the morning to have breakfast with them. Jane leaves before nine. She sells ornaments in a Christmas shop, and Jackson is gone by the time she returns in the afternoon. David is in kindergarten all day. Jackson tends bar until long after midnight. Sometimes he steals a bottle of blended whiskey and brings it home with him. He wears saddle shoes and a wedding ring. His clothes are poor but he has well-shaped hands and nails. Jane is usually asleep when Jackson gets in bed beside her. He goes at her without turning on the light.

"I don't want to wake you up," he says.

Jackson is from Virginia. Once, a photograph of him in period dress appeared in *The New Yorker* for a VISIT WILLIAMSBURG advertisement. They have saved the magazine. It is in their bookcase with their books.

Jackson packs his hair down hard with water when he leaves the house. The house is always a mess. It is not swept. There are crumbs and broken toys beneath all the furniture. There are cereal bowls everywhere, crusty with soured milk. There is hair everywhere. The dog sheds. It is a collie, three years older than David. It is Jane's dog. She brought him with her into this marriage, along with her Mexican bowls and something blue.

Jane could be pretty but she doesn't know how to arrange her hair. She has violet eyes. And she prefers that color. She has three pots of violets in the living room on Jackson's old chess table. They flourish. This is sometimes mentioned by Jackson. Nothing else flourishes as well here.

Whenever Jackson becomes really angry with Jane, he takes off his glasses and breaks them in front of her. They seem always to be the most valuable thing at hand. And they are replaceable, although the act causes considerable inconvenience.

Jane and David eat supper together every night. Jane eats like a child. Jane is closest to David in this. They are children together, eating junk. Jane has never prepared a meal in this house. She is as though in a seasonal hotel. This is not her life; she does not have to be this. She refuses to become familiar with this house, with this town. She is a guest here. She has no memories. She is waiting. She does not have to make anything of these moments. She is a stranger here.

She is waiting for Jackson to become an architect. His theories of building are realistic but his quest is oneiric, he tells her. He sometimes talks about "sites."

They are getting rid of the dog. Jackson has been putting ads in the paper. He is enjoying this. He has been advertising for weeks. The dog is free and many people call. Jackson refuses all callers. For three weekends now, he and Jane have talked about nothing except the dog. They will simplify their life and they cannot stop thinking about it, this dog, this act, this choice that lies before them.

The dog has crammed itself behind the pipes beneath the kitchen sink. David squats before him, blowing gently on his nose. The dog thumps his tail on the linoleum.

"We're getting rid of you, you know," David says.

It is Saturday evening and someone has stopped at the house to see the dog.

"Is he a full-blooded collie," the person asks. "Does he have papers?"

"He doesn't say." Jackson smiles.

After all these years, six, Jane is a little confused by Jackson. She sees this as her love for him. What would her love for him be if it were not this? In turn, she worries about her love for David. Jane does not think David is nice-looking. He has many worries, it seems. He weeps, he has rashes, he throws up. He has pale hair, pale skin. She does not know how she can go through all these days, each day, embarrassed for her son.

Jane and Jackson lie in bed.

"I love Sundays," Jane says.

Jackson wears a T-shirt. Jane slips her hand beneath it and strokes his chest. She is waiting. She sometimes fears that she is waiting for the waiting to end, fears that she seeks and requires only that recognition and none other. Jackson holds her without opening his eyes.

It is Sunday. Jane pours milk into a pancake mix.

Jackson says, "David, I want you to stop crying so much and I want you to stop pretending to bake in Mommy's cupcake tins." Jackson is angry, but then he laughs. After a moment, David laughs too.

That afternoon, a woman and a little girl come to the house about the dog.

"I told you on the phone, I'd give you some fresh eggs for him," the woman says, thrusting a child's sand bucket at Jane. "Even if you decide not to give the dog to us, the eggs are still yours." She pauses at Jane's hesitation. "Adams," the woman says. "We're here for the ad."

Jackson waves her to a chair and says, "Mrs. Adams, we seek no personal aggrandizement from our pet. Our only desire is that he be given a good home. A great many people have contacted us and now we must make a difficult decision. Where will he inspire the most contentment and where will he find canine fulfillment?"

Jane brings the dog into the room.

"There he is, Dorothy!" Mrs. Adams exclaims to the little girl. "Go over and pet him or something."

"It's a nice dog," Dorothy says. "I like him fine."

"She needs a dog," Mrs. Adams says. "Coming over here, she said, 'Mother, we could bring him home today in the back of the car. I could play with him tonight.' Oh, she sure would like to have this dog. She lost her dog last week. Kicked to death by one of the horses. Must have broken every bone in his fluffy little body."

"What a pity!" Jackson exclaims.

"And then there was the accident," Mrs. Adams goes on. "Show them your arm, Dorothy. Why, I tell you, it almost came right off. Didn't it, darling?"

The girl rolls up the sleeve of her shirt. Her arm is a mess, complexly rearranged, a yellow matted wrinkle of scar tissue.

"Actually," Jackson says, "I'm afraid my wife has promised the dog to someone else."

After they leave, Jackson says, "These farm people crack me up."

The dog walks slowly back to the kitchen, swinging his high foolish hips. David wanders back to the breakfast table and picks up something, some piece of food. He chews it for a moment and then spits it out. He kneels down and spits it into the hot-air register.

"David," Jane says. She looks at his face. It is calm and round, a child's face.

It is evening. On television, a man dressed as a chef, holding six pies, falls down a flight of stairs. The incident is teaching numbers.

SIX, the screen screams.

"Six," David says.

Jane and Jackson are drinking whiskey and apple juice. Jane is wondering what they did for David's last birthday, when he was five. Did they have a little party?

"What did we do on your last birthday, David?" Jane asks.

"We gave him pudding," Jackson says.

"That's not true," Jane says, worried. She looks at David's face.

SIX TOCKING CLOCKS, the television sings.

"Six," David says.

Jane's drink is gone. "May I have another drink?" she asks politely, and then gets up to make it for herself. She knocks the ice cubes out of the tray and smashes them up with a wooden spoon. On the side of the icebox, held in place by magnets, is a fragment from a poem, torn from a book. It says, *The dead must fall silent when one sits down to a meal.* She wonders why she put it there. Perhaps it was to help her diet.

Jane returns to the couch and David sits beside her. He says, "You say 'no' and I say 'yes.'"

"No," Jane says.

"Yes," David yells, delighted.

"No."

"Yes."

"No."

"Yes."

"Yes."

David stops, confused. Then he giggles. They play this game all the time. Jane is willing to play it with him. It is easy enough to play. Jackson and Jane send David to a fine kindergarten and are always buying him chalk and crayons. Nevertheless, Jane feels unsure with David. It is hard to know how to act when one is with the child, alone.

The dog sits by a dented aluminum dish in the bright kitchen. Jackson is opening a can of dog food.

"Jesus," he says, "what a sad, stupid dog."

The dog eats his food stolidly, gagging a little. The fur beneath his tail hangs in dirty beards.

"Jesus," Jackson says.

Jane goes to the cupboard, wobbling slightly. "I'm going to kill that dog," she says. "I'm sick of this." She puts down her drink and takes a can of Drāno out of the cupboard. She takes a pound of hamburger that is thawing in a bowl and rubs off the soft pieces onto a plate. She pours Drāno over it and mixes it in.

"It is my dog," Jane says, "and I'm going to get rid of him for you."

David starts to cry.

"Why don't you have another drink?" Jackson says to Jane. "You're so vivacious when you drink."

David is sobbing. His hands flap in the air. Jackson picks him up. "Stop it," he says. David wraps his legs around his father's chest and pees all over him. Their clothing turns dark as though, together, they'd been shot. "Goddamn it," Jackson shouts. He throws his arms out. He stops holding the child but his son clings to him, then drops to the floor.

Jane grabs Jackson's shoulder. She whispers in his ear, something so crude, in a tone so unfamiliar, that it can only belong to all the time before them. Jackson does not react to it. He says nothing. He unbuttons his shirt. He takes it off and throws it in the sink. Jane has thrown the dog food there. The shirt floats down to it from his open fist.

Jane kneels and kisses her soiled son. David does not look at her. It is as though, however, he is dreaming of looking at her.

The Wedding

ELIZABETH ALWAYS WANTED TO READ FABLES TO HER LITTLE girl but the child only wanted to hear the story about the little bird who thought a steam shovel was its mother. They would often argue about this. Elizabeth was sick of the story. She particularly disliked the part where the baby bird said, "You are not my mother, you are a *snort*, I want to get out of here!" At night, at the child's bedtime, Sam would often hear them complaining bitterly to each other. He would preheat the broiler for dinner and freshen his drink and go out and sit on the picnic table. In a little while, the screen door would slam and Elizabeth would come out, shaking her head. The child had frustrated her again. The child would not go to sleep. She was upstairs, wandering around, making "cotton candy" in her bone-china bunny mug. "Cotton candy" was Kleenex sogged in water. Sometimes Elizabeth would tell Sam the story that she had prepared for the child. The people in Elizabeth's fables were always looking for truth or happiness and they were always being given mirrors or lumps of coal. Elizabeth's stories were inhabited by wolves and cart horses and solipsists.

"Please relax," Sam would say.

"Sam," the child called, "have some of my cotton candy. It's delicious."

Elizabeth's child reminded Sam of Hester's little Pearl even though he knew that her father, far from being the "Prince of the Air," was a tax accountant. Elizabeth spoke about him occasionally. He had not shared the previous year's refund with her even though they had filed jointly and half of the year's income had been hers. The tax accountant told Elizabeth that she didn't know how to do anything right. Elizabeth, in turn, told her accountant that he was always ejaculating prematurely.

"Sam," the child called, "why do you have your hand over your heart?"

"That's my Scotch," Sam said.

. . .

Elizabeth was a nervous young woman. she was nervous because she was not married to Sam. This desire to be married again embarrassed her, but she couldn't help it. Sam was married to someone else. Sam was always married to someone.

Sam and Elizabeth met as people usually meet. Suddenly, there was a deceptive light in the darkness. A light that blackly reminded the lonely of the darkness. They met at the wedding dinner of the daughter of a mutual friend. Delicious food was served and many peculiar toasts were given. Sam liked Elizabeth's aura and she liked his too. They danced. Sam had quite a bit to drink. At one point, he thought he saw a red rabbit in the floral centerpiece. It's true, it was Easter week, but he worried about this. They danced again. Sam danced Elizabeth out of the party and into the parking lot. Sam's car was nondescript and tidy except for a bag of melting groceries.

Elizabeth loved his kisses. On the other hand, when Sam saw Elizabeth's brightly flowered scanty panties, he thought he'd faint with happiness. He was a sentimentalist.

"I love you," Elizabeth thought she heard him say.

Sam swore that he heard Elizabeth say, "Life is an eccentric privilege."

This worried him but not in time.

They began going out together. elizabeth promised to always take the babysitter home. At first, Elizabeth and Sam attempted to do vile and imaginative things to each other. This culminated one afternoon when Sam spooned a mound of tiramisu between Elizabeth's legs. At first, of course, Elizabeth was nervous. Then she stopped being nervous and began watching Sam's sweating, good-looking shoulders with real apprehension. Simultaneously, they both gave up. This seemed a good sign. The battle is always between the pleasure principle and the reality principle, is it not? Imagination is not what it's cracked up to be. Sam decided to forget the petty, bourgeois rite of eating food out of another's orifices for a while. He decided to just love Elizabeth instead.

. . .

"DID YOU KNOW THAT CHARLES DICKENS WANTED TO MARRY LIT-tle Red Riding Hood?"

"What!" Sam exclaimed, appalled.

"Well, as a child he wanted to marry her," Elizabeth said.

"Oh," Sam said, relieved.

ELIZABETH HAD A HOUSE AND HER LITTLE GIRL. SAM HAD A house and a car and a Noank sloop. The houses were thirteen hundred miles apart. They spent the winter in Elizabeth's house in the South and they drove up to Sam's house for the summer. The trip took two and a half days. They had done it twice now. It seemed about the same each time. They bought peaches and cigarettes and fireworks. The child would often sit on the floor in the front seat and talk into the air-conditioning vent.

"Emergency," she'd say. "Come in, please."

ON THE MOST RECENT TRIP, SAM HAD CALLED HIS LAWYER FROM a Hot Shoppe on the New Jersey Turnpike. The lawyer told him that Sam's divorce had become final that morning. This had been Sam's third marriage. He and Annie had seemed very compatible. They tended to each other realistically, with affection and common sense. Then Annie decided to go back to school. She became interested in animal behaviorism. Books accumulated. She was never at home. She was always on field trips, in thickets or on beaches, or visiting some ornithologist in Barnstable.

"Annie, Annie," Sam had pleaded. "Let's have some people over for drinks. Let's prune the apple tree. Let's bake the orange cake you always made for my birthday."

"I have never made an orange cake in my life," Annie said.

"Annie," Sam said, "don't they have courses in seventeenth-century romantic verse or something?"

"You drink too much," Annie said. "You get quarrelsome every night at nine. Your behavior patterns are severely limited."

Sam clutched his head with his hands.

"Plus you are reducing my ability to respond to meaningful occurrences, Sam."

Sam poured himself another Scotch. He lit a cigarette. He applied a mustache with a piece of picnic charcoal.

"I am Captain Blood," he said. "I want to kiss you."

"When Errol Flynn died, he had the body of a man of ninety," Annie said. "His brain was unrealistic from alcohol."

She had already packed the toast rack and the pewter and rolled up the Oriental rug.

"I am just taking this one Wanda Landowska recording," she said. "That's all I'm taking in the way of records."

Sam, with his charcoal mustache, sat very straight at his end of the table.

"The variations in our life have ceased to be significant," Annie said.

SAM'S HOUSE WAS ON A HILL OVERLOOKING A COVE. THE COVE was turning into a saltwater marsh. Sam liked marshes but he thought he had bought property on a deepwater cove where he could take his boat in and out. He wished that he were not involved in witnessing his cove turning into a marsh. When he had first bought the place, he was so excited about everything that he had a big dinner party at which he served *soupe de poisson* using only the fish he had caught himself from the cove. He could not, it seems, keep himself from doing this each year. Each year, the *soupe de poisson* did not seem as nice as it had the year before. About a year before Annie left him, she suggested that they should probably stop having that particular dinner party.

WHEN SAM RETURNED TO THE TABLE IN THE HOT SHOPPE ON the New Jersey Turnpike after learning about his divorce, Elizabeth didn't look at him.

"I have been practicing different expressions, none of which seem appropriate," Elizabeth said.

"Well," Sam said.

"I might as well be honest," Elizabeth said.

Sam looked at his toast. He did not feel lean and young and unencumbered.

"In the following sentence, the same word is used in each of the missing spaces, but pronounced differently." Elizabeth's head was bowed. She was reading off the place mat. "Don't look at yours now, Sam," she said, "the answer's on it." She slid his place mat off the table, accidentally spilling coffee on his cuff. "*A prominent _____ and man came into a restaurant at the height of the rush hour. The waitress was _____ to serve him immediately as she had _____.*"

Sam looked at her. She smiled. He looked at the child. The child's eyes were closed and she was hmming. Sam paid the bill. The child went to the bathroom. An hour later, just before the Tappan Zee Bridge, Sam said, "*Notable.*"

"What?" Elizabeth said.

"*Notable.* That's the word that belongs in all three spaces."

"You looked," Elizabeth said.

"Goddamn it," Sam yelled. "I did not look!"

"I knew this would happen," Elizabeth said. "I knew it was going to be like this."

IT IS A VERY HOT NIGHT. ELIZABETH HAS POISON IVY ON HER wrists. Her wrists are covered with calamine lotion. She has put Saran Wrap over the lotion and secured it with a rubber band. Sam is in love. He smells the wonderfully clean, sun-and-linen smell of Elizabeth and her calamine lotion.

Elizabeth is going to tell a fairy story to the child. Sam tries to convince her that fables are sanctimonious and dully realistic.

"Tell her any one except the 'Frog King,'" Sam whispers.

"Why can't I tell her that one?" Elizabeth says. She is worried.

"The toad stands for male sexuality," Sam whispers.

"Oh, Sam," she says, "that's so superficial. That's a very superficial analysis of the animal-bridegroom stories."

Sam growls, biting her softly on the collarbone.

"Oh, Sam," she says.

· · ·

SAM'S FIRST WIFE WAS VERY PRETTY. SHE HAD THE FLATTEST stomach he had ever seen and very black, very straight hair. He adored her. He was faithful to her. He wrote both their names on the flyleaves of all his books. They went to Europe. They went to Mexico. In Mexico they lived in a grand room in a simple hotel opposite a square. The trees in the square were pruned in the shape of perfect boxes. Each night, hundreds of birds would come home to the trees. Beside the hotel was the shop of a man who made coffins. So many of the coffins seemed small, for children. Sam's wife grew depressed. She lay in bed for most of the day. She pretended she was dying. She wanted Sam to make love to her and pretend that she was dying. She wanted a baby. She was all mixed up.

Sam suggested that it was the ions in the Mexican air that made her depressed. He kept loving her but it became more and more difficult for them both. She continued to retreat into a landscape of chaos and warring feelings.

Her depression became general. They had been married for almost six years but they were still only twenty-four years old. Often they would go to amusement parks. They liked the bumper cars best. The last time they had gone to the amusement park, Sam had broken his wife's hand when he crashed head-on into her bumper car. They could probably have gotten over the incident had they not been so bitterly miserable at the time.

IN THE MIDDLE OF THE NIGHT, THE CHILD RUSHES DOWN THE hall and into Elizabeth and Sam's bedroom.

"Sam," the child cries, "the baseball game! I'm missing the baseball game."

"There is no baseball game," Sam says.

"What's the matter? What's happening!" Elizabeth cries.

"Yes, yes," the child wails. "I'm late, I'm missing it."

"Oh, what is it!" Elizabeth cries.

"She's having an anxiety attack," Sam says.

The child puts her thumb in her mouth and then takes it out again.

"She's too young for anxiety attacks," Elizabeth says. "It's only a dream." She takes the child back to her room. When she comes back, Sam is sitting up against the pillows, drinking a glass of Scotch.

"Why do you have your hand over your heart?" Elizabeth asks.

"I think it's because it hurts," Sam says.

ELIZABETH IS TRYING TO STUFF ANOTHER FABLE INTO THE CHILD. She is determined this time. Sam has just returned from setting the mooring for his sailboat. He is sprawled in a hot bath, listening to the radio.

Elizabeth says, "There were two men wrecked on a desert island and one of them pretended he was home while the other admitted—"

"Oh, Mummy," the child says.

"I know that one," Sam says from the tub. "They both died."

"This is not a primitive story," Elizabeth says. "Colorless, anticlimactic endings are typical only of primitive stories."

Sam pulls his knees up and slides his head underneath the water. The water is really blue. Elizabeth had dyed curtains in the tub and stained the porcelain. Blue is Elizabeth's favorite color. Slowly, Sam's house is turning blue. Sam pulls the plug and gets out of the tub. He towels himself off. He puts on a shirt, a tie and a white summer suit. He laces up his sneakers. He slicks back his soaking hair. He goes into the child's room. The lights are out. Elizabeth and the child are looking at each other in the dark. There are fireflies in the room.

"They come in on her clothes," Elizabeth says.

"Will you marry me?" Sam asks.

"I'd love to," she says.

SAM CALLS HIS FRIENDS UP, BEGINNING WITH PETER, HIS OLDEST friend.

"I am getting married," Sam says.

There is a pause, then Peter finally says, "Once more the boat departs."

❧

IT IS HARDER TO GET MARRIED THAN ONE WOULD THINK. SAM has forgotten this. For example, what is the tone that should be established for the party? Elizabeth's mother believes that a wedding cake is very necessary. Elizabeth is embarrassed about this.

"I can't think about that, Mother," she says. She puts her mother and the child in charge of the wedding cake. At the child's suggestion, it has a jam center and a sailboat on it.

Elizabeth and Sam decide to get married at the home of a justice of the peace. Her name is Mrs. Custer. Then they will come back to their own house for a party. They invite a lot of people to the party.

"I have taken out *obey*," Mrs. Custer says, "but I have left in *love* and *cherish*. Some people object to the *obey*."

"That's all right," Sam says.

"I could start now," Mrs. Custer says. "But my husband will be coming home soon. If we wait a few moments, he will be here and then he won't interrupt the ceremony."

"That's all right," Sam says.

They stand around. Sam whispers to Elizabeth, "I should pay this woman a little something, but I left my wallet at home."

"That's all right," Elizabeth says.

"Everything's going to be fine," Sam says.

They get married. They drive home. Everyone has arrived, and some of the guests have brought their children, who run around with Elizabeth's child. One little girl has long red hair and painted green nails.

"I remember you," the child says. "You had a kitty. Why didn't you bring your kitty with you?"

"That kitty bought the chops," the little girl says.

Elizabeth overhears this. "Oh, my goodness," she says. She takes her daughter into the bathroom and closes the door.

"There is more than the seeming of things," she says to the child.

"Oh, Mummy," the child says, "I just want my nails green like that girl's."

"Elizabeth," Sam calls. "Please come out. The house is full of people. I'm getting drunk. We've been married for one hour and fifteen minutes." He closes his eyes and leans his forehead against the door. Miraculously, he enters. The closed door is not locked. The child escapes by the same entrance, happy to be free. Sam kisses Elizabeth by the blue tub. He kisses her beside the sink and before the full-length mirror. He kisses her as they stand pressed against the windowsill. Together, in their animistic embrace, they float out the window and circle the house, gazing down at all those who have not found true love, below.

The Yard Boy

THE YARD BOY WAS A SPIRITUAL MATERIALIST. HE LIVED IN the Now. He was free from the karmic chain. Being enlightened wasn't easy. It was very hard work. It was manual labor, actually.

The enlightened being is free. He feels the sorrow and sadness of those around him but does not necessarily feel his own. The yard boy felt that he had been enlightened for about two months, at the most.

The yard boy had two possessions. One was a pickup truck. The other was a stuffed and mounted plover he had found in the take-it-or-leave-it shed at the dump. The bird was now in the room he rented. The only other thing in the room was a bed. The landlady provided sheets and towels. Sometimes when he came back from work hot and sweaty with little bits of leaves and stuff caught in his hair, the landlady would give him a piece of homemade key lime pie.

The yard boy was content. He had hard muscular arms and a tanned back. He had compassion. He had a girlfriend. When he thought about it, he supposed that having a girlfriend was a cop-out to the security he had eschewed. This was a preconception, however, and a preconception was the worst of all the forms of security. The yard boy believed he was in balance on this point. He tried to see things the way they were from the midst of nowhere, and he felt that he had worked out this difficulty about the girlfriend satisfactorily. The important thing was to be able to see through the veils of preconception.

The yard boy was a handsome fellow. He seldom spoke. He was appealing. Now that he was a yard boy his hands smelled of 6-6-6. His jeans smelled of tangelos. He was honest and truthful, a straightforward person who did not distinguish between this and that. For the girlfriend he always had a terrific silky business that was always at the ready.

The yard boy worked for several very wealthy people. In the morning of every day he got into his pickup and drove over the causeways to the Keys, where he mowed and clipped and cut and hauled. He talked to the plants. He always told them what he was going to do before he did it so they would have a chance to prepare themselves. Plants have lived in the Now for a long time but they still have to have some things explained to them.

AT THE WILSONS' HOUSE THE YARD BOY CLIPS A SUCKER FROM A grapefruit tree. It is February. Even so, the tree doesn't like it much. Mrs. Wilson comes out and watches the yard boy while he works. She has her son with her. He is about three. He doesn't talk yet. His name is Tao. Mrs. Wilson is wealthy and can afford to be wacky. What was she supposed to do, after all, she asked the yard boy once, call her kid George? Larry? For god's sake.

Her obstetrician had told her at the time that he had never seen a more perfectly shaped head.

The Wilsons' surroundings are splendid. Mrs. Wilson has splendid clothes, a splendid figure. She has a wonderful Cuban cook. The house is worth three-quarters of a million dollars. The plantings are worth a hundred thousand dollars. Everything has a price. It is fantastic. A precise worth has been ascribed to everything. Every worm and aphid can be counted upon. It costs a certain amount of money to eradicate them. The sod is laid down fresh every year. For weeks after the lawn is installed, the seams are visible and then the squares of grass gather together and it becomes, everywhere, in sun or shade, a smooth, witty and improbable green like the color of a parrot.

Mrs. Wilson follows the yard boy around as he tends to the hibiscus, the bougainvillea, the poinciana, the Java flower, the flame vine. They stand beneath the mango, looking up.

"Isn't it pagan?" Mrs. Wilson says.

Close the mouth, shut the doors, untie the tangles, soften the light, the yard boy thinks.

Mrs. Wilson says, "I've never understood nature, all this effort. All this will . . ." She flaps her slender arms at the reeking of odors, the rioting colors. Still, she looks up at the mangoes, hanging. Uuuuuh, she thinks.

Tao is standing between the yard boy and Mrs. Wilson with an oleander flower in his mouth. It is pink. Tao's hair is golden. His eyes are blue.

The yard boy removes the flower from the little boy's mouth. "Poisonous," the yard boy says.

"What is it!" Mrs. Wilson cries.

"Oleander," the yard boy says.

"Cut it down, dig it out, get rid of it," Mrs. Wilson cries. "My precious child!" She imagines Tao being kidnapped, held for an astronomical ransom by men with acne.

Mrs. Wilson goes into the house and makes herself a drink. The yard boy walks over to the oleander. The oleander trembles in the breeze. The yard boy stands in front of it for a few minutes, his clippers by his side.

Mrs. Wilson watches him from the house. She sips her drink and rubs the glass over her hot nipples. The ice clinks. The yard boy raises the clippers and spreads them wide. The bolt connecting the two shears breaks. He walks over to the house, over to where Mrs. Wilson stands behind glass doors. The house weighs a ton with the glass. The house's architect was the South's most important architect, Mrs. Wilson once told the yard boy. Everything he made was designed to give a sense of freedom and space. Everything was designed to give the occupants the impression of being outside. His object was to break down definitions, the consciousness of boundaries. Mrs. Wilson told the yard boy the architect was an idiot.

Behind the glass, Mrs. Wilson understands the difficulty. Behind Mrs. Wilson's teeth is a tongue that tastes of bourbon.

"I'll drive you downtown and we can get a new whatever," she says. She is determined.

She and he and Tao get into Mrs. Wilson's Mercedes SL350. Mrs. Wilson is a splendid driver. She has taken the Mercedes up to 130, she tells the yard boy. The engine stroked beautifully at 130, no sound of strain at all.

She drives past the beaches, over the causeways. She darts in and out of traffic with a fine sense of timing. Behind them, occasionally, old men in tiny cars jump the curb in fright. Mrs. Wilson glances at them in the rearview mirror, seeming neither satisfied nor dissatisfied. She puts her hand on the yard boy's knee. She rubs his leg.

Tao scrambles from the back into the front seat. He gets on the other side of the yard boy. He bites him.

I am living in a spiritual junkyard, thinks the yard boy. I must make it into a simple room with one beautiful object.

Sweat runs down the yard boy's spine. Tao is gobbling at his arm as though it is junket.

"What is going on!" yells Mrs. Wilson. She turns the Mercedes around in the middle of the highway. An ice-cream truck scatters a tinkle of music and a carton of Fudgsicles as it grinds to a stop. Mrs. Wilson is cuffing Tao as she speeds back home. Her shaven armpit rises and falls before the yard boy's eyes.

"Save the oleander!" she yells at both of them. "What do I care!"

In the driveway she runs around to Tao's side of the car and pinches the child's nose. He opens his mouth. She grabs him by the hair and carries him suspended into the house.

The yard boy walks to his truck, gets in and drives off. The world is neither nest nor playground, the yard boy thinks.

THE YARD BOY LIES IN HIS ROOM THINKING ABOUT HIS GIRL-friend.

Open up, give in, allow some space, sprinkle and pour, he thinks.

THE YARD BOY IS MOWING THE GRASS AROUND JOHNNY DAKOTA'S swimming pool. Dakota is into heroin and intangible property. As he is working, the yard boy hears a big splash behind him. He looks into the swimming pool and sees a rock on the bottom of it. He finishes mowing the grass and then he gets a net and fishes the rock out. It is as big as his hand and gray, with bubbly streaks of iron and metal running through it. The yard boy thinks it is a meteorite. It would probably still be smoldering with heat had it not landed in the swimming pool.

It is interesting but not all that interesting. The possibility of its surviving the earth's atmosphere is one-tenth of one percent. Other things are more interesting than this. Nevertheless, the yard boy shows it to Johnny Dakota, who might want to place it in a taped-up box in his house to prevent the air from corroding it.

Johnny Dakota looks up at the sky, then at the piece of space junk and then at the yard boy. He is a sleek, fit man. Only his eyes and his hands look old. His hands have deep ridges in them and smashed nails. He once told the yard boy that his mother had died from plucking a wild hair from her nose while vacationing in Calabria. His father had been felled by an incident in Chicago. The darkness is always near, he had told the yard boy.

Johnny Dakota usually takes his swim at this time of the morning. He is wearing his swim trunks and flip-flops. If he had been in the pool he could have been brained. Once his mother had dreamed of losing a tooth and two days later her cousin dropped dead.

Johnny Dakota is angry. Anyone could tell. His face is dark. His mouth is a thin line. He gives the yard boy two twenties and tells him to bury the rock in the backyard. He tells him not to mention this to anyone.

The yard boy takes the rock and buries it beneath a fiddle-leaf fig at the north end of the house. The fig tree is distressed. It's magnetic, that's the only thing known about this rock. The fig tree is almost as upset as Johnny Dakota.

THE YARD BOY LIES IN HIS ROOM. HIS GIRLFRIEND IS GIVING HIM a hard time. She used to visit him in his room several nights a week but now she doesn't. He will take her out to dinner. He will spend the two twenties on a fantastic dinner.

The yard boy is disgusted with himself. The spider's web is woven into the wanting, he thinks. He has desire for his girlfriend. His mind is shuttling between thoughts of the future and thoughts of the past. He is out of touch with the sharp simplicity and wonderfulness of the moment. He looks around him. He opens his eyes wide. The yard boy's jeans are filthy. A green insect crawls in and out of the scapular feathers of the plover.

The yard boy goes downstairs. He gives the plover to his land-lady. She seems delighted. She puts it on a shelf in the pantry with her milk-glass collection. The landlady has white hair, a wen and old legs that end in sneakers. She wants the yard boy to look at a plant she has just bought. It is in a big green plastic pot in the sunshine of her kitchen. Nothing is more obvious than the hidden, the yard boy thinks.

"This plant is insane," the yard boy says.

The landlady is shocked. She backs off a little from the plant, a rabbit's-foot fern.

"It has seen something terrible," the yard boy says.

"I bought it at that place I always go," the landlady says.

The yard boy shakes his head. The plant waves a wrinkly leaf and drops it.

"Insane," the landlady asks. She would like to cry. She has no family, no one.

"Mad as a hatter," the yard boy says.

THE RESTAURANT THAT THE YARD BOY'S GIRLFRIEND CHOOSES IS not expensive. It is a fish restaurant. The plates are plastic. There is a bottle of hot sauce on each table. The girlfriend doesn't like fancy.

The yard boy's girlfriend is not talking to him. She has not been talking to him for days, actually. He knows he should be satisfied with whatever situation arises but he is having a little difficulty with his enlightenment.

THE YARD BOY'S LANDLADY HAS PUT HER RABBIT'S-FOOT FERN out by the garbage cans. The yard boy picks it up and puts it in the cab of his truck. It goes wherever he goes now.

The yard boy gets a note from his girlfriend. It says:

> My ego is too healthy for real involvement with you. I don't like you. Good-bye.
>
> *Alyce*

. . .

THE YARD BOY WORKS FOR MR. CROWN, AN ILLUSTRATOR WHO lives in a fine house on the bay. Across the street, someone is building an even finer house on the gulf. Mr. Crown was once the most renowned illustrator of Western art in the country. In his studio he has George Custer's jacket. Sometimes the yard boy poses for Mr. Crown. The year before, a gentleman in Cody, Wyoming, bought Mr. Crown's painting of an Indian who was the yard boy for fifty thousand dollars. This year, however, Mr. Crown is not doing so well. He has been reduced to illustrating children's books. His star is falling. Also, the construction across the street infuriates him. The new house will block off his view of the sun as it slides daily into the water.

Mr. Crown's publishers have told him that they are not interested in cowboys. There have been too many cowboys for too long.

The yard boy is spraying against scale and sooty mold.

"I don't need the money but I am insulted," Mr. Crown tells the yard boy.

Mr. Crown goes back into the house. The yard boy takes a break to get a drink of water. He sits in the cab of his truck and drinks from a plastic jug. He sprinkles some water on the rabbit's-foot fern. The fern sits there on the seat, dribbling a little vermiculite, crazier than hell.

The fern and the yard boy sit.

It is not a peaceful spot to sit. The racket of the construction on the gulf is considerable. Nonetheless, the yard boy swallows his water and attempts to dwell upon the dignity and simplicity of the moment.

Then there is the sound of gunfire. The yard boy cranes his neck out of the window of his pickup truck and sees Mr. Crown firing from his studio at the workers across the street. It takes the workers several moments to realize that they are being shot at. The bullets make big mealy holes in the concrete. The bullets whine through the windows that will exhibit the sunset. The workers all give a howl and try to find cover. The yard boy curls up behind the wheel of his truck. The little rushy brown hairs on the fern's stalks stick straight out.

A few minutes later the firing stops. Mr. Crown goes back to the drawing board. No one is hurt. Mr. Crown is arrested and posts a large bond. Charges are later dropped. The house across the street is built. Still, Mr. Crown seems calmer now. He gives up illustrating. When he wants to look at something, he looks at the bay. He tells the yard boy he is putting sunsets behind him.

THE YARD BOY AND THE RABBIT'S-FOOT FERN DRIVE FROM LAWN to lawn in the course of their days, the fern tipping forward a little in its green pot, the wind folding back its leaves. In the wind, its leaves curl back like the lips of a Doberman pinscher.

The yard boy sees things in the course of his work that he wouldn't dream of telling the fern even though the fern is his only confidant. The fern has a lot of space around it in which anything can happen but it doesn't have much of an emotional life because it is insane. Therefore, it makes a good confidant.

The yard boy has always been open. He has always let be and disowned. Nevertheless, he has lost the spontaneity of his awakened state. He is sad. He can feel it. The fern can feel it too, which makes it gloomier than ever. Even so, the fern has grown quite fond of the yard boy. It wants to help him any way it can.

The yard boy doesn't rent a room anymore. He lives in his truck. Then he sells his truck. He and the rabbit's-foot fern sit on the beach. The fern lives in the shade of the yard boy. The yard boy doesn't live in the Now at all anymore. He lives in the past. He thinks of his childhood. As a child he had a comic-book-collection high of 374 with perfect covers. His parents had loved him. His parents had another son, whom they loved too. One morning this son had fallen out of a tree onto the driveway and played with nothing but a spoon and saucepan for the next twenty-five years. When the yard boy has lived in the past as much as is reliable, he lives in the future. It is while he is living in the future that his girlfriend walks by on the beach. She is wearing a long wet T-shirt that says, I'M NOT A TOURIST I LIVE HERE. The rabbit's-foot fern alerts the yard boy and they both stare at her as she walks by.

It is a beautiful day. The water is a smooth green, broken occasionally by porpoises rising. Between the yard boy and his girlfriend is sand a little less white than the clouds. Behind the yard boy are plantings of cabbage palms and succulents and Spanish bayonets. The bayonets are harsh and green with spikes that end in black tips like stilettos.

Act but do not rely upon one's own abilities, thinks the yard boy. He chews at his nails. The moon can shine in a hundred different bowls, he thinks. What a lot of junk the yard boy thinks. He is as lost in the darkness of his solid thoughts as a yard boy can be. He watches his girlfriend angrily as she sashays by.

The rabbit's-foot fern brightens at the yard boy's true annoyance. Its fuzzy long-haired rhizomes clutch its pot tightly. The space around it simmers, it bubbles. Each cell mobilizes its intent of skillful and creative action. It turns its leaves toward the Spanish bayonets. It straightens and sways. Straightens and sways. A moment passes. The message of retribution is received along the heated air. The yard boy watches as the Spanish bayonets uproot themselves and move out.

Shepherd

IT HAD BEEN THREE WEEKS SINCE THE GIRL'S GERMAN SHEP-
herd had died. He had drowned. The girl couldn't get over it. She sat
on the porch of her boyfriend's beach house and looked at the water.

It was not the same water. The house was on the Gulf of Mexico.
The shepherd had drowned in the bay.

The girl's boyfriend had bought his house just the week before. It
had been purchased furnished with mismatched plates and glasses, several large oak beds and an assortment of bamboo furniture.

The girl had a house of her own on the broad seawalled bay that
had big windows overlooking shaggy bougainvillea bushes. There were
hardly any studs in the frame and the whole house had shaken when
the dog ran through it.

The girl's boyfriend's last name was Chester and everyone called
him that. He wore sunglasses the color of champagne bottles. Chester
had wide shoulders, great hands and one broken marriage, on which he
didn't owe a dime.

"You have fallen into the butter dish," the girl's friends told her.

Three days before the shepherd had drowned, Chester had asked
the girl to marry him. They had known each other almost a year. "Let's
get married," he said. They had taken a Quaalude and gone to bed.
That had been three weeks and three days ago. They were going to be
married in four days. Time is breath, the girl thought.

The shepherd was brown and black with a blunt, fabulous face. He
had a famous trick. When the girl said, "Do you love me?" he would leap
up, all fours, into her arms. And he was light, so light, containing his
great weight deep within himself, like a dream of weight.

The girl had had him since he was two months old. She had bought
him from a breeder in Miami, a man who had once been a priest. The
girl's shepherd came from a litter of five with excellent bloodlines. The

mother was graceful and friendly, the father more solemn and alert. The breeder who had once been a priest made the girl spend several minutes alone with each puppy and asked her a great many questions about herself. She had never thought about herself much. When she had finally selected her puppy, she sat in the kitchen with the breeder and drank a Pepsi. The puppy stumbled around her feet, nibbling at the laces of her sneakers. The breeder smoked and talked to the girl with a great deal of assurance. The girl had been quite in awe of him.

He said, "We are all asleep and dreaming, you know. If we could ever actually comprehend our true position, we would not be able to bear it, we would have to find a way out."

The girl nodded. She was embarrassed. People would sometimes speak to her like this, intimate and alarming, as though she were passionate or thoughtful or well read. The puppy smelled wonderful. She picked him up and held him.

"We deceive ourselves. All we do is dream. Good dreams, bad dreams . . ."

"The ways that others see us is our life," the girl said.

"Yes!" the breeder exclaimed.

THE GIRL SAT MOVING SLOWLY ON THE PORCH GLIDER. SHE IMAG- ined herself standing laughing, younger and much nicer, the shepherd leaping into her arms. Her head buzzed and rustled. The bourbon bobbed around the flamingo's lowered head on the gaudy glass. The shepherd's drowned weight in her arms had been a terrible thing, ter- rible. She and Chester were both dressed rather elaborately because they had just returned from dinner with two friends, a stockbroker and his girlfriend, an art dealer. The girl was very thin and very blond. There were fine blond hairs on her face. The small restaurant where they ate appeared much larger than it was by its use of mirrored walls. The girl watched the four of them eating and drinking in the mirrors. The stockbroker spoke of money, of what he could do for his friends. "I love my work," he said.

"The art I handle," his girlfriend said, "is intended as a stimulus for discussion. In no way is it to be taken as an aesthetic product."

The girl had asked her for the untouched steak tournedos that their

waiter had wrapped up in aluminum foil, the foil twisted into the shape
of a swan. The girl remembered carrying the meat into the house for
the shepherd and seeing the torn window screen. She remembered feeling the stillness in her house as it flowed into her eyes.

THE GIRL LOOKED AT THE GULF. IT WAS A DAZZLING DAY WITH NO
surf. The beach was deserted. The serious tanners were in tanning par-
lors, bronzing evenly beneath sunlamps, saving time.

The girl wished the moment were still to come, that she were there,
then, waiting, her empty arms outstretched, saying, "Do you love me?"
Dogs hear sounds that we cannot, thought the girl. Dogs hear callings.

Chester had dug a deep square hole beneath the largest of the bougainvillea bushes and the girl had laid her dog down into it.

Their pale clothes became dirty from the drowned dog's coat. The
girl had thrown her dress away. Chester had sent his suit to the dry
cleaner.

Chester liked the dog, but it was the girl's dog. A dog can only belong to one person. When Chester and the girl made love in her house,
or when the girl was out for the evening, she kept the shepherd inside,
closed up on a small porch with high screened windows. He had taken
to leaping out of his pen, a clearing enclosed with Cyclone fencing and
equipped with old tires. It was supposed to be his playground, an exercise area that would keep away boredom and loneliness when the girl
wasn't with him. It was a tall fence, but the shepherd had found a way
over it. He had escaped, again and again, so the girl had begun locking him up in the small porch room. The girl had never witnessed his
escape, from either of these places, but she imagined him leaping, gathering himself and plunging upward. He could leap so high—there was
such lightness in him, such faith in the leaping.

On the beach, at Chester's, the waves glittered so with light that the
girl could not bear to look at them. She finished the bourbon, took the
empty glass to the kitchen and put it in the sink.

When the girl and the shepherd had first begun their life together,
they had lived around Mile 47 in the Florida Keys. The girl worked
in a small marine laboratory there. Her life was purely her own and

the dog's. Life seemed slow and joyous, and remembering those days the girl felt she had been on the brink of something extraordinary. She remembered the shepherd, his exuberance, energy, dignity. She remembered the shepherd and remembered being, herself, good. She lived aware of happiness.

The girl pushed her hands through her hair. The gulf seemed to stick in her throat.

There had been an abundance of holy things then. Once the world had been promising. But then there had been a disappearance of holy things.

A friend of Chester's had suggested hypnotism. He was quite enthusiastic about it. The girl would have a few sessions with this hypnotist that he knew, and she would forget the dog. Not forget, exactly. Rather, certain connections would not be made. The girl would no longer recall the dog in the context of her grief. The hypnotist had had great success with smokers.

Tonight they were going to have dinner with this man and his wife. The girl couldn't bear the thought of it. They would talk and talk. They would talk about real estate and hypnotism and coke. Tonight, they would go to a restaurant that had recently become notorious when an elderly woman had died from burns received when the cherries jubilee she was being served set fire to her dress. They would all order flaming desserts. They would go dancing afterward.

Animals are closer to God than we, the girl thought, but they are lost to him. Her arms felt heavy. The sun was huge, moving ponderously toward the horizon. People were gathering on the beach to watch it go down. They were playing their radios. When the sun touched the horizon, it took three minutes before it disappeared. An animal can live for three minutes without air. It had taken the shepherd three minutes to die after however long he had been swimming in the deep water off the smooth seawall. The girl remembered walking into the house with the meat wrapped in the foil in the shape of a swan, and seeing the broken screen. The house was full of mosquitoes. Chester put some soft ice in a glass and poured a nightcap. Chester always looked out of place in the girl's house. The house wasn't worth anything, it was the land that was valuable. The girl went outside, calling, past the empty pen, calling, down to the bay, seeing the lights of the better houses along the seawall. A neighbor had called the sheriff's department and the lights from the deputy's car shone on the ground on the dark dog.

A buzzer sounded in the beach house. Chester had had the whole house wired. In the week he had owned it, he had put in central air-conditioning, replaced all the windows with one-way glass and installed an elaborate infrared alarm system. The buzzer, however, was just a local signal. It stopped. It had been just the door opening, just Chester coming home. Chester activated the total system when they were out or when they were sleeping. The girl thought of invisible frequencies monitoring undisturbed air. The girl found offensive the notion that she could be spared pain, humiliation or loss by microwaves. She contemplated for a moment the desire Chester had for a complete home security system. There wasn't anything in the house worth stealing. Chester was protecting space. For a moment, the girl found offensive the touch of Chester's hand on her hair.

"Why aren't you dressed," he asked.

The girl looked at him, and then down at herself, at the thin T-shirt and hibiscus-flowered shorts. I am getting too old to wear this shit, the girl thought. The porch was cooling down fast in the twilight. She shivered and rubbed her arms.

"Why?" the girl said.

Chester sighed. "We're going out to dinner with the Tynans."

"I don't want to go out to dinner with the Tynans," the girl said.

Chester put his hands in his pockets. "You've got to snap out of this," he said.

"I'm flying," the girl said. "I have flown." She thought of the shepherd leaping, the lightness. He had escaped from her. She hadn't gotten any-place.

Chester said, "I've consoled you the best I can."

"There is no consolation," the girl said. "There is no recovery. There is no happy ending."

"We're the happy ending," Chester said. "Give us a break."

The sky was red, the water a dull silver. "I can't bear to see the Tynans again," the girl said. "I can't bear to go to another restaurant and see the sneeze guard over the salad bar."

"Don't scream at me, darling. Doesn't any of that stuff you take ever calm you down? I'm not the dog that you can scream at."

"What?" the girl said.

Chester sat down on the glider. He put his hand on her knee. "I think you're wonderful, but I think a little self-knowledge, a little *realism*, is in order here. You would stand and *scream* at that dog, darling."

The girl looked at his hand, patting her knee. It seemed an impossibly large, ruddy hand.

"I wasn't screaming," she said. The dog had a famous trick. The girl would ask, "Do you love me?" and he would leap up, all fours, into her arms. Everyone had been amazed.

"The night it happened, you looked at the screen and you said you'd *kill* him when he got back."

The girl stared at the hand stroking and rubbing her knee. She felt numb. "I never said that."

"It was a justifiable annoyance, darling. You must have repaired that screen half a dozen times. He was becoming a discipline problem. He was beginning to make people feel uncomfortable."

"Uncomfortable?" the girl said. She stood up. The hand dropped away.

"We cannot change any of this," Chester said. "If it were in my power, I would. I would do anything for you."

"You didn't stay with me that night, you didn't lie down beside me!" The girl walked in small troubled circles around the room.

"I stayed for *hours*, darling. But nobody could sleep on that bed. The sheets were always sandy and covered with dog hairs. That's why I bought a house, for the beds." Chester smiled and reached out to her. She turned and walked through the house, opening the door, tripping the buzzer. "Oh, you must stop this!" Chester called.

When she reached her own house, she went into the bedroom and lay down there. There was a yawning silence all around her, like an enormous hole. Silence was a thing entrusted to the animals, the girl thought. Many things that human words have harmed are restored again by the silence of animals.

The girl lay on her side, then turned onto her back. She thought of the bougainvillea, of the leaves turning into flowers over the shepherd's grave. She thought of the shepherd by her bed, against the wall, sleeping quietly, his faith in her at peace.

There was a pop, a small explosion in her head that woke her. She lurched up, gasping, from a dream that the shepherd had died. And for an instant, she hovered between two dreams, twice deceived. She saw herself leaping, only to fall back. The moonlight spilled into the clearing.

"I did love you, didn't I?" the girl said. She saw herself forever leaping, forever falling back. "And didn't you love me?"

Train

NSIDE, THE AUTO TRAIN WAS VIOLET. BOTH LITTLE GIRLS WERE pleased because it was their favorite color. Violet was practically the only thing they agreed on. Danica Anderson and Jane Muirhead were ten years old. They had traveled from Maine to Washington, D.C., by car with Jane's parents and were now on the train with Jane's parents, 109 other people and 42 automobiles en route to Florida, where they lived. It was September. Danica had been with Jane since June. Danica's mother was getting married again and she had needed the summer months to settle down and have everything nice for Dan when she saw her in September. In August, her mother had written Dan and asked what she could do to make things nice for her when she got back. Dan replied that she would like a good wall-hung pencil sharpener and satin sheets. She would like cowboy bread for supper. Dan supposed that she would get none of these things. Her mother hadn't even asked her what cowboy bread was.

The girls explored the entire train, north to south. They saw everyone but the engineer. Then they sat down in their violet seats. Jane made faces at a cute little toddler holding a cloth rabbit until he started to cry. Dan took out her writing materials and began writing to Jim Anderson. She was writing him a postcard.

Jim, she wrote, *I miss you and I will see you any minute. When I see you we will go swimming right away.*

"That is real messy writing," Jane said. "It's all scrunched together. If you were writing to anyone other than a dog, they wouldn't be able to read it at all."

Dan printed her name on the bottom of the card and embellished it all with X's and O's.

"Your writing to Jim Anderson is dumb in about twelve different ways. He's a *golden retriever*, for god's sake."

Dan looked at her friend mildly. She was used to Jane yelling at her and expressing disgust and impatience. Jane had once lived in Manhattan. She had developed certain attitudes. Jane was a treasure from the city of New York currently on loan to the state of Florida, where her father, for the last two years, had been engaged in running down a perfectly good investment in a marina and dinner theater. Jane liked to wear scarves tied around her head. She claimed to enjoy grapes and brown sugar and sour cream for dessert more than ice cream and cookies. She liked artichokes. She *adored* artichokes. She *adored* the part in the New York City Ballet's *Nutcracker Suite* where the Dewdrops and the candied Petals of Roses dance to the "Waltz of the Flowers." Jane had seen the *Nutcracker* four *times*, for god's sake.

Dan and Jane and Jane's mother and father had all lived with Jane's grandmother in her big house in Maine all summer. The girls hadn't seen that much of the Muirheads. The Muirheads were always "cruising." They were always "gunk-holing," as they called it. Whatever that was, Jane said, for god's sake. Jane's grandmother's house was on the ocean and she knew how to make pizza—'za, she called it—and candy and sail a canoe. She sang hymns. She sewed sequins on their jeans and made them say grace before dinner. After they said grace, Jane's grandmother would ask forgiveness for things done and left undone. She would, upon request, lie down and chat with them at night before they went to sleep. Jane was crazy about her grandmother and was quite a nice person in her presence. One night, at the end of summer, Jane had had a dream in which men dressed in black suits and white bathing caps had broken into her grandmother's house and taken all her possessions and put them in the road. In Jane's dream, rain fell on all her grandmother's things. Jane woke up weeping. Dan had wept too. Jane and Dan were friends.

The train had not yet left the station even though it was two hours past the posted departure time. An announcement had just been made that said that a two-hour delay was built into the train's schedule.

"They make up the time at night," Jane said. She plucked the postcard from Dan's hand. "This is a good one," she said. "I think you're sending it to Jim Anderson just so you can save it yourself." She read aloud, "This is a photograph of the Phantom Dream Car crashing through a wall of burning television sets before a cheering crowd at the Cow Palace in San Francisco."

At the beginning of summer, Dan's mother had given her one hundred dollars, four packages of new underwear and three dozen stamped postcards. Most of the cards were plain but there were a few with odd pictures on them. Dan's mother wanted to hear from her twice weekly throughout the summer. She had married a man named Jake, who was a carpenter. Jake had already built Dan several bookcases. This seemed to be the extent of what he knew how to do for her.

"I only have three left now," Dan said, "but when I get home I'm going to start my own collection."

"I've been through that phase," Jane said. "It's just a phase. I don't think you're much of a correspondent. You wrote, 'I got sunburn. Love, Dan' ... 'I bought a green Frisbee. Love, Dan' ... 'Mrs. Muirhead has swimmer's ear. Love, Dan' ... 'Mr. Muirhead went water-skiing and cracked his rib. Love, Dan' ... When you write to people you should have something to say."

Dan didn't reply. She had been Jane's companion for a long time, and was wearying of what Jane's mother called her effervescence.

Jane slapped Dan on the back and hollered, "Danica Anderson! What is a clod like yourself doing on this fabulous journey!"

Together, as the train began to move, the girls made their way to the Starlight Lounge in Car 7, where Mr. and Mrs. Muirhead told them they would be enjoying cocktails. They hesitated in the car where the train's magician was with his audience, watching him while he did the magic silks trick, the cut and restored handkerchief trick, the enchanted saltshaker trick and the dissolving quarter trick. The audience, primarily retirees, screamed with pleasure.

"I don't mind the tricks," Jane whispered to Dan, "but the patter drives me crazy."

The magician was a young man with a long spotted face. He did a lot of card forcing. Again and again, he called the card that people chose from a shuffled deck. Each time that the magician was successful, the audience participant looked astonished and thrilled. Jane and Dan passed on through.

"You don't really choose," Jane said. "He just makes you think you choose. He does it all with his pinkie." She pushed Dan forward into the Starlight Lounge, where Mrs. Muirhead was on a banquette staring out the window at a shed and unkempt bush that were sliding slowly past. She was drinking a martini. Mr. Muirhead was several tables away talking to a young man wearing jeans and a yellow jacket. Jane did not sit down. "Mummy," she said, "can I have your olive?"

"Of course not," Mrs. Muirhead said, "it's soaked in gin."

Jane, Dan in tow, went to her father's table. "Daddy," Jane demanded, "why aren't you sitting with Mummy? Are you and Mummy having a fight?"

Dan was astonished at this question. Mr. and Mrs. Muirhead fought continuously and as bitterly as vipers. Their arguments were baroque, stately and, although frequently extraordinary, never enlightening. At breakfast, they would be quarreling over an incident at a cocktail party the night before or a dumb remark made fifteen years ago. At dinner, they would be howling over the fate, which they called by many names, that had delivered each of them to the other. Forgiveness, charity and cooperation were qualities unknown to them. They were opponents *pur sang*. Dan was sure that one morning, Jane would be called from her classroom and told as gently as possible by Mr. Mooney, the school principal, that her parents had splattered each other's brains all over the lanai.

Mr. Muirhead looked at the children sorrowfully and touched Jane's cheek.

"I am not sitting with your mother because I am sitting with this young man here. We are having a fascinating conversation."

"Why are you always talking to young men," Jane asked.

"Jane, honey," Mr. Muirhead said, "I will answer that." He took a swallow of his drink and sighed. He leaned forward and said earnestly, "I talk to so many young men because your mother won't let me talk to young women." He remained hunched over, patting Jane's cheek for a moment, and then leaned back.

The young man extracted a cigarette from his jacket and hesitated. Mr. Muirhead gave him a book of matches. "He does automobile illustrations," Mr. Muirhead said.

The young man nodded. "Belly bands. Pearls and flakes. Flames. All custom work."

Mr. Muirhead smiled. He seemed happier now. Mr. Muirhead loved conversations. He loved "to bring people out." Dan supposed that

Jane had picked up this pleasant trait from her father and distorted it in some perversely personal way.

"I bet you have a Trans Am yourself," Jane said.

"You are so-o-o right," the young man said. He extended his hand, showing a large gaudy stone in a setting that seemed to be gold. "Same color as this ring," he said.

Dan could still be impressed by adults. Their mysterious, unreliable images still had the power to attract and confound her, but Jane was clearly not interested in the young man. She demanded much of life. She had very high standards when she wanted to. Mr. Muirhead ordered the girls ginger ales and the young man and himself another round of drinks. Sometimes the train mysteriously would stop and even reverse, so they would pass unfamiliar scenes once more. The same green pasture filled with slanty light, the same row of clapboard houses, each with the shades of their windows drawn against the heat, the same boats on their trailers, waiting on dry land. The moon was rising beneath a spectacular lightning and thunder storm. People around them were commenting on it. Close to the train, a sheen of dark birds flew low across a dirt road.

"Birds are only flying reptiles, I'm sure you're all aware," Jane said suddenly.

"What a horrible thought!" Mr. Muirhead said. His face had become a little slack, and his hair somewhat disarranged.

"It's true, it's true," Jane sang. "Sad but true."

"You mean like lizards and snakes," the young man asked. He snorted and shook his head.

"*Glorified* reptiles, certainly," Mr. Muirhead said, recovering a bit of his sense of time and place.

Dan suddenly felt lonely. It was not homesickness, although she would have given anything at that moment to be poking around in her little aluminum boat with Jim Anderson. But she wouldn't be living any longer in the place she thought of as home. The town was the same but the place was different. The house where she had been a little tiny baby and had lived her whole life belonged to someone else now. Over the summer, her mother and Jake had bought another house that he was going to fix up.

"Reptiles have scales," the young man said, "or else they're long and slimy."

Dan felt like bawling. She could feel the backs of her eyes swelling up like cupcakes. She was surrounded by strangers saying crazy things. Even her own mother often said crazy things in a reasonable way that made Dan know she was a stranger too. Dan's mother told Dan everything. Her mother told her she wouldn't have to worry about having brothers or sisters. Her mother discussed the particular nature of the problem with her. Half the things she told her, Dan didn't want to know. There would be no brothers and sisters. There would be Dan and her mother and Jake, sitting around the house together, caring deeply for one another, sharing a nice life together, not making any mistakes.

Dan excused herself and started toward the lavatory on the level below. Mrs. Muirhead called to her as she approached and handed her a folded piece of paper. "Would you be kind enough to give this to Mr. Muirhead," she asked. Dan returned to Mr. Muirhead and gave him the note and then went down to the lavatory. She sat on the little toilet and cried as the train rocked along.

After a while, she heard Jane's voice saying, "I hear you in there, Danica Anderson. What's the matter with you?"

Dan didn't say anything.

"I know it's you," Jane said.

Dan blew her nose, pushed the button on the toilet and said, "What did the note say?"

"I don't know," Jane said. "Daddy ate it."

"He ate it!" Dan exclaimed. She opened the door of the stall and went to the sink. She washed her hands and splashed her face with water. She giggled. "He really ate it?"

"Everybody is looped in that Starlight Lounge," Jane said, then patted her hair with a hairbrush. Jane's hair was full of tangles and she never brushed hard enough to get them out. She looked at Dan by looking in the mirror. "Why were you crying?"

"I was thinking about your grandma," Dan said. "She said that one year she left the Christmas tree up until Easter."

"Why were you thinking about my grandma!" Jane yelled.

"I was thinking about her singing," Dan said, startled. "I like her singing."

In her head, Dan could hear Jane's grandmother singing about Death's dark waters and sinking souls, about Mercy Seats and the Great Physician. She could hear the voice rising and falling through the thin walls of the Maine house, borne past the dark screens and into the night.

"I don't want you thinking about my grandma," Jane said, pinching Dan's arm.

Dan tried not to think of Jane's grandma. Once, she had seen her fall coming out of the water. The beach was stony. The stones were round and smooth and slippery. Jane's grandmother had skinned her arm.

The girls went into the corridor and saw Mrs. Muirhead standing there. Mrs. Muirhead was deeply tanned. She had put her hair up in a twist and a wad of cotton was noticeable in her left ear. The three of them stood together, bouncing and nudging against one another with the motion of the train.

"My ear is killing me," Mrs. Muirhead said. "I think there's something they're not telling me. It crackles and snaps in there. It's like a bird breaking seeds in there." She touched the bone between cheekbone and ear. "I think that doctor I was seeing should lose his license. He was handsome and competent, certainly, but on my last visit he was vacuuming my ear and his secretary came in to ask him a question and she put her hand on his neck. She stroked his neck, his secretary! While I was sitting there having my ear vacuumed!" Mrs. Muirhead's cheeks were flushed.

The three of them gazed out the window. The train must have been clipping along, but things outside, although gone in an instant, seemed to be moving slowly. Beneath a streetlight, a man was kicking his pickup truck.

"I dislike trains," Mrs. Muirhead said. "I find them depressing."

"It's the oxygen deprivation," Jane said, "coming from having to share the air with all these people."

"You're such a snob, dear." Mrs. Muirhead sighed.

"We're going to supper now," Jane said.

"Supper," Mrs. Muirhead said. "Ugh."

The children left her looking out the window, a disconsolate, pretty woman wearing a green dress with a line of frogs dancing around it.

The dining car was almost full. The windows reflected the eaters. The countryside was dim and the train pushed through it.

Jane steered them to a table where a man and woman silently labored over their meal.

"My name is Crystal," Jane offered, "and this is my twin sister, Clara."

"Clara!" Dan exclaimed. Jane was always inventing drab names for her.

"We were triplets," Jane went on, "but the other died at birth. Cord got all twisted around his neck or something."

The woman looked at Jane and smiled.

"What is your line of work?" Jane persisted brightly.

There was silence. The woman kept smiling, then the man said, "I don't do anything, I don't have to do anything. I was injured in a peacetime accident and they brought me to the base hospital and worked on reviving me for forty-five minutes. Then they gave up. They thought I was dead. Four hours later, I woke up in the mortuary. The Army gives me a good pension." He pushed his chair away from the table and left.

Dan looked after him, astonished, a cold roll raised halfway to her mouth. "Was your husband really dead for all that while," she asked.

"My husband, ha!" the woman said. "I'd never laid eyes on that man before the six-thirty seating."

"I bet you're a professional woman who doesn't believe in men," Jane said slyly.

"Crystal, how did you guess! It's true, men are a collective hallucination of women. It's like when a group of crackpots get together on a hilltop and see flying saucers." The woman picked at her chicken.

Jane looked surprised, then said, "My father went to a costume party once wrapped from head to foot in aluminum foil."

"A casserole," the woman offered.

"No! A spaceman, an alien astronaut!"

Dan giggled, remembering when Mr. Muirhead had done that. She felt that Jane had met her match with this woman.

"What do you do!" Jane fairly screamed. "You won't tell us!"

"I do drugs," the woman said. The girls shrank back. "Ha," the woman said. "Actually, I test drugs for pharmaceutical companies. And I do research for a perfume manufacturer. I am involved in the search for human pheromones."

Jane looked levelly at the woman.

"I know you don't know what a pheromone is, Crystal. To put it grossly, a pheromone is a smell that a person has that can make another person do or feel a certain thing. It's an irresistible signal."

Dan thought of mangrove roots and orange groves. Of the smell of gas when the pilot light blew out on Jane's grandmother's stove. She liked the smell of the Atlantic Ocean when it dried upon your skin and the smell of Jim Anderson's fur when he had been rained upon. There were smells that could make you follow them, certainly.

Jane stared at the woman, tipping forward slightly in her seat.

"Relax, will you, Crystal, you're just a child. You don't even *have* a smell yet," the woman said. "I test all sorts of things. Sometimes I'm part of a control group and sometimes I'm not. You never know. If you're part of the control group, you're just given a placebo. A placebo, Crystal, is something that is nothing, but you don't know it's nothing. You think you're getting something that will change you or make you feel better or healthier or more attractive or something, but you're not really."

"I know what a placebo is," Jane muttered.

"Well that's terrific, Crystal, you're a prodigy." The woman removed a book from her handbag and began to read it. The book had a denim jacket on it that concealed its title.

"Ha!" Jane said, rising quickly and attempting to knock over a glass of water. "My name's not Crystal!"

Dan grabbed the glass before it fell and hurried after her. They returned to the Starlight Lounge. Mr. Muirhead was sitting with another young man. This one had a blond beard and a studious manner.

"Oh, this is a wonderful trip!" Mr. Muirhead said exuberantly. "The wonderful people you meet on a trip like this! This is the most fascinating young man. He's a writer. Been everywhere. He's putting together a book on cemeteries of the world. Isn't that some subject? I told him anytime he's in our town, stop by our restaurant, be my guest for some stone crab claws."

"Hullo," the young man said to the girls.

"We were speaking of Père-Lachaise, the legendary Parisian cemetery," Mr. Muirhead said. "So wistful. So grand and romantic. Your mother and I visited it, Jane, when we were in Paris. We strolled through it on a clear crisp autumn day. The desires of the human heart have no boundaries, girls. The mess of secrets in the human heart are without number. Witnessing Père-Lachaise was a very moving experience. As we strolled, your mother was screaming at me, Jane. Do you know why, honeybunch? She was screaming at me because back in New York, I had garaged the car at the place on East Eighty-Fourth Street. Your mother said that the people in the place on East Eighty-Fourth Street never turned the ignition all the way off to the left and were always running down the battery. She said there wasn't a soul in all of New York City who didn't know that the people running the garage on East Eighty-Fourth Street were idiots who were always ruining batteries. Before Père-Lachaise, girls, this young man and I were discussing the Panthéon, just outside of Guanajuato in Mexico. It so happens that I am also familiar with the Panthéon. Your mother wanted some tiles for the foyer so we went to Mexico. You stayed with Mrs. Murphy, Jane. Remember? It was Mrs. Murphy who taught you how to make egg salad. In any case, the Panthéon is a walled cemetery, not unlike the Campo Santo in Genoa, Italy, but the reason everybody goes there is to see the mummies. Something about the exceptionally dry air in the mountains has preserved the bodies and there's a little museum of mummies. It's grotesque, of course, and it certainly gave me pause. I mean it's one thing to think we will all gather together in a paradise of fadeless splendor like your grandma thinks, lamby-lettuce, and it's another thing to think as the Buddhists do that latent possibilities withdraw into the heart at death but do not perish, thereby allowing the being to be reborn, and it's one more thing, even, to believe like a goddamn scientist in one of the essential laws of physics which states that no energy is ever lost. It's one thing to think any of those things, girls, but it's quite another to be standing in that little museum looking at those miserable mummies. The horror and indignation were in their faces still. I almost cried aloud, so vivid was my sense of the fleetingness of this life. We made our way into the fresh air of the courtyard and I bought a pack of cigarettes at a little stand which sold postcards and film and such. I reached into my pocket for my lighter and it wasn't there. It seemed that I had lost my lighter. The lighter was a very good one that your mother had bought me the Christmas before, Jane, and your mother started screaming at me. There was a very gentle, warm rain falling, and there were bougainvillea petals on the walks. Your mother grasped my arm and reminded me that the lighter had been a gift from her. Your mother reminded me of the blazer she had bought for me. I spilled buttered popcorn on it at the movies and you can still see the spot. She reminded me of the hammock she bought for my fortieth birthday, which I allowed to rot in the rain. She recalled the shoulder bag she bought me, which I detested, it's true. It was somehow left out in the yard and I mangled it with the lawn mower. Descending the cobbled hill into Guanajuato, your mother recalled every one of her gifts to me, offerings both monetary and of the heart. She pointed out how I had mishandled and betrayed every one."

No one said anything.

"Then," Mr. Muirhead continued, "there was the San Cataldo Cemetery in Italy."

"That hasn't been completed yet," the young man said hurriedly. "It's a visionary design by the architect Aldo Rossi. In our conversation, I was just trying to describe the project to you."

"You can be assured," Mr. Muirhead said, "that when the project is finished and I take my little family on a vacation to Italy, as we walk, together and afraid, strolling through the hapless landscape of the San Cataldo Cemetery, Jane's mother will be screaming at me."

"Well, I must be going," the young man said. He got up.

"So long," Mr. Muirhead said.

"Were they really selling postcards of the mummies in that place," Dan asked.

"Yes, sweetie pie, they were," Mr. Muirhead said. "In this world there is a postcard of everything. That's the kind of world this is."

The crowd was getting boisterous in the Starlight Lounge. Mrs. Muirhead came down the aisle toward them and with a deep sigh, sat beside her husband. Mr. Muirhead gesticulated and formed words silently with his lips as though he was talking to the girls.

"What?" Mrs. Muirhead said.

"I was just telling the girls some of the differences between men and women. Men are more adventurous and aggressive with greater spatial and mechanical abilities. Women are more consistent, nurturant and aesthetic. Men can see better than women, but women have better hearing," Mr. Muirhead said.

"Very funny," Mrs. Muirhead said.

The girls retired from the melancholy regard Mr. and Mrs. Muirhead had fixed upon each other, and wandered through the cars of the train, occasionally returning to their seats to fuss in the cluttered nests they had created there. Around midnight, they decided to revisit the game car, where, earlier, people had been playing backgammon, Diplomacy, anagrams, crazy eights and Clue. They were still at it, variously throwing down queens of diamonds, moving troops through Asia Minor and accusing Colonel Mustard of doing it in the conservatory with a wrench. Whenever there was a lull in the playing, they talked about the accident.

"What accident?" Jane demanded.

"Train hit a Buick," a man said. "Middle of the night." The man had big ears and a tattoo on his forearm.

"There aren't any good new games," a woman complained. "Haven't been for years and years."

"Did you fall asleep?" Jane said accusingly to Dan.

"When could that have happened?" Dan said.

"We didn't see it," Jane said, disgusted.

"Two teenagers escaped without a scratch," the man said. "Lived to laugh about it. They are young and silly but it's no joke to the engineer. The engineer has a lot of paperwork to do after he hits something. The engineer will be filling out forms for a week." The man's tattoo said MOM AND DAD.

"Rats," Jane said.

The children returned to the darkened dining room, where *Superman* was being shown on a small television set. Jane instantly fell asleep. Dan watched Superman spin the earth backward so he could prevent Lois Lane from being smothered in a rockslide. The train shot past a group of old lighted buildings, SEWER KING, a sign said. When the movie ended, Jane woke up.

"When we lived in New York," she said muzzily, "I was sitting in the kitchen one afternoon doing my homework and this girl came in and sat down at the table. Did I ever tell you this? It was the middle of the winter and it was snowing. This person just came in with snow on her coat and sat right down at the table."

"Who was she," Dan asked.

"It was me, but I was old. I mean I was about thirty years old or something."

"It was a dream," Dan said.

"It was the middle of the afternoon, I tell you! I was doing my homework. She said, 'You've never lifted a finger to help me.' Then she asked me for an aspirin."

After a moment, Dan said, "It was probably the cleaning lady."

"Cleaning lady! Cleaning lady, for god's sake. What do you know about cleaning ladies!"

Dan felt her hair bristle as though someone were running a comb through it back to front, and realized she was mad, madder than she'd been all summer, for all summer she'd only felt humiliated when Jane was nasty to her.

"Listen up," Dan said, "don't talk to me like that anymore."

"Like what," Jane said coolly.

Dan stood up and walked away while Jane was saying, "The thing I don't understand is how she ever got into that apartment. My father had about a dozen locks on the door."

Dan sat in her seat in the quiet, dark coach and looked out at the night. She tried to recollect how it seemed dawn happened. Things just sort of rose out, she guessed she knew. There was nothing you could do about it. She thought of Jane's dream in which the men in white bathing caps were pushing all her grandma's things out of the house and into the street. The inside became empty and the outside became full. Dan was beginning to feel sorry for herself. She was alone, with no friends and no parents, sitting on a train between one place and another, scaring herself with someone else's dream in the middle of the night. She got up and walked through the rocking cars to the Starlight Lounge for a glass of water. After 4:00 a.m. it was no longer referred to as the Starlight Lounge. They stopped serving drinks and turned off the electric stars. It became just another place to sit. Mr. Muirhead was sitting there, alone. He must have been on excellent terms with the stewards because he was drinking a Bloody Mary.

"Hi, Dan!" he said.

Dan sat opposite him. After a moment she said, "I had a very nice summer. Thank you for inviting me."

"Well, I hope you enjoyed your summer, sweetie," Mr. Muirhead said.

"Do you think Jane and I will be friends forever?" Dan asked.

Mr. Muirhead looked surprised. "Definitely not. Jane will not have friends. Jane will have husbands, enemies and lawyers." He cracked ice noisily with his white teeth. "I'm glad you enjoyed your summer, Dan, and I hope you're enjoying your childhood. When you grow up, a shadow falls. Everything's sunny and then this big goddamn *wing* or something passes overhead."

"Oh," Dan said.

"Well, I've only heard that's the case, actually," Mr. Muirhead said. "Do you know what I want to be when I grow up?" He waited for her to smile. "When I grow up I want to become an Indian so I can use my Indian name."

"What is your Indian name?" Dan asked, smiling.

"My Indian name is He Rides a Slow Enduring Heavy Horse."

"That's a nice one," Dan said.

"It is, isn't it?" Mr. Muirhead said, gnawing ice.

Outside, the sky was lightening. Daylight was just beginning to flourish on the city of Jacksonville. It fell without prejudice on the slaughterhouses, Dairy Queens and courthouses, on the car lots, Sabal palms and a billboard advertisement for pies.

The train went slowly around a long curve, and looking backward, past Mr. Muirhead, Dan could see the entire length of it moving ahead. The bubble-topped cars were dark and sinister in the first flat and hopeful light of the morning.

Dan took the three postcards she had left out of her bookbag and looked at them. One showed Thomas Edison beneath a banyan tree. One showed a little tar-paper shack out in the middle of the desert in New Mexico where men were supposed to have invented the atomic bomb. One was a "quickie" card showing a porpoise balancing a grape-fruit on the top of his head.

"Oh, I remember those," Mr. Muirhead said, picking up the "quickie" card. "You just check off what you want." He read aloud, "How are you?

I am fine ( ) lonesome ( ) happy ( ) sad ( ) broke ( ) flying high ( )." Mr. Muirhead chuckled. He read, "I have been good ( ) no good ( ). I saw the Gulf of Mexico ( ) the Atlantic Ocean ( ) the Orange Groves ( ) Interesting Attractions ( ) You in My Dreams ( )."

"I like this one," Mr. Muirhead said, chuckling.

"You can have it," Dan said. "I'd like you to have it."

"You're a nice little girl," Mr. Muirhead said. He looked at his glass and then out the window. "What do you think was on that note Mrs. Muirhead had you give me," he asked. "Do you think there's something I've missed?"

The Excursion

JENNY LIES A LITTLE. SHE IS JUST A LITTLE GIRL, A CHILD WITH fears. She fears that birds will fly out of the toilet bowl. Starlings with slick black wings. She fears trees and fishes and the bones in meat. She lies a little but it is not considered serious. Sometimes it seems she forgets where she is. She is lost in a place that is not her childhood. Sometimes she will say to someone, Mrs. Coogan at the Capt'n Davy Nursery School, for example, that her mother is dead, her father is dead, even her dog, Tonto, is dead. She will say that she has no toys, that she lives with machinery she cannot run, that she lives in a house with no windows, no view of the street, that she lives with strangers. She has to understand everything herself.

Poor Mrs. Coogan! She pats Jenny's shoulder. Jenny wears pretty and expensive dresses with blue sneakers. The effect is charming. She has blond hair falling over a rather low brow and an interesting, mobile face. She does everything too fast. She rushes to bathtimes and meal-times and even to sleep. She sleeps rapidly with deep, heartbreaking sighs. Such hurry is unnecessary. It is as though she rushes forward to meet even her memories.

Jenny does not know how to play games very well. When the others play, she is still. She stands with her stomach thrust out, watching the others with a cool, inward gaze. Sometimes, something interrupts her, some urgent voice, perhaps, or shout, and she makes a startled, curious skip. Her brown eyes brim with confusion. She turns pale or very red. Yes, sometimes Jenny has bad days. The crayons are dead, the swings are dead, even little Johnny Lewis, who sits so patiently on his mat at snack time, will be dead. He is thirsty and when Mrs. Coogan gives him a cup of juice, Jenny is glad for his sake.

"I am so happy Johnny Lewis got his juice!" she cries.

Poor Mrs. Coogan. The child is such a puzzle.

"I don't care for the swimming," Jenny tells her, even though Mrs. Coogan doesn't take her little group swimming. She takes them for a walk. Down to the corner, where the school bus carrying the older children goes by.

"Perhaps you'll like it when you get a little older, when you get a little better at it," Mrs. Coogan says.

Jenny shakes her head. She thinks of all the nakedness, milling and bobbing and bumping against her in the flat, warm, dark water. She says this aloud.

"Oh, my dear," Mrs. Coogan says.

"I don't understand about the swimming," Jenny says.

Jenny's father picks her up at four. He always has a present for her, and today it is a watch. It's only a toy watch, but it has moving parts and the manufacturer states that if it is not abused it will keep fairly reasonable time.

Mrs. Coogan says to Jenny's father, "All children fib a little. It's their nature. Their lives are incompatible with the limits imposed upon their experience."

Jenny feels no real insecurity while Mrs. Coogan speaks, but she is a little anxious. She is with a man. She doesn't smell very good. Outside other men are striking the locked door with sticks.

"Leña," they call. "Leña."

Jenny's father frowns at Mrs. Coogan. He does not wish to be aware that Jenny lies. To him, it is a terrible risk of oneself to lie. It risks control, peace, self-knowledge, even, perhaps, the proper acceptance of love. He is a thoughtful, reasonable man. He loves his only child. He wills her safe passage through the world. He does not wish to acknowledge that lying gives a beat and structure to Jenny's life that the truth has not yet justified. Jenny's imagination depresses him. He senses an ultimatum in it.

Jenny runs to the car. Her father is not with her. He is behind her. Suddenly the child realizes this and whips around to catch him with her eyes. Once again, she succeeds.

Jenny's mother is in the front seat, checking over her grocery list. Jenny kisses her and shows her the big, colorful watch. A tiny girl sits on a swing within the watch's face. When Jenny winds it, the girl starts swinging, the clock starts to run.

Jenny sits in the back. The car moves out into the street. She hears a mother somewhere crying. Some mother, calling, "Oh, come back and let me rock you on your little swing!"

Jenny says nothing. She is propelled by sidereal energies. Loving, for her, will not be a free choosing of her destiny. It will be the discovery of the most fateful part of herself. She is with a man. When he kisses her, he covers her throat with his hand. He rubs his fingers lightly down the tendons of her neck. He holds her neck in his big hand as he kisses her over and over again.

"Raisin bran or Cheerios," Jenny's mother asks. "Cheddar or Swiss?"

Jenny is just a little girl. She worries that there will not be enough jam, not enough cookies. When she walks with her mother through the supermarket, she nervously pats her mother's arm.

Now, at home, Jenny reads. She is precocious in this. When she first discovered that she could read, she did not tell anyone about it. The words took on the depths of patient, dangerous animals, and Jenny cautiously lived alone with them for a while. Now, however, everyone realizes that she can read, and they are very proud of her. Jenny reads in the newspaper that in San Luis Obispo, California, a seventeen-year-old girl came out of a clothing store, looked around horrified, screamed and died. The newspaper said that several years previous to this, the girl's sister had woken early, given a piercing scream and died. The newspaper said that the parents now fear for the welfare of their other two daughters.

Women suffer from the loss of a secret once known. Jenny will realize this someday. Now, however, she merely thinks, What is the dread that women have?

Jenny gets up and goes to her room. A stuffed bear is propped on her bureau. She takes it to the kitchen and gives it some orange juice. Then she takes it to the bathroom and puts it on the toilet seat for a moment. Then she puts it to bed.

Jenny wakes crying in the night and rushes into her parents' room. She is not sure of the time; she is not sure if they will be there. Of course they are there. Jenny is just a child. On a bedside table are her mother's reading glasses and a little vase of marigolds. Deeply hued, yellow, red and orange. Her parents are very patient. She is a normal little girl with fears, with nightmares. The nightmares do no real harm, that is, they will not alter her life. She is afraid that she is growing, that she will grow too much. She returns to her room after being comforted, holding one of the little flowers.

The man likes flowers, although he dislikes Jenny's childishness. He removes Jenny's skimpy cotton dress. He puts the flowers between her breasts, between her legs. The house is full of flowers. It is Mexico on the Day of the Dead. Millions of marigolds have been woven into carpets and placed on the graves. Jenny's mouth hurts, her stomach hurts. Yes, the man dislikes her childishness. He kneels beside her, his hands on her hips, and forces her to look at his blank, warm face. It is a youthful face, although he is certainly no longer a young man. Jenny had seen him when he was younger, drunk, blue-eyed. It doesn't matter. He doesn't age. He has had other loves and he has behaved similarly with them all. How could it be otherwise? Even so, Jenny knows that she has originated with him, that anything before him was nostalgia for this. Even so, there are letters, variously addressed, interchangeably addressed, it would seem. These letters won't be kept. It isn't the time, but they are here now, in a jumble, littered with the toys. Jenny reads them as though in a dream. This is Jenny! As in a dream too, she is less reasonable but capable of better judgment.

I won't stay here. It is a tomb, this town, and the streets are full of whores, women with live mice or snakes or fish in the clear plastic heels of their shoes. Death and the whores are everywhere, walking in these bright, horrible shoes.

How unhappy Jenny's mother would be if she were to see this letter! She comes into the child's room in the morning and helps her tie her shoes.

"You do it like this," she says, crossing the laces, "and then you do this, you make a bunny ear here, see."

Her mother holds her on her lap while she teaches her to tie her shoes. Jenny is so impatient. She wants to cry as she sees her mother's eager fingers. Jenny's nightie is damp and sweaty. Her mother takes it off and goes to the sink, where she washes it with sweet-smelling soap. Then she makes Jenny's breakfast. Jenny is not hungry. She takes the food outside and scatters it on the ground. The grass covers it up. Jenny goes back to her room. Everything is neatly put away. Her mother has made the bed. Jenny takes everything out again, her toy stove and typewriter and phone, her puppets and cars, the costly and minute dollhouse furnishings. Everything is there: a tiny papier-mâché pot roast dinner, lamps, rugs, andirons, fans, everything. The cupboards are full of play bread, the play pool is full of water.

Jenny's face is tense and intimate. She knows everything, but how aimless and arbitrary her knowledge is! For she has only desire; she has always had only the desire for this, her sleek, quiescent lover. He is so cold and so satisfying for there is no discovery in him. She goes to the bed and curls up beside him. He is dark and she is light. There are no shadings in Jenny's world. He is a tall, dark tree rooted in the stubborn night, and she is a flame seeking him—unstable, transparent. They are in Oaxaca. If they opened the shutters they would see the stone town. The town is made of a soft, pale green stone that makes it look as though it has been rained upon for centuries. Shadows in the shapes of men fall from the buildings. Everything is cool, almost rotten. In the markets, the fruit beads with water; the fragile feathered skulls of the birds are moist to the touch.

The man sleeks her hair back behind her ears. She is not so pretty now. Her face is uneven, her eyes are closed.

"You're asleep," he says. "You're making love to me in your sleep." She is nothing, nowhere. There is something exquisite in this, in the way, now, that he holds her throat. The pressure is so familiar. She yearns for this.

But he turns from her. He leaves.

Jenny pretends sleep. She plays that she is sleeping. She is fascinated with her sleep, where everything takes place as though it were not so. Nothing is concealed. On stationery from the Hotel Principal there is written:

Nobody to blame. Call 228

She sits at a small desk, drinking beer and reading. She is reading about the Aztecs. She notes the goddess Tlazolteotl, the goddess of filth and fecundity, of human moods, sexual love and confession. Jenny sits very straight in the chair. Her neck is long, full, graceful. But she feels out of breath. The high, clear air here makes her pant. The man pants too while he climbs the steep, stone steps of the town. He smokes too much. At night, when they return from drinking, he coughs flecks of blood onto the bathroom mirror. The blood is on the tiles, in the basin. Jenny closes her own mouth tightly as she hears him gag. Breath is outside her, expelled, not doing her any good. She stands beside the man as he coughs. There is not much blood but it seems to be everywhere, late at night, after they have been drinking, everywhere except on the man's clothes. He is impeccable about his clothes. He always wears a gray lightweight suit and a white shirt. He has two suits and they are both gray, and he has several shirts and they are all white. He is always the same. Even in his nakedness, his force, he is smooth, furled, closed. He is simple to her. There is no other path offered. He offers her the death of his sterility. His sexuality is the source of life, and his curse is death. He offers her nothing except his dying.

She wets her hands and wipes off the mirror. She cannot really imagine him dead. She is just a child embracing the crisis of a woman. The death she sees is that of herself in his emptiness. And he fills her with it. He floods her with emptiness. She grasps his thick, longish hair. She feels as if she is floating through his hair, falling miraculously away from danger into death. Safe at last.

"Jenny, Jenny, Jenny," her mother calls.

"I want a baby," Jenny says. "Can I have a baby?"

"Of course," her mother says, "when you get to be a big girl and fall in love."

Jenny will write on the stationery of the Hotel Principal:

The claims of love and self-preservation are opposed.

The man looks over her shoulder. He is restless, impatient to get going. They are going to the baths outside of town, in the mountains. A waterfall thuds into a long stone basin that has been artificially heated. It is a private club, crowded with Americans and wealthy Mexicans. When Jenny and the man arrive at the baths, they first go to a tiny stone cubicle, where the man strips. He hangs his clothes carefully from the wooden pegs fixed in the stone. Jenny looks outside, where a red horse grazes from a long, woven tether. There is water trickling over the face of the hillside. There is very little grass. The water sparkles around the horse's hooves. The man turns Jenny from the window and begins to undress her. She is like a little child with artless limbs. He rolls her pants down slowly. He slips her sweater off. He does everything slowly. Her clothes fall to the floor, which is wet with something that smells sweet. With one hand, the man holds her arms firmly behind her back. He doesn't do anything to her. She cannot smell him or even feel his breath. She can see his face, which is a little stern but not frightening. It holds no disappointment for her. She tries to move closer to him, but his grip on her arms prevents her. She begins to tremble. Her body feels his stroking, his touch, even though he does nothing. Her body starts to beat, to move in the style of their lovemaking. She becomes confused, the absence of him in her is so strong.

Later, the man goes out to the pool. Jenny hates the baths, but they come here several times a week on the man's insistence. She dresses and goes out to the side of the pool and watches the man swim back and forth. There are many people here, naked or nearly so, tossing miniature footballs back and forth. She sees the man grasp the ankles of a woman and begin to tow her playfully through the water. The woman wears silver earrings. Her hair is silver, her pubic hair is silver. Her mouth is a thickly frosted white. The water foams on her skin in tiny translucent bubbles. The woman laughs and moves her legs up in a scissors grip around the man's waist. Jenny sees him kiss her.

Another man, a Mexican, comes up to Jenny. He is bare-chested and wears white trousers and tall, yellow boots. He absently plucks at his left nipple while he looks at her.

"Ford Galaxie," he says at last. He takes a ring of car keys from his pocket and jerks his head toward the mountains.

"No," Jenny says.

"Galaxie," the Mexican says. "Galaxie. *Rojo.*"

Jenny sees the car, its red shell cold in the black mountains, drawn through the landscape of rock and mutilated maguey. Drawn through, with her inside, quietly transported.

"No," she says. She hates the baths. The tile in the bottom of the pool is arranged in the shape of a bird, a heron with thin legs and a huge, flat head. Her lover stands still in the water now, looking at her, amused.

"Jenny," her mother laughs. "You're such a dreamer. Would you like to go out for supper? You and Daddy and I can go to the restaurant that you like."

For it is just the summer. That is all it is, and Jenny is only five. In the house they are renting on Martha's Vineyard, there is a dinghy stored in the rafters of the living room. The landlord is supposed to come for it and take it down, but he does not. Jenny positions herself beneath the dinghy and scatters her shell collection over her legs and chest. She pretends that she has been cast out of it and floated to the bottom of the sea.

"Jenny-cake, get up now," her mother says. The child rises heavily from the floor. The same sorrow undergone for nothing is concluded. Again and again, nothing.

"Oh, Jenny-cake," her mother says sadly, for Jenny is so quiet, so pale. They have come to the island for the sunshine, for play, to offer Jenny her childhood. Her childhood eludes them all. What guide does Jenny follow?

"Let's play hairdresser," her mother says. "I'll be the hairdresser and you be the little girl."

Jenny lets her comb and arrange her hair.

"You're so pretty," her mother says.

But she is so melancholy, so careless with herself. She is bruised everywhere. Her mother parts her hair carefully. She brings out a dish of soapy water and brushes and trims Jenny's nails. She is put in order. She is a tidy little girl in a clean dress going out to supper on a summer night.

"Come on, Jenny," her mother urges her. "We want to be back home while it's still light." Jenny moves slowly to the door that her father is holding open for them.

"I have an idea," her mother says. "I'll be a parade and you be the little girl following the parade."

Jenny is so far away. She smiles to keep her mother from prattling on. She is what she will be. She has no energy, no talent, not even for love. She lies facedown, her face buried in a filthy sheet. The man lies beside her. She can feel his heart beating on her arm. Pounding like something left out of life. A great machine, a desolate engine, taking over for her, moving her. The machine moves her out the door, into the streets of the town.

There is a dance floor in the restaurant. Sometimes Jenny dances with her father. She dances by standing on top of his shoes while he moves around the floor. The restaurant is quite expensive. The menu is written in chalk on a blackboard that is then rolled from table to table. They go to this restaurant mostly because Jenny likes the blackboard. She can pretend that this is school.

There is a candle on each table, and Jenny blows it out at the beginning of each meal. This plunges their table into deep twilight. Sometimes the waitress relights the candle, and Jenny blows it out again. She can pretend that this is her birthday over and over again. Her parents allow her to do this. They allow her to do anything that does not bring distress to others. This usually works out well.

Halfway through their dinner, they become aware of a quarrel at the next table. A man is shouting at the woman who sits beside him. He does not appear angry, but he is saying outrageous things. The woman puts her hand gently on the side of his head. He does not shrug it off nor does it appear that he allows the caress. The woman's hand falls back in her lap.

"We're spoiling the others' dinner," the woman says.

"I don't care about the others," the man says. "I care about you."

The woman's laugh is high and uneasy. Her face is serene, but her hands tremble. The bones glow beneath her taut skin. There is a sense of blood, decay, the smell of love.

"Nothing matters except you," the man says again. He reaches across the table toward her and knocks over the flowers, the wine. "What do you care what others think?" he says.

"I don't know why people go out if they're not intending to have a nice time," Jenny's mother whispers. Jenny doesn't speak. The man's curses tease her ears. The reality of the couple, now gone, cheats her eyes. She gazes fixedly at the abandoned table, at the wreckage there. Everywhere there is disorder. Even in her parents' eyes.

"Tomorrow we're going sailing," her father says. "It's going to be a beautiful day."

"I would say that woman had a problem there," Jenny's mother says.

Outside, the sunset has dispersed the afternoon's fog. The sun makes long paddle strokes through the clouds. At day's end, the day creaks back to brightness like a swinging boom. Jenny walks down the street between her parents. At the curb, as children do, she takes a little leap into space, supported, for the moment, by their hands.

And now gone for good, this moment. It is night again.

"It's been night for a long time," the man says. He is shaving at the basin. His face, to about an inch below his eyes, is a white mask of lather. His mouth is a dark hole in the mask.

Jenny's dizzy from drinking. The sheets are white, the walls are white. One section of the room has a raised ceiling. It rises handsomely to nothing but a single lightbulb, shaded by strips of wood. The frame around the light is very substantial. It is as though the light were caged. The light is like a wild thing up there, pressed against the ceiling, a furious bright creature with slanty wings.

In the room there is a chair, a table, a bureau and a bed. There is a milk shake in a glass on a tin tray. On the surface of the milk, green petals of mold reach out from the sides toward the center.

"Clean yourself up and we'll go out," the man says.

Jenny moves obediently to the basin. She hangs her head over the round black drain. She splashes her hands and face with water. The drain seems very complex. Grids, mazes, avenues of descent, lacings and webs of matter. At the very bottom of the drain she sees a pinpoint of light. She's sure of it. Children lie there in that light, sleeping. She sees them so clearly, their small, sweet mouths open in the light.

"We know too much," Jenny says. "We all know too much almost right away."

"Clean yourself up better than that," the man says.

"You go ahead. I'll meet you there," Jenny says. For she has plans for the future. Jenny has lived in nothing if not the future all her life. Time had moved between herself and the man, but only for years. What does time matter to the inevitability of relations? It is inevitability that matters to lives, not love. For had she not always remembered him? And seen him rising from a kiss? Always.

When she is alone, she unties the rope that ties her luggage together. The bag is empty. She has come to this last place with nothing, really. She has been with this man for a long time. There had always been less of her each time she followed him. She wants to do this right, but her fingers fumble with the rope. It is as though her fingers were cold, the rope knotted and soaked with seawater. It is so difficult to arrange. She stops for a moment and then remembers in a panic that she has to go to the bathroom. That was the most important thing to remember. She feels close to tears because she almost forgot.

"I have to go to the bathroom," she cries.

Her mother leads her there.

"This is not a nice bathroom," her mother says. Water runs here only at certain times of the day. It is not running now. There are rags on the floor. The light falling through the window is dirty.

"Help me, Mother," Jenny says.

Her stomach is so upset. She is afraid she will soil herself. She wants to get out in the air for a moment and clear her head. Her head is full of lies. Outside the toilet, out there, she remembers, is the deck of the motor sailer. The green sails that have faded to a style of blue are luffing, pounding like boards in the wind. She closes the door to the toilet. Out here is the Atlantic, rough and blue and cold. Of course there is no danger. The engines are on; they are bringing the people back to the dock. The sails have the weight of wood. There is no danger. She is all right. She is just a little girl. She is with her mother and father. They are on vacation. They are cruising around the island with other tourists. Her father has planned an excursion for each day of their vacation. Now they are almost home. No one is behaving recklessly. People sit quietly on the boat or move about measuredly, collecting tackle or coiling lines or helping children into their sweaters.

Jenny sees the man waiting on the dock. The boat's engines whine higher as the boat is backed up, as it bumps softly against the canvas-wrapped pilings. The horrid machine whines higher and higher. She steps off into his arms.

He kisses her as he might another. She finds him rough, hurtful at first, but then his handling of her becomes more gentle, more sure in the knowledge that she is willing.

His tongue moves deeply, achingly in her mouth. His loving becomes autonomous now. It becomes, at last, complete.

Winter Chemistry

IT WAS THE MIDDLE OF JANUARY AND THERE WAS NOTHING TO look forward to. The radio station went off at dusk and dusk came early in the afternoon and then came the dark and nothing to watch but a bleached-out moon lying over fields slick as a frosted cake, and nothing to hear at all.

There was nothing left of Christmas but the cold that slouched and pressed against the people. Their blood was full of it. And their eyes and the food that they ate. The people walked the streets wearing woolen masks as though they were gangsters, or deformed. Old ladies died of breaks and foolish wounds in houses where no one came, and fish froze in the quiet of their rivers.

The cold didn't invent anything like the summer has a habit of doing and it didn't disclose anything like the spring. It lay powerfully encamped—waiting, altering one's ambitions, encouraging ends. The cold made for an ache, a restlessness and an irritation, and thinking that fell in odd and unemployable directions.

Judy Cushman and Julep Lee were the best of friends. Each knew things that the other did not, and each had a different manner of going after the things that she wanted. Each loved the handsome chemistry teacher of the high school. Love had different beginnings but always the same end. Someone was going to get hurt. Julep was too discreet to admit this for she tried not to think of shabby things.

They were fourteen and the only thing that was familiar to them was the town and the way they spent their lives there, which they hated.

They slept a great deal and always talked about the same things and made brownies and popcorn and drank Coca-Cola. Julep always made a great show of drinking Coca-Cola because she claimed that her father had given her three shares of stock in it the day she was born.

Judy would laugh about this whenever she thought to. "On the day I was born," she'd say, "I received the gifts of beauty and luck."

Their schoolbooks lay open and unread, littered with crumbs and nail trimmings. Every night that didn't bring a blizzard, they would spy on the chemistry teacher, for they were fourteen and could only infrequently distinguish what they did from what they merely dreamed about.

The chemistry teacher had enormous trembling eyes like a deer and a name in your mouth sweet as a candy bar. DEBEVOISE. He was tall and languid and unmarried and handsome. He lived alone in a single rented room on the second floor of a large house on the coast. The house was the last one on a street that abruptly became a field of pines and stones. Every night the girls would come to the field and, crouching in a hollow, watch him through a pair of cheap binoculars. For a month they had been watching him move woodenly around the small room and still they did not know what it was they wanted to happen. The walls of the room were painted white and he sat at a white desk with his shirtsleeves rolled down to his wrists. The only thing that was on the desk was a tiny television set with a screen the size of a book. He watched it and drank from a glass. Sometimes he would run his own hands through his own dark hair.

Judy Cushman and Julep Lee felt that loving him was a success in itself.

But still they had no idea what they waited for in the snow. The rocks dug into their skinny shanks. Their ears went deaf with the cold. At times, Judy thought that she wanted him to bring a woman up there. Or perhaps do something embarrassing or dirty all by himself. But she was not sure about this.

As for Julep, she seldom said things that she had not already said once long before, so there was no way of knowing what she thought.

JULEP WAS THE THINNEST HUMAN BEING IN TOWN, ALL ANGLES and bruises and fierce joinings. Even her lips were hard and spare and bloodless as bone. Her hair was such a pale, parched blond that it looked white and her brows and lashes were the same color, although her eyes, under heavy round lids that worked slowly as a doll's, were brown.

Her parents had moved from the South to the North when she was four years old, and she had lived on the same bitter and benumbed coast ever since. She steered her way through each new day incredulously, as though she had been kidnapped and sent to some grim prison yard in another world. She couldn't employ the cold to any advantage so she dreamed of heat, of a sun fierce enough to melt the monstrous town and set her free. She talked about the sun as though it were a personal friend of hers, waiting in the next room for her to get ready and go out with it.

Julep was a Baptist, a clarinetist in the band, a forward on the six-girl basketball team that was famous throughout the state, undefeated, unthreatened, unsmiling. She had scabs on her knees, a blue silk uniform in her locker, fingernails split and ragged from the gritty leather ball. Julep was an innocent.

JUDY CUSHMAN TOO WAS AN INNOCENT, BUT HAD A TENDENCY TO see things in a greedy, rutting way. Judy was tiny and tough and wore a garter belt. Almost every one of her eyebrow hairs was plucked from her head and her hair was stacked over a foot high, for her older sister was a hairdresser who taught her half of everything she knew.

Judy was full and sleek and a favorite with the boys and she would tell Julep things that Julep almost died hearing. She would say, "Last night Tommy Saloma exposed himself to my eyes only in the rumpus room of his house," and Julep would almost faint. She would say, "Billy Colter touched my breast in the library," and Julep would gasp and hold her head at an unnaturally high angle for she felt that if she didn't, everything inside her would stream terribly from her mouth, everything she was made of, falling out of her onto the floor in front of them.

Judy always told her friend the most awful things she could think of, true or false, and made promises that she would not keep and insulted and disappointed and teased her as much as possible. Julep allowed this and was always deeply affected and bewildered by this, which flattered Judy enormously. This pleasure compensated for the fact that Julep had white hair that Judy would have given anything in the world to have. It annoyed her that her friend had such strange and devastating hair and didn't know how to cut or curl it properly.

After school, they would often go to Julep's house. They usually went there rather than to Judy's because Julep's room was bigger. Judy's room was just a closet with a bright lightbulb and a studio bed and the smell of underwear.

"LOOK NOW," JUDY SAID, PEELING OFF A STRIP OF SCOTCH TAPE from her bangs, "we've got to broaden our conversational base. Why don't we talk about men or movies? Or even mixed drinks?"

Julep said, "We don't know anything about those things." She looked at the worn black Bible on her bedside table. She had read there that the sun would someday become black as a sackcloth of hair and the moon would turn red as blood. This was because of the evil in people, and Julep worried that this would happen to the sun before she had a chance to get back to where it was again.

"You don't know anything is all." Judy plucked at her sweater and smiled the bittersweet smile she found so crushing on the lips of the girl models of the fashion magazines. Her new breasts rose and fell eerily beneath her sweater.

"I know that someday you're gonna poke someone's eye out with those things," Julep said, pointing at her friend's chest. "If I were you, I'd be worried sick."

Judy yawned. Julep stared out the window. The sun was still up but nowhere in sight. The air was blue and the snow falling through it was blue, and the trees were as black as though they had been burned.

"I'm leaving," Judy said abruptly, then swept out of Julep's bedroom and downstairs to the kitchen.

Julep rubbed at the frost forming inside the windowpane with a thin yellowish nail that was bleeding beneath the quick. She felt her head sweating. If she pressed her hands to it, it would pop like a too-heavy tick on a dog. If hell were hot then heaven must be freezing cold. She backed away from the window and thudded down the stairs.

Judy had drawn on her boots and coat. She waved coyly at Julep.

"Well, aren't we going over there tonight to watch him?" Julep asked nervously, swinging her eyes heavily toward her friend. Looking often cost Julep a great deal of effort, as though her eyes were boxes of bricks she had to push around in front of her.

"No," Judy said, for she wanted to punish Julep for her dullness. Her books were lying on the kitchen table beside a small dish that said LET ME HOLD YOUR TEA BAG. Judy rolled her eyes and then shook her head at Julep. Julep's father owned a little grocery and variety store down the street, and in the window of it was a hand-lettered sign.

WHY MAKE THE RICH RICHER
PATRONIZE THE POOR
THANK YOU

"How can you stand to live in such a dump," she asked. "With such dummies?" Julep didn't know. Judy left and walked through the heavy snow to dumb Julep's father's dumb store, where she bought a package of gum and lifted a mascara and eyeliner set.

Julep ate supper. Chowder, bread, two glasses of milk and three pieces of cake. She felt that she was feeding something inside her that belonged in a pen in the zoo. A plow traveled up the street, its orange light chopping through the blackness. She went to bed early, for she had tests and a basketball game the next day. She thought of the tropical ocean, of enormous white flowers on yellow stalks motionless in the sun. Things would carry distantly over the water there. Things would start out from ugly places and never reach Julep at all.

JUDY CUSHMAN AND JULEP LEE HAD BECOME FRIENDS THE SUMMER before when they were on the beach. It was a bitter, shining Maine day and they were alone except for two people drowning just beyond the breaker line. The two girls sat on the beach eating potato chips, unable to decide if the people were drowning or if they were just having a good time. Even after they disappeared, the girls could not believe they had really done it. They went home and the next day read about it in the newspapers. From that day on, they spent all their time together, even though they never mentioned the incident again.

．　．　．

Debevoise was thirty-four and took no part in adventure. He didn't care for women and he couldn't care for men. He lived in a corner second-story room of a rambling boardinghouse. The room had two windows, one of which overlooked the field and the other, the sea. There were no curtains on the windows and he never pulled the shades. He ate breakfast with the elderly owners, lunch every noon at the high school and drove to a hotel in the next town for dinner every night. He was stern and deeply tanned and exceptionally good-looking. As for the teaching, he barely recognized his students as human beings, considering them all mentally bludgeoned by the unremitting landscape. He couldn't imagine chemistry doing any better or worse by them than anything else.

And the girls felt hopeless, stubborn and distraught, for they had come a long way on just a whisper more than nothing.

They could approach the house either by walking up the beach and climbing the metal rungs welded into the rock, which was dangerous and gave them no cover, or by walking through the little town and across the field. Their post was a small depression beside an enormous pine, the branches of which swept the ground. Farther away was the rim of rocks they had assembled as another hiding place. Every night they could see everything from either one of these locations.

Every night the chemistry teacher was projected brightly behind the square window glass and watching him was like seeing something in a museum. The girls would often close their eyes and even doze off for a time, and the snow would fall on them and freeze in their hair. Sometimes he would take off all his clothes and walk around the room, punching at the wall but never hitting it. Seeing him naked was never as exciting as the girls kept on imagining it would be since no one had ever told them what to feel about this.

Even so, Julep would come back to the house smiling, as though someone had made a very exciting promise to her. No one was there to notice this, for her mother was always locked in her room, powdered and rouged and in a lacy bed jacket like an invalid, watching TV and eating ice cream from the store, and her father had been sleeping for hours, twitching and suicidal, dreaming of meat going bad in faulty freezers.

On the nights when the girls saw the chemistry teacher without his clothes, Judy pretended to swoon with delight but actually felt hostile toward this vision, which was both improbable and irresistible. His body was brown all over and did not seem real. The boys she knew were so comprehensible. Of Debevoise, she understood nothing. She could pretend he was a movie star, beside her, naked, about to press his tongue against her teeth. Mr. Debevoise was going to put a bruise on her neck! He was going to take her hand and place it on his belt!! But she could not really believe these things.

THE MORNING AFTER JUDY HAD REFUSED TO GO SPYING, JULEP woke with a headache and a terrible thirst. She thought for a moment that she had taken up the watch all by herself and something awful had happened to her. As soon as she stepped outside, someone was going to tell her about it.

The sky had pieces of black running through it like something that had died during the night. Walking to school, Julep suddenly started to cry. Her throat ached and her head felt heavy. She pulled savagely at her colorless hair, arranging it so it fell more directly into and around her eyes. She stood in front of the school, her arms dangling, looking at her feet. She looked and looked, shocked. There she began. There were her boots, tall scuffed riding boots, her only winter footwear, which let in the damp, staining her feet each day the color of her socks. Then came her chapped knees, yellow and gray from spills on the gymnasium floor. Then her frayed and ugly coat. Her insides, too, were not what she would wish, for she knew that she was convulsively arranged—a steaming mess of foods and soft scarlet parts, Bible quotes, chemistry equations and queer bumpings and pains as though there was something down in her frantic to get out.

Debevoise, she knew, was pure and warm with not a speck of debris about him.

Julep walked inside and moved down the busy halls like a wraith, meek and bony and awkward, her towhead glowing like a lamp. The class before chemistry was endless. The cold seeped past the window-sills and over the plastic rosebud on the teacher's desk.

The classroom fell away and she was alone with Debevoise in a rubber raft on a clear green ocean. Small sweet fish nibbled on one another without rancor and parts of them fell off with no blood attached. Julep's knees touched his and they both had cameras and were taking pictures of each other. The sun was burning a hole in the top of her head . . .

NO ONE EVER PLAYED IN THE SNOW OR USED IT FOR ANYTHING. It came too often and it stayed too long. In the cafeteria, the windows were even with the ground and crisscrossed with a steel mesh to protect the glass from objects flying through the air and across the ground. The snow was higher than the windows. Judy sat alone at a long wooden table. Old food and bobby pins were lodged in its cracks. The cafeteria was a terrible place that everyone recklessly frequented. When Judy saw her friend's narrow nervous frame move jerkily across the room she decided on the spot that she would forgive her and they would resume watching Debevoise that very night. Afterward, they would go to Julep's room and drink gin and Coca-Cola. They would have highballs and she would make Julep talk about men whether she wanted to or not. Julep could provide the Coca-Colas since she was making money on drinking them.

Julep sat down and looked at Judy shyly. The chemistry teacher walked past them and sat at the faculty table on the other side of the room. He wore a lemon-colored suit, a dark blue shirt, a deep yellow tie and the fixed smirk that was his usual workaday expression.

They watched him respectfully. Julep closed her eyes. With her eyes shut, Julep looked sick and unconscious, beyond the range of instruction.

"What would you have him do if you had your choice?" Judy whispered. Julep said nothing. Judy tapped her fingers on the table and whispered more loudly, "The way you're sitting there and the way you're looking, you look for all the world as though you'd just gotten raped."

Julep's eyes fell open, blurred and out of focus for several seconds as though they'd been somewhere other than her head for the last few years. "You could ruin the heavenly city itself," she finally said.

. . .

JUDY CALLED HER HEAVENLY CITY FOR THE REST OF THE AFTER-noon. In the chemistry laboratory, she muttered so much that her titra-tion experiments were ruined. Julep poured the chemicals in the trough of running water that flowed down the center of the slate worktable, and pressed her hands to her roaring head. She could feel Debevoise standing silently beside her, smell the cologne and the new shirt. His bright clothing rested on the rim of her eye like a giddy tropical bird.

After classes, in the gymnasium, Julep sat on a bench behind the scorer in her shining uniform and the high white sneakers she'd won in a statewide free-throw contest the year before. She could not remember why she had become obsessed with playing basketball. She taped up her wrists.

Judy was a fan in the bleachers, surrounded by boys. The boys were all running combs through their hair and all wore jeans and hunting boots. "Heavenly City!" Judy shouted. "Heavenly City!"

Julep watched the girls from the other team. They caught the bas-ketball delicately, as though it were covered with some dreadful slime.

On the court she played extravagantly, her hard white head cresting above the others crowded beneath the board, her bony elbows shocking the girls in the ribs. Her nostrils filled with dust and the tapping heat of the radiators. Julep's team was far ahead. The cords of the net creaked as the ball floated through. Basketball was serious business and Julep felt no levity. Life was what you figured out for yourself.

"Heavenly City, Heavenly City!" Judy persisted from the stands. "Look to your right!" All the boys around her looked soberly down on the court and chewed great wads of gum. "Look to your right," Judy shrieked.

Julep moved her eyes gingerly along the sidelines. The opposing for-wards had the ball and were moving it cautiously around on the other half of the court. She stood panting and slightly bent, looking through the stands until her weary eyes rested on Debevoise. He was smiling kindly and looking at her. His dark handsome face was smooth and empty of habitual boredom and disgust, and his lips, in the instant that she saw him, seemed to be moving toward an expression that she had not known he possessed. It was then that the ball hit her squarely in the head and she fell to her knees. She heard a noise from the bleachers, something corrosive and impersonal, a rush and a hissing bubble as though her head had opened up and a wave was coming through it. A titter and blurred silence. As someone helped her up and off the court, she could see the chemistry teacher, smiling into his hands as though his jaws were about to crack.

Julep walked home slowly in a freezing dusk, her coat in her arms. Her brain was pumping madly, although her heart was still.

Judy came over at eight o'clock, a bottle of gin zipped up in the lining of her coat. She had found it lodged behind the record player in her house. The bottle was very dusty and about two inches of its contents were gone. Judy didn't know if it was still good or not.

Julep was in the bathroom, pressing a hot washcloth against her left eye. Almost all the white had disappeared into a soak of red. Judy did not speak to her about the embarrassment of the basketball game. She thought Julep was crazy to get so excited about playing a boys' game and she was also suspicious that too much of that sort of thing would change her friend's hormones. Magazines told her terrible things and she believed in most of them.

Judy went to the kitchen for glasses and something to mix with the gin. From behind a closed door, she heard a television going and a woman's voice above it. "No," the voice said. "No, that bum is up to no good." There was a shot, then a bump and rising music. "I told you," the voice said. Judy gathered up a handful of stale cookies and went up to Julep. The cookies were in the shape of stars and burned at the edges.

"Holiday relics," Julep said, mopping at her eye.

They each drank a glass of gin and then walked through the town, which was all one color with hardly anything moving in it, and the night was very cold and clear. Beyond the field, the sea was flat as a highway in the moonlight.

"I feel just amazing," Judy said in a high, wet voice.

Julep said nothing. She felt only hot and ponderous, as she had when she woke up that morning. She arranged her head scarf over her injured eye. Every once in a while, the eye seemed to roll backward and study her instead of bearing outward toward the night.

They settled beneath the giant tree and Judy fumblingly took the binoculars from her coat. She dropped them in the snow and giggled as she dug them out. She thought that Julep was just trying to be smart and had no doubt poured her gin into the rug or something when she wasn't watching. She pushed against her rudely and raised the binoculars.

"God," she said loudly. "He's nude again."

Julep sat hunched, her arms around her knees. Her clothes were soaked with sweat and rivulets of perspiration ran from the corners of her mouth.

"You're yelling," Julep said. "Someone will hear you." She tried to think of her own nakedness and what it might mean to somebody, even herself, but she had never paid any attention to her own body. Her eye shuddered and then became a piece of raw meat lying tamely in her head.

Debevoise was clamping a sunlamp above his bed. He turned it on and then lay on his back with his hands beneath his head. The bulb hung over him blankly for a moment and then lit shrilly. Almost at the same instant, the door of the house opened and a flashlight beam bored over the field. Judy gave a small shriek and pushed herself backward against the tree trunk.

"Who's there!" a man demanded. "I know you're there." Behind the voice were a pink hallway and an old woman standing in a shawl, her hand in a fist moving across her mouth. There seemed deadening light everywhere. The sea and snow and sunlamp and now the old man walking toward them. The girls knelt beneath the tree like jacked deer.

"Don't go over there, Ernest," the old woman said.

The man stopped and moved the light in a wide arc. "It ain't the first time you been here. You come out or there's going to be trouble."

"Ernest," the old woman said fretfully, turning the porch light off and on as though she were guiding in a ship. Judy and Julep bolted, stumbling across the field, spinning off tree limbs, their hands over their faces. "Hey!" they heard behind them. "Hey! You get outta here."

JULEP WAS SICK FOR THREE WEEKS AND NEVER MOVED FROM THE bed. She could hear children on their horses, cantering in the streets. She could hear the plows. She drank soup and sniffed herself beneath the damp bedclothes. She felt that she was an exceedingly fragile organism lying beneath complex layers of mulch. Her face was shrunken and without structure, as though something were burning it up and coring it out from within. The snow fell eternally out of a withered sky, and inside, Julep, beyond the range of dream or reasoning, continued to burn.

She couldn't decide if it had been coming for a long time and she had just gotten in the way of it or if it had always been there with her and she had only now recognized it.

Ever since the afternoon of the basketball game, she could not remember how she had once regarded Debevoise. He was the pain and the heat of her head, and no longer something she could think about.

Judy also could not bear to think about Debevoise. It frightened her to think they might be caught. Everyone would think she was queer. The girls would laugh and the boys would take advantage of her whereas now they fought over her and loved her and were scared half to death of her. She was glad that Julep was sick and they didn't have to sit around in the snow. She would never admit that she was being cautious or afraid, but she would tell Julep after she got well that she was bored and had learned everything she wanted to know about Debevoise.

Judy would come to visit Julep but didn't like to look at her. Once, Judy said, "He asked about you, you know."

Julep smiled politely and studied the hem of her sheet.

"He asked if you had moved and I said no, you were sick and then he said girls keep themselves too skinny these days as a fashion and they don't eat the right foods and get sick."

When Julep returned to school, everything was tiny, as in a dream, and moving with blinding speed. She could not keep up with it all, her muscles, having rested for so long, useless for anything. In the laboratory, she spilled potassium permanganate, staining her hands a deep brown. She watched her hands accompany her now like a dark disease, like a man's hands, soaked and sordid.

She felt cold.

JULEP NOW WENT OUT ALONE TO WATCH DEBEVOISE. JUDY WAS surprised and she became defensive and intrigued, imagining that Julep was at last succeeding in something they had not been able to accomplish together.

"I can't imagine anything going on that we haven't already seen," she said peevishly. "The only thing that could happen is if one of us got up right there in that room with him and we were looking out of that window instead of looking into it. You're going to get sick out there and freeze and go unconscious."

Julep looked at her wrecked hands and rubbed at them briefly with a piece of flannel she had started to carry around with her.

Judy was suspicious. She worried that something interesting had happened. "You've got to have somebody caring for you all the time," she said. "I'm going to go with you one more time but then I'm never going again and I'm going to stop you from going there too." How she would do this last thing, she didn't know. She could tell on Julep, she supposed. That would stop it all dead. She looked at Julep righteously and Julep looked back.

The night was black, moonless and starless, with only the snow shining dully with its own light, and the ice hanging in webs from the trees. They walked with their hands strung out in front of their faces and their elbows sticking out, shuffling a little so they wouldn't trip.

The ground was ice-buckled and had lots of hollows. Judy's knees dipped and, jaw joggling, she bit her tongue. She had fallen out of practice, out of step with the land and her reason for being on it. Julep walked steadily ahead and Judy followed, somewhere in a movie, war, a lusted-after orphan, in full bloom and in danger all the time. If only Julep had imagination, she thought, she wouldn't get so involved in things.

They settled down beside the tree, in a new and deeper ditch, with a stone base and the sides smooth ice, alarmingly, impossibly, like a home.

The second floor was in darkness.

"He's not even here," Judy said accusingly.

Julep's grainy face stuck out of her wool wrappings. "He's here," she said.

"Well, what's he doing in the dark!" Judy shouted. "Have you been watching him do something in the dark?" She was getting angry. They crouched in a cloud of her perfume. She felt like throttling Julep, who was tilted slightly toward her, in a trance and satisfied, dumb and patient. She looked toward the house, feeling Debevoise moving thunderously in the dark and making no sense to her. She was getting so angry she thought she would burst. She gave a little squeal and stamped her feet, then stood up and started back across the field. She was kicking her feet out in front of her, moving so fast that she thought when she felt her boots sliding away that she could still catch up with them before she fell, but her legs kept moving forward while the rest of her slid back and she tipped over with a crack.

She lay there whimpering. Unlike Julep, she had never hurt herself in her life. She had never been bruised or sick or burned and nothing had ever broken. She remained on her back, prodding herself gently, singing to herself in a little girl's voice. She was suddenly pulled roughly to her feet and shaken hard. Debevoise had grabbed her by the coat front and was pushing her back and forth, pinching her breasts, pushing and pulling at her as though to a musical beat, his face riding from side to side only inches in front of her, almost like it was his head that was wagging and not her own. His face was raging. It seemed on the verge of flying apart. He was saying several simple words to her but she could not seem to understand them. He would propel her back as he said each word and then yank her toward him in the silence between the words and it was as though someone was turning a radio on and off.

Then she simply stopped rocking, and with his hands still on her coat he toppled toward her, turning her slightly to the left as he fell so that they both sank side by side in the snow. His head settled and then broke slowly through a crust of ice. One eye filled up with snow while the other continued to stare at her.

Julep, a rock in each hand, took several steps forward and knelt beside him. There were two wounds in the back of his well-shaped head. She raised her hands again, dropping them with a slow, hard force against his skull. They made almost no sound. The eye that was still staring at Judy seemed to shake. His mouth was closed tightly but there was blood coming from between his lips. Judy pushed herself away. His hands remained on her coat, but then dropped off as she crept backward to a tree and clung to it, whimpering.

Julep had lost her mittens. The backs of her hands were cold from the snow, but her mottled palms were hot from the man's broken head. She lay down beside him, feeling white and glistening, turned inside out, scrubbed down and aired. She ran her hands over the thin shirt he wore, feeling his collarbone, his ribs, the tight muscles of his stomach. She unbuttoned his shirt and felt his nipples, which were hard, withered, much like her own. She pressed her lips against his chest and tasted salt, then lay her colorless famished head upon his shoulder, which was as warm as though he'd lived all his days in the sun.

Shorelines

WANT TO EXPLAIN. THERE ARE ONLY THE TWO OF US, THE CHILD and me. I sleep alone. Jace is gone. My hair is wavy, my posture good. I drink a little. Food bores me. It takes so long to eat. Being honest, I must say I drink. I drink, perhaps, more than moderately, but that is why there is so much milk. I have a terrible thirst. Rum and Coke. Grocery wine. Anything that cools. Gin and juices of all sorts. My breasts are always aching, particularly the left, the earnest one, which the baby refuses to favor. First comforts must be learned, I suppose. It's a matter of exposure.

I have tried to be clean about my person since the child. I wash frequently, rinse my breasts before feeding, keep my hands away from my eyes and mouth . . . but it's hard to keep oneself up. I have tried to think only harmonious thoughts since the child, but the sun on the water here, that extravagant white water, the sun brings such dishevelment and confusion.

I am tall. I have a mole by my lip. When I speak, the mole vanishes. I address myself to the child quite frequently. He is an infant, only a few months old.

I say things like, "What would you like for lunch? A marmalade crepe? A peanut-butter cupcake?"

Naturally, he does not answer. As for myself, I could seldom comply with his agreement. I keep forgetting to buy the ingredients. There was a time when I had everything on hand. I was quite the cook once. Pompano stuffed with pecans. Quiche Lorraine. And curry! I was wonderful with curries. I had such imaginative accompaniments. The whole thing no bigger than a saucer sometimes, yet perfect!

.   .   .

WE LIVE IN THE SUN HERE, ON THE BEACH, IN THE SOUTH. IT IS so hot here. I will tell you exactly how hot it is. It is too hot for orange trees. People plant them but they do not bear. I sleep alone now. I will be honest. Sometimes I wake in the night and realize that I have called upon my body. I am repelled but I do not become distraught. I remove my hands firmly. I raise and lower them to either side of the bed. It seems a little self-conscious, a little staged, to bring my hands away like that. But hands, what do they have to do with any of us?

The heat is the worst at night. I go damp with fever here at night, and I dream. Once I dreamed of baking a bat in the oven. I can't imagine myself dreaming such a thing.

I try to keep the child cool at night. I give him ice to play with. He accepts everything I have to offer. He is always with me. He is in my care.

I knew when Jace had started the baby. It's true what you've heard. A woman knows.

It has always been Jace only. We were children together. We lived in the same house. It was a big house on the water. Jace remembers it precisely. I remember it not as well. There were eleven people in that house and a dog beneath it, tied night and day to the pilings. Eleven of us and always a baby. It doesn't seem reasonable now when I think of it, but there were always eleven of us and always a baby. The diapers and the tiny clothes, hanging out to dry, for years!

Jace was older than me by a year and a day and I went everywhere with him.

My momma tried to bring me around. She said, "One day you're going to be a woman. There are ways you'll have to behave."

But we were just children. It was a place for children and we were using it up. The sharks would come up the inlet in the morning rains and they'd roll so it would seem the water was boiling. Our breath was wonderful. Everything was wonderful. We would box. Underneath the house, with the dog's rope tangling around our legs, Jace and I would box, stripped to the waist. Red and yellow seaweed would stream from the rope. The beams above us were soft blue with mold. Even now, I can feel exactly what it felt like to be cool and out of the sun.

Jace's fists were like flowers.

. . .

JACE IS THIN AND QUICK. HIS JEANS ARE WHITE WITH MY WASH-ing. I have always done my part. Wherever we went, I planted. If the soil was muck, I would plant vegetables; if dry, herbs; if sandy, strawberries. We always left before they could be harvested. We were always moving on, down the coast. But we always had bread to eat. I made good crusty bread. I had a sourdough starter that was seventy-one years old.

We have always lived on the water. Jace likes to hear it. We have been on all the kinds of water there are in the South. Once we lived in the swamp. The water there was a creamy pink. Air plants covered the trees like tufts of hair. All the life was in the trees, in the nests swinging from high branches.

I didn't care for the swamp, although it's true the sun was no problem there.

In Momma's house, a lemon tree grew outside the window of the baby's room. The fruit hung there for color mostly. Sometimes Momma made a soup. The tree was quite lovely and it flourished. It had been planted over the grease trap of the sink. I am always honest when I can be. It was swill that made it grow.

Here there is nothing of interest outside the child's room. Just the sand and the dunes. The dunes cast no shadow and offer no relief from the sun. A small piece of the gulf is visible and it flickers like glass. It's as though the water is signaling some message to my child in his crib.

WE DO NOT WAIT FOR JACE TO COME BACK. WE DO NOT WAIT FOR anything. We do not want anything. Jace, on the other hand, wants and wants. There is nothing he would not accept. He has many trades. Once he was a deep-sea diver. He dove for sponges out of Tarpon Springs. He dove every day, all of one spring and all of one summer. There was a red tide that year that drove people almost mad. Your eyes would swell, your throat would burn. Everything was choking. The water was like chewing gum. The birds went inland. All the fish and turtles died. I wouldn't hear about it. I was always a sensitive woman. Jace would lie in bed, smoking, his brown arms on the white sheets, his pale hair on the pressed pillowcases. Yes, everything was spotless once, and in order.

He said, "The fastest fish can't swim out of it. Not even the barracuda."

I wouldn't hear it. I did not like suffering.

"The bottom was covered with fish," he said. "I couldn't see the sponges for the acres of fish."

I began to cry.

"Everything is all right," he said. He held me. "No one cares," he said. "Why are you crying?"

There were other jobs Jace had. He built and drove. He would be gone for a few weeks or a few months and then he would come back. There were some things he didn't tell me.

THE BEACH LAND HERE BELONGS TO THE NAVY. IT HAS BELONGED to them for many years, though its purpose has been forgotten. There are a few trees near the road, but they have no bark or green branches. I point this out to the child, directing his gaze to the blasted scenery. "The land is unwholesome," I say. He refuses to agree. I insist, although I am not one for words.

"Horsetail beefwood can't be tolerated here," I tell him, "although horsetail beefwood is all the land naturally bears. Now if they had a decorative bent," I tell him, "they would plant palms, but there are no palms."

The baby's head is a white globe beneath my heart. He exhausts me, even though his weight is little more than that of water on my hands. He is a frail child. So many precautions are necessary. My hands grow white from holding him.

I am so relieved that Jace is gone. He has a perfect memory. His mouth was so clean, resting on me, and I was so quiet. But then he'd start talking about Momma's house.

"Wasn't life nice then?" he'd say. "And couldn't we see everything there was to see? And didn't life just make the finest sense?"

Even without Jace, I sometimes feel uneasy. There is something I feel I have not done.

.   .   .

It was the third month I could feel the child best. they move, you know, to face their stars.

There is a small town not far from here. i loathe the town and its people. They are watchful country people. The town's economy is dependent upon the prison. The prison is a good neighbor, they say. It is unobtrusive, quiet. When an execution is necessary, the executioner arrives in a white Cadillac and he is unobtrusive, too, for the Cadillac is an old one and there are a great many white cars here. The cars are white because of the terrible heat. The man in the Cadillac is called the engineer and no one claims to know his name.

The townspeople are all handy. They are all very willing to lend a helping hand. They hire prison boys to work in their yards. You can always tell the prison boys. They look so hungry and serene.

Martha is the only one of the townspeople who talks to me. The rest nod or smile. Martha is a comfy woman with a nice complexion, but her hair is the color of pork. She is always touching my arm, directing my attention to things she believes I might have overlooked, a sale on gin, for example, or frozen whipped puddings.

"You might could use a sweet or two," she says. "Fill you out."

Her face is big and friendly and her hands seem clean and dry. She is always talking to me. She talks about her daughter, who hasn't lived with her for many years. The daughter lives in a special home in the next state. Martha says, "She had a bad fever and she stopped being good."

Martha's hand on my shoulder feels like a nurse's hand, intimate and officious. She invites me to her home and I accept, over and over again. She is inviting me in for tea and conversation and I am always opening the door to her home. I am forever entering her rooms, walking endlessly across the shiny wooden floors.

"I don't want to be rich," Martha says. "I want only enough to have a friend over for a piece of pie or a highball. And I would like a frost-free refrigerator. Even in the winter, I have to defrost ours once a week. I have to take everything out and then spread the newspapers and get the bowl and sponge and then I have to put everything back."

"Yes," I say.

Martha's hands are moving among the cheap teacups. "It seems a little senseless," she says.

There are small table fans in the house, stirring the air. The rooms smell of drain cleaner and mold and mildew preventives. When the fans part the curtains to the west, an empty horse stall and a riding ring are visible. Martha crowns my tea with rum, like a friend.

"This is a fine town," Martha says. "Everyone looks out for his neighbor. Even the prison boys are good boys, most of them up just for stealing copper wire or beating on their women's fellows."

I hold the child tight. You know a mother's fears. He is fascinated by the chopping blades of the little fans, by the roach tablets behind the sofa cushions. Outside, as well, he puts his hands to everything.

"I imagine the wicked arrive at that prison only occasionally," I say.

"Hardly ever," Martha agrees.

I AM TRYING TO EXPLAIN TO YOU. I AM ALWAYS INSIDE THIS WOM-an's house. I am always speaking reasonably with this Martha. I am so tired and so sad and I am lying on a bed drinking tea. It is not Martha's bed. It is, I suppose, a bed for her guests. I am lying on a bedspread that is covered by a large embroidered peacock. Underneath the bed is a single medium-size mixing bowl. In the light socket is a night-light in the shape of a rose. I feel wonderful in this room in many ways. I feel like a column of air. I would like to audition for something. I am so clean inside.

"My husband worries about you," Martha says. She takes the cup away. "We are all good people here," she says. "We all lead good lives."

"What does your husband do, then?" I say. I smile because I do not want her to think I am confused. Actually, I've met the man. He placed his long hands on my stomach, on my thighs.

"We are not unsubtle here," Martha says, tapping her chest.

I met the man and when I met him in this house he was putting in new pine boards over the cement floors. When I arrived, he stopped, but that was what he was doing. He had a gun that shot nails into the concrete. Each nail cost a quarter. The expense distressed Martha and she mentioned it in my hearing. Men resume things, you know. He went back to it. As I lay on the bed, I could hear the gun being fired and I awoke quickly, frightened the noise might awaken the child. You know a mother's presumptions. There was the smell of sawdust and smoke from the nail gun.

"I wouldn't have thought we'd have to worry about you," Martha says unhappily.

WHEN I RETURNED FROM MARTHA'S HOUSE THE FIRST TIME, I passed a farmer traveling on the beach road in his rusty car. Strapped to the roof was a sandhill crane, one wing raised, pumped full of air and sailing in the moonlight. They kill these birds for their meat. The meat, they say, tastes just like chicken. I have found that almost everything tastes like chicken.

THERE IS A GARAGE NOT FAR FROM TOWN WHERE JACE USED TO buy gas. I stopped there once. There was a large wire meshed cage outside, by the pumps. A sign on it said BABY FLORIDA RATTLERS. Inside were dozens of blue and pink baby rattles on a dirt floor. It gave me a headache. The deception. The largeness of the cage.

AT NIGHT I TAKE THE CHILD AND WALK OVER THE BEACH TO THE water's edge, where it is cool. The child is at peace here, beside the water, and it is here, most likely, where Jace will find us when he comes back. When Jace comes back it will be at night. He always comes in on the heat, at night.

"Darling," I can hear him say, "even as a little boy, I was all there ever was for you."

I can see it quite clearly. I will be on the shoreline, nursing, and Jace will come back in on the heat, all careless and easy, and "Darling," he'll shout into the wind, into the white roil of water behind us. "Darling, darling," Jace will shout, "where you been, little girl?"

The Farm

IT WAS A DARK NIGHT IN AUGUST. SARAH AND TOMMY WERE going to their third party that night, the party where they would actually sit down to dinner. They were driving down Mixtuxet Avenue, a long black street of trees that led out of the village, away from the shore and the coastal homes into the country. Tommy had been drinking only soda that night. Every other weekend, Tommy wouldn't drink. He did it, he said, because he could.

Sarah was telling a long story as she drove. She kept asking Tommy if she had told it to him before, but he was noncommittal. When Tommy didn't drink, Sarah talked and talked. She was telling him a terrible story that she had read in the newspaper about an alligator at a jungle-farm attraction in Florida. The alligator had eaten a child who'd crawled into its pen. The alligator's name was Cookie. Its owner shot it immediately. The owner was sad about everything—the child, the parents' grief, Cookie. He was quoted in the paper as saying that shooting Cookie was not an act of revenge.

When Tommy didn't drink, Sarah felt cold. She was shivering in the car. There were goose pimples on her tanned, thin arms. Tommy sat beside her smoking, saying nothing.

There had been words between them earlier. The parties here had an undercurrent of sexuality. Sarah could almost hear it, flowing around them all, carrying them all along. In the car, on the night of the accident, Sarah was at that point in the evening when she felt guilty. She wanted to make things better, make things nice. She had gone through her elated stage, her jealous stage, her stubbornly resigned stage and now she felt guilty. Had they talked about divorce that night, or had that been before, on other evenings? There was a flavor she remembered in their talks about divorce, a scent. It was hot, as Italy had been hot when they were there. Dust, bread, sun, a burning at the back of the throat from too much drinking.

But no, they hadn't been talking about divorce that night. The parties had been crowded. Sarah had hardly seen Tommy. Then, on her way to the bathroom, she had seen him sitting with a girl on a bed in one of the back rooms. He was telling the girl about condors, about hunting for condors in small, light planes.

"Oh, but you didn't hurt them, did you," the girl asked. She was someone's daughter, a little overweight but with beautiful skin and large green eyes.

"Oh no," Tommy assured her, "we weren't hunting to hurt."

Condors. Sarah looked at them sitting on the bed. When they noticed her, the girl blushed. Tommy smiled. Sarah imagined what she looked like, standing in the doorway.

That had been at the Steadmans'. The first party was at the Perrys'. The Perrys never served food. Sarah had two or three drinks there. The bar was set up beneath the grape arbor and everyone stood outside. It had still been light at the Perrys' but at the Steadmans' it was dark and people drank inside. Everyone spoke about the end of summer as though it were a bewildering and unnatural event.

They had stayed at the Steadmans' longer than they should have and now they were going to be late for dinner. Nevertheless, they were driving at a moderate speed through a familiar landscape, passing houses that they had been entertained in many times. There were the Salts and the Hollands and the Greys and the Dodsons. The Dodsons kept their gin in the freezer and owned two large and dappled crotch-sniffing dogs. The Greys imported southerners for their parties. The women all had lovely voices and knew how to make spoon bread and pickled tomatoes and artillery punch. The men had smiles when they'd say to Sarah, "Why, let me get you another. You don't have a thing in that glass, I swear." The Hollands gave the kind of dinner party where the shot was still in the duck and the silver should have been in a vault. Little whiskey was served but there was always excellent wine. The Salts were a high-strung couple. Jenny Salt was on some type of medication for tension and often dropped the canapés she attempted to serve. She and her husband, Pete, had a room in which there was nothing but a large dollhouse where witty mâché figures carried on assignations beneath tiny clocks and crystal chandeliers. Once, when Sarah was examining the dollhouse's library, where two figures were hunched over a chess game that was just about to be won, Pete had always said, on the twenty-second move, he told Sarah that she had pretty eyes. She moved away from him immediately. She closed her eyes. In another room, with the other guests, she talked about the end of summer.

On that night, at the end of summer, the night of the accident, Sarah was still talking as they passed the Salts' house. She was talking about Venice. She and Tommy had been there once. They drank in the plaza and listened to the orchestras. Sarah quoted D. H. Lawrence on Venice . . . *Abhorrent, green, slippery city* . . . But she and Tommy had liked Venice. They drank standing up at little bars. Sarah had a cold and she drank grappa and the cold had disappeared for the rest of her life.

After the Salts' house, the road swerved north and became very dark. There were no lights or houses for several miles. There were stone walls, an orchard of sickly peach trees, a cider mill. There was the St. James Episcopal Church, where Tommy took their daughter, Martha, to Sunday school. The Sunday school was oddly fundamental. There were many arguments among the children and their teachers as to the correct interpretation of Bible story favorites. For example, when Lazarus rose from the dead, was he still sick? Martha liked the fervor at St. James. Each week, her dinner graces were becoming more impassioned and fantastic. Martha was seven.

Each Sunday, Tommy takes Martha to her little classes at St. James. Sarah can imagine the child sitting there at a low table with her jar of crayons. Tommy doesn't go to church himself and Martha's classes are two hours long. Sarah doesn't know where Tommy goes. She suspects he is seeing someone. When they come home on Sundays, Tommy is sleek, exhilarated. The three of them sit down to the luncheon Sarah has prepared.

Over the years, Sarah suspects, Tommy has floated to the surface of her. They are swimmers now, far apart on the top of the sea.

Sarah at last fell silent. The road seemed endless as in a dream. They seemed to be slowing down. She could not feel her foot on the accelerator. She could not feel her hands on the wheel. Her mind was an untidy cupboard filled with shining bottles. The road was dark and silvery and straight. In the space ahead of her, there seemed to be something. It beckoned, glittering. Sarah's mind cleared a little. She saw Martha with her hair cut oddly short. She saw Tommy choosing a succession of houses, examining the plaster, the floorboards, the fireplaces, deciding where windows should be placed or walls knocked down. The sea was white and flat. It did not command her to change her life. It demanded nothing of her. She saw Martha sleeping, her paint-smudged fingers curled. She saw Tommy in the city with a woman, riding in a cab. The woman wore a short fur jacket and Tommy stroked it as he spoke. She saw a figure in the road ahead, its arms raised before its face as though to block out the sight of her. The figure was a boy who wore dark clothing, but his hair was bright, his face was shining. She saw her car leap forward and run him down where he stood.

TOMMY HAD TAKEN RESPONSIBILITY FOR THE ACCIDENT. HE HAD told the police he was driving. The boy apparently had been hitchhiking and had stepped out into the road. At the autopsy, traces of a hallucinogen were found in his system. The boy was fifteen years old and his name was Stevie Bettencourt. No charges were filed.

"My wife," Tommy told the police, "was not feeling well. My wife," he said, "was in the passenger seat."

Sarah stopped drinking immediately after the accident. She felt nauseated much of the time. She slept poorly. The bones in her hands ached. She remembered this was how she'd felt the last time she had stopped drinking. That had been two years before. She remembered why she'd stopped and also why she'd started again. She had stopped because she'd done a cruel thing to her little Martha. It was spring and she and Tommy were giving a dinner party. Sarah had two martinis in the late afternoon when she was preparing dinner and then she had two more martinis with her guests. Martha had come downstairs to say a polite good night to everyone as she had been taught. She had put on her nightie and brushed her teeth. Sarah poured a little more gin in her glass and went upstairs with her to brush out her hair and put her to bed. Martha had long, thick blond hair, of which she was very proud. On that night she wore it in a ponytail secured by an elasticized holder with two small colored balls on the ends. Sarah's fingers were clumsy and she could not get it off without pulling Martha's hair and making her cry. She got a pair of scissors and carefully began snipping at the stubborn elastic. The scissors were large, like shears, and they had been difficult to handle. A foot of Martha's gathered hair had abruptly fallen to the floor. Sarah remembered trying to pat it back into place on the child's head.

So Sarah had stopped drinking the first time. She did not feel renewed. She felt exhausted and wary. She read and cooked. She realized how little she and Tommy had to talk about. Tommy drank Scotch when he talked to her at night. Sometimes Sarah would silently count as he spoke to see how long the words took. When he was away and he telephoned her, she could hear the ice tinkling in the glass.

Tommy was in the city four days a week. He often changed hotels. He would bring Martha little bars of soap wrapped in the different colored papers of the hotels. Martha's drawers were full of the soaps scenting her clothes. When Tommy came home on the weekends he would work on the house and they would give parties at which Tommy was charming. Tommy had a talent for holding his liquor and for buying old houses, restoring them and selling them for three times what he had paid for them. Tommy and Sarah had moved six times in eleven years. All their homes had been fine old houses in excellent locations two or three hours from New York. Sarah would stay in the country while Tommy worked in the city.

For three weeks, Sarah did not drink. Then it was her birthday. Tommy gave her a slim gold necklace and fastened it around her neck. He wanted her to come to New York with him, to have dinner, see a play, spend the night with him in the fine suite the company had given him at the hotel. They had gotten a babysitter for Martha, a marvelous capable woman. Sarah drove. Tommy had never cared for driving. His hand rested on her thigh. Occasionally, he would slip his hand beneath her skirt. Sarah was sick with the thought that he touched other women like this.

By the time they were in Manhattan, they were arguing. They had been married for eleven years. Both had had brief marriages before. They could argue about anything. In midtown, Tommy stormed out of the car as Sarah braked for a light. He took his suitcase and disappeared.

Sarah drove carefully for many blocks. When she had the opportunity, she would pull to the curb and ask someone how to get to Connecticut. No one seemed to know. Sarah thought she was probably phrasing the question poorly but she didn't know how else to present it. After half an hour, she somehow found the hotel where Tommy was staying. The doorman parked the car and she went into the lobby. She looked into the hotel bar and saw Tommy in the dimness, sitting at a small table. He jumped up and kissed her passionately. He rubbed his hands up and down her sides. "Darling, darling," he said, "I want you to have a happy birthday."

Tommy ordered drinks for both of them. Sarah sipped hers slowly at first but then she drank it and he ordered others. The bar was subdued. There was a piano player who sang about the lord of the dance. The words seemed like those of a hymn. The hymn made her sad but she laughed. Tommy spoke to her urgently and gaily about little things. They laughed together like they had when they were first married. They had always drunk a lot together then and fallen asleep, comfortably and lovingly entwined.

They went to their room to change for the theater. The maid had turned back the beds. There was a fresh rose in a bud vase on the writing desk. They had another drink in the room and got undressed. Sarah awoke the next morning curled up on the floor with the bedspread tangled around her. Her mouth was sore. There was a bruise on her leg. Sarah crept into the bathroom and turned on the shower. She sat in the tub while the water beat against her. Pinned to the outside of the shower curtain was a note from Tommy, who had gone to work. *Darling,* the note said, *we had a good time on your birthday. I can't say I'm sorry we never got out. I'll call you for lunch. Love.*

Sarah turned the note inward until the water made the writing illegible. When the phone rang just before noon, she didn't answer it.

THERE IS A CERTAIN TYPE OF CONVERSATION ONE HEARS ONLY when drunk and it is like a dream, full of humor and threat and significance, deep significance. And how one witnesses things when drunk is different as well. It is like putting a face mask against the surface of the sea and looking into things, into their baffled and guileless hearts.

When Sarah had been a drinker, she felt she had a fundamental and inventive grasp of situations, but now that she no longer drank, she found herself in the midst of a great and impenetrable silence that she could in no way interpret.

It was a small village. Many of the people who lived there didn't even own cars. The demands of life were easily met and it was pretty there besides. It was divided between those who had always lived there and owned fishing boats and restaurants and the city people who had more recently discovered the area as a summer place and winter weekend investment. On the weekends, the New Yorkers would come up with their houseguests and their pâté and cheeses and build fires and go cross-country skiing. Tommy came home to Sarah on weekends. They did things together. They agreed on where to go. During the week she was on her own.

Once, alone, she saw a helicopter carrying a tree in a sling across the sound. The wealthy could afford to leave nothing behind.

Once, with the rest of the town, she saw five boats burning in their storage shrouds. Each summer resort has its winter pyromaniac.

Sarah did not read anymore. Her eyes hurt when she read and her hands ached all the time. During the week, she marketed and walked and cared for Martha.

It was three months after Stevie Bettencourt was killed when his mother visited Sarah. She came to the door and knocked on it and Sarah let her in.

Genevieve Bettencourt was Sarah's age, although she looked rather younger. She had been divorced almost from the day that Stevie was born. She had another son named Bruce, who lived with his father in Nova Scotia. She had an old powder-blue Buick parked on the street in front of Sarah's house. The Buick had one white door.

The two women sat in Sarah's handsome, sunny living room. It was very calm, very peculiar, almost thrilling. Genevieve looked all around the room. Off the living room were the bedrooms. The door to Sarah and Tommy's was closed but Martha's door was open. She had a little hanging garden against the window. She had a hamster in a cage. She had an enormous bookcase filled with dolls and books.

Genevieve said to Sarah, "That room wasn't there before. This used to be a lobster pound. I know a great deal about this town. People like you have nothing to do with what I know about this town. Do you remember the way things were, ever?"

"No," Sarah said.

Genevieve sighed. "Does your daughter look like you or your husband?"

"No one's ever told me she looked like me," Sarah said quietly.

"I did not want my life to know you," Genevieve said. She removed a hair from the front of her white blouse and dropped it to the floor. She looked out the window at the sun. The floor was of a very light and varnished pine. Sarah could see the hair lying there.

"I'm so sorry," Sarah said. "I'm so very, very sorry." She stretched her neck and put her head back.

"Stevie was a mixed-up boy," Genevieve said. "They threw him off the basketball team. He took pills. He had bad friends. He didn't study and he got a D in geometry and they wouldn't let him play basketball."

She got up and wandered around the room. She wore green rubber boots, dirty jeans and a beautiful, hand-knit sweater. "I once bought all my fish here," she said. "The O'Malleys owned it. There were practically no windows. Just narrow high ones over the tanks. Now it's all windows, isn't it? Don't you feel exposed?"

"No, I . . ." Sarah began. "There are drapes," she said.

"Off to the side, where you have your garden, there are whale bones if you dig deep enough. I can tell you a lot about this town."

"My husband wants to move," Sarah said.

"I can understand that, but you're the real drinker, after all, aren't you, not him."

"I don't drink anymore," Sarah said. She looked at the woman dizzily.

Genevieve was not pretty but she had a clear, strong face. She sat down on the opposite side of the room. "I guess I would like something," she said. "A glass of water." Sarah went to the kitchen and poured a glass of Vichy for them both. Her hands shook.

"We are not strangers to one another," Genevieve said. "We could be friends."

"My first husband always wanted to be friends with my second husband," Sarah said after a moment. "I could never understand it." This had somehow seemed analogous when she was saying it but now it did not. "It is not appropriate for us to be friends," she said.

Genevieve continued to sit and talk. Sarah found herself concentrating desperately on her articulate, one-sided conversation. She suspected that the words Genevieve was using were codes for other words, terrible words. Genevieve spoke thoughtlessly, dispassionately, with erratic flourishes of language. Sarah couldn't believe that they were chatting about food, men, the red clouds massed above the sea.

"I have a friend who is a designer," Genevieve said. "She hopes to make a great deal of money someday. Her work has completely altered her perceptions. Every time she looks at a view, she thinks of sheets. 'Take out those mountains,' she will say, 'lighten that cloud a bit and it would make a great sheet.' When she looks at the sky, she thinks of lingerie. Now when I look at the sky, I think of earlier, happier times when I'd looked at the sky. I've never been in love, have you?"

"Yes," Sarah said, "I'm in love."

"It's not a lucky thing, you know, to be in love."

There was a soft scuffling at the door and Martha came in. "Hello," she said. "School was good today. I'm hungry."

"Hello, dear," Genevieve said. To Sarah, she said, "Perhaps we can have lunch sometime."

"Who is that?" Martha asked Sarah after Genevieve had left.

"A neighbor," Sarah said. "One of Mommy's friends."

WHEN SARAH TOLD TOMMY ABOUT GENEVIEVE COMING TO VISIT her, he said, "It's harassment. It can be stopped."

It was Sunday morning. They had just finished breakfast and Tommy and Martha were drying the dishes and putting them away. Martha was wearing her church-school clothes and she was singing a song she had learned the Sunday before.

" ... I'm going to a Mansion on the Happy Day Express ... " she sang.

Tommy squeezed Martha's shoulders. "Go get your coat, sweetie," he said. When the child had gone, he said to Sarah, "Don't speak to this woman. Don't allow it to happen again."

"We didn't talk about that."

"What else could you talk about? It's weird."

"No one talks about that. No one, ever."

Tommy was wearing a corduroy suit and a tie Sarah had never seen before.

"I've done everything I could to protect you, Sarah, to help you straighten yourself out. It was a terrible thing but it's over. You have to get over it. Now, just don't see her again. She can't cause trouble if you don't speak to her."

Sarah stopped looking at Tommy's tie. She moved her eyes to the potatoes she had peeled and put in a bowl of water.

Martha came into the kitchen and held on to her father's arm. Her hair was long and thick, but it was getting darker. It was as though it had never been cut.

After they left, Sarah put the roast in the oven and went into the living room. The large window was full of the day, a colorless windy day without birds. Sarah sat on the floor and ran her fingers across the smooth, varnished wood. Beneath the expensive flooring was cold cement. Tanks had once lined the walls. Lobsters had crept back and forth across the mossy glass. The phone rang. Sarah didn't look at it, suspecting it was Genevieve. Then she picked it up.

"Hello," said Genevieve. "I thought I might drop by. It's a bleak day, isn't it. Cold. Is your family at home?"

"They go out on Sunday," Sarah said. "It gives me time to think. My husband takes our daughter to church."

"What do you think about?" The woman's voice seemed far away. Sarah strained to hear her.

"I'm supposed to cook. When they come back we have a noonday dinner."

"I can prepare clams in forty-three different ways," Genevieve said.

"This is a roast. A roast pork."

"Well, may I come over?"

"All right," Sarah said.

She continued to sit on the floor, waiting for Genevieve, looking at the water beneath the sky. The water on the horizon was a wide, satin ribbon. She wished that she had the courage to swim on such a bitter, winter day. To swim far out and rest, to hesitate and then to return.

Her life was dark, unexplored. Her abstinence had drained her. She felt sluggish, robbed. Her body had no freedom.

She sat, seeing nothing, the terrible calm light of the day around her. The things she remembered were so far away, bathed in a different light. Her life seemed so remote to her. She had sought happiness in someone, knowing she could not find it in herself, and now her heart was strangely hard. She rubbed her head with her hands.

Her life with Tommy was broken, irreparable. Her life with him was over. His infidelities kept getting mixed up in her mind with the death of the boy, with Tommy's false admission that he had been driving when the boy died. Sarah couldn't understand anything. Her life seemed so random, so needlessly constructed and now threatened in a way that did not interest her.

"Hello," Genevieve called. She had opened the front door and was standing in the hall. "You didn't hear my knock."

Sarah got up. She was to entertain this woman. She felt anxious, adulterous. The cold rose from Genevieve's skin and hair. Sarah took her coat and hung it in the closet. The fresh cold smell lingered on her hands.

Sarah moved into the kitchen. She took a package of rolls out of the freezer.

"Does your little girl like church," Genevieve asked.

"Yes, very much."

"It's a stage," said Genevieve. "I'm Catholic myself. As a child, I used to be fascinated by the martyrs. I remember a picture of St. Lucy, carrying her eyes like a plate of eggs, and St. Agatha. She carried her breasts on a plate."

Sarah said, "I don't understand what we're talking about. I know you're just using these words, that they mean other words, I—"

"Perhaps we could take your little girl to a movie sometime, a matinee, after she gets out of school."

"Her name is Martha," Sarah said. She saw Martha grown up, her hair cut short once more, taking rolls out of the freezer, waiting.

"Martha, yes," Genevieve said. "Have you wanted more children?"

"No," Sarah said. Their conversation was illegal, unspeakable. Sarah couldn't imagine it ever ending. Her fingers tapped against the ice-cube trays. "Would you care for a drink?"

"A very tall glass of vermouth," Genevieve said. She was looking at a little picture that Martha had made and Sarah had tacked to the wall. It was a very badly drawn horse. "I wanted children. I wanted to fulfill myself. One can never fulfill oneself. I think it is an impossibility."

Sarah made Genevieve's drink very slowly. She did not make one for herself.

"When Stevie was Martha's age, he knew everything about whales. He kept notebooks. Once, on his birthday, I took him to the whaling museum in New Bedford." She sipped her drink. "It all goes wrong somewhere," she said. She turned her back on Sarah and went into the other room. Sarah followed her.

"There are so many phrases for *dead*, you know," Genevieve was saying. "The kids think them up, or they come out of music or wars. Stevie had one that he'd use for dead animals and rock stars. He'd say they'd 'bought the farm.'"

Sarah nodded. She was pulling and peeling at the nails of her hands.

"I think it's pretty creepy. A dark farm, you know. Weedy. Run-down. Broken machinery everywhere. A real job."

Sarah raised her head. "You want us to share Martha, don't you," she said. "It's only right, isn't it?"

" . . . the paint blown away, acres and acres of tangled, black land, a broken shutter over the well."

Sarah lowered her head again. Her heart was cold, horrified. The reality of the two women, placed by hazard in this room, this bright functional tasteful room that Tommy had created, was being tested. Reality would resist, for days, perhaps weeks, but then it would yield. It would yield to this guest, this visitor, for whom Sarah had made room.

"Would you join me in another drink?" Genevieve asked. "Then I'll go."

"I mustn't drink," Sarah said.

Genevieve went into the kitchen and poured more vermouth for herself. Sarah could smell the meat cooking. From another room, the clock chimed.

"You must come to my home soon," Genevieve said. She did not sit down. Sarah looked at the pale green liquid in the glass.

"Yes," Sarah said, "soon."

"We must not greet one another on the street, however. People are quick to gossip."

"Yes," Sarah said. "They would condemn us." She looked heavily at Genevieve, full of misery and submission.

There was knocking on the door. "Sarah," Tommy's voice called, "why is the door locked?" She could see his dark head at the window.

"I must have thrown the bolt," Genevieve said. "It's best to lock your house in the winter, you know. It's the kids mostly. They get bored. Stevie was a robber once or twice, I'm sure." She put down her glass, took her coat from the closet and went out. Sarah heard Martha say, "That's Mommy's friend."

Tommy stood in the doorway and stared at Sarah. "Why was she here? Why did you lock the door?"

Sarah imagined seeing herself naked. She said, "There are robbers."

Tommy said, "If you don't feel safe here, we'll move. I've been looking at a wonderful place about twenty miles from here, on a cove. It only needs a little work. It will give us more room. There's a barn, some fence. Martha could have a horse."

Sarah looked at him with an intent, halted expression, as though she were listening to a dialogue no one present was engaged in. Finally, she said, "There are robbers. Everything has changed."

Escapes

W
HEN I WAS VERY SMALL, MY FATHER SAID, "LIZZIE, I WANT to tell you something about your grandfather. Just before he died, he was alive. Fifteen minutes before."

I had never known my grandfather. This was the most extraordinary thing I had ever heard about him.

Still, I said, No.

"No!" my father said. "What do you mean, 'No.'" He laughed.

I shook my head.

"All right," my father said, "it was one minute before. I thought you were too little to know such things, but I see you're not. It was even less than a minute. It was one *moment* before."

"Oh, stop teasing her," my mother said to my father.

"He's just teasing you, Lizzie," my mother said.

IN WARM WEATHER ONCE WE DROVE UP INTO THE MOUNTAINS, my mother, my father and I, and stayed for several days at a resort lodge on a lake. In the afternoons, horse races took place in the lodge. The horses were blocks of wood with numbers painted on them, moved from one end of the room to the other by ladies in ball gowns. There was a long pier that led out into the lake and at the end of the pier was a nightclub that had a twenty-foot-tall champagne glass on the roof. At night, someone would pull a switch and neon bubbles would spring out from the lit glass into the black air. I very much wanted such a glass on the roof of our own house and I wanted to be the one who, every night, would turn on the switch. My mother always said about this, "We'll see."

I saw an odd thing once, there in the mountains. I saw my father pretending to be lame. This was in the midst of strangers in the gift shop of the lodge. The shop sold hand-carved canes, among many other things, and when I came in to buy bubble gum in the shape of cigarettes, to which I was devoted, I saw my father hobbling painfully down the aisle, leaning heavily on a dully gleaming yellow cane, his shoulders hunched, one leg turned out at a curious angle. My handsome, healthy father, his face drawn in dreams. He looked at me. And then he looked away as though he did not know me.

My mother was a drinker. Because my father left us, I assumed he was not a drinker, but this may not have been the case. My mother loved me and was always kind to me. We spent a great deal of time together, my mother and I. This was before I knew how to read. I suspected there was a trick to reading, but I did not know the trick. Written words were something between me and a place I could not go. My mother went back and forth to that place all the time, but couldn't explain to me exactly what it was like there. I imagined it to be a different place.

As a very young child, my mother had seen the magician Houdini. Houdini had made an elephant disappear. He had also made an orange tree grow from a seed right on the stage. Bright oranges hung from the tree and he had picked them and thrown them out into the audience. People could eat the oranges or take them home, whatever they wanted.

"How did he make the elephant disappear," I asked.

"He disappeared in a puff of smoke," my mother said. "Houdini said that even the elephant didn't know how it was done."

"Was it a baby elephant," I asked.

My mother sipped her drink. She said that Houdini was more than a magician, he was an escape artist. She said that he could escape from handcuffs and chains and ropes.

"They put him in straitjackets and locked him in trunks and threw him in swimming pools and rivers and oceans and he escaped," my mother said. "He escaped from water-filled vaults. He escaped from coffins."

I said that I wanted to see Houdini.

"Oh, Houdini's dead, Lizzie," my mother said. "He died a long time ago. A man punched him in the stomach three times and he died."

Dead. I asked if he couldn't get out of being dead.

"He met his match there," my mother said.

She said that he turned a bowl of flowers into a pony who cantered around the stage.

"He sawed a lady in half too, Lizzie." Oh, how I wanted to be that lady, sawed in half and then made whole again!

My mother spoke happily, laughing. We sat at the kitchen table and my mother was drinking from a small glass that rested snugly in her hand. It was my favorite glass too but she never let me drink from it. There were all kinds of glasses in our cupboard but this was the one we both liked. This was in Maine. Outside, in the yard, was our car, which was an old blue convertible.

"Was there blood," I asked.

"No, Lizzie, no. He was a magician!"

"Did she cry, that lady," I wanted to know.

"I don't think so," my mother said. "Maybe he hypnotized her first."

It was winter. My father had never ridden in the blue convertible, which my mother had bought after he had gone. The car was old then, and was rusted here and there. Beneath the rubber mat on my side, the passenger side, part of the floor had rusted through completely. When we went anywhere in the car, I would sometimes lift up the mat so I could see the road rushing past beneath us and feel the cold round air as it came up through the hole. I would pretend that the coldness was trying to speak to me, in the same way that words written down tried to speak. The air wanted to tell me something, but I didn't care about it, that's what I thought. Outside, the car stood in the snow.

I had a dream about the car. My mother and I were alone together as we always were, linked in our hopeless and uncomprehending love of each other, and we were driving to a house. It seemed to be our destination but we arrived only to move on. We drove again, always returning to the house, which we would circle and leave, only to arrive at it again. As we drove, the inside of the car grew hair. The hair was gray and it grew and grew. I never told my mother about this dream just as I had never told her about my father leaning on the cane. I was a secretive person. In that way, I was like my mother.

I wanted to know more about Houdini. "Was Houdini in love," I asked. "Did he love someone?"

"Bess," my mother said. "He loved his wife, Bess."

I went and got a glass and poured some ginger ale in it and I sipped my ginger ale as slowly as I had seen my mother sip her drink many, many times. Even then, I had the gestures down. I sat opposite her, very still and quiet, pretending.

But then I wanted to know if there was magic in the way he loved her. Could he make her disappear. Could he make both of them disappear, was the way I put my question.

"No one knew anything about Bess except that Houdini loved her," my mother said. "He never turned their love into loneliness, which would have been beneath him of course."

We ate our supper and after supper my mother would have another little bit to drink. Then she would read articles from the newspaper aloud to me.

"My goodness," she said, "what a strange story. A hunter shot a bear who was carrying a woman's pocketbook in its mouth."

"Oh, oh," I cried. I looked at the newspaper and struck it with my fingers. My mother read on, a little oblivious to me. The woman had lost her purse years before on a camping trip. Everything was still inside it, her wallet and her compact and her keys.

"Oh," I cried. I thought this was terrible. I was frightened, thinking of my mother's pocketbook, how she always carried it always, and the poor bear too.

"Why did the bear want to carry a pocketbook," I asked.

My mother looked up from the words in the newspaper. It was as though she had come back into the room I was in.

"Why, Lizzie," she said.

"The poor bear," I said.

"Oh, the bear is all right," my mother said. "The bear got away."

I did not believe this was the case. She herself said the bear had been shot.

"The bear escaped," my mother said. "It says so right here," and she ran her finger along a line of words. "It ran back into the woods to its home." She stood up and came around the table and kissed me. She smelled then like the glass that was always in the sink in the morning, and the smell reminds me still of daring and deception, hopes and little lies.

I shut my eyes and felt I could not hear my mother. I saw the bear holding the pocketbook, walking through the woods with it, feeling fine and different and pretty too, then stopping to find something in it, wanting something, moving its big paw through the pocketbook's small things.

"Lizzie," my mother called to me. My mother did not know where I was, which alarmed me. I opened my eyes.

"Don't cry, Lizzie," my mother said. She looked as though she were about to cry too. This was how it often was at night, late in the kitchen, with my mother.

My mother returned to the newspaper and began to turn the pages. She called my attention to the drawing of a man holding a hat with stars sprinkling out of it. It was an advertisement for a magician who would be performing not far away. We decided we would see him. My mother knew just the seats she wanted for us, good seats, on the aisle, close to the stage. We might be called up on the stage, she said, to be part of the performance. Magicians often used people from the audience, particularly children. I might even be given a rabbit.

I wanted a rabbit.

I put my hands on the table and I could see the rabbit between them. He was solid white in the front and solid black in the back as though he were made up of two rabbits. There are rabbits like that. I saw him there, before me on the table, a nice rabbit.

My mother went to the phone and ordered two tickets, and not many days after that, we were in our car driving to Portland for the matinee performance. I very much liked the word *matinee*. Matinee, matinee, I said. There was a broad hump on the floor between our seats and it was here where my mother put her little glass, the glass often full, never, it seemed, more than half empty. We chatted together and I thought we must have appeared interesting to others as we passed by in our convertible in winter. My mother spoke about happiness. She told me that the happiness that comes out of nowhere, out of nothing, is the very best kind. We paid no attention to the coldness, which was speaking in the way that it had, but enjoyed the sun beating through the windshield on our pale hands.

My mother said that Houdini had black eyes and that white doves flew from his fingertips. She said that he escaped from a block of ice.

"Did he look like my father, Houdini," I asked. "Did he have a mustache."

"Your father didn't have a mustache," my mother said, laughing. "Oh, I wish I could be more like you."

Later, she said, "Maybe he didn't escape from a block of ice, I'm not sure about that. Maybe he wanted to, but he never did."

We stopped for lunch somewhere, a dark little restaurant along the road. My mother had cocktails and I myself drank something cold and sweet. The restaurant was not very nice. It smelled of smoke and dampness as though once it had burned down, and it was so noisy that I could not hear my mother very well. My mother looked like a woman in a bar, pretty and disturbed, hunched forward saying, Who do you think I look like, will you remember me? She was saying all manner of things. We lingered there, and then my mother asked the time of someone and seemed surprised. My mother was always surprised by time. Outside, there were woods of green fir trees, whose lowest branches swept the ground, and as we were getting back into the car, I believed I saw something moving far back in the darkness of the woods beyond the slick, snowy square of the parking lot. It was the bear, I thought. Hurry, hurry, I thought. The hunter is playing with his children. He is making them something to play in as my father had once made a small playhouse for me. He is not the hunter yet. But in my heart I knew the bear was gone and the shape was just the shadow of something else in the afternoon.

My mother drove very fast but the performance had already begun when we arrived. My mother's face was damp and her good blouse had a spot on it. She went into the ladies' room and when she returned the spot was larger, but it was water now and not what it had been before. The usher assured us that we had not missed much. The usher said that the magician was not very good, that he talked and talked, he told a lot of jokes and then when you were bored and distracted, something would happen, something would have changed. The usher smiled at my mother. He seemed to like her, even know her in some way. He was a small man, like an old boy, balding. I did not care for him. He led us to our seats, but there were people sitting in them and there was a small disturbance as the strangers rearranged themselves. We were both expectant, my mother and I, and we watched the magician intently. My mother's lips were parted, and her eyes were bright. On the stage were a group of children about my age, each with a hand on a small cage the magician was holding. In the cage was a tiny bird. The magician would ask the children to jostle the cage occasionally and the bird would flutter against the bars so that everyone would see it was a real thing with bones and breath and feelings too. Each child announced that they had a firm grip on the bars. Then the magician put a cloth over the cage, gave a quick tug and both cage and bird vanished. I was not surprised. It seemed just the kind of thing that was going to happen. I decided to withhold my applause when I saw that my mother's hands too were in her lap. There were several more tricks of the magician's invention, certainly nothing I would have asked him to do. Large constructions of many parts and colors were wheeled onto the stage. There were doors everywhere that the magician opened and slammed shut. Things came and went, all to the accompaniment of loud music. I was confused and grew hot. My mother too moved restlessly in the next seat. Then there was an intermission and we returned to the lobby.

"This man is a far, far cry from the great Houdini," my mother said.

"What were his intentions, exactly," I asked.

He had taken a watch from a man in the audience and smashed it for all to see with a hammer. Then the watch, unharmed, had reappeared behind the man's ear.

"A happy memory can be a very misleading thing," my mother said. "Would you like to go home?"

I really did not want to leave. I wanted to see it through. I held the glossy program in my hand and turned the pages. I stared hard at the print beneath the pictures and imagined all sorts of promises being made.

"Yes, we want to see how it's done, don't we, you and I," my mother said. "We want to get to the bottom of it."

I guessed we did.

"All right, Lizzie," my mother said, "but I have to get something out of the car. I'll be right back."

I waited for her in a corner of the lobby. Some children looked at me and I looked back. I had a package of gum cigarettes in my pocket and I extracted one carefully and placed the end in my mouth. I held the elbow of my right arm with my left hand and smoked the cigarette for a long time and then I folded it up in my mouth and I chewed it for a while. My mother had not yet returned when the performance began again. She was having a little drink, I knew, and she was where she went when she drank without me, somewhere in herself. It was not the place where words could take you but another place even. I stood alone in the lobby for a while, looking out into the street. On the sidewalk outside the theater, sand had been scattered and the sand ate through the ice in ugly holes. I saw no one like my mother who passed by. She was wearing a red coat. Once she had said to me, You've fallen out of love with me, haven't you, and I knew she was thinking I was someone else, but this had happened only once.

I HEARD THE MUSIC FROM THE STAGE AND I FINALLY RETURNED to our seats. There were not as many people in the audience as before. Onstage with the magician was a woman in a bathing suit and high-heeled shoes holding a chain saw. The magician demonstrated that the saw was real by cutting up several pieces of wood with it. There was the smell of torn wood for everyone to smell and sawdust on the floor for all to see. Then a table was wheeled out and the lady lay down on it in her bathing suit, which was in two pieces. Her stomach was very white. The magician talked and waved the saw around. I suspected he was planning to cut the woman in half and I was eager to see this. I hadn't the slightest fear about this at all. I did wonder if he would be able to put her together again or if he would only cut her in half. The magician said that what was about to happen was too dreadful to be seen directly, that he did not want anyone to faint from the sight, so he brought out a small screen and placed it in front of the lady so that we could no longer see her white stomach, although everyone could still see her face and her shoes. The screen seemed unnecessary to me and I would have preferred to have been seated on the other side of it. Several people in the audience screamed. The lady who was about to be sawed in half began to chew on her lip and her face looked worried.

It was then that my mother appeared on the stage. She was crouched over a little, for she didn't have her balance back from having climbed up there. She looked large and strange in her red coat. The coat, which I knew very well, seemed the strangest thing. Someone screamed again, but more uncertainly. My mother moved toward the magician, smiling and speaking and gesturing with her hands, and the magician said, "No,

I can't of course, you should know better than this, this is a performance, you can't just appear like this, please sit down . . ."

My mother said, "But you don't understand I'm willing, though I know the hazards and it's not that I believe you, no one would believe you for a moment but you can trust me, that's right, your faith in me would be perfectly placed because I'm not part of this, that's why I can be trusted because I don't know how it's done . . ."

Someone near me said, "Is she kidding, that woman, what's her plan, she comes out of nowhere and wants to be cut in half . . ."

"Lady," the magician said, and I thought a dog might appear for I knew a dog named Lady who had a collection of colored balls.

My mother said, "Most of us don't understand I know and it's just as well because the things we understand that's it for them, that's just the way we are . . ."

She probably thought she was still in that place in herself, but everything she said were the words coming from her mouth. Her lipstick was gone. Did she think she was in disguise, I wondered.

"But why not," my mother said, "to go and come back, that's what we want, that's why we're here and why can't we expect something to be done you can't expect us every day we get tired of showing up every day you can't get away with this forever then it was different but you should be thinking about the children . . ." She moved a little in a crooked fashion, speaking.

"My god," said a voice, "that woman's drunk."

"Sit down, please!" someone said loudly.

My mother started to cry then and she stumbled and pushed her arms out before her as though she were pushing away someone who was trying to hold her, but no one was trying to hold her. The orchestra began to play and people began to clap. The usher ran out onto the stage and took my mother's hand. All this happened in an instant. He said something to her, he held her hand and she did not resist his holding it, then slowly the two of them moved down the few steps that led to the stage and up the aisle until they stopped beside me for the usher knew I was my mother's child. I followed them, of course, although in my mind I continued to sit in my seat. Everyone watched us leave. They did not notice that I remained there among them, watching too.

We went directly out of the theater and into the streets, my mother weeping on the little usher's arm. The shoulders of his jacket were of cardboard and there was gold braid looped around it. We were being taken away to be murdered, which seemed reasonable to me. The usher's ears were large and he had a bump on his neck above the collar of his shirt. As we walked he said little soft things to my mother that gradually seemed to be comforting her. I hated him. It was not easy to walk together along the frozen sidewalks of the city. There was a belt on my mother's coat and I hung on to that as we moved unevenly along.

"Look, I've pulled myself through," he said. "You can pull yourself through." He was speaking to my mother.

We went into a coffee shop and sat down in a booth. "You can collect yourself in here," he said. "You can sit here as long as you want and drink coffee and no one will make you leave." He asked me if I wanted a donut. I would not speak to him. If he addressed me again, I thought, I would bite him. On the wall over the counter were pictures of sandwiches. I did not want to be there and I did not take off either my mittens or my coat. The little usher went up to the counter and brought back coffee for my mother and a donut on a plate for me. "Oh," my mother said, "what have I done?" and she swung her head from side to side.

"I could tell right away about you," the usher said. "You've got to pull yourself together. It took jumping off a bridge for me and breaking both legs before I got turned around. You don't want to let it go that far."

My mother looked at him. "I can't imagine," my mother said.

Outside, a child passed by, walking with her sled. She looked behind her often and you could tell she was admiring how the sled followed her so quickly on its runners.

"You're a mother," the usher said to my mother, "you've got to pull yourself through."

His kindness made me feel he had tied us up with rope. At last he left us and my mother laid her head down on the table and fell asleep. I had never seen my mother sleeping and I watched her as she must once have watched me, as everyone watches a sleeping thing, not knowing how it would turn out or when. Then slowly I began to eat the donut with my mittened hands. The sour hair of the wool mingled with the tasteless crumbs and this utterly absorbed my attention. I pretended someone was feeding me.

AS IT HAPPENED, MY MOTHER WAS NOT ABLE TO PULL HERSELF through, but this was later. At the time, it was not so near the end and when my mother woke we found the car and left Portland, my mother saying my name. "Lizzie," she said. "Lizzie." I felt as though I must be with her somewhere and that she knew that too, but not in that old blue convertible traveling home in the dark, the soft, stained roof ballooning up as I knew it looked like it was from outside. I got out of it, but it took me years.

Rot

LUCY WAS WATCHING THE STREET WHEN AN OLD FORD THUN-
derbird turned in to their driveway. She had never seen the car
before and her husband, Dwight, was driving it. One of Dwight's old
girlfriends leapt from the passenger seat and ran toward the house. Her
name was Caroline, she had curly hair and big white teeth, more than
seemed normal, and Lucy liked her the least of all of Dwight's old girlfriends.

"I was the horn," Caroline said. "That car doesn't have one so I was
it. I'd yell out the window, 'Watch out!'"

"Were you the brakes too or just the horn," Lucy asked.

"It has brakes," Caroline said, showing her startling teeth. She went
into the living room and said, "Hello, rug." She always spoke to the rug
lying there. The rug was from Mexico with birds of different colors flying across it. All of the birds had long, white eyes. Dwight and Caroline
had brought the rug back from the Yucatán when they had gone snor-
keling there years before. Some of the coves were so popular that the
fish could scarcely be seen for all the suntan oil floating in the water. At
Garrafón in Isla Mujeres, Dwight told Lucy, he had raised his head and
seen a hundred people bobbing facedown over the rocks of the reef and
a clean white tampon bobbing there among them. Caroline had said at
the time, "It's disgusting, but it's obviously some joke."

Caroline muttered little things to the rug, showing off, Lucy thought,
although she wasn't speaking Spanish to it, she didn't know Spanish.
Lucy looked out the window at Dwight sitting in the Thunderbird.
It was old with new paint, black, with a white top and portholes and
skirts. He looked a little big for it. He got out abruptly and ran to the
house as though through rain, but there was no rain. It was a still day
in spring, just before Easter, with an odious weight to the air. Recently,
when they had been coming inside, synthetic stuff from Easter baskets

had been traveling in with them, the fake nesting matter, the pastel and crinkly stuff of Easter baskets. Lucy couldn't imagine where they kept picking it up from, but no festive detritus came in this time.

Dwight gave her a hard, wandering kiss on the mouth. Lately, it was as though he were trying out kisses, trying to adjust them.

"You'll tell me all about this, I guess," Lucy said.

"Lucy," Dwight said solemnly.

Caroline joined them and said, "I've got to be off. I don't know the time, but I bet I can guess it to within a minute. I can do that," she assured Lucy. Caroline closed her eyes. Her teeth seemed still to be looking out at them, however. "Five-ten," she said after a while. Lucy looked at the clock on the wall, which showed ten minutes past five. She shrugged.

"That car is some cute," Caroline said, giving Dwight a little squeeze. "Isn't it some cute?" she said to Lucy. "Your Dwight's been tracking this car for days."

"I bought it from the next of kin," Dwight said.

Lucy looked at him impassively. She was not a girl who was quick to alarm.

"I was down at the Aquarium last week looking at the fish," Dwight began.

"Oh, that Aquarium," Lucy said.

The Aquarium was where a baby seal had been put to sleep because he was born too ugly to be viewed by children. He had not been considered viewable so off he went. The Aquarium offended Lucy. "I like fish," Dwight had told Lucy when she asked why he spent so much of his free time at the Aquarium. "Men like fish."

"And when I came out into the parking lot, next to our car was this little Thunderbird and there was a dead man sitting behind the wheel."

"Isn't that something!" Caroline exclaimed.

"I was the first to find him," Dwight said. "I'm no expert but that man was gone."

"What did this dead man look like," Lucy asked Dwight.

He thought for a moment, then said, "He looked like someone in the movies. He had a large head."

"In any case," Lucy said a little impatiently.

"In any case," Dwight said, "this car just jumped at me, you know how some things do. I knew I just had to have this car, it was just so pretty. This car is almost cherry," Dwight said, gesturing out at it, "and now it's ours."

"That car is not almost cherry," Lucy said. "A man died in it. I would say that this car was about as un-cherry as you can get." She went on vehemently like this for a while.

Caroline gazed at her, her lips parted, her teeth making no judgment. Then she said, "I've got to get back to my lonely home." She did not live far away. Almost everybody they knew, and a lot of people they didn't, lived close by. "Now you two have fun in that car, it's a sweet little car." She kissed Dwight and he patted her back in an avuncular fashion as he walked her to the door. The air outside had a faint, thin smell of fruit and rubber. A siren screamed through it.

When Dwight returned, Lucy said, "I don't want a car a man died in for my birthday."

"It's not your birthday coming up, is it?"

Lucy admitted it was not, although Dwight often planned for her birthday months in advance. She blushed.

"It's funny how some people live longer than others, isn't it," she finally said.

WHEN DWIGHT HAD FIRST SEEN LUCY, HE WAS TWENTY-FIVE years old and she was a four-month-old baby.

"I'm gonna marry you," Dwight said to the baby. People heard him. He was tall and had black hair, and was wearing a leather jacket that a girlfriend had sewed a silk liner into. It was a New Year's Eve party at this girlfriend's house and the girl was standing beside him. "Oh, right," she said. She didn't see anything particularly intriguing about this baby. They could make better babies than this, she thought. Lucy lay in a white wicker basket on a sofa. Her hair was sparse and her expression solemn. "You're gonna be my wife," Dwight said. He was very good with babies and good with children too. When Lucy was five, her favorite things were pop-up books in which one found what was missing by pushing or pulling or turning a tab, and for her birthday Dwight bought her fifteen of these, surely as many as had ever been produced. When she was ten he bought her a playhouse and filled it with balloons. Dwight was good with adolescents as well. When she was fourteen, he rented her a horse for a year. As for women, he had a special touch with them, as all his girlfriends would attest. Dwight wasn't faithful to Lucy as she was growing up, but he was attentive and devoted. Dwight kept up the pace nicely. And all the time Lucy was stoically growing up, learning how to dress herself and read, letting her hair grow, then cutting it all off, joining clubs and playing records, doing her algebra, going on dates, Dwight was out in the world. He always sent her little stones from the places he visited and she ordered them by size or color and put them in and out of boxes and jars until there came to be so many she grew confused as to where each had come from. At about the time Lucy didn't care if she saw another little stone in her life, they got married. They bought a house and settled in. The house was a large, comfortable one, large enough, was the inference, to accommodate growth of various sorts. Things were all right. Dwight was like a big strange book where Lucy just needed to turn the pages and there everything was already.

THEY WENT OUT AND LOOKED AT THE THUNDERBIRD IN THE WANing light.

"It's a beauty, isn't it," Dwight said. "Wide whites, complete engine dress." He opened the hood, exposing the gleaming motor. Dwight was happy, his inky eyes shone. When he slammed the hood shut there was a soft rattling as of pebbles being thrown.

"What's that," Lucy asked.

"What's what, my sweet?"

"That," Lucy said, "on the ground." She picked up a piece of rust, as big as her small hand and very light. Dwight peered at it. As she was trying to hand it to him, it dropped and crumbled.

"It looked so solid, I didn't check underneath," Dwight said. "I'll have some body men come over tomorrow and look at it. I'm sure it's no problem, just superficial stuff."

She ran her fingers behind the rocker panel of the door and came up with a handful of flakes.

"I don't know why you'd want to make it worse," Dwight said.

The next morning, two men were scooting around on their backs beneath the T-Bird, poking here and there with screwdrivers and squinting at the undercarriage. Lucy, who enjoyed a leisurely breakfast, was still in the kitchen, finishing it. As she ate her cereal, she studied the milk carton, a panel of which made a request for organs. Lucy was aware of a new determination in the world to keep things going. She rinsed her bowl and went outside just as the two men had slipped from beneath the car and were standing up, staring at Dwight. Gouts and clots of rust littered the drive.

"This for your daughter here?" one of them said.

"No," Dwight said irritably.

"I wouldn't give this to my daughter."

"It's not for anyone like that!" Dwight said.

"Bottom's just about to go," the other one said. "Riding along, these plates give, floor falls out, your butt's on the road. You need new pans at least. Pans are no problem." He chewed on his thumbnail. "It's rusted out too where the leaf springs meet the frame. Needs some work, no doubt about that. Somebody's done a lot of work but it needs a lot more work for sure. Donny, get me the Hemmings out of the truck."

The other man ambled off and returned with a thick brown catalog.

"Maybe you should trade up," the first man said. "Get a car with a solid frame."

Dwight shook his head. "You can't repair it?"

"Why sure we can repair it!" Donny said. "You can get everything for these cars, all the parts, you got yourself a classic here!" He thumbed through the catalog until he came to a page that offered the services of something called The T-Bird Sanctuary. The Sanctuary seemed to be a wrecking yard. A grainy photograph showed a jumble of cannibalized cars scattered among trees. It was the kind of picture that looked as though it had been taken furtively with a concealed camera.

"I'd trade up," the other man said. "Lookit over here, this page here, Fifty-seven T-Bird supercharged, torch red, total body-off restoration, nothing left undone, ready to show . . ."

"Be still, my heart," Donny said.

"You know if you are going to stick with this car you got," the other man said, "and I'm not advising you to, you should paint it the original color. This black ain't original." He opened the door and pointed at a smudge near the hinges. "See here, powder blue."

Lucy returned to the house. She stood inside, thinking, looking out at the street. When she had been a little girl walking to school, she had once found an envelope on the street with her name on it, but there hadn't been anything in the envelope.

"We're getting another opinion," Dwight said when he came in. "We're taking it over to Boris, the best in the business."

They drove to the edge of town, to where another town began, to a big brown building there. Lucy enjoyed the car. It handled very well, she thought. They hurtled along, even though bigger cars passed them.

Boris was small, bald and stern. The German shepherd that stood beside him seemed remarkably large. His paws were delicately rounded but each was the size of a football. There was room, easily, for another German shepherd inside him, Lucy thought. Boris drove the Thunderbird onto a lift and elevated it. He walked slowly beneath it, his hands on his hips. Not a hair grew from his head. He lowered the car down and said, "Hopeless." When neither Lucy nor Dwight spoke, he shouted, "Worthless. Useless." The German shepherd sighed as though he had heard this prognosis many times.

"What about where the leaf springs meet the frame?" Lucy said. The phrase enchanted her.

Boris moved his hands around and then clutched and twisted them together in a pleading fashion.

"How can I make you nice people understand that it is hopeless? What can I say so that you will hear me, so that you will believe me? Do you like ripping up one-hundred-dollar bills? Is this what you want to do with the rest of your life? What kind of masochists are you? It would be wicked of me to give you hope. This car is unrestorable. It is full of rust and rot. Rust is a living thing, it breathes, it eats and it is swallowing up your car. These quarters and rockers have already been replaced, once, twice, who knows how many times. You will replace them again. It is nothing to replace quarters and rockers! How can I save you from your innocence and foolishness and delusions. You take out a bad part, say, you solder in new metal, you line-weld it tight, you replace the whole rear end, say, and what have you accomplished, you have accomplished only a small part of what is necessary, you have accomplished hardly anything! I can see you feel dread and nausea at what I'm saying but it is nothing compared to the dread and nausea you will feel if you continue in this unfortunate project. Stop wasting your thoughts! Rot like this cannot be stayed. This brings us to the question, What is man? with its three subdivisions, What can he know? What ought he do? What may he hope? Questions which concern us all, even you, little lady."

"What!" Dwight said.

"My suggestion is to drive this car," Boris said in a calmer tone, "enjoy it, but for the spring and summer only, then dump it, part it out. Otherwise, you'll be putting in new welds, more and more new welds, but always the collapse will be just ahead of you. Years will pass and then will come the day when there is nothing to weld the weld to, there is no frame, nothing. Once rot, then nothing." He bowed, then retired to his office.

Driving home, Dwight said, "You never used to hear about rust and rot all the time. It's new, this rust and rot business. You don't know what's around you anymore."

Lucy knew Dwight was depressed and tried to look concerned, though in truth she didn't care much about the T-Bird. She was distracted by a tune that was going through her head. It was a song she remembered hearing when she was a little baby, about a tiny ant being at his doorway. She finally told Dwight about it and hummed the tune.

"Do you remember that little song," she asked.

"Almost," Dwight said.

"What was that about anyway," Lucy asked. "The tiny ant didn't do anything, he was just waiting at his doorway."

"It was just nonsense stuff you'd sing to a little baby," Dwight said. He looked at her vaguely and said, "My sweet . . ."

LUCY CALLED UP HER FRIEND DAISY AND TOLD HER ABOUT THE black Thunderbird. She did not mention rot. Daisy was ten years older than Lucy and was one of the last of Dwight's girlfriends. Daisy had recently had one of her legs amputated. There had been a climbing accident and then she had just let things go on for too long. She was a tall, boyish-looking woman who before the amputation had always worn jeans. Now she slung herself about in skirts, for she found it disturbed people less when she wore a skirt, but when she went to the beach she wore a bathing suit, and she didn't care if she disturbed people or not because she loved the beach, the water, so still and so heavy, hiding so much.

"I didn't read in the paper about a dead man just sitting in his car like that," Daisy said. "Don't they usually report such things? It's unusual, isn't it?"

Lucy had fostered Daisy's friendship because she knew Daisy was still in love with Dwight. If someone, God, for example, had asked Daisy if she'd rather have her leg back or Dwight, she would have said, "Dwight." Lucy felt excited about this and at the same time mystified and pitying. Knowing it always cheered Lucy up when she felt out of sorts.

"Did I tell you about the man in the supermarket with only one leg," Daisy asked. "I had never seen him before. He was with his wife and baby and instead of being in the mother's arms the baby was in a stroller so the three of them took up a great deal of room in the aisle, and when I turned down the aisle I became entangled with this little family. I felt that I had known this man all my life, of course. People were smiling at us. Even the wife was smiling. It was dreadful."

"You should find someone," Lucy said without much interest.

Daisy's leg was in ashes in a drawer in a church garden, waiting for the rest of her.

"Oh no, no," Daisy said modestly. "So!" she said. "You're going to have another car!"

It was almost suppertime and there was the smell of meat on the air. Two small, brown birds hopped across the patchy grass and Lucy watched them with interest for birds seldom frequented their neighborhood. Whenever there were more than three birds in a given place, it was considered an infestation and a variety of measures were taken, which reduced their numbers to an acceptable level. Lucy remembered that when she was little, the birds that flew overhead sometimes cast shadows on the ground. There were flocks of them at times and she remembered hearing the creaking of their wings, but she supposed that was just the sort of thing a child might remember, having seen or heard it only once.

She set the dining room table for three as this was the night each spring when Rosette would come for dinner, bringing shad and shad roe, Dwight's favorite meal. Rosette had been the most elegant of Dwight's girlfriends, and the one with the smallest waist. She was now married to a man named Bob. When Rosette had been Dwight's girlfriend, she had been called Muffin. For the last five springs, ever since Lucy and Dwight had been married, she would have the shad flown down from the North and she would bring it to their house and cook it. Yet even though shad was his favorite fish and he only got it once a year, Dwight would be coming home a little late this night because he was getting another opinion on the T-Bird. Lucy no longer accompanied him on these discouraging expeditions.

Rosette appeared in a scant, white cocktail dress and red high-heeled shoes. She had brought her own china, silver, candles and wine. She reset the table, dimmed the lights and made Lucy and herself large martinis. They sat, waiting for Dwight, speaking aimlessly about things. Rosette and Bob were providing a foster home for two delinquents, whose names were Jerry and Jackie.

"What awful children," Rosette said. "They're so homely too. They were cuter when they were younger, now their noses are really long and their jaws are odd-looking too. I gave them bunny baskets this year and Jackie wrote me a note saying that what she really needed was a prescription for birth-control pills."

When Dwight arrived, Rosette was saying, "Guilt's not a bad thing to have. There are worse things to have than guilt." She looked admiringly at Dwight and said, "You're a handsome eyeful." She made him a martini, which he drank quickly, then she made them all another one. Drinking hers, Lucy stood and watched the T-Bird in the driveway. It was a dainty car, and the paint was so black it looked wet. Rosette prepared the fish with great solemnity, bending over Lucy's somewhat dirty broiler. They all ate in a measured way. Lucy tried to eat the roe one small egg at a time but found that this was impossible.

"I saw Jerry this afternoon walking down the street carrying a weed whacker," Dwight said. "Does he do yard work now? Yard work's a good occupation for a boy."

"Delinquents aren't always culprits," Rosette said. "That's what many people don't understand, but no, Jerry is not doing yard work, he probably stole that thing off someone's lawn. Bob tries to talk to him but Jerry doesn't heed a word he says. Bob's not very convincing."

"How is Bob?" Lucy asked.

"Husband Bob is a call I never should have answered," Rosette said.

Lucy crossed her arms over her stomach and squeezed herself with delight because Rosette said the same thing each year when she was asked about Bob.

"Life with Husband Bob is a long twilight of drinking and listless anecdote," Rosette said.

Lucy giggled, because Rosette always said this, too.

THE NEXT DAY, DWIGHT TOLD LUCY OF HIS INTENTIONS TO BRING the T-Bird into the house. "She won't last long on the street," he said. "She's a honey but she's tired. Elements are hard on a car and it's the elements that have done this sweet little car in. We'll put her in the living room, which is underfurnished anyway, and it will be like living with a work of art right in our living room. We'll keep her shined up and sit inside her and talk. It's very peaceful inside that little car, you know."

The T-Bird looked alert and coquettish as they spoke around it.

"That car was meant to know the open road," Lucy said. "I think we should drive it till it drops." Dwight looked at her sorrowfully and she widened her eyes, not believing she had said such a thing. "Well," she said, "I don't think a car should be in a house, but maybe we could bring it in for a little while and then if we don't like it we could take it out again."

He put his arms around her and embraced her and she could hear his heart pounding away in his chest with gratitude and excitement.

Lucy called Daisy on the telephone. The banging and sawing had already begun. "Men go odd differently than women," Daisy said. "That's always been the case. For example, I read that men are exploring how to turn the earth around toxic waste dumps into glass by the insertion of high-temperature electric probes. A woman would never think of something like that."

Dwight worked feverishly for days. He removed the picture window, took down the wall, shored up the floor, built a ramp, drained the car of all its fluids so it wouldn't leak on the rug, pushed it into the house, replaced the studs, put back the window, erected fresh Sheetrock and repainted the entire room. In the room, the car looked like a big doll's car. But it didn't look bad inside the house at all and Lucy didn't mind it being there, although she didn't like it when Dwight raised the hood. She didn't care for the hood being raised one bit and always lowered it when she saw it was up. She thought about the Thunderbird most often at night when she was in bed lying beside Dwight and then she would marvel at its silent, unseen presence in the room beside them, taking up space, so strange and shining and full of rot.

They would sit frequently in the car, in their house, not going anywhere, looking through the windshield out at the window and through the window to the street. They didn't invite anyone over for this. Soon, Dwight took to sitting in the car by himself. Dwight was tired. It was taking him a while to bounce back from the carpentry. Lucy saw him there one day behind the wheel, one arm bent and dangling over the glossy door, his eyes shut, his mouth slightly open, his hair as black as she had ever seen it. She couldn't remember the first time she had noticed him, really noticed him, the way he must have first noticed her when she'd been a baby.

"I wish you'd stop that, Dwight," she said.

He opened his eyes. "You should try this by yourself," he said. "Just try it and tell me what you think."

She sat for some time in the car alone, then went into the kitchen, where Dwight stood, drinking water. It was a gray day, with a gray careless light falling everywhere.

"I had the tiniest feeling in there that the point being made was that something has robbed this world of its promise," Lucy said. She did not have a sentimental nature.

Dwight was holding a glass of water, frowning a little at it. Water poured into the sink and down the drain, part of the same water he was drinking. On the counter was a television set and on the screen men were wheeling two stretchers out of a house and across a lawn and on each stretcher was a long still thing covered in a green cloth. The house was a cement-block house with two metal chairs on the porch with little cushions on them, and under the roof's overhang a basket of flowers swung.

"Is this the only channel we ever get?" Lucy said. She turned the water faucet off.

"It's the news, Lucy."

"I've seen this news a hundred times before. It's always this kind of news."

"This is the Sun Belt, Lucy."

That he kept saying her name began to irritate her. "Well, Dwight," she said. "Dwight, Dwight, Dwight."

Dwight looked at her mildly and went back to the living room. Lucy trailed after him. They both looked at the car and Lucy said to it, "I'd like an emerald ring. I'd like a baby boy."

"You don't ask it for things, Lucy," Dwight said.

"I'd like a Porsche Carrera," Lucy said to it.

"Are you crazy or what!" Dwight demanded.

"I would like a little baby," she mused.

"You were a little baby once," Dwight said.

"Well, I know that."

"So isn't that enough?"

She looked at him uneasily, then said, "Do you know what I used to like that you did? You'd say, 'That's my wife's favorite color . . .' or 'That's just what my wife says . . .'" Dwight gazed at her from his big, inky eyes. "And of course your wife was me!" she exclaimed. "I always thought that was kind of sexy."

"We're not talking sex anymore, Lucy," he said. She blushed.

Dwight got into the Thunderbird and rested his hands on the wheel. She saw his fingers pressing against the horn rim but it made no sound.

"I don't think this car should be in the house," Lucy said, still fiercely blushing.

"It's a place where I can think, Lucy."

"But it's in the middle of the living room! It takes up practically the whole living room!"

"A man's got to think, Lucy. A man's got to prepare for things."

"Where did you think before we got married?" she said crossly.

"All over, Lucy. I thought of you everywhere. You were part of everything."

Lucy did not want to be part of everything. She did not want to be part of another woman's kissing, for example. She did not want to be part of Daisy's leg, which she was certain, in their time, had played its part and been something Dwight had paid attention to. She did not want to be part of a great many things that she could mention.

"I don't want to be part of everything," she said.

"Life is different from when I was young and you were a little baby," Dwight said.

"I never did want to be part of everything," she said excitedly.

Dwight worked his shoulders back into the seat and stared out the window.

"Maybe the man who had this car before died of a broken heart, did you ever think of that?" Lucy said. When he said nothing, she said, "I don't want to start waiting on you again, Dwight." Her face had cooled off now.

"You wait the way you have to," Dwight said. "You've got to know what you want while you're waiting." He patted the seat beside him and smiled at her. It wasn't just a question of moving this used-up thing out again, she knew that. Time wasn't moving sideways in the manner it had always seemed to her to move but was climbing upward, then falling back, then lurching in a circle like some poisoned, damaged thing. Eventually, she sat down next to him. She looked through the glass at the other glass, then past that.

"It's raining," Lucy said.

There was a light rain falling, a warm spring rain. As she watched, it fell more quickly. It was silverish, but as it fell faster it appeared less and less like rain and she could almost hear it rattling as it struck the street.

The Skater

ANNIE AND TOM AND MOLLY ARE LOOKING AT BOARDING schools. Molly is the applicant, fourteen years old. Annie and Tom are the mom and dad. This is how they are referred to by the admissions directors. "Now if Mom and Dad would just make themselves comfortable while we steal Molly away for a moment ..." Molly is stolen away and Tom and Annie drink coffee. There are cookies on a plate. Colored slides are flashed on a screen showing children earnestly learning and growing and caring through the seasons. These things have been captured. Rather, it's clear that's what they're getting at. The children's faces blur in Tom's mind. And all those autumn leaves. All those laboratories and playing fields and bell towers.

It is winter and there is snow on the ground. They have flown in from California and rented a car. Their plan is to see seven New England boarding schools in five days. Icicles hang from the admissions building. Tom gazes at them. They are lovely and refractive. They are formed and then they vanish. Tom looks away.

Annie is sitting on the other side of the room, puzzling over a mathematics problem. There are sheets of problems all over the waiting room. These are to keep parents and kids on their toes as they wait. The cold, algebraic problems are presented in little stories. Five times as many girls as boys are taking music lessons or trees are growing at different rates or ladies in a bridge club are lying about their ages. The characters and situations are invented only to be exiled to measurement. Watching Annie search for solutions makes Tom's heart ache. He remembers a class he took once himself, almost twenty years ago, a class in myth. In mythical stories, it seems, there were two ways to disaster. One of them was to answer an unanswerable question. The other was to fail to answer an answerable question.

Down a corridor there are several shut doors and behind one is
Molly. Molly is their living child. Tom and Annie's other child, Martha, has been dead a year. Martha was one year older than Molly. Now
they're the same age. Martha choked to death in her room on a piece of
bread. It was early in the morning and she was getting ready for school.
The radio was playing and two disc jockeys called the Breakfast Flakes
chattered away between songs.

THE WEATHER IS BAD, THE ROADS ARE SLIPPERY. FROM THE BACK-
seat, Molly says, "He asked what my favorite ice cream was and I said,
'Quarterback Crunch.' Then he asked who was President of the United
States when the school was founded and I said, 'No one.' Wasn't that
good?"

"I hate trick questions," Annie says.

"Did you like the school," Tom asks.

"Yeah," Molly says.

"What did you like best about it?"

"I liked how our guide—you know, Peter—just walked right across
the street that goes through the campus and the cars just stopped. You
and Mom were kind of hanging back, looking both ways and all, but
Peter and I just trucked right across."

Molly was chewing gum that smelled like oranges.

"Peter was cute," Molly says.

TOM AND ANNIE AND MOLLY SIT AROUND A SMALL TABLE IN
their motel room. Snow accumulates beyond the room's walls. They
are nowhere. The brochure that the school sent them states that the
school is located thirty-five miles from Boston. Nowhere! They are all
exhausted and merely sit there regarding their beverages. The television
set is chained to the wall. This is indicative, Tom thinks, of considerable
suspicion on the part of the management. There was also a four-dollar
deposit on the room key. The management, when Tom checked in, was
in the person of a child about Molly's age, a boy eating from a bag of
potato chips and doing his homework.

"There's a kind of light that glows in the bottom of the water in an atomic reactor that exists nowhere else, do you know that?" the boy said to Tom.

"Interesting," Tom said.

"Yeah," the boy said, and marked the book he was reading with his pencil.

The motel room is darkly paneled and there is a painting of a moose between the two large beds. The moose is knee-deep in a lake with his head raised. Annie goes into the bathroom and washes her hands and face. It was her idea that Molly go away to school. She wants Molly to be free. She doesn't want her to be afraid. She fears that she is making her afraid, as she herself is afraid. Annie hears Molly and Tom talking in the other room and then she hears Molly laugh. She raises her fingers to the window frame and feels the cold seeping in. She adjusts the lid to the toilet tank. It shifts slightly. She washes her hands again. She goes into the room and sits on one of the beds.

"What are you laughing about?" she says. She means to be offhand, but her words come out heavily.

"Did you see the size of that girl's radio in the dorm room we visited?" Molly says, laughing. "It was the biggest radio I'd ever seen. I told Daddy there was a real person lying in it, singing." Molly giggles. She pulls her turtleneck sweater up to just below her eyes.

Annie laughs, then she thinks she has laughed at something terrible, the idea of someone lying trapped and singing. She raises her hands to her mouth. She had not seen a radio large enough to hold anyone. She saw children in classes, in laboratories in some brightly painted basement. The children were dissecting sheep's eyes. "Every winter term in biology you've got to dissect sheep's eyes," their guide said wearily. "The colors are really nice, though." She saw sacks of laundry tumbled down a stairwell with names stenciled on them. Now she tries not to see a radio large enough to hold anyone singing.

AT NIGHT, TOM DRIVES IN HIS DREAMS. HE DREAMS OF ICE, OF slick treachery. All night he fiercely holds the wheel and turns in the direction of the skid.

In the morning when he returns the key, the boy has been replaced by an old man with liver spots the size of quarters on his hands. Tom thinks of asking where the boy is, but then realizes he must be in school learning about eerie, deathly light. The bills the old man returns to Tom are soft as cloth.

IN CALIFORNIA, THEY LIVE IN A CANYON. MARTHA'S ROOM IS NOT situated with a glimpse of the ocean like some of the other rooms. It faces a rocky ledge where owls nest. The canyon is cold and full of small birds and bitter-smelling shrubs. The sun moves quickly through it. When the rocks are touched by the sun, they steam. All of Martha's things remain in her room—the radio, the posters and mirrors and books. It is a "guest" room now, although no one ever refers to it as such. They still call it "Martha's room." But it has become a guest room, even though there are never any guests.

THE RENTAL CAR IS WITHOUT DISTINCTION. IT IS A FOUR-DOOR sedan with automatic transmission and a poor turning radius. Martha would have been mortified by it. Martha had a boyfriend who, with his brothers, owned a monster truck. The Super Swamper tires were as tall as Martha, and all the driver of an ordinary car would see when it passed by was its colorful undercarriage with its huge shock and suspension coils, its long yellow stabilizers. For hours on a Saturday they would wallow in sloughs and rumble and pitch across stony creek beds, and then they would wash and wax the truck or, as James, the boyfriend, would say, dazzle the hog. The truck's name was Bear. Tom and Annie didn't care for James, and they hated and feared Bear. Martha loved Bear. She wore a red and white peaked cap with MONSTER TRUCK stenciled on it. After Martha died, Molly put the cap on once or twice. She thought it would help her feel closer to Martha but it didn't. The sweatband smelled slightly of shampoo, but it was just a cap.

TOM PULLS INTO THE FROZEN FIELD THAT IS THE PARKING LOT for the Northwall School. The admissions office is very cold. The receptionist is wearing an old worn chesterfield coat and a scarf. Someone is playing a hesitant and plaintive melody on a piano in one of the nearby rooms. They are shown the woodlot, the cafeteria and the arts department, where people are hammering out their own silver bracelets. They are shown the language department, where a class is doing tarot card readings in French. They pass a room and hear a man's voice say, "Matter is a sort of blindness."

While Molly is being interviewed, Tom and Annie walk to the barn. The girls are beautiful in this school. The boys look a little dull. Two boys run past them, both wearing jeans and denim jackets. Their hair is short and their ears are red. They appear to be pretending they're in a drama that's being filmed. They dart and feint. One stumbles into a building while the other crouches outside, tossing his head and scowling, throwing an imaginary knife from hand to hand.

Annie tries a door to the barn but it is latched from the inside. She walks around the barn in her high heels. The hem of her coat dangles. She wears gloves on her pale hands. Tom walks beside her with his hands in his pockets. A flock of starlings fly overhead in an oddly tight formation. A hawk flies above them. The hawk will not fall upon them, clenched like this. If one would separate from the flock, then the hawk could fall.

"I don't know about this 'matter is a sort of blindness' place," Tom says. "It's not what I had in mind."

Annie laughs but she's not paying attention. She wants to get into the huge barn. She tugs at another door. Dirt smears the palms of her gloves. Then, suddenly, the wanting leaves her face.

"Martha would like this school, wouldn't she?" she says.

"We don't know," Tom says. "Please don't, Annie."

"I feel that I've lived my whole life in one corner of a room," Annie says. "That's the problem. It's just having always been in this one corner. And now I can't see anything. I don't even know the room, do you see what I'm saying?"

Tom nods but he doesn't see the room. The sadness in him has become his blood, his life flowing in him. There's no room for him.

In the admissions building, Molly sits in a wooden chair facing her interviewer, Miss Plum, who teaches composition and cross-country skiing.

"You asked if I believe in *aluminum*," Molly asks.

"Yes, dear. Uh-huh, I did," Miss Plum says.

"Well, I suppose I'd have to *believe* in it," Molly says.

ANNIE HAS A LARGE CARDBOARD FILE THAT HOLDS COMPART-mentalized information on the schools they're visiting. The rules and regulations for one school are put together in what is meant to look like an American passport. In the car's backseat, Molly flips through the book, annoyed.

"You can't do anything in this place!" she says. "The things on your walls have to be framed and you can only cover sixty percent of the wall space. You can't wear jeans." Molly gasps. "And you have to eat breakfast!" Molly tosses the small book onto the floor, on top of the ice scraper. She gazes glumly out the window at an orchard. She is sick of the cold. She is sick of discussing her "interests." White fields curve by. Her life is out there somewhere, fleeing from her while she is in the backseat of this stupid car. Her life is never going to be hers. She thinks of it raining, back home in the canyon, rain falling upon rain. Her legs itch and her scalp itches. She has never been so bored. She thinks that the worst thing she has done so far in her life was to lie in a hot bath one night, smoking a cigarette and saying *I hate God*. That was the very worst thing. It's pathetic. She bangs her knees irritably against the front seat.

"You want to send me far enough away," she says to her parents. "I mean, it's the other side of the dumb continent. Maybe I don't even want to do this," she says.

She looks at the thick sky holding back snow. She doesn't hate God anymore. She doesn't even think about God. Anybody who would let a kid choke on a piece of bread . . .

THE NEXT SCHOOL HAS CHAPEL FOUR TIMES A WEEK AND AN IN-door hockey rink. In the chapel, two fir trees are held in wooden boxes. Wires attached to the ceiling hold them upright. It is several weeks before Christmas.

"When are you going to decorate them," Molly asks Shirley, her guide. Shirley is handsome and rather horrible. The soles of her rubber boots are a bright, horrible orange. She looks at Molly.

"We don't decorate the trees in the chapel," she says.

Molly looks at the tree stumps bolted into the wooden boxes. Beads of sap pearl golden on the bark.

"This is a very old chapel," Shirley says. "See those pillars? They look like marble, but they're just pine, painted to look like marble." She isn't being friendly, she's just saying what she knows. They walk out of the chapel, Shirley soundlessly, on her horrible orange soles.

"Do you play hockey," she asks.

"No," Molly says.

"Why not?"

"I like my teeth," Molly says.

"You *do?*" Shirley says in mock amazement. "Just kidding," she says. "I'm going to show you the hockey rink anyway. It's new. It's a big deal."

Molly sees Tom and Annie standing some distance away beneath a large tree draped with many strings of extinguished lights. Her mother's back is to her, but Tom sees her and waves.

Molly follows Shirley into the still, odd air of the hockey rink. No one is on the ice. The air seems distant, used up. On one wall is a big painting of a boy in a hockey uniform. He is in a graceful, easy posture, skating alone on bluish ice toward the viewer, smiling. He isn't wearing a helmet. He has brown hair and wide golden eyes. Molly reads the plaque beneath the painting. His name is Jimmy Watkins and he had died six years before at the age of seventeen. His parents had built the rink and dedicated it to him.

Molly takes a deep breath. "My sister, Martha, knew him," she says.

"Oh yeah?" Shirley says with interest. "Did your sister go here?"

"Yes," Molly says. She frowns a little as she lies. Martha and Jimmy Watkins of course know each other. They know everything but they have secrets too.

The air is not like real air in here. Neither does the cold seem real. She looks at Jimmy Watkins, bigger than life, skating toward them on his black skates. It is not a very good painting. Molly thinks that those who love Jimmy Watkins must be disappointed in it.

"They were very good friends," Molly says.

"How come you didn't tell me before that your sister went here?"

Molly shrugs. She feels happy, happier than she has in a long time. She has brought Martha back from the dead and put her in school. She has given her a room, friends, things she must do. It can go on and on. She has given her a kind of life, a place in death. She has freed her.

"Did she date him or what," Shirley asks.

"It wasn't like that," Molly says. "It was better than that."

She doesn't want to go much further, not with this girl whom she dislikes, but she goes a little further.

"Martha knew Jimmy better than anybody," Molly says.

She thinks of Martha and Jimmy Watkins being together, telling each other secrets. They will like each other. They are seventeen and fourteen, living in the single moment that they have been gone.

MOLLY IS WITH HER PARENTS IN THE CAR AGAIN ON A WINDING road, going through the mountains. Tonight they will stay in an inn that Annie has read about and tomorrow they will visit the last school. Several large rocks, crusted with dirty ice, have slid onto the road. They are ringed with red cones and traffic moves slowly around them. The late low sun fiercely strikes the windshield.

"Bear could handle those rocks," Molly says. "Bear would go right over them."

"Oh, that truck," Annie says.

"That truck is an ecological criminal," Tom says.

"Big Bad Bear," Molly says.

Annie shakes her head and sighs. Bear is innocent. Bear is only a machine, gleaming in a dark garage.

Molly can't see her parents' faces. She can't remember how they looked when she was little. She wants to ask them about Martha. She wants to ask them if they are sending her so far away so they can imagine that Martha is just far away too. But she knows she will never ask such a question. There are secrets now. The dead have their secrets and the living have their secrets with the dead. This is the way it must be.

. . .

MOLLY HAS HER THINGS. AND SHE SETS THEM UP EACH NIGHT IN the room she's in. She lays a little scarf across the bureau first, and then her things on top of it. Painted combs for her hair, a little dish for her rings. They are the only guests at the inn, an old rambling structure on a lake. In a few days, the owner will be closing it down for the winter. It's too cold for such an old place in the winter, the owner says. He had planned to keep it open for skating on the lake when he first bought it and had even remodeled part of the cellar as a skate room. There is a bar down there, a wooden floor and shelves of old skates in all sizes. Window glass runs the length of one wall just above ground level and there are spotlights that illuminate a portion of the lake. But winter isn't the season here. The pipes are too old and there aren't enough guests.

"Is this the deepest lake in the state," Annie asks. "I read that somewhere, didn't I?" She has her guidebooks, which she examines each night. Everywhere she goes, she buys books.

"No," the inn's owner says. "It's not the deepest, but it's deep. You should take a look at that ice. It's beautiful ice."

He is a young man, balding, hopelessly proud of his ice. He lingers with them, having given them thick towels and new bars of soap. He offers them soup for supper, fresh baked bread and pie. He offers them his smooth, frozen lake.

"Do you want to skate," Tom asks his wife and daughter. Molly shakes her head.

"No," Annie says. She takes a bottle of Scotch from her suitcase. "Are there any glasses," she asks the man.

"I'm sorry," the man says, startled. "They're all down in the skate room, on the bar." He gives a slight nod and walks away.

Tom goes down into the cellar for the glasses. The skates, their runners bright, are jumbled on the shelves. The frozen lake glitters in the window. He pushes open the door and there it is, the ice. He steps out onto it. Annie, in their room, waits without taking off her coat. Tom takes a few quick steps and then slides. He is wearing a suit and tie, his good shoes. It is a windy night and the trees clatter with the wind and the old inn's sign creaks on its chains. Tom slides across the ice, his hands pushed out, then he holds his hands behind his back, going back and forth in the space where the light is cast. There is no skill without the skates, he knows, and probably no grace without them either, but it is enough to be here under the black sky, cold and light and moving. He wants to be out here. He wants to be out here with Annie.

From a window, Molly sees her father on the ice. After a moment, she sees her mother moving toward him, not skating but slipping forward, making her way. She sees their heavy awkward shapes embrace.

Molly sees them, already remembering it.

Lu-Lu

HEATHER WAS SITTING WITH THE DUNES, DON AND DEBBIE, beside their swimming pool. The Dunes were old. Heather, who lived next door in a little rented house, was young and desperate. They were all suntanned and drinking gin and grapefruit juice, trying to do their best by the prolifically fruiting tree in the Dunes' backyard. The grapefruits were organic, and pink inside. They shone prettily by the hundreds between leaves curled and bumpy and spotted from spider mite and aphid infestation.

Before Heather and the Dunes on a glass-topped table was the bottle of gin, two-thirds gone, three grapefruits and a hand juicer. The label on the bottle had a picture of a little old lady who gazed out at them sternly. Beneath the table, their knees were visible, Heather's young dimpled ones and the Dunes' knobby ones. The knees looked troubled, even baffled, beneath the glass.

"We could take her to Mexico," Don said. "Lu-Lu would love Mexico, I bet." He was wearing a dirty blue billed cap with a fish leaping on it.

"Not Baja, though," Debbie said. Her left arm was bandaged from where she'd burned it on the stove. "Too many RVs there. All those old geezers with nothing better to do in their twilight years than to drive up and down Baja. They'd flatten Lu-Lu in a minute."

"I've heard those volcanic islands off Bahia Los Angeles are full of snakes," Heather said.

The Dunes looked at her, shocked.

After a moment, Debbie said, "Lu-Lu wouldn't like that at all."

"She don't know any other snakes," Don added.

He poured more gin in all the glasses.

"Do you remember tequila, my dear?" he said to Debbie. He turned his old wrinkled face toward her.

"The beverage of Mexico," Debbie said solemnly.

"On the back of each label is a big black crow," Don said. "You can see it real good when the liquor's gone."

"The Mexicans are a morbid people," Debbie said.

"What I like best about snakes," Heather said, "is how they move without seeming to. They *move*, but they seem to be moving *in place*. Then suddenly they're *gone*." She snapped her fingers wetly.

"That's the thing you like best about 'em?" Don said morosely. "Better things than that to like."

Heather looked at her fingers. How did they get so damp, she wondered.

"We got inquiries as far away as San Diego, did we tell you?" Don said. "San Diego wants her real bad."

Debbie raised her chin high and shook her head back and forth. The stringy tendons in her neck trembled. "Never!" she said. "People would stare and make comments." She shuddered. "I can hear them!"

"She's got second sight, Debbie has," Don confided to Heather. "It don't use her as a vehicle much, though."

Debbie had shut her eyes and was wobbling back and forth in her chair. "San Diego!" She groaned. "A cement floor. A room with nothing in it but Lu-Lu. Nothing! No pictures, no plants ... and people staring at her through the glass. There's a little sign telling about her happy life here in Tampa and a little about her personality, but not much, and her dimensions and all ... And I can see one big fat guy holding an ice-cream sandwich in one hand and a little girl by the other and he's saying, 'Why that thing weighs fifteen pounds more than Daddy!'" Debbie gave a little yelp and dug in her ears with her fingers.

"Second sight's no gift," Don said.

"We're so old," Debbie wailed.

Don tapped the elbow of her good arm solicitously and nodded at her drink.

"We're so old," Debbie said, taking a sip. "Can't take care of ourselves nor the ones we love."

"And Heather here is young," Don said. "Don't make no difference."

"We live in the wrong time, just like Lu-Lu," Debbie said.

"Lu-Lu should have lived in the Age of Reptiles," Heather said slowly. Speaking seemed to present certain problems. She looked at the stern old lady on the gin bottle.

"She would have loved it," Don said.

"Those were the days," Debbie said. "Days of doomed grandeur."

"You know what I was reading about the other day?" Don said. "I was reading about the Neanderthals."

Debbie looked at Don proudly. Heather scratched her shoulder. The sun beat down on the crooked part in her hair. Why has love eluded me, she wondered.

"They weren't us, I read. They were a whole different species. But we're the only species that are supposed to have souls, am I right? But the Neanderthals, it turned out, buried their dead Neanderthals with bits of food and flint chips and such, and even flowers. They found the graves."

"Now how could they know there were flowers?" Debbie said.

"I forget," Don said impatiently. "I'm seventy-six, I can't remember everything." He thought for a moment. "They got ways," he said.

Debbie Dune was silent. She smoothed the little skirt of her bathing suit.

"My point is that those things might not have had souls but they *thought* they had souls."

"That's a very pretty story," Heather said slowly.

The Dunes looked at her.

"The flowers and all," Heather said.

"I don't know what you're saying, Don," Debbie said politely.

"What I'm saying," Don said, "is who's to say what's got a soul and what hasn't."

"Another thing I like about snakes," Heather said, "is how they can occupy themselves for long stretches of time doing nothing."

"I think," Debbie said, "that what it boils down to soul-wise is simple. If things cry, they got souls. If they don't, they don't."

"Lu-Lu don't cry," Don said.

"That's right," Debbie said pluckily.

"May I get some more ice," Heather asked.

"Oh, that's a good idea, honey. Do get some more ice," Debbie said.

Heather stood up, carefully passed the swimming pool and went into the kitchen. Lu-Lu was there, drinking from a pan of milk.

"Hello, Lu-Lu," Heather said. Deaf as a post, she thought.

She opened the freezer and took out a tray of ice. She looked inside the refrigerator and saw a dozen eggs and a box of shredded wheat. I should do something for these poor old people, Heather thought. Make them a quiche or something. She nibbled on a biscuit of shredded wheat and watched Lu-Lu drink her milk. Lu-Lu stared at her as she watched.

Heather walked outside. It was hot. The geraniums growing from Crisco cans looked peaked.

"Whoops," Debbie said. "I guess we need more gin now with all this ice."

"This is a difficult day for us," Don said. "It is a day of decision."

"The gin's right on the counter there beneath the emergency phone numbers," Debbie said.

Heather went back into the kitchen. Lu-Lu was still working away at the milk.

"Lu-Lu's eating," Heather said, outside again.

"She don't eat much," Don said.

"No, she don't," Debbie said. "But she does like her rats. You know when she swallows a rat, she keeps it in her gullet for a while and that rat is fine. That rat's snug as if it were in its own little hole."

"That rat's oblivious," Don said. "That rat thinks it might even have escaped."

"Her gullet's like a comfy little waiting room to the chamber of horrors beyond it," Debbie said.

"You know in Mexico, in that big zoo in Mexico City, once a month they feed the boas and everybody turns out to watch. They feed 'em live chickens."

"*Such* a morbid people," Debbie said.

Heather looked across the Dunes' yard into the one behind her little rented house. Her diaphanous nightie hung on the clothesline, barely moving. Time to go, Heather thought. She sat in her chair, chewing on her sun-blistered lip.

Lu-Lu slithered toward them. She placed her spade-like head on Debbie's knee.

"Poor dear doesn't know what's going to happen next," Debbie said.

"We know neither the time nor the hour," Don said. "None of us."

He peered through the glass-topped table at Lu-Lu. "Is she clouding up again?"

"She molted less than four months ago," Debbie said. "It's your eyes that are clouding up."

"She looks kind of milky to me," Don said.

"Don't you wish!" exclaimed Debbie. She winked at Heather. "Don gets the biggest kick out of Lu-Lu shedding her skin."

Don grinned shyly. He took off his billed cap and put it back on again.

"We got her skins hanging up in the lanai," Debbie said to Heather. "Have you seen them?"

Heather shook her head. They all three got up and lurched toward the lanai, a small screened room looking out over where they had been. Lu-Lu followed behind. There, thumbtacked to the mildewed ceiling, were half a dozen chevron-patterned gray and papery skins rustling and clicking in the breeze.

"In order to do this really right, you'd need a taller room," Debbie said. "I've always wanted a nice tall room and I've never gotten one. With a nice tall room they could hang in all their glory."

"There's nothing prettier than Lu-Lu right after she molts," Don said. "She's so shiny and new!"

Heather went over to Lu-Lu's old skins. There were Lu-Lu's big empty mouth and eyes. Heather pushed her face closer and sniffed. The skins smelled salty, she thought. Then she thought they couldn't possibly smell like anything she could describe.

"They got a prettier sound than those tinny wind chimes," Don said. "Anybody can buy themselves one of those. What's the sense of it? They don't last forever, though."

"I almost called Lu-Lu Draco, but I'm glad I didn't," Debbie said.

"Draco would have been a big mistake all right," Don agreed.

"You'll never guess what Don used to be," Debbie said.

Heather felt sleepy and anxious at the same time. She took several tiny, restless steps.

"He was a pastry chef," Debbie said.

Heather looked at the Dunes. Never would she have imagined Don Dune to be a pastry chef.

The disclosure seemed to exhaust Debbie. Her good arm paddled through the air toward Don. "I have to go to bed now," she said.

"My dear," Don said, crooking his elbow gallantly in her direction.

Heather followed them into their small, brown bedroom. Everything was brown. It seemed cool and peaceful. Lu-Lu remained on the lanai, wrapped around a hassock.

Heather turned back the sheets and the Dunes crawled in, wearing their bathing suits.

"When I was a little girl," Debbie said, "nothing was more horrible to me than having to go to bed while it was still light."

Don took off his cap and patted his head. "Even my hair feels drunk," he said.

"I would like to take Lu-Lu and make a new life for myself," Heather announced.

The Dunes lay in bed, the dark sheets pulled up to their chins.

"If you go off with Lu-Lu," Debbie said, "you've got to love her good, because Lu-Lu can't show she loves you back."

"Snakes ain't demonstrative as a rule," Don added. "They've got no obvious way of showing attachment."

"She'll be able to recognize your footsteps after a while," Debbie said.

Heather was delighted.

"Will she get into my car, do you think?" Heather asked.

"Lu-Lu's a good rider," Debbie said. "A real good rider. I always wanted to drive her into a big uncharted desert, but I never did."

"We'll find a desert," Heather said with enthusiasm.

"Debbie don't think she's ever wanted much, but she has," Don said. He sighed.

"We'd better get started," Heather said. She smoothed the sheet and tucked it in under the mattress.

"Bless you, honey," Debbie said drowsily.

"Spoon a little jelly in Lu-Lu's milk sometimes," Don said. "She enjoys that."

Heather left the bedroom and hurried across the yard to her driveway. Her car stalled several times as she coaxed it across the lawn toward the Dunes' swimming pool. She opened all the doors to the car, and then the doors to the Dunes' house. She was rushing all around inside herself. Lu-Lu stared fixedly at her from the lanai.

"Come, Lu-Lu!" Heather cried.

Already her own house looked as if it had been left for good. The nightie dangled on the clothesline. Leave it there, she thought. Ugly nightie with its yearnings. She wondered if Lu-Lu would want dirt for their trip. She found Don's shovel and threw some earth into the backseat of the car. She didn't know how she was going to coax Lu-Lu in. She sat on the hood of the car and stared at Lu-Lu. Dusk was growing into dark. How do you beckon to something like this, she wondered; something that can change everything, your life.

The Little Winter

S HE WAS IN THE AIRPORT, WAITING FOR HER FLIGHT TO BE
called, when a woman came to a phone near her chair. The woman
stood there, dialing, and after a while began talking in a flat, aggrieved
voice. Gloria couldn't hear everything by any means, but she did hear
her say, "If anything happens to this plane, I hope you'll be satisfied."
The woman spoke monotonously and without mercy. She was tall and
disheveled and looked the very picture of someone who recently had
ceased to be cherished. Nevertheless, she was still being mollified on
the other end. Gloria heard with astounding clarity the part about the
plane being repeated several times. The woman then slammed down
the receiver and boarded Gloria's flight, flinging herself down in a
first-class seat. Gloria proceeded to the rear and sat quietly, thinking
that every person is on the brink of eternity every moment, that the
means of leaving this world are innumerable and often inconceivable.
She thought in this manner for a while, then ordered a drink.

The plane pushed through the sky and the drink made her think of
how, as a child, she had enjoyed chewing on the collars of her dresses.
The first drink of the day did not always bring this to mind, but frequently it did. Then she began thinking of the desert she was leaving
behind and how much she liked it. Once she had liked the sea and felt
she could not live without it, but now she missed it almost not at all.

The plane continued. Gloria ordered another drink, no longer
resigned to believing that the woman was going to blow up the plane.
Now she began thinking of her plans. She was going to visit Jean, a
friend of hers who was having a hard time—a fourth divorce, after
all, but Jean had a lot of energy—yet that was only for a day or two.
Jean had a child named Gwendal. Gloria hadn't seen them for years
and probably wouldn't even recognize Gwendal. Then she would just

keep moving around until it happened. She was thinking of buying a dog. She'd had a number of dogs but hadn't had very good luck with them. This was the thing about pets, of course, you knew that something dreadful was going to befall them, that it was not going to end well. Two of her dogs had been hit by cars, one had been epileptic and another was diagnosed early on as having hip dysplasia. Vets had never done very well by Gloria's dogs, much as doctors weren't doing very well by Gloria now. She thought frequently about doctors, though she wasn't going to see them anymore. Under the circumstances, she probably shouldn't acquire a dog, but she felt she wanted one. Let the dog get stuck for a change, she thought.

At the airport, Gloria rented a car. She decided to drive just outside Jean's town and check in to a motel. Jean was a talker. A day with Jean would be enough. A day and a night would be too much. Just outside Jean's town was a monastery where the monks raised dogs. Maybe she would find her dog there tomorrow. She would go over to the monastery early in the morning and spend the rest of the day with Jean. But that was it. Other than that, there wasn't much of a plan.

The day was cloudy and there was a great deal of traffic. The land falling back from the highway was green and still. It seemed to her a slightly lugubrious landscape, obelisks and cemeteries, thick drooping forests, the evergreens dying from the top down. Of course there was hardly any place to live these days. A winding old road ran parallel to the highway and Gloria turned off and drove along it until she came to a group of cabins. They were white with little porches but the office was in a structure built to resemble a tepee. There was a dilapidated miniature-golf course and a wooden tower from the top of which you could see into three states. But the tower leaned and the handrail curving optimistically upward was splintered and warped, and only five steps from the ground a rusted chain prevented further ascension. Gloria liked places like this.

In the tepee, a woman in a housedress stood behind a pink Formica counter. A glass hummingbird coated with greasy dust hung in one window. Gloria could smell meat loaf cooking. The woman had red cheeks and white hair, and she greeted Gloria extravagantly, but as soon as Gloria paid for her cabin the woman became morose. She gazed at

Gloria glumly, as though perceiving her as one who had already walked off with the blankets, the lamp and the painting of the waterfall.

The key Gloria had been given did not work. It fit into the lock and turned, but did not do the job of opening the door. She walked back to the office and a small dog with short legs and a fluffy tail fell into step beside her. Back in the tepee, Gloria said, "I can't seem to make this key work." The smell of the meat loaf was now clangorous. The woman was old, but she came around the counter fast.

The dog was standing in the middle of the turnabout in front of the cabins.

"Is that your dog," Gloria asked.

"I've never seen it before," the woman said. "It sure is not," she added. "Go home!" she shrieked at the dog. She turned the key in the lock of Gloria's cabin and then gave the door a sharp kick with her sneaker. The door flew open. She stomped back to the office. "Go home!" she screamed again at the dog.

Gloria made herself an iceless drink in a paper cup and called Jean.

"I can't wait to see you," Jean said. "How are you?"

"I'm all right," Gloria said.

"Tell me."

"Really," Gloria said.

"I can't wait to see you," Jean said. "I've had the most god-awful time. I know it's silly."

"How is Gwendal doing?"

"She never liked Chuckie anyway. She's Luke's, you know. But she's not a bit like Luke. You know Gwendal."

Gloria barely remembered the child, who would be almost ten by now. She sipped from the paper cup and looked through the screen at the dog, who was gazing over the ruined golf course to the valley beyond.

"I don't know how I manage to pick them," Jean was saying. She was talking about the last one.

"I'll be there by lunch tomorrow," Gloria said.

"Not until then! Well, we'll bring some lunch over to Bill's and eat with him. You haven't met him, have you? I want you to meet him."

Bill was Jean's first ex-husband. She had just bought a house in the town where two of her old ex-husbands and her new ex-husband lived. Gloria knew she had quite a day cut out for herself tomorrow. Jean gave her directions and Gloria hung up and made herself a fresh drink in the paper cup. She stood out on the porch. Dark clouds had massed over the mountains. Traffic thundered invisibly past in the distance, beyond the trees. In the town in the valley below, there were tiny hard lights in the enlarging darkness. The light, which had changed, was disappearing, but there was still a lot of it. That's the way it was with light. If you were out in it while it was going you could still see enough for longer.

She woke midmorning with a terrible headache. She was not supposed to drink but what difference did it make, really. It didn't make any difference. She took her pills. Sometimes she thought it had been useless for her to grow older. She was now forty. She lay in the musty cabin. Everything seemed perfectly clear. Then it seemed equivocal again. She dressed and went to the office, where she paid for another night. The woman took the money and looked at Gloria worriedly as though she were already saying good-bye to the welcome mat she had just bought, and that old willow chair with the cushion.

It began to rain. The road to the monastery was gravel and wound up the side of a mountain. There were orchards, fields of young corn . . . the rain fell on it all in a fury. Gloria drove slowly, barely able to make out the road. She imagined it snowing out there, not rain but snow, filling everything up. She imagined thinking *it was dark now but still snowing*—a line like that, as in a story. A line like that was lovely, she thought. When she was small they had lived in a place where the little winter came first. That's what everyone called it. There was "the little winter," then there were pleasant days, sometimes weeks. Then the big winter came. She was on the monastery's grounds now and there were wooden buildings with turreted roofs and minarets. Someone had planted birches. She parked by a sign that said INFORMATION/GIFT SHOP and dashed from the car to the door. She was laughing and shaking the water from her hair as she entered.

The situation was that there were no dogs available, or rather that the brother whose duty was the dogs, who knew about the dogs, was away and would not return until tomorrow. She could come back tomorrow. The monk who told her this had a beard and wore a soiled apron. His interest in her questions did not seem intense. He had appeared from a back room, a room that seemed part smokehouse, part kitchen. This was the monk who smoked chickens, hams and cheese. There was always cheese in this life. The monastery had a substantial mail-order business; the monks smoked things, the nuns made cheese-cakes. He seemed slightly impatient with Gloria. He had given up a great deal, no doubt, in order to be here. The gift shop was crowded with half-price icons and dog beds. In a corner there was a refrigerated case filled with the nuns' cheesecakes. Gloria looked in there, at the stacks of white boxes.

"The Deluxe is a standard favorite," the monk said. "The Kahlúa is encased in a chocolate cookie-crumb crust, the rich liqueur from the sunny Caribbean blending naturally with the nuns' original recipe." The monk droned on as if at matins. "The Chocolate is a must for chocolate fanciers. The Chocolate Amaretto is considered by the nuns to be their pièce de résistance."

Gloria bought the Chocolate Amaretto and left. How gloomy, she thought. The experience had seemed vaguely familiar, as though she had surrendered passively to it in the past. She supposed it was a belief in appearances. She put the cheesecake in the car and walked around the grounds. It was raining less heavily now, but even so her hair was plastered to her skull. She passed the chapel and then turned back and went inside. She picked up a candlestick and jammed it into her coat pocket. This place made her mad. Then she took the candlestick out and set it on the floor. Outside, she wandered around hearing nothing but the highway, which was humming like something in her head. She finally found the kennels and opened the door and went in. This is how she thought it would be, nothing closed to her at all. There were four dogs, all young ones, maybe three months old, German shepherds. She watched them for a while. It would be easy to take one, she thought. She could just do it.

She drove back down the mountain into town, where she pulled into a shopping center that had a liquor store. She bought gin and some wine for Jean, then drove down to Jean's house in the valley. She felt tired. There was something pounding behind her eyes. Jean's house was a dirty peach color with a bush in front. Everything was pounding, the house, even the grass. Then the pounding stopped.

.   .   .

"Oh my god," jean exclaimed. "you've brought the pièce de résistance!" Apparently everyone was familiar with the nuns' cheese-cakes. Jean and Gloria hugged each other. "You look good," Jean said. "They got it all, thank god, right? The things that happen anymore . . . there aren't even names for half of what happens, I swear. You know my second husband, Andy, the one who died? He went in and never came out again and he just submitted to it, but no one could ever figure out what *it* was. It was something complicated and obscure and the only thing they knew was that he was dying from it. It might've been some insect that bit him. But the worst thing—well, not the worst thing, but the thing I remember because it had to do with me, which is bad of me, I suppose, but that's just human nature. The worst thing was what happened just before he died. He was very fussy. Everything had to be just so."

"This is Andy," Gloria said.

"Andy," Jean agreed. "He had an excellent vocabulary and was very precise. How I got involved with him I'll never know. But he was my husband and I was devastated. I *lived* at the hospital, week after week. He liked me to read to him. I was there that afternoon and I had adjusted the shade and plumped the pillows and I was reading to him. And there he was, quietly slipping away right then, I guess, looking back on it. I was reading and I got to this part about someone being the master of a highly circumscribed universe and he opened his eyes and said, Circumscribed. What, darling? I said. And he said, Circum-scribed, not circumcised . . . you said circumcised. And I said, I'm sure I didn't, darling, and he gave me this long look and then he gave a big sigh and died. Isn't that awful?"

Gloria giggled, then shook her head.

Jean's eyes darted around the room, which was in high disorder. Peeling wallpaper, cracked linoleum. Cardboard boxes everywhere. Shards of glass had been swept into one corner and a broken croquet mallet propped one window open. "So what do you think of this place?" Jean said.

"It's some place," Gloria said.

"Everyone says I shouldn't have. It needs some work, I know, but I found this wonderful man, or he found me. He came up to the door and looked at all this and I said, Can you help me? Do you do work like this? And he nodded and said, I puttah. Isn't that wonderful! I puttah . . ."

Gloria looked at the sagging floor and the windows loose in their frames. The mantel was blackened by smoke and grooved with cigarette burns. It was clear that the previous occupants had led lives of grinding boredom here and with little composure. He'd better start puttahing soon, Gloria thought. "Don't marry him," she said, and laughed.

"Oh, I know you think I marry everybody," Jean said, "but I don't. There have only been four. The last one, and I mean the last, was the worst. What a rodent Chuckie was. No, he's more like a big predator, a crow or a weasel or something. Cruel, lazy, deceitful." Jean shuddered. "The best thing about him was his hair." Jean was frequently undone by hair. "He has great hair. He wears it in a sort of fifties full flattop."

Gloria felt hollow and happy. Nothing mattered much. "You actually bought this place?" she said.

"Oh, it's crazy," Jean said, "but Gwendal and I needed a home. I've heard that *faux* is the new trend. I'm going to do it all *faux* when I get organized. Do you want to see the upstairs? Gwendal's room is upstairs. Hers is the neatest."

They went up the stairs to a room where a fat girl sat on a bed writing in a book.

"I'm doing my autobiography," Gwendal said, "but I think I'm going to change my approach." She turned to Gloria. "Would you like to be my biographer?"

Jean said, "Say hello to Gloria. You remember Gloria."

Gloria gave the girl a hug. Gwendal smelled good and had small pale eyes. The room wasn't clean at all, but there was very little in it. Gloria supposed it was the neatest. Conversation lagged.

"Let's go out and sit on the lawn," Jean suggested.

"I don't want to," Gwendal said.

The two women went downstairs. Gloria needed to use the bathroom but Jean said she had to go outside as the plumbing wasn't all it should be at the moment. There was a steep brushy bank behind the house and Gloria crouched there. The day was clear and warm now. At the bottom of the bank, a flat stream moved laboriously around vine-covered trees. The mud glistened in the sun. Blackberries grew in the brush. This place had a lot of candor, Gloria thought.

Jean had laid a blanket on the grass and was sitting there, eating a wedge of cheesecake from a plastic plate. Gloria decided on a drink over cake.

"We'll go to Bill's house for lunch," Jean said. "Then we'll go to Fred's house for a swim." Fred was an old husband too. Gwendal's father was the only one who wasn't around. He lived in Las Vegas. Andy wasn't around either, of course.

Gwendal came out of the house into the sloppy yard. She stopped in the middle of a rhubarb patch, exclaiming silently and waving her arms.

Jean sighed. "It's hard being a single mother."

"You haven't been single for long," Gloria said.

Jean laughed loudly at this. "Poor Gwendal," she said. "I love her dearly."

"A lovely child," Gloria murmured.

"I just wish she wouldn't make up so much stuff sometimes."

"She's young," Gloria said, finishing her drink. Really, she hardly knew what she was saying. "What *is* she doing?" she asked Jean.

Gwendal leapt quietly around in the rhubarb.

"Whatever it is, it needs to be translated," Jean said. "Gwendal needs a good translator."

"She's pretending something or other," Gloria offered, thinking she would very much like another drink.

"I'm going to put on a fresh dress for visiting Bill," Jean said. "Do you want to change?"

Gloria shook her head. She was watching Gwendal. When Jean went into the house, the girl trotted over to the blanket. "Why don't you kidnap me," she said.

"Why don't you kidnap *me?*" Gloria said, laughing. What an odd kid, she thought. "I don't want to kidnap you," she said.

"I'd like to see your house," Gwendal said.

"I don't have a house. I live in an apartment."

"Apartments aren't interesting," Gwendal said. "Dump it. We could get a van. The kind with the ladder that goes up the back. We could get a wheel cover that says MESS WITH THE BEST, LOSE LIKE THE REST."

There was something truly terrifying about girls on the verge of puberty, Gloria thought. She laughed.

"You drink too much," Gwendal said. "You're always drinking something."

This hurt Gloria's feelings. "I'm dying," she said. "I have a brain tumor. I can do what I want."

"If you're dying you can do anything you want?" Gwendal said. "I didn't know that. That's a new one. So there are compensations."

Gloria couldn't believe she'd told Gwendal she was dying. "You're fat," she said glumly.

Gwendal ignored this. She wasn't all that fat. Somewhat fat, perhaps, but not grotesquely so.

"Oh, to hell with it," Gloria said. "You want me to stop drinking, I'll stop drinking."

"It doesn't matter to me," Gwendal said.

Gloria's mouth trembled. I'm drunk, she thought.

"Some simple pleasures are just a bit too simple, you know," Gwendal said.

Gloria had felt she'd been handling her upcoming death pretty well, but now she wasn't sure. In fact she felt awful. What was she doing spending what might be one of her last days sitting on a scratchy blanket in a weedy yard while an unpleasant child insulted her? Her problem was that she had never figured out exactly where she wanted to go to die. Some people knew and planned accordingly. The desert, say, or Nantucket. Or a good hotel somewhere. But she hadn't figured it out. En route was the closest she'd come.

Gwendal said, "Listen, I have an idea. We could do it the other way around. Instead of you being my biographer, I'll be yours. *Gloria by Gwendal.*" She wrote it in the air with her finger. She did not have a particularly flourishing hand, Gloria noted. "Your life as told to Gwendal Crawley. I'll write it all down. At least that's something. We can always spice it up."

"I haven't had a very interesting life," Gloria said modestly. But it was true, she thought. When her parents had named her, they must have been happy. They must have thought something was going to happen now.

"I'm sure you must be having some interesting reflections, though,"

Gwendal said. "And if you're really dying, I bet you'll feel like doing everything once." She was wringing her hands in delight.

Jean walked toward them from the house.

"C'mon," Gwendal hissed. "Let me go with you. You didn't come all this way just to stay here, did you?"

"Gloria and I are going to visit Bill," Jean said. "Let's all go," she said to Gwendal.

"I don't want to," Gwendal said.

"If I don't see you again, good-bye," Gloria said to Gwendal.

The kid stared at her.

JEAN WAS DRIVING, TURNING HERE AND THERE, PASSING THE houses of those she had once loved.

"That's Chuckie's house," Jean said. "The one with the hair." They drove slowly by, looking at Chuckie's house. "Charming on the outside but sleazy inside, just like Chuckie. He broke my heart, literally broke my heart. Well, his foot is going to slide in due time, as they say, and I want to be around for that. That's why I've decided to stay." She said a moment later, "It's not really."

They passed Fred's house. Everybody had a house.

"Fred has a pond," Jean said. "We can go for a swim there later. I always use Fred's pond. He used to own a whole quarry, can you imagine? This was before our time with him, Gwendal's and mine, but kids were always getting in there and drowning. He put up big signs and barbed wire and everything but they still got in. It got to be too much trouble, so he sold it."

"Too much trouble!" Gloria said.

Death seemed preposterous. Totally unacceptable. Those silly kids, Gloria thought. She was elated and knew that she would soon feel tired and uneasy, but maybe it wouldn't happen this time. The day was bright, clean after the rain. Leaves lay on the streets, green and fresh.

"Those were Fred's words, too much trouble. Can't I pick them? I can really pick them." Jean shook her head.

They drove to Bill's house. Next to it was a pasture with horses in it. "Those aren't Bill's horses, but they're pretty, aren't they," Jean said.

"You're going to love Bill. He's gotten a little strange but he always was a little strange. We are who we are, aren't we. He carves ducks."

Bill was obviously not expecting them. He was a big man with long hair wearing boxer shorts and smoking a cigar. He looked at Jean warily.

"This used to be the love of my life," Jean said. To Bill, she said, "This is Gloria, my dearest friend."

Gloria felt she should demur, but smiled instead. Her condition didn't make her any more honest, she had found.

"Beautiful messengers, bad news," Bill said.

"We just thought we'd stop by," Jean said.

"Let me put on my pants," he said.

The two women sat in the living room, surrounded by wooden ducks. The ducks, exquisite and oppressive, nested on every surface. Bufflehead, canvasback, scaup, blue-winged teal. Gloria picked one up. It looked heavy but was light. Shoveler, mallard, merganser. The names kept coming to her.

"I forgot the lunch so we'll just stay a minute," Jean whispered. "I was *mad* about this man. Don't you ever wonder where it all goes?"

Bill returned, wearing trousers and a checked shirt. He had put his cigar somewhere.

"I *love* these ducks," Jean said. "You're getting so good."

"You want a duck," Bill said.

"Oh, yes!" Jean said.

"I wasn't offering you one. I just figured that you did." He winked at Gloria.

"Oh, you," Jean said.

"Take one, take one." Bill sighed.

Jean picked up the nearest duck and put it in her lap.

"That's a harlequin," Bill said.

"It's bizarre, I love it." Jean gripped the duck tightly.

"You want a duck?" Bill said to Gloria.

"No," Gloria said.

"Oh, take one!" Jean said excitedly.

"Decoys have always been particularly abhorrent to me," Gloria said, "since they are objects designed to lure a living thing to its destruction with the false promise of safety, companionship and rest."

They both looked at her, startled.

"Wow, Gloria," Jean said.

"These aren't decoys," Bill said mildly. "People don't use them for decoys anymore, they use them for decoration. There are hardly any ducks left to hunt. Ducks are on their way out. They're in a free fall."

"Diminishing habitat," Jean said.

"There you go," Bill said.

Black duck, pintail, widgeon. The names kept moving toward Gloria, then past.

"I'm more interested in creating dramas now," Bill said. "I'm getting away from the static stuff. I want to make dramatic moments. They have to be a little less than life-sized, but otherwise it's all there . . . the whole situation." He stood up. "Just a second," he said.

Once he was out of the room, Jean turned to her. "Gloria?" she said.

Bill returned carrying a large object covered by a sheet. He set it down on the floor and took off the sheet.

"I like it so far," Jean said after a moment.

"Interpret away," Bill said.

"Well," Jean said, "I don't think you should make it too busy."

"I said interpret, not criticize," Bill said.

"I just think the temptation would be to make something like that too busy. The temptation would be to put stuff in all those little spaces."

Bill appeared unmoved by this possible judgment, but he replaced the sheet.

IN THE CAR, JEAN SAID, "WASN'T THAT *AWFUL*. HE SHOULD STICK to ducks."

According to Bill, the situation the object represented seemed to be the acceptance of inexorable fate, this acceptance containing within it, however, a heroic gesture of defiance.

This was the situation, ideally always the situation, and it had been transformed, more or less abstractly, by Bill, into wood.

"He liked you."

"Jean, why would he like me?"

"He was flirting with you, I think. Wouldn't it be something if you two got together and we were all here in this one place?"

"Oh, my *god*," Gloria said, putting her hands over her face. Jean glanced at her absentmindedly. "I should be getting back," Gloria said. "I'm a little tired."

"But you just got here, and we have to take a swim at Fred's. The pond is wonderful, you'll love the pond. Actually, listen, do you want to go over to my parents' for lunch? My mother can make us something nice."

"Your parents live around here too," Gloria asked.

Jean looked frightened for a moment. "It's crazy, isn't it? They're so sweet. You'd love my parents. Oh, I wish you'd talk," she exclaimed. "You're my friend. I wish you'd open up some."

They drove past Chuckie's house again. "Whose car is that now?" Jean wondered.

"I remember trying to feed my mother a spoonful of dust once," Gloria said.

"Why?" Jean said. "Tell!"

"I was little, maybe four. She told me that I had grown in her stomach because she'd eaten some dust."

"No!" Jean said. "The things they tell you when they know you don't know."

"I wanted there to be another baby, someone else, a brother or a sister. So I had my little teaspoon. Eat this, I said. It's not a bit dirty. Don't be afraid."

"How out of control!" Jean cried.

"She looked at it and said she'd been talking about a different kind of dust, the sort of dust there was on flowers."

"She was just getting in deeper and deeper, wasn't she?" Jean said. She waited for Gloria to say more but the story seemed to be over.

IT WAS DARK WHEN SHE GOT BACK TO THE CABINS. THERE WERE no lights on anywhere. She remembered being happy off and on that day, and then looking at things and finding it all unkind. It had gotten harder for her to talk, and harder to listen too, but she was alone now and felt a little better. Still, she didn't feel right. She knew she would never be steady. It would never seem all of a piece for her. It would come and go until it stopped.

She pushed open the door and turned on the lamp beside the bed. There were three sockets in the lamp but only one bulb. There had been more bulbs in the lamp last night. She also thought there had been more furniture in the room, another chair. Reading would have been difficult, if she had wanted to read, but she was tired of reading, tired of books. After they had told her the first time and even after they had told her the other times in different ways, she had wanted to read, she didn't want to just stand around gaping at everything, but she couldn't pick the habit up again, it wasn't the same.

The screen in the window was a mottled bluish green, a coppery, oceanic color. She thought of herself as a child with the spoonful of dust, but it was just a memory of her telling it now.

In the middle of the night she woke, soaked with sweat. Someone was right outside, she thought. Then this feeling vanished. She gathered up her things and put everything in the car. She did this all hurriedly, and then drove quickly to Jean's house. She parked out front and turned the lights off. After a few moments, Gwendal appeared. She was wearing an ugly dress and carrying a suitcase. There were creases down one side of her face as though she'd been sleeping hard before she woke. "Where to first?" Gwendal said.

What they did first was to drive to the monastery and steal a dog. Gloria suspected that a fatal illness made her more or less invisible, and this seemed to be the case. She drove directly to the kennel, went in and walked out with a dog. She put him in the backseat and they drove off.

"We'll avoid the highway," Gloria said. "We'll stick to the back roads."

"Fine with me," Gwendal said.

Neither of them spoke for miles, then Gwendal said, "Would you say he's handsome and he knows it?"

"He's a dog," Gloria said. Gwendal was really mixed up. She was worse than her mother, Gloria thought.

They pulled into a diner and had breakfast. Then they went to a store and bought notebooks, pencils, dog food and gin. They bought sunglasses. It was full day now. They kept driving until dusk. They were quite a distance from Jean's house. Gloria felt sorry for Jean. She liked to have everyone around her, even funny little Gwendal, and now she didn't.

Gwendal had been sleeping. Suddenly she woke up. "Do you want to hear my dream?" she asked.

"Absolutely," Gloria said.

"Someone, it wasn't you, told me not to touch this funny-looking animal, it wasn't him," Gwendal said, gesturing toward the dog. "Every time I'd pat it, it would bite off a piece of my arm or a piece of my chest. I just had to keep going 'It's cute' and keep petting it."

"Oh," Gloria said. She had no idea what to say.

"Tell me one of your dreams," Gwendal said, yawning.

"I haven't been dreaming lately," Gloria said.

"That's not good," Gwendal said. "That shows a lack of imagination. Readiness, it shows a lack of readiness, maybe. Well, I can put the dreams in later. Don't worry about it." She chose a pencil and opened the notebook. "OK," she said. "Married?"

"No."

"Any children?"

"No."

"Allergies?"

Gloria looked at her.

"Do you want to start at the beginning or work backward from the Big Surprise," Gwendal asked.

They were on the outskirts of a town, stopped at a traffic light. Gloria looked straight ahead. Beginnings. She couldn't remember any beginnings.

"Hey," someone said. "Hey!"

She looked to her left at a dented car full of young men. One of them threw a can of beer at her. It bounced off the door and they sped off, howling.

"Everyone knows if someone yells 'Hey' you don't look at them," Gwendal said.

"Let's stop for the night," Gloria said.

"How are you feeling," Gwendal asked ... not all that solicitously, Gloria thought.

They pulled into the first motel they saw. Gloria fed the dog and had a drink while Gwendal bounced on the bed. He seemed a most equable dog. He drank from the toilet bowl and gnawed peaceably on the bed rail. Gloria and Gwendal ate pancakes in an empty restaurant and strolled around a swimming pool that had a filthy rubber cover rolled across it. Back in the room, Gloria lay down on one bed while Gwendal sat on the other.

"Do you want me to paint your nails or do your hair," Gwendal asked.

"No," Gloria said. She was recalling a bad thought she'd had once, a very bad thought. It had caused no damage, however, as far as she knew.

"I wouldn't know how to do your hair, actually," Gwendal said.

With a little training, Gloria thought, this kid could be a mortician.

That night Gloria dreamed. She dreamed she was going to the funeral of some woman who had been indifferent to her. There was no need for her to be there. She was standing with a group of people. She felt like a criminal, undetected, but she felt chosen, too, to be there when she shouldn't be. Then she was lying across the opening of a cement pipe. When she woke, she was filled with relief, knowing she would forget the dream immediately. It was morning again. Gwendal was outside by the unpleasant pool, writing in her notebook.

"*This was happiness then,*" she said, scribbling away.

"Where's the dog," Gloria asked. "Isn't he with you?"

"I don't know," Gwendal said. "I let him out and he took off for parts unknown."

"What do you mean!" Gloria said. She ran back to the room, went to the car, ran across the cement parking lot and around the motel. Gloria didn't have any name to call the dog with. It had just disappeared without having ever been hers. She got Gwendal in the car and they drove down the roads around the motel. She squinted, frightened, at black heaps along the shoulder and in the littered grass, but it was tires, rags, tires. Cars sped by them. Along the median strip, dead trees were planted at fifty-foot intervals. The dog wasn't anywhere that she could find. Gloria glared at Gwendal.

"It was an accident," Gwendal said.

"You have your own ideas about how this should be, don't you?"

"He was kind of a distraction," Gwendal said.

Gloria's head hurt. Back in the desert, just before she had made this trip, she had had her little winter. Her heart had pounded like a fist on a door. But it was false, all false, for she had survived it.

Gwendal had the hateful notebook on her lap. It had a splatter black cover with the word *Composition* on it. "Now we can get started," she said. "Today's the day. Favorite color," she asked. "Favorite show tune?" A childish blue barrette was stuck haphazardly in her hair, exposing part of a large, pale ear.

Gloria wasn't going to talk to her.

After a while, Gwendal said, *"They were unaware that the fugitive was in their midst."* She wrote it down. Gwendal scribbled in the book all day long and asked Gloria to buy her another one. She sometimes referred to Gloria's imminent condition as the Great Adventure.

Gloria was distracted. Hours went by and she was driving, though she could barely recall what they passed. "I'm going to pull in early tonight," she said.

The motel they stopped at late that afternoon was much like the one before. It was called the Motel Lark. Gloria lay on one bed and Gwendal sat on the other. Gloria missed having a dog. A dog wouldn't let the stranger in, she thought sentimentally. Whereas Gwendal would in a minute.

"We should be able to talk," Gwendal said.

"Why should we be able to talk?" Gloria said. "There's no reason we should be able to talk."

"You're not open is your problem. You don't want to share. It's hard to imagine what's real all by yourself, you know."

"It is not!" Gloria said hotly. They were bickering like an old married couple.

"This isn't working out," Gloria said. "This is crazy. We should call your mother."

"I'll give you a few more days, but it's true," Gwendal said. "I thought this would be a more mystical experience. I thought you'd tell me something. You don't even know about makeup. I bet you don't even know how to check the oil in that car. I've never seen you check the oil."

"I know how to check the oil," Gloria said.

"How about an electrical problem? Would you know how to fix an electrical problem?"

"No!" Gloria yelled.

Gwendal was quiet. She stared at her fat knees.

"I'm going to take a bath," Gloria said.

She went into the bathroom and shut the door. The tile was turquoise and the stopper to the tub hung on a chain. This was the Motel Lark, she thought. She dropped the rubber stopper in the drain and ran the water. A few tiles were missing and the wall showed a gray, failed adhesive. She wanted to say something but even that wasn't it. She didn't want to say anything. She wanted to realize something she couldn't say. She heard a voice, it must have been Gwendal's, in the bedroom. Gloria lay down in the tub. The water wasn't as warm as she expected. *Your silence is no deterrent to me, Gloria,* the voice said. She reached for the hot-water faucet but it ran in cold. If she let it run, it might get warm, she thought. That's what they say. Or again, that might be it.

Health

PAMMY IS IN AN UNPLEASANT TEXAS CITY, THE CITY WHERE she was born, in the month of her twelfth birthday. It is cold and cloudy. Soon it will rain. The rain will wash the film of ash off the car she is traveling in, volcanic ash that has drifted across the Gulf of Mexico all the way from the Yucatán. Pammy is a stocky blue-eyed blonde, a daughter being taken in her father's car to her tanning lesson.

This is her father's joke. She is being taken to a tanning session, twenty-five minutes long. She had requested this for her birthday, ten tanning sessions in a health spa. She had also asked for and received new wheels for her skates. They are purple Rannallis. She had dyed her stoppers to match although the stoppers were a duller, cruder purple. Pammy wants to be a speed skater but worries that she doesn't have the personality for it. "You've gotta have gravel in your gut to be in speed," her coach said. Pammy has mastered the duck walk but still doesn't have a good, smooth crossover, and sometimes she fears that she never will.

Pammy and her father, Morris, are following a truck that is carrying a jumble of television sets. There is a twenty-four-inch console facing them on the open tailgate, restrained by rope, with a bullet hole in the exact center of the screen.

Morris drinks coffee from a plastic-lidded cup that fits into a bracket mounted just beneath the car's radio. Pammy has a friend, Wanda, whose stepfather has the same kind of plastic cup in his car, but he drinks bourbon and water from his. Wanda had been adopted when she was two months old. Pammy is relieved that neither her father nor Marge, her mother, drinks. Sometimes they have wine. On her birthday, even Pammy had wine with dinner. Marge and Morris seldom argue and she is grateful for this. This morning, however, she had seen them quarrel. Once again, her mother had borrowed her father's hairbrush and left long, brown hairs in it. Her father had brushed them out with a comb over the clean kitchen sink. Her father had left a nest of brown hair in the white sink.

In the car, the radio is playing a song called "Tainted Love," a song Morris likes to refer to as "Rancid Love." The radio plays constantly when Pammy and her father drive anywhere. Morris is a good driver. He enjoys driving still, after years and years of it. Pammy looks forward to learning how to drive now, but after a few years, who knows? She can't imagine it being that enjoyable after a while. Her father is skillful here, on the freeways and streets, and on the terrifying, wide two-lane highways and narrow mountain roads in Mexico, and even on the rutted, soiled beaches of the Gulf Coast. One weekend, earlier that spring, Morris had rented a Jeep in Corpus Christi and he and Pammy and Marge had driven the length of Padre Island. They sped across the sand, the only people for miles and miles. There was plastic everywhere.

"You will see a lot of plastic," the man who rented them the Jeep said, "but it is plastic from all over the world."

Morris had given Pammy a driving lesson in the Jeep. He taught her how to shift smoothly, how to synchronize acceleration with the depression and release of the clutch. "There's a way to do things right," Morris told her, and when he said this she was filled with a sort of fear. They were just words, she knew, words that anybody could use, but behind words were always things, sometimes things you could never tell anyone, certainly no one you loved, frightening things that weren't even true.

"I'm sick of being behind this truck," Morris says. The screen of the injured television looks like dirty water. Morris pulls to the curb beside a Japanese market. Pammy stares into the market, where shoppers wait in line at a cash register. Many of the women wear scarves on their heads. In school, in social studies class, she is reading eyewitness accounts of the aftermath of the atomic bombing of Hiroshima. She reads about young girls running from their melting city, their hair burned off, their burned skin in loose folds, crying, "Stupid Americans." Morris sips his coffee, then turns the car back onto the street now free from fatally wounded television sets.

Pammy gazes at the backs of her hands, which are tan but not, she feels, quite tan enough. They are a dusky peach color. This will be her fifth tanning lesson. In the health spa, there are ten colored photographs on the wall showing a woman in a bikini, a pale woman being transformed into a tanned woman. In the last photograph she has plucked the bikini slightly away from her hip bone to expose a sliver of white skin and she is smiling down at the sliver.

Pammy tans well. Without a tan, her face seems grainy and uneven for she has freckles and rather large pores. Tanning draws her together, completes her. She has had all kinds of tans—golden tans, pool tans, even a Florida tan that looked yellow back in Texas. She had brought all her friends the same present from Florida—small plywood crates filled with tiny oranges that were actually chewing gum. The finest tan Pammy has ever had, however, was in Mexico six months ago. She went there with her parents for two weeks and had gotten the truly remarkable tan and also tuberculosis. This has caused some tension between Morris and Marge as it had been Morris's idea to swim at the spas in the mountains rather than in the pools at the more established hotels. It was believed that Pammy had become infected at one particular public spa just outside the small dusty town where they had gone to buy tiles, tiles of a dusky orange with blue rays flowing from the center that are now in the kitchen of their home, where each morning Pammy drinks her juice and takes three hundred milligrams of isoniazid.

"Here we are," Morris says. The health spa is in a small, concrete-block building with white columns, salvaged from the wrecking of a mansion, adorning the front. Along the street there are gift shops, palmists and an exterminating company. This was not the company that had tented Wanda's house for termites. That had been another company. When Pammy was in Mexico getting tuberculosis, Wanda and her parents had gone to San Antonio for a week while their house was being tented. When they returned, they'd found a dead robber in the living room, with the things he was stealing piled neatly nearby. He had died from inhaling the deadly gas used by the exterminators.

"Mommy will pick you up," Morris says. "She has a class this afternoon so she might be a little late. Just stay inside until she comes."

Morris kisses her on the cheek. He treats her like a child. He treats Marge like a mother, her mother.

Marge is thirty-five but still a student. She takes courses in art history and film at one of the city's universities, the same university where Morris teaches petroleum science. Years ago when Marge had first been a student, before she met Morris or Pammy was born, she had been in Spain, in a museum studying a Goya, and a piece of the painting had fallen at her feet. She had quickly placed it in her pocket and now has it on her bureau in a small glass box. It is a wedge of greenish violet paint, as large as a thumbnail. It is from one of Goya's nudes.

Pammy gets out of the car and goes into the health spa. There is no equipment here except for the tanning beds, twelve of them in eight small rooms. Pammy has never had to share a room with anyone. If asked to, she would probably say no, hoping this wouldn't hurt the other person's feelings. The receptionist is an old, vigorous woman behind a scratched metal desk, wearing a black jumpsuit and feather earrings. Behind her are shelves of powders and pills in squat brown bottles with names like DYNAMIC STAMINA BUILDER and DYNAMIC SUPER STRESS-END and LIVER CONCENTRATE ENERGIZER.

The receptionist's name is Aurora. Pammy thinks the name is magnificent and is surprised that it belongs to such an old woman. Aurora leads her to one of the rooms at the rear of the building. The room has a mirror, a sink, a small stool, a white rotating fan and the bed, a long bronze coffin-like apparatus with a lid. Pammy is always startled when she sees the bed with its frosted ultraviolet tubes, its black vinyl headrest. In the next room, someone coughs. Pammy imagines people lying in all the rooms, wrapped in white light, lying quietly as though they were being rested for a long, long journey. Aurora takes a spray bottle of disinfectant and a scrap of toweling from the counter above the sink and cleans the surface of the bed. She twists the timer and the light leaps out.

"There you are, honey," Aurora says. She pats Pammy on the shoulder and leaves.

Pammy pushes off her sandals and undresses quickly. She leaves her clothes in a heap, her sweatshirt on top of the pile. Her sweatshirt is white with a transfer of a skater on the back. The skater is a man wearing a helmet and kneepads, side-surfing and goofy-footed. She lies down and with her left hand pulls the lid to within a foot of the bed's cool surface. She can see the closed door and the heap of clothing and her feet. Pammy considers her feet to be her ugliest feature. They are skinny and the toes are too far apart. She and Wanda had painted their toes the same color, but Wanda's feet were pretty and hers were not. Pammy thought her feet looked like they belonged to a dead person and there wasn't anything she could do about them. She closes her eyes.

Wanda, who reads a lot, told Pammy that tuberculosis was a romantic disease, one suffered only by artists and poets and "highly sensitive individuals."

"Oh, yeah," her stepfather had said. "Tuberculosis has mucho cachet."

Wanda's stepfather is always joking, Pammy thinks. She feels Wanda's parents are pleasant enough but she's always a little uncomfortable around them. Wanda wasn't the first child they adopted. There had been another baby, but it was learned that the baby's background had been misrepresented. Or perhaps it had been a boring baby. In any case the baby had been returned and they got Wanda. Pammy doesn't think Wanda's parents are very steadfast. She is surprised that they don't make Wanda nervous.

The tanning bed is warm but not uncomfortably so. Pammy lies with her arms straight by her sides, palms down. She hears voices in the hall and footsteps. When she first began coming to the health spa, she was afraid that someone would open the door to the room she was in by mistake. She imagined exactly what it would be like. She would see the door open abruptly out of the corner of her eye, then someone would say "Sorry" and the door would close again. But this had not happened. The voices pass by.

Pammy thinks of Snow White lying in her glass coffin. The queen had deceived her how many times? Three? She had been in disguise, but still. And then Snow White had choked on an apple. In the restaurants she sometimes goes to with her parents there are posters on the walls that show a person choking and another person trying to save him.

Snow White lay in a glass coffin, not naked of course but in a gown, watched over by dwarfs. But surely they had not been real dwarfs. That was just a word that had been given to them.

When Pammy had told Morris that tuberculosis was a romantic disease, he said, "There's nothing romantic about it. Besides, you don't have it."

It seems to be a fact that she both has and doesn't have tuberculosis.

Pammy had been given the tuberculin skin test along with her class-mates when she began school in the fall and within forty-eight hours had a large swelling on her arm.

"Now that you've come in contact with it, you don't have to worry about getting it," the pediatrician had said in his office, smiling.

"You mean the infection constitutes immunity," Marge said.

"Not exactly," the pediatrician said, shaking his head, still smiling.

Her lungs are clear. She is not ill but has an illness. The germs are in her body but in a resting state, still alive though rendered powerless. Outwardly, she is the same, but within, a great drama has taken place and Pammy feels herself in possession of a bright, secret and unspeak-able knowledge.

She knows other things too, things that would break her parents' hearts, common, ugly, easy things. She knows a girl in school who stole money from her mother's purse and bought a personal massager. She knows another girl whose brother likes to wear her clothes. She knows a boy who threw a can of motor oil at his father and knocked him unconscious.

Pammy stretches. Her head tingles. Her body is about a foot and a half off the floor and appears almost gray in the glare from the tubes. She has heard of pills you could take to acquire a tan. Just take two pills a day and after twenty days you'd have a wonderful tan that could be maintained by continuing to take the pills. You ordered them from Canada. It was some kind of food-coloring substance. How gross, Pammy thinks. When she had been little she bought a quarter of an acre of land in Canada by mail for fifty cents. That was two years ago.

Pammy hears voices from the room next to hers, coming through the thin wall. A woman talking rapidly says, "Pete went up to Detroit two days ago to visit his brother who's dying up there in the hospi-tal. Cancer. The brother's always been a nasty type, very unpleasant. Younger than Pete and always mean. Tried to commit suicide twice. Then he learns he has cancer and decides he doesn't want to die. Car-ries on and on. Is miserable to everyone. Puts the whole family through hell, but nothing can be done about it, he's dying of cancer. So Pete goes up to see him his last days in the hospital and you know what happens? Pete's wallet gets stolen. Right out of a dying man's room. Five hundred dollars in cash and all our credit cards. That was yesterday. What a day."

Another woman says, "If it's not one thing, it's something else."

Pammy coughs. She doesn't want to hear other people's voices. It is as though they are throwing away junk, the way some people use words, as though one word were as good as another.

"Things happen so abruptly anymore," the woman says. "You know what I mean?"

Pammy does not listen and does not open her eyes for if she did she would see this odd bright room with her clothes in a heap and herself lying motionless and naked. She does not open her eyes because she prefers imagining that she is levitating on a stage in a coil of pure energy. If one thought purely enough, one could create one's own truth. That's how people accomplished astral travel, walked over burning coals, cured warts. There was a girl in Pammy's class at school, Bonnie Black, a small owlish-looking girl who was a Christian Scientist. She raised rabbits and showed them at fairs, and was always wearing the ribbons they had won to school, pinned to her blouse. She had warts all over both hands, but one day Pammy noticed that the warts were gone and Bonnie Black told her they'd disappeared after she clearly realized that in her true being as God's reflection, she couldn't have warts.

It seemed that people were better off when they could concentrate on something, hold something in their mind for a long time and really believe it. Pammy had once seen a radical skater putting on a show at the opening of a shopping mall. He leapt over cars and pumped up the sides of buildings. He did flips and spins. A disc jockey who was set up for the day in the parking lot interviewed him. "I'm really impressed with your performance," the disc jockey said, "and I'm impressed that you never fall. Why don't you fall?" The skater was a thin boy in baggy cutoff jeans. "I don't fall," the boy said, looking hard at the microphone, "because I've got a deep respect for the concrete surface and because when I make a miscalculation, instead of falling I turn it into a new trick."

Pammy thinks it is wonderful that the boy was able to tell himself something that would keep him from thinking he might fall.

The door to the room opened. Pammy had heard the turning of the knob. At first she lies without opening her eyes, willing the sound of the door shutting, but she hears nothing, only the ticking of the bed's timer. She swings her head quickly to the side and looks at the door. A man is standing there, staring at her. She presses her right hand into a fist and lays it between her legs. She puts her left arm across her breasts.

"What?" she says to the figure, frightened. In an instant she is almost panting with fear. She feels the repetition of something painful and known, but she has not known this, not ever. The figure says nothing and pulls the door shut. With a flurry of rapid ticking, the timer stops. The harsh lights of the bed go out.

Pammy pushes the lid back and hurriedly gets up. She dresses hastily and smooths her hair with her fingers. She looks at herself in the mirror, her lips parted. Her teeth are white behind her pale lips. She stares at herself. She can be looked at and not discovered. She can speak and not be known. She opens the door and enters the hall. There is no one there. The hall is so narrow that by spreading her arms she can touch the walls with her fingertips. In the reception area by Aurora's desk, there are three people, a stoop-shouldered young woman and two men. The woman was signing up for a month of unlimited tanning, which meant that after the basic monthly fee she only had to pay a dollar a visit. She takes her checkbook out of a soiled handbag, which is made out of some silvery material, and writes a check. The men look comfortable lounging in the chairs, their legs stretched out. They know each other, Pammy guesses, but do not know the woman. One of them has dark spiky hair like a wet animal's. The other wears a tight red T-shirt. Neither is the man she had seen in the doorway.

"What time do you want to come back tomorrow, honey," Aurora asks Pammy. "You certainly are coming along nicely. Isn't she coming along nicely?"

"I'd like to come back the same time tomorrow," Pammy says. She raises her hand to her mouth and coughs slightly.

"Not the same time, honey. Can't give you the same time. How about an hour later?"

"All right," Pammy says. The stoop-shouldered woman sits down in a chair. There are no more chairs in the room. Pammy opens the door and steps outside. It has rained and the pavement is dark and shining. She walks slowly down the street and smells the rain lingering in the trees. By a store called Imagine, there's a clump of bamboo with some beer cans glittering in its ragged, grassy center. Imagine sells neon palm trees and silk clouds and stars. It sells greeting cards and chocolate in shapes children aren't allowed to see and it sells children's stickers and shoelaces. Pammy looks in the window at a satin pillow in the shape of a heart with a heavy zipper running down the center of it. Pammy turns and walks back to the building that houses the tanning beds. Her mother pulls up in their car. "Pammy!" she calls. She is leaning toward the window on the passenger side, which she has rolled down. She unlocks the car's door. Pammy gets in and the door locks again.

The car speeds down the street and Pammy sits in it, a little stunned. Her father will teach her how to drive, and she will drive around. Her mother will continue to take classes at the university. Whenever she meets someone new, she will mention the Goya. "I have a small Goya," she will say, and laugh. Pammy will grow older, she is older already. But the world will remain as young as she was once, infinite in its possibilities, and uncaring. She never wants to see that figure looking at her again, staring so coldly, but she knows she will, for already its features are becoming more indistinct, more general. It could be anything. And it will be somewhere else now, something else. She coughs, but it is not the cough of a sick person because Pammy is a healthy girl. It is the kind of cough a person might make if they were at a party and there was no one there but strangers.

White

BLISS AND JOAN WERE GIVING A FAREWELL PARTY FOR THE
Episcopal priest and his family, who had been called by God to the
state of Michigan. They had invited some mutual friends and couples
with children the same age as the priest's children. Bliss did not go to
church and had never met the priest, but he approved of any party
given for whatever reason and felt that Joan had something of a fascina-
tion with the man, whose name was Daniel. Joan had always imagined
that Daniel might tell her something, although he never had, and now
he was leaving.

This was in New England, where they had lived for three years.
Joan was a fourth-generation Floridian who missed the garish sunsets
and the sound of armadillos crashing through the palmetto scrub. She
remembered wearing live lizards hanging from her earlobes when she
was a child. She remembered Gator, a pony her father had bought for
her. Joan's father owned a grapefruit grove. Her grandfather had run
a fishing camp, and her great-grandfather had been a guide who shot
flamingos and spoonbills and ibis and gathered eggs for naturalists.

Bliss had been born in Florida too. Now he's a dentist. People think
that dentists are acquisitive and don't care, but Bliss cares.

Bliss and Joan have no children. Twice, Joan gave birth to a baby
but both times the baby died before he was six months old. There was
a sweet smell on the baby's diaper, a smell rather like that of maple
sugar, and in a few hours the baby was dead. Bliss has a single deviant
gene that matches a single deviant gene of Joan's. When a doctor told
him at the hospital that the deaths were not as mysterious as they first
appeared to be, Bliss struck him before he could say anything more,
once with his left hand and again with his right. The doctor fell to the
floor but got up quickly and walked away down the white corridor,
leaving Bliss alone, his arms aching.

After the death of their second child, they had moved to New England. In Florida, Joan's depression had been compounded by unpleasant dreams of her great-grandfather. He appeared in her dreams exactly as he did in her father's photo album—a skinny man in a wide hat, rough clothes and rubber boots, standing with his shotgun. In a recurrent dream, he was a waiter in a pleasant, rosily lit dining room serving her soup in which birds in all stages of incubation floated. In another frequent dream, he was not visible, yet Joan sensed his presence beneath the vision of hundreds of flamingos flying through a dark sky, flying, as they do, in a serpentine manner, as though they were crawling through the air.

In New England, Joan discovered that if she slept while it was light she didn't dream, so she slept in the afternoons and stayed up all night, putting together immense puzzles of Long Island Sound. She lived in terror, actually, but it was rootless, because the worst had already happened. She referred to the days behind her as "those so-called days."

The day of the party was a Saturday, and Bliss had shopped with Joan for the liquor and food. As they were turning in to their driveway, their car was struck in the rear by a woman in an old Triumph. Joan and Bliss got out and looked at the rear of their car, which was undamaged, and then at the Triumph, which also appeared undamaged.

The woman was weeping. "I'm sorry," she wailed. "Oh, I'm so sorry. This is my husband's car."

"No harm done," Bliss said.

The woman tore at her hair. She was very pretty.

Joan was unaffected by trivial unpleasantries. She drove to the house, while Bliss remained standing by the Triumph. Joan unloaded the car and then went outside with a large bag of Hershey's Kisses. She hid the Kisses all around the lawn, in the interstices of the stone walls and on the lower branches of trees for the children at the party to find.

"Well, Donna certainly has a tale to tell," Bliss said, coming up to her. He unwrapped the foil from a Kiss and tossed the chocolate into his mouth.

"Donna, the TR person," Joan said.

"I invited her to the party. Is that all right?"

"Sure," Joan said. Bliss often invited strangers to their parties. Sometimes they were very nice people.

"Her husband had a stroke and is divorcing her. He insists on it." Bliss rolled the foil into a tiny ball, looked at it, then dropped it in his pocket.

"We won't get divorced," Joan said.

"Never," Bliss said. He went into the house to set out the glasses and plates. Joan walked around outside, hiding the rest of the candy. In the yard next door, a Doberman puppy with bandages on his ears and tail was playing with a rubber ice-cream sundae. His aluminum run extended the length of the yard. He had a druggy name, the name of some amphetamine. Joan had heard his owner calling him. The owner was a muscular man with a mustache who drove an elaborate four-wheel-drive vehicle. The puppy's fashionable name made him seem transitory, even doomed.

At 5:00 p.m., Joan and Bliss went upstairs to their bedroom. The room was simple and pleasant with plain wide-board floors and white furniture, a little cell of felicity. There was a single framed poster of wildflowers on the white walls. It seemed to Joan the kind of room in which someone was supposed to be getting better. Joan lay on the bed and watched Bliss change his clothes for the party. She smiled for an instant, then shut her eyes. The passion they felt for each other had turned to unease some time ago.

"Maybe you'd love me if I were a priest," Bliss said.

Joan's eyes were shut. She saw the green lawn below them extending in time to her parents' house, herself as the child her own children would never remind her of. She saw the barn where her father kept the chemicals and sprays for the groves. Inside, tacked on one wall, was a large foldout from an insecticide manufacturer's brochure depicting all the ills that citrus was heir to. Beneath each picture of an insect was a picture of the horrible damage it could do. As a child, she had thrilled to it—flyspecked, yellowing, curling around the rusted nails that secured it. That such cruel and destructive forces could exist and be named amazed her, and that the means to control them could be at hand seemed preposterous. She saw it often, as now, clearly; the meticulous detail, the particularity of each proffered blight.

"It's a question of language," Bliss said. " 'The periapical granuloma is one of the most common of all sequelae of pulpitis'—it's not the kind of language that sends a person forth into the world feeling loved, forgiven and renewed."

"It's not very comforting," Joan agreed, opening her eyes.

"Really," Bliss said, "I'm sick of teeth. You wouldn't believe what goes on in people's mouths. I want to abandon dentistry and go into the ministry. I have already chosen my style," Bliss said, addressing her face in the mirror. "Yesterday, when Peter Carlyle was in—he's the acute suppurative osteomyelitis—I said, 'This day only is ours.'"

"Did he agree?"

"He certainly did," Bliss said. "That is, he nodded slightly and groaned. Would you like a drink?"

"Sure," Joan said. "It's a party."

Bliss went downstairs and reappeared a few moments later with a glass of bourbon and ice. Joan ran a bath and sat in the tub, listening to the cars coming up the driveway, the slamming of doors and people's greetings. She did not touch the bourbon. She thought about Daniel, his voice, his prematurely gray hair. He had big feet. The shoes he wore in church seemed enormous. Joan went to church several times a week and sat, rose or knelt in accordance with the service. She sat in the back, in a pew where someone had once outlined a flower in the brocade of the kneeling bench with green crayon. In each pew, by the hymnal rack, was a smaller rack holding printed information cards and a small sharpened pencil. One could introduce oneself, ask questions, request a hymn, seek counseling. Joan did none of these things. She sat quietly in church, her head tilted upward, listening, feeling vain, unfixed, distracted. With Daniel she felt she was close to something, some comprehension of what there was left for her to want. Bliss was right, she thought, to be jealous of Daniel, although she and the priest were little more than acquaintances. And Daniel, of course, doesn't know anything about her—he doesn't know the past, about the babies, he doesn't know her breasts, her lips. He doesn't know the terrible way she thinks, like Bliss knows.

Joan got out of the tub. Wide veins were darkly visible on her hands and feet. She painted her nails chalk-colored, put on a flowered dress and went down to the party on the lawn. There were several dozen adults there and half a dozen children sitting meditatively in a circle.

Joan approached them slowly, wondering what was in the heart of the circle. A baby bird? A Ouija board? But from a distance she saw it was a bowl of pretzels. The sky was pale and the ragged crown of the trees, dark. She gazed at the children without really seeing them. If someone had demanded that she describe them, she could not. She and Bliss gave a great many parties and were reciprocally invited to many. There was nothing to it, really.

A man named Tim Barnes came up to her and kissed her cheek. Tim liked to sail. He enjoyed narrow rivers and winding estuaries. He had fashioned a story around the time his mast went through the branches of a tree, and often he would tell it. When he told it, he would say, "I proceeded, looking like Birnam Wood."

Once, during another party, Tim had said to Joan, "I dream about you, and when I wake up I'm angry. What do you think?"

People were talking and laughing. Joan had a tendency to look at their mouths. Their teeth seemed good. Bliss had made the acquaintance of many of these people professionally. She imagined Bliss solving their mouths, making them attractive, happy, her friends.

Next door, the Doberman trotted back and forth the length of his run, watching them. He had an abrupt, rocking gait. His paws, striking the soft dirt, made no sound.

People were talking about whether or not they wanted to survive a nuclear war.

"I certainly wouldn't," Tim Barnes's wife said.

"I don't believe we're talking about nuclear war just like our parents did in the fifties," a woman named Petey said.

Joan saw a clutch of candy at the base of a slender crab apple tree. She should have hidden something less bright. She had to remember to tell the children that they were supposed to look for the candy. She thought of her father spraying water on his citrus before a freeze. The next morning, the globes of fruit would be white and shining and rotting in the clear sunny air. Florida was not a serious state.

"The first thing our government is going to do after the Big B is to implement their post-attack taxation plan," Tim Barnes said.

"I mean," his wife said, "who wants to survive only to pay forty or fifty percent?"

"You have to protect the banking system," Tim said. "You have to reestablish the productive base."

"I have to greet the guest of honor," Joan said. The group, for the most part, chuckled. Joan walked toward Daniel, who was standing at the bottom of the lawn. He had a drink in one hand and a pretzel rod in the other and was gazing into a bed of delphiniums. Several yards away, Donna, the TR person, was talking to Bliss.

"People need dentists," Joan heard her assure him, "they really do."

"Joan!" Daniel exclaimed as she drew near. "What a beautiful garden." He wore a green shirt and a poplin suit. His large feet were encased in sneakers. "Cast completely in blue and white. Very discriminating, very elegant. It must have been difficult."

Joan looked at her garden, which gave her no pleasure. She had designed it and cared for it. She knew some things. It didn't matter.

"White is a distinctively modern color," Daniel said, finishing his drink. "It takes the curse off things."

"Its neutrality is its charm," Joan said.

The priest sighed. "I want to clarify what I just said, Joan. You can't imagine how tired I am. Claire was so tired, she couldn't make it. The hustle-bustle of moving is exhausting. She's going to write you a note. You will definitely receive a note from her. I meant, and this is not in regard to your garden, which is stunning, that white is often used to make otherwise unacceptable things acceptable. In general."

"Some people feel that flowers are in bad taste," Joan said.

"Isn't that astounding," Daniel said. "Someone told me that once in regard to the altar and I found it astounding." He rolled his glass between his hands and nodded toward the puppy, who was resting on his haunches now, regarding the group in the dimming light.

"Your cats must be afraid of that Doberman," he said.

"I don't have cats."

"I'm sorry, I thought you had two cats. Perhaps it's Joan Pillsbury who has the cats."

One of Daniel's sons came up to them and said, "Dad, there's nothing to do here." Daniel looked at him. Joan told the boy about the hidden candy and in a moment the small group of children had scattered across the yard with shrill cries. An instant later, they had found it all and returned to the small piece of earth that they had appropriated for themselves. They displayed the amount, then ate it.

"That was fun," the priest said. "They all certainly enjoyed that."

"Dentists talk a lot, don't they," Donna said to Bliss. "I mean, I've always wondered, why are dentists so garrulous?"

"Look," Bliss said, "my wife has turned on the moon." The two couples had drifted together and now looked upward at a full, close, mauve moon.

"My wife fell from that tree once, you know," Bliss said, addressing Daniel, pointing toward a large maple.

"You didn't," the priest said to Joan. He shook his head.

"Uh-huh," Bliss said. "Several years ago."

"How did it happen?" Daniel said, weaving his eyes among the branches, down the trunk to the ground beneath it as though he expected to see her splayed form there, outlined in lime by some secular authority. "Was one of your cats up there with his eye on the sparrow?" He chuckled.

"I would've broken my neck," Donna said. She laughed but her eyes were wet. Her mouth trembled a little.

"Nothing happened," Joan said. "Here I am."

"I understand what you're saying, Joan," Daniel said. "You took a little rest but now you're back among us."

Donna looked at Joan, then at the priest.

"I believe you married us," Donna said to Daniel. "St. Stephen's, right? Harry and Donna Sutton?"

"Hello," Daniel said warmly.

"We weren't members. You just fit us in."

There was a pause while they all sipped their drinks.

"Do you know that at any given moment there are approximately five hundred and eighty-four million unfilled carious lesions in the teeth of the U.S. population?" Bliss said.

Donna laughed, then turned and walked unsteadily to one of the long stone benches on the lawn. She lay on the bench and crossed her ankles.

"You'd like Donna," Bliss said to Joan. "You know where she's from? Panama City."

"How are she and Harry doing," Daniel asked.

"Time has wrought its meanness on their attachment," Bliss said. "You know what I told her? I told her, to God both the day and the night are alike, so are the first and last of our days."

"My, that's very good," Daniel said, "but a bit cold."

"I told her sufficient to the day is the evil thereof."

"One of the great lines, certainly."

"Are you of the school that thinks of man as a vapor, a fantastic vapor, or a shadow, even the dream of a shadow?" Bliss asked.

"Stop," Joan said. She stifled a yawn because she wanted to appear rude.

"A bubble," Daniel said. "We subscribe to the bubble theory."

"Excuse me, Father," Bliss said. "I'm sure this happens to you all the time, people asking you questions on an emergency basis at cocktail parties."

Daniel stretched his neck and smiled at Joan.

Bliss took several swallows of his drink. "An interesting thing happened today," he said. "Joan's father sent us a letter. It began briskly enough, 'Dear Joan and Bliss.' But then there was nothing, not a thing. Just a page, blank as the day is long. Well, we puzzled over that one, you can imagine."

"Faith illuminates that letter for us," Daniel said. "Love is the great translator. On the other hand, how's Dad's eyesight? Does he buy good-quality pens or does he buy them ten for two dollars?"

"The man refuses to be a guest." Bliss laughed. "Actually, I don't know why I made that up about the letter."

"I'm a little giddy tonight myself," Daniel said. "I suppose it's the thrill of saddling up and moving on."

Bliss put his hand on Joan's back and lightly touched her hair. For an instant Joan hated him, and in another instant felt sick, drowning. She saw the party set up beneath the trees, illuminated by candles stuck in paper bags of sand. People were eating ribs and salad from large china plates. Donna remained lying on her back on the bench, her arms dangling, her hands, loosely curved, touching the grass. Joan pulled away from Bliss and walked over to her. The girl's eyes were open and she wore shiny pants, pegged and zippered at the ankles. Her blouse looped out over her belt.

"Can I get you something to eat?" Joan asked. She was solicitous and incurious. But people were supposed to be making connections like these all the time, she thought, all through their lives.

Donna sat up abruptly. "I shouldn't be behaving like this, should I? I'm making a fool of myself, aren't I?" Joan sat beside her on the bench. "My husband's sick and doesn't want me anymore," she said. "When he was well he was always saying he didn't want me to have a baby yet. He said he wanted to wait a while before we had a baby. Men always act as though the same baby is waiting out there in the dark each month, did you ever notice that?"

At the edge of the party, Amanda Sherrill, her long peach-colored hair shining and swinging, demonstrated a hip-slimming exercise to a small exuberant group. She grasped the seat of a lawn chair and extended her left leg upward in a slow arc.

"Oh, my goodness," Jack Buttrick screamed.

"Your husband is very pleasant," Donna said. "He's funny, isn't he? And you're pleasant. It was very nice of you to invite me here. I'd been driving around in Harry's car and crying to myself, and then I hit you. You were so nice about it." She looked at Joan uneasily. "Your husband thinks we're a little alike," she said. "I never would've guessed you were from the South. Do you miss Florida?"

"My father always used to call it Floridon't," Joan said. This was how it was supposed to be, she thought. Memory and conversation, clarification and semblance, miscalculation and repentance, skim and rest.

Donna laughed, showing considerable gum. Bliss isn't going to be able to do much about that, Joan thought. "I'll get us something to eat," she said. She walked toward the house, having no intention of getting anyone anything to eat.

Joan went up to the second floor, entered the bedroom and closed the door. She stood by the window and looked down into the adjoining yard. The muscular young man with the mustache had gone into the pen and was playing with the Doberman puppy, who spun in tight, exhilarated circles. The owner put his hands on the dog's shoulders and pushed him from side to side. Joan stood by the window, watching. Moonlight fell across the ribbon of earth where the man and the dog playfully pulled and turned and rose against each other. Then the man grasped the dog by the collar and led him into the house and the pen was empty.

Some time later, Bliss came into the room. He stood behind her and put his arms around her. His face was damp and his hair smelled of cigarette smoke.

"Do you remember when we drove up here," Joan said, "when it was finished?"

"Don't whisper," Bliss said.

"We left everything behind and drove all through the night and in the morning we stopped at this little picnic grove by a river and there were two old people there and they were washing this big white dog in the river. A big old white dog. They washed him so carefully and then dried him with a towel. He was what they had."

"Everyone's about to leave," Bliss said. "Let's go down and say good night."

"I don't want to be like those old people," Joan said.

"Never," Bliss said. "Let's go down and say good night. Just this one more time."

The Blue Men

BOMBER BOYD, AGE THIRTEEN, TOLD HIS NEW ACQUAINTANCES that summer that his father had been executed by the state of Florida for the murder of a sheriff's deputy and his drug-sniffing dog.

"It's a bummer he killed the dog," a girl said.

"Guns, chair or lethal injection?" a boy asked.

"Chair," Bomber said. He was sorry he had mentioned the dog in the same breath. The dog had definitely not been necessary.

"Lethal injection is fascist, man," a small, fierce-looking boy said. "Who does lethal injection?"

"Florida, Florida, Florida," the girl murmured. "We went to Key West once. We did sunset. We did Sloppy's. We bought conch-shell lamps with tiny plastic flamingos and palm trees lit up inside by tiny lights." The girl's hair was cut in a high Mohawk that rose at least half a foot in the air. She was pale, her skin flawless except for one pimple artfully flourishing above her full upper lip.

"Key West isn't Florida," a boy said.

There were six of them standing around, four boys and two girls. Bomber stood there with them, waiting.

MAY WAS IN HER GARDEN LOOKING THROUGH A STACK OF A HUNdred photographs that her son and daughter-in-law had taken years before when they visited Morocco. Bomber had been four at the time and May had taken care of him all that spring. There were pictures of camels, walled towns, tiled staircases and large vats of colored dyes on rooftops. May turned the pictures methodically. There were men washing their heads in a marble ablutions basin. On a dusty road there was the largest pile of carrots May had ever seen. May had been through the photographs many times. She slowly approached the one that never ceased to trouble her, a picture of her child in the city of Fez. He wore khaki pants and a polo shirt and was squatting beside a blanket on which teeth were arranged. It had been explained to May that there were many self-styled dentists in Morocco who pulled teeth and then displayed them on plates they then sold. In the photograph, her son looked healthy, muscular and curious, but there was something unfamiliar about his face. It had begun there, May thought, somehow. She put the photographs down and picked up a collection of postcards from that time, most of them addressed to Bomber. May held one close to her eyes. Men in blue burnooses lounged against their camels, the desert wilderness behind them. On the back was written, *The blue men! We wanted so much to see them but we never did.*

MAY AND BOMBER WERE TRYING OUT THEIR LIFE TOGETHER IN A new town. They had only each other, for Bomber's mother was resting in California, where she would probably be resting for quite some time, and May's husband, Harold, was dead. In the new town, which was on an island, May had bought a house and planted a pretty little flower garden. She had two big rooms upstairs that she rented out by the week to tourists. One was in yellow and the other in rose. May liked to listen to the voices in the rooms, but as a rule her tourists didn't say much. Actually, she strained to hear at times. She was not listening for sounds of love, of course. The sounds of love were not what mattered, after all.

Once, as she was standing in the upstairs hallway polishing a small table, her husband's last words had returned to her. Whether they had been spoken again by someone in the room, either in the rose room or the yellow room, she did not quite know, but there they were. *That doctor is so stuck on himself* . . . the same words as Harold's very last ones.

The tourists would gather seashells and then leave them behind when they left. They left them on the bureaus and on the windowsills and May would pick them up and take them back to the beach. On nights when she couldn't sleep she would walk downtown to a bar where the young people danced, the Lucky Kittens, and have a glass of beer. The Lucky Kittens was a loud and careless place where there was dancing all night long. May sat alone at a table near the door, an old lady, dignified and out of place.

BOMBER WAS DOWN AT THE DOCK, WATCHING TOURISTS ARRIVE on the ferry. The tourists were grinning and ready for anything, they thought. Two boys were playing catch with a tennis ball on the pier, the older one wearing a college sweatshirt. The younger one sidled back and forth close to the pier's edge, catching in both hands the high, lobbed throws the other boy threw. The water was high and dark and flecked with oil, and they were both laughing like lunatics. Bomber believed they were brothers and enjoyed watching them.

A girl moved languidly across the dock toward him. She was the pale girl with the perfect pimple and she touched it delicately as she walked. Her shaved temples had a slight sheen of baby powder on them. Her name was Edith.

"I've been thinking," Edith said, "and I think that what they should do, like, a gesture is enough. Like for murderers they could make them wear black all the time. They could walk around but they'd have to be always in black and they'd have to wear a mask of some sort."

Sometimes Bomber thought of what had happened to his father as an operation. It was an operation they had performed. "A mask," he said. "Hey." He crossed his arms tight across his chest. He thought Edith's long, pale face beautiful.

She nodded. "A mask," she said. "Something really amazing."

"But that wouldn't be enough, would it," Bomber asked.

"They wouldn't be able to take it off," Edith said. "There'd be no way." There was a pale vein on her temple, curving like a piece of string. "We didn't believe what you told us, you know," she said. "There was this kid, his name was Alex, and he had a boat. And he said he took this girl water-skiing who he didn't like, and they were water-skiing in this little cove where swans were and he steered her right in the middle of the swans and she just creamed them, but he wasn't telling the truth. He's such a loser."

"Which one's Alex," Bomber asked.

"Oh, he's around," Edith said.

They were silent as the passengers from the ferry eddied around them. They watched the two boys playing catch, the younger one darting from side to side, never looking backward to calculate the space, his eyes only on the softly slowly falling ball released from his brother's hand.

"That's nice, isn't it?" Edith said. "That little kid is so trusting it's kind of holy, but if his trust were misplaced it would really be holy."

Bomber wanted to touch the vein, the pimple, the shock of dark, waxed hair, but he stood motionless, slouched in his clothes. "Yeah," he said.

"Like, you know, if he fell in," Edith said.

ONE SUNDAY, MAY WENT TO CHURCH. IT WAS A DENOMINATION that, as she gratefully knew, would bury anyone. She sat in a pew behind three young women and studied their pretty blond hair, their necks and their collars and their zippers. One of the girls scratched her neck. A few minutes later, she scratched it again. May bent forward and saw a small tick crawling on the girl. She carefully picked it off with her fingers. She did it with such stealth that the girl didn't even know that May had touched her. May pinched the tick vigorously between her fingernails for some time and then dropped it to the floor, where it vanished from her sight.

After the service, there was a coffee hour. May joined a group around a table that was dotted with plates of muffins, bright cookies and glazed cakes. When the conversation lagged, she said, "I've just returned from Morocco."

"How exotic!" a woman exclaimed. "Did you see the Casbah?" The group turned toward May and looked at her attentively.

"There are many casbahs," May said. "I had tea under a tent on the edge of the Sahara. The children in Morocco all want aspirin. '*Boom-boom la tête,*' they say, '*boom-boom la tête.*' Their little hands are dry as paper. It's the lack of humidity, I suppose."

"You didn't go there by yourself, did you," a woman asked. She panted as she spoke.

"I went alone, yes," May said.

The group hummed appreciatively. May was holding a tiny blueberry muffin in her hand. She couldn't remember picking it up. It sat cupped in the palm of her hand, the paper around it looking like the muffin itself. May had been fooled by such muffins in public places in the past. She returned it to the table.

"I saw the blue men," May said.

The group looked at her, smiling. They were taller than she and their heads were tilted toward her.

"Most tourists don't see them," May said. "They roam the deserts. Their camels are pale beige, almost white, and the men riding them are blue. They wear deep blue floating robes and blue turbans. Their skin is even stained blue where the dye has rubbed off."

"Are they wanderers," someone asked. "What's their purpose?"

May was startled. She felt as though the person were regarding her with suspicion.

"They're part of the mystery," she said. "To see them is to see part of the mystery."

"It must have been a sight," someone offered.

"Oh yes," May said, "it was."

After some moments, the group dispersed and May left the church and walked home through the town. She liked the town, which was cut off from other places. People came here only if they wanted to. You couldn't find this place by accident. The town seemed to be a place to visit and most people didn't stay on. There were some, of course, who had stayed on. May liked the clear light of the town and the trees rounded by the wind. She liked the trucks and the Jeeps with the dogs riding in them. When the trucks were parked, the dogs would stare solemnly down at the pavement as though something there was astounding.

May felt elated, almost feverish. She had taken up lying rather late in life, but with enthusiasm. Bomber didn't seem to notice, even though he had, in May's opinion, a hurtful obsession with the truth. When May got back to her house, she changed from her good dress into her gardening dress. She looked at herself in the mirror. I'm in charge of this person, she thought. "You'd better watch out," she said to the person in the mirror.

·   ·   ·

BOMBER'S FRIENDS DON'T DRINK OR SMOKE OR EAT MEAT. THEY are bony and wild. In the winter, a psychiatrist comes into their class-rooms and says, You think that suicide is an escape and not a perma-nent departure, but the truth is that it is a permanent departure. They know that! Their eyes water with boredom. Their mothers used to lie to them when they were little about dead things, but they know bet-ter now. It's stupid to wait for the dead to do anything new. But one of their classmates had killed himself, so the psychiatrist would come back every winter.

"They planted a tree," Edith said, "you know, in this kid's memory at school, and what this kid had done was to hang himself from a tree." She rolled her eyes. "I mean, this school. You're not going to believe this school."

Edith and Bomber sat on opposite sides of May's parlor, which was filling with twilight. Edith wore a pair of men's boxer shorts, lace-up boots and a lurid Hawaiian shirt. "This is a nice house," Edith said. "It smells nice. I see your granny coming out of the Kittens sometimes. She's cute."

"A thing I used to remember about my dad," Bomber said, "was that he gave me a tepee once when I was little and he pitched it in the mid-dle of the living room. I slept in it every night for weeks, right in the middle of the living room. It was great. But it actually wasn't my dad who had done that at all, it was my gramma."

"Your granny is so cute," Edith said. "I know I'd like her. Do you know Bobby?"

"Which one's Bobby," Bomber asked.

"He's the skinny one with the tooth that overlaps a little. He's the sort of person I used to like. What he does is he fishes. There's not a fish he can't catch."

"I can't do that," Bomber said.

"Oh, you don't have to do anything like that now," Edith said.

THE LAST THINGS MAY HAD BROUGHT HER SON WERE A DARK suit and a white shirt. They told her she could if she wished, and she had. She had brought him many things in the two years before he died—candy and cigarettes, books on all subjects—and lastly she had brought these things. She had bought the shirt new and then washed it at home several times so it was soft and then she had driven over to that place. It was a cool, misty morning and the air smelled of chemicals from the mills miles away. Dew glittered on the wires and on the grasses and the fronds of palms. She sat opposite him in the tall, narrow, familiar room, its high windows webby with steel, and he had opened the box with the shirt in it. Together they had looked at it. Together, mutely, they had bent their heads over it and stared. Their eyes had fallen into it as though it were a hole. They watched the shirt and it seemed to shift and shrink as though to accommodate itself to some ghastly and impossible interstice of time and purpose.

"What a shirt," her child said.

"Give it back," May whispered. She was terribly frightened. She had obliged some lunatic sense of decorum, and dread—the dread that lay beyond the fear of death—seized her.

"This is the one, I'm going out in this one," her child said. He was thin, his hair was gray.

"I wasn't thinking," May said. "Please give it back, I can't think about any of this."

"I was born to wear this shirt," her child said.

IN THE LUCKY KITTENS, OVER THE BAR, WAS A LARGE PAINTING of kittens crawling out of a sack. The sack was huge, out of proportion to the sea and the sky behind it. When May looked at it for a time, the sack appeared to tremble. One night, as she was walking home, someone brushed against her, almost knocking her down, and ran off with her purse. Her purse had fifteen dollars in it and in it too were the postcards and pictures of Morocco. May continued to walk home, her left arm still feeling the weight of the purse. It seemed heavier now that it wasn't there. She pushed herself forward, looking, out of habit, into the handsome homes along the street. The rooms were artfully lit as though on specific display for the passerby. No one was ever seen in them. At home, she looked at herself in the mirror for bruises. There were none, although her face was deeply flushed.

"You've been robbed," she said to the face.

She went into her parlor. On the floor above, in either the rose room or the yellow room, someone shifted around. Her arm ached. She turned off the light and sat in the dark, rubbing her arm.

"The temperature of the desert can reach one hundred and seventy-five degrees," she said aloud. "At night, it can fall below freezing. Many a time I awoke in the morning to find a sheet of ice over the water in the glass beside my bed." It was something that had been written on one of the cards. She could see it all, the writing, the words, plain as day.

Some time later, she heard Bomber's voice. "Gramma," he said, "why are you sitting in the dark?" The light was on again.

"Hi!" May said.

"Sometimes," Bomber said, "she lies out in the garden and the fog rolls in, and she stays right out there."

"The fog will be swirling around me," May said, "and Bomber will say, 'Gramma, the fog's rolled in and there you are!'" She was speaking to a figure beside Bomber with a flamboyant crest of hair. The figure was dressed in silk lounging pajamas and a pair of black work boots with steel toes.

"Gramma," Bomber said, "this is Edith."

"Hi!" Edith said.

"What a pretty name," May said. "There's a hybrid lily called Edith that I like very much. I'm going to plant an Edith bulb when fall comes."

"Will it come up every year," Edith asked.

"Yes," May said.

"That is so cool," Edith said.

A FEW DAYS AFTER SHE HAD BEEN ROBBED, MAY'S PURSE WAS RE-turned to her. It was placed in the garden, just inside the gate. Every-thing was there, but the bills were different. May had had a ten and a five and the new ones were singles. The cards were there. May touched one and looked at the familiar writing on the back. *It never grows dark in the desert*, the writing said. *The night sky is a deep and intense blue as though the sun were shut up behind it.* Her child had been a thoughtful tourist once, sending messages home, trying to explain things she would never see. He had never written from the prison. The thirst for explanation had left him. May thought of death. It was as though someone were bending over her, trying to blow something into her mouth. She shook her head and looked at her purse. "Where have you been?" she said to the purse. The pictures of Morocco were there. She looked through them. All there. But she didn't want them anymore. Things were never the same when they came back. She closed the purse up and dropped it in one of her large green trash cans, throwing some clipped, brown flowers over it so it was concealed. It was less than a week later that everything was returned to her again, once more placed inside the gate. People went through the dump all the time, she imagined, to see what they could find. In town, the young people began calling her by name. "May," they'd say, "good morning!" They'd say, "How's it going, Gramma?" She was the condemned man's mother, and Bomber was the condemned man's son, and it didn't seem to matter what they did or didn't do, it was he who had been accepted by these people, and he who was allowing them to get by.

EDITH WAS SPENDING MORE AND MORE TIME AT MAY AND BOMBER's house. She had dyed her hair a peculiar brown color and wore scarves knotted around her neck.

"I like this look," Edith said. "It looks like I'm concealing a tracheotomy, doesn't it?"

"Your hair's good," Bomber said.

"You know what the psychiatrist at school says?" Edith said. "He says you think you want death when all you want is change."

"What is with this guy," Bomber asked. "Is there really a problem at that place or what?"

"Oh there is, absolutely," Edith said. "You look a little like your granny. Did your dad look like her?"

"A little, I guess," Bomber said.

"You're such a sweet boy," Edith said. "Such a sweet, bad boy. I really love you."

The summer was over. The light had changed, and the leaves on the trees hung still. At the Lucky Kittens, the dancing went on, but not so many people danced. When May went there, they wouldn't take her money and May submitted to this. She couldn't help herself, it seemed.

Edith helped around the house. She washed the windows with vinegar and made chocolate desserts. One evening she said, "Do you still, like, pay income tax?"

May looked at the girl and decided to firmly lie. "No," she said.

"Well, that's good," Edith said. "It would be pretty preposterous to pay taxes after what they did."

"Of course," May said.

"But you're paying in other ways," Edith said.

"Please, dear," May said, "it was just a mistake. It doesn't mean anything in the long run," she said, dismayed at her words.

"I'll help you pay," Edith said.

WITH THE COOL WEATHER, THE TOURISTS STOPPED COMING. When school began, Edith asked if she could move into the yellow room. She didn't get along with her parents, she had been moving about, staying here and there with friends, but she had no real place to live, could she live in the yellow room?

May was fascinated by Edith. She did not want her in the house, above her, living in the yellow room. She felt that she and Bomber should move on, that they should try their new life together somewhere else, but she knew that this was their new life. This was the place where it appeared they had gone.

"Of course, dear," May said.

She was frightened and this surprised her, for she could scarcely believe she could know fright again after what happened to them, but there it was, some thing beyond the worst thing—some disconnection, some demand. She remembered telling Edith that she was going to plant bulbs in the garden when fall came, but she wasn't going to do it, certainly not. "No," May said to her garden, "don't even think about it." Edith moved into the yellow room. It was silent there, but May didn't listen either.

Something happened later that got around. May was driving, it was night, and the car veered off the road. Edith and Bomber were with her. The car flipped over twice, miraculously righted itself and skidded back onto the road, the roof and fenders crushed. This was observed by a policeman who followed them for over a mile in disbelief before he pulled the car over. None of them were injured and at first they denied that anything unusual had happened at all. May said, "I thought it was just a dream, so I kept on going."

The three seemed more visible than ever after that, for they drove the car in that damaged way until winter came.

The Last Generation

H E WAS NINE.

"Nine," his father would say, "there's an age for you. When I was nine . . ." and so on.

His father's name was Walter and he was a mechanic at a Chevrolet garage in Tallahassee. He had a seventeen-year-old brother named Walter, Jr., and he was Tommy. The boys had no mother, she'd been killed in a car wreck a while before.

It had not been her fault.

The mother had taken care of houses that people rented on the river. She cleaned them and managed them for the owners. Just before she died, there had been this one house where the toilet got stopped up. "I told the plumber," Tommy's mother told them, "that I wanted to know just what was in that toilet because I didn't trust those tenants. I knew there was something deliberate there, not normal. I said, You tell me what you find there and when he called back he said, Well, you wanted to know what I found there and it was meat fat and paper towels."

She had been very excited about what the plumber had told her. Tommy worried that his mother had still been thinking about this when she died, that she'd been driving along still marveling about it—meat fat and paper towels!—and that then she had been struck, and died.

She had slowed for an emergency vehicle that was tearing through an intersection with its lights flashing and a truck had crashed into her from behind. The emergency vehicle had a destination but there hadn't even been an emergency at the time. It was supposed to be stationed at the stock-car races and it was late. The races—the first of the season—were just about to begin at the time of the wreck. Walter, Jr., was sitting in the old bleachers with a girl, waiting for the start, and the announcer had just called for the drivers to fire up their engines. There had been an immense roar in the sunny, dusty field, and a great cloud of insects had flown up from the rotting wood of the bleachers. The girl beside Walter, Jr., had screamed and spilled her Coke all over him. There had been thousands of these insects, which were long, red flying ants of some sort with transparent wings.

Tommy had not seen the alarming eruption of insects. He had been home, putting together a little car from a kit and painting it with silver paint.

Tommy liked rope. Sometimes he ate dirt. Lightning storms thrilled him. He was small for his age, a weedy child. He wore blue jeans with deeply rolled cuffs for growth, although he grew slowly. Weeks often went by when he didn't grow at all.

The house they lived in on the river was a two-story house with a big porch, surrounded by trees. There was a panel in the ceiling that gave access to a particularly troublesome water pipe. The pipe would leak whenever it felt like it but not all the time. Apparently it had been placed by the builders at such an angle that it could be neither replaced nor repaired. Walter had placed a bucket in the crawl space between Tommy's ceiling and the floor above to catch water, and this he emptied every few weeks. Tommy believed something existed up there that needed water, as all living things do, some quiet, listening, watching thing that shared his room with him. At the same time, he knew there was nothing there. Walter would throw the water from the bucket into the yard. It was important to Tommy that he always be there to see the bucket being brought down, emptied, then replaced.

In the house, with other photographs, was one of Tommy and his mother taken when he was six. It had been taken on the bank of the same river the rest of them still lived on, but not the same place. This had been farther upstream. Tommy was holding a fish by the tail. His mother had black hair and she was smiling at him and he was looking at the fish. He was holding the fish upside down and it was not very large but still large enough to keep, apparently. Tommy was told that he had caught the fish and that his mother had fried it up just for him in a pan with butter and salt and that he had eaten it, but Tommy could remember none of this. What he remembered was that he had found the fish, which was not true.

Tommy loved his mother but he didn't miss her. He didn't like his father much, and never had. He liked Walter, Jr.

Walter, Jr., had a mustache and his own Chevy truck. He liked to ride around at night with his friends and sometimes he would take Tommy along. The big boys would drink beer and holler at people in Ford trucks and, in general, carry on as they tore along the river roads. Once they all saw a naked woman in a lighted window. The headlights swept past all kinds of things. One night, one of the boys pointed at a mailbox.

"Look, that's a three-hundred-dollar mailbox!"

"Mailbox can't be three hundred dollars," one of the other boys yelled.

"I seen it advertised. It's totally indestructible. Door can't be pulled off. Ya hit it with a ball bat or a two-by-four, it just busts up the wood, don't hurt the box. Toss an M-80 in there, won't hurt the box."

"What's an M-80," Tommy asked.

The big boys looked at him.

"He don't know what an M-80 is," one of them said.

Walter, Jr., stopped the truck and backed it up. They all got out and stared at the mailbox. "What kind of mail you think these people get anyway?" Walter, Jr., said.

The boys pushed at the box. "It's just asking for it, isn't it," one of the boys said. They laughed and shrugged, and one of them pissed on it. Then they got back in the truck and drove away.

Walter, Jr., had girlfriends too. For a time, his girl was Audrey, only Audrey. She had thick hair and very white, smooth skin and Tommy thought she was beautiful. Together, he thought, she and his brother were like young gods who made the world after many trials and tests, accomplishing everything only through wonders and self-transformations. In reality, the two were quite an ordinary couple. If anything, Audrey was peculiar looking, even ugly.

"If you marry my brother, I'll be your brother-in-law," Tommy told her.

"Ha," she said.

"Why don't you like me?" He adored her, he knew she had some power over him.

"Who wants to know?"

"Me. I want to know. Tommy."

"Who's that?" And she would laugh, twist him over, hang him upside down by the knees so he swung like a monkey, dump him on his feet again and give him a stale stick of gum.

Then Walter, Jr., began going out with other girls.

"He dropped me," Audrey told Tommy, "just like that."

It was the end of the summer that his mother had died at the start of. Her clothes still hung in the closet. Audrey came over every day and she and Tommy would sit on the porch of the house on the river in two springy steel chairs painted piggy pink.

Audrey told him, "You can't trust anybody." And, "Don't agree to anything."

When Walter, Jr., walked by, he never glanced at her. It was as though Audrey wasn't there. He would walk by whistling, his hair dark and crispy, his stomach flat as a board. He wore sunglasses, even though the summer had been far from bright. It had been cool and damp. The water in the river was yellow with the rains.

"Does your dad miss the Mom," Audrey asked Tommy.

"Uh-huh."

"Who misses her the most?"

"I don't know," Tommy said. "Dad, I think."

"That's right," Audrey said. "That's what true love is. Wanting something that's missing."

She brought him presents. She gave him a big book about icebergs. He knew she had stolen it. They looked at the book together and Audrey read parts of it aloud.

"Icebergs were discovered by monks," Audrey said. "That's not exactly what it says here, but I'm trying to make it easier for you. Icebergs were discovered by monks who thought they were floating crystal castles." She pointed toward the river. "Squeeze your eyes up and look at the river. It looks like a cloud lying on the ground instead, see?"

He squeezed up his eyes. He could not see it.

"I like clouds," he said.

"Clouds aren't as pretty as they used to be," Audrey said. "That's a known fact."

Tommy looked back at the book. It was a big book, with nothing but pictures of icebergs or so it seemed. How could she have stolen it? She turned the pages back and forth, not turning them in any order that he could see.

"Later explorers came and discovered the sea cow," she read. "The sea cows munched seaweed in the shallows of the Bering Strait. They were colossal and dim-witted, their skin was like the bark of ancient oaks. Discovered in 1741, they were extinct by 1768."

"I don't know what extinct is," Tommy said.

"Seventeen sixty-eight was the eighteenth century. Then there was the nineteenth century and the twentieth century and we are now in the twenty-first century. This is the century of destruction. The earth's been around for four point six billion years and it may take only fifty more years to kill it."

He thought for a while. "I'll be fifty-nine," he said. "You'll be sixty-five."

"We don't want to be around when the earth gets killed," Audrey said.

She went into the kitchen and helped herself to two Popsicles from the freezer. They ate them quickly, their lips and tongues turned red.

"Do you want me to give you a kiss?" Audrey said.

He opened his mouth.

"Look," she said. "You don't drool when you kiss. How'd you learn such a thing?"

"I didn't," he said.

"Never mind," she said. "We don't ever have to kiss. We're the last generation."

Walter made his boys supper every night when he came home from work. He set the table, poured the milk.

"Well, men," he would say, "here we are." He would begin to cry. "I'm sorry, men," he'd say.

The sun would be setting in a mottled sky over the wet woods and the light would linger in a smeared radiance for a while.

Tommy would scarcely be able to sleep at night, waiting for the morning to come and go so it would be the afternoon and he would be with Audrey, rocking in the metal chairs.

"The last generation has got certain responsibilities," Audrey said, "though you might think we wouldn't. We should know nothing and want nothing and be nothing, but at the same time we should want everything and know everything and be everything."

Upstairs, in his room, Walter, Jr., was lifting weights. They could hear him hoarsely breathing, gasping.

Audrey's strange, smooth face looked blank. It looked empty.

"Did you love my brother," Tommy asked. "Do you still love him?"

"Certainly not," Audrey said. "We were just passing friends."

"My father says we are all passing guests of God."

"He says that kind of thing because the Mom left so quick." She snapped her fingers.

Tommy was holding tight to the curved metal arms of the chair. He put his hands up to his face and sniffed them. He had had dreams of putting his hands in Audrey's hair, hiding them there, up to his wrists. Her hair was the color of gingerbread.

"Love isn't what you think anyway," Audrey said.

"I don't," Tommy said.

"Love is ruthless. I'm reading a book for English class, *Wuthering Heights*. Everything's in that book, but mostly it's about the ruthlessness of love."

"Tell me the whole book," Tommy said.

"Emily Brontë wrote *Wuthering Heights*. I'll tell you a story about her."

He picked at a scab on his knee.

"Emily Brontë had a bulldog named Keeper that she loved. His only bad habit was sleeping on the beds. The housekeeper complained about this and Emily said that if she ever found him sleeping on the clean white beds again, she would beat him. So Emily found him one evening sleeping on a clean white bed and she dragged him off and pushed him in a corner and beat him with her fists. She punished him until his eyes were swelled up and he was bloody and half blind, and after she punished him, then she nursed him back to health."

Tommy rocked on his chair, watching Audrey. He stopped picking. The scab didn't want to come off.

"She had a harsh life," Audrey said, "but she was fair."

"Did she tell him later that she was sorry," Tommy asked.

"No. Absolutely not."

"Did Keeper forgive her?"

"Dogs can't think that way."

"I've never had a dog," Tommy said.

"I had a dog when I was little. She was a golden retriever. She looked exactly like all golden retrievers. Her size was the same, the color of her fur, and her large, sad eyes. Her behavior was the same. She was devoted, expectant and yet resigned. Do you see what I mean? But I liked her a lot. She was special to me. When she died, I wanted them to bury her under my window, but you know what they said to me? They said, The best place to bury a dog is in your heart."

She looked at him until he finally said, "That's right."

"That's a crock," she said. "A crock of you know what. Don't agree to so much stuff. You've got to watch out."

"All right," he said, and shook his head.

Sometimes, Audrey visited him at school. He told her when his recess was and she would walk over to the playground and talk with him through the playground's chain-link fence. Once she brought a girl-friend with her. Her name was Flan and she wore large clothes, a long, wide skirt and a big sweater with little animals running in rows. There were only parts of the little animals where the body of the sweater met the sleeves and collar.

"He's like a little doll, like, isn't he," Flan said.

"Now don't go and scare him," Audrey said.

Flan had a cold. She held little wadded tissues to her mouth and eyes. The tissues were blue and pink and green and she would dab at her face with them and push them back in her pockets but one spilled out and fluttered in the weeds beside the school-yard fence. It didn't blow away and stayed there, fluttering.

"I ain't scaring him. Where'd you get all them moles around your neck?" she said to Tommy.

"What do you mean, where'd he get them?" Audrey said. "He didn't get them from anywhere."

"Don't you worry about them moles?" the girl persisted.

"Naw," Tommy said.

"You're a brave little guy, aren't you," Flan said. "There's other stuff, I know. I'm not saying it's all moles." She tugged at the front of the fright-ful sweater. "Audrey gave me this sweater. She stole it. You know how she steals things and after a while she puts them back? But I like this so it's not going to get put back."

Tommy gazed unhappily at the sweater and then at Audrey.

"Sometimes putting stuff back is the best part," Audrey said. "Sometimes it isn't."

"Audrey can steal anything," Flan said.

"Can she steal a house," Tommy asked.

"He's so *cute*," Flan shrieked.

"I gotta go in," Tommy said. Behind him, in the school yard, the children were playing a peculiar game, running, crouching, calling. There didn't seem to be any rules. He trotted toward them and heard Flan say, "He's a cute little guy, isn't he."

Tommy never saw Flan again and he was glad of that. He asked Audrey if Flan was in the last generation.

"Yes," Audrey said. "She sure is."

"Is my brother in the last generation too?"

"Technically he is, of course," Audrey said. "But he's not really. He has too much stuff."

"I have stuff," Tommy said. He had his little cars. "You've given me stuff."

"But you don't have possessions because what I gave you I stole. Anyway, you'll stop caring about that soon. You'll forget all about it, but Walter, Jr., really likes possessions and he likes to think about what he's going to do. He has his truck and his barbells and those shirts with the pearl buttons."

"He wants a pair of lizard boots for his birthday," Tommy said.

"Isn't that pathetic?" Audrey said.

Every night, Walter would come home from work, scrub down his hands and arms, set the table, pour the milk. The boys sat on either side of him. The chair where their mother used to sit looked out at the yard, at a woodpile there.

"Men," Walter began, "when I was your age, I didn't know . . ." He shook his head, his eyes filling with tears.

He had been forgetting to empty the bucket in the space above Tommy's room. A pale stain had spread across the ceiling. Tommy showed it to Audrey.

"That's nice," she said, "the shape, all dappled brown and yellow like that, but it doesn't really tell you anything. It's just part of the doomed reality all around us." She climbed up and brought the bucket down.

"A monk would take this water and walk into the desert and pour it over a dry and broken stick there," she said. "That's why people become monks, because they get sick of being around doomed reality all the time."

"Let's be monks," he said.

"Monks love solitude," Audrey said. "They love solitude more than anything. When monks started out, long, long ago, they were waiting for the end of time."

"But the end of time didn't happen, did it," Tommy asked.

"It was too soon then. They didn't know what we know today."

She wore silver sandals. Once she had broken a strap on the sandal and Tommy had fixed it with his Hot Stuff instant glue.

"Someday we could have a little boy just like you," she said, "and we'd call him Tommy Two."

But he was not fond of this idea. He was afraid that it would come out of him somehow, this Tommy Two, that he would make it and be ashamed. So, together, they dismissed the notion.

One day, Walter, Jr., said to him, "Look, Audrey shouldn't be hanging around here all the time. She's weird. She's no mommy, believe me."

"I don't need a mommy," Tommy said.

"She's mad at me and she's trying to get back at me through you. She's just practicing on you. You don't want to be practiced on, do you? She's just a very unhappy person."

"I'm unhappy," Tommy said.

"You need to get out and play some games. Soccer, maybe."

"Why?" Tommy said. "I don't like Daddy."

"You're just trying that out," Walter, Jr., said. "You like him well enough."

"Audrey and me are the last generation and you're not," Tommy said.

"What are you talking about?"

"You should be but you're not. Nothing can be done about it."

"Let's drive around in the truck," Walter, Jr., said.

Tommy still enjoyed riding around in the truck. They passed by the houses their mother had cleaned. They looked all right. Someone else was cleaning them now.

"You don't look good," Walter, Jr., said. "You're too pale. You mope around all the time."

Inside the truck, the needle of the black compass on the dashboard trembled. The compass box was filled with what seemed like water. Maybe it was water. Tommy was looking at everything carefully, but trying not to think about it. Audrey was teaching him how to do this. He remembered at some point to turn toward his brother and smile, and this made his brother feel better, it was clear.

The winter nights were cool. Audrey and Tommy still sat in their chairs at dusk on the porch but now they wrapped themselves in blankets.

"Walter, Jr., is dating a lot anymore," Audrey said. "It's nice we have these evenings to ourselves but we should take little trips, you know? I have a lot to show you. Have you ever been to the TV tower north of town?"

The father, Walter, was already in bed. He worked and slept. He'd saved the fragments of soap his wife had left behind in the shower. He had wrapped them in tissue paper and placed them in a drawer. But he was sleeping in the middle of the bed these nights, hardly aware of it.

"No," Tommy said. "Is it in the woods?"

"It's a lot taller than the woods and it's not far away from here. It's called Tall Timbers. It's right smack in the middle of birds' migration routes. Thousands of birds run into it every year, all kinds of them. We can go out there and look at the birds."

Tommy was puzzled. "Are the birds dead?"

"Yes," she said. "In an eleven-year period, thirty thousand birds of a hundred and seventy species have been found at the base of the tower."

"Why don't they move it?"

"They don't do things like that," Audrey said. "It would never occur to them."

He did not want to see the birds around the tower. "Let's go," he said anyway.

"We'll go in the spring. That's when the birds change latitudes. That's when they move from one place to another. There's a little tiny warbler bird that used to live around here in the spring, but people haven't seen it for years. They haven't found it at the base of any of the transmission towers. They used to find it there, that's how they knew it wasn't extinct."

"Monks used to live on top of tall towers," Tommy said, for she had told him this. "If a monk stayed up there, he could keep the birds away, he could wave his arms around or something so they wouldn't hit."

"Monks live in a cool, crystalline half darkness of the mind and heart," Audrey said. "They couldn't be bothered with that."

They rocked in their chairs on the porch. The porch had been painted a succession of colors. Where the chairs had scraped the wood there was light green, dark green, blue, red. Bugs crawled around the lights.

"If I got sick, would you stay with me," Tommy asked.

"I'm not sure. It would depend."

"My mommy would have stayed."

"Well, you never know," Audrey said. "You got to realize mommies get tired. They're willing to let things go sometimes. They get to thinking and they're off."

"Do you have a mommy," he asked cautiously.

"Technically I do," Audrey said, "but she's gone as your mommy, actually. Before something's gone, it had to have been there, right? Even so, I don't feel any rancor about her. It's important not to feel rancor."

"I don't feel rancor," Tommy said.

Then, one afternoon, Walter came home from his work at the garage and it was as though he had woken from a strange sleep. He didn't appear startled by his awakening. His days and nights of grief came to an end with a shock no harder than that of a boat's keel grounding on a river's shore. He stopped weeping. He put his wife's things in cardboard boxes and stored the boxes. In fact, he stored them in the space above Tommy's room.

"Why's that girl here all the time," Walter asked. "She's not still Walter, Jr.'s girlfriend, is she? She shouldn't be here all the time."

"Audrey's my friend," Tommy said.

"She's not a nice girl. She's too old to be your friend."

"Then I'm too young to be your friend."

"No, honey, you're my son."

"I don't like you," Tommy said.

"You love me but you don't like me, is that it?" Walter was thinner and cleaner. He spoke cheerfully.

Tommy considered this. He shook his head.

At school, at the edge of the playground, Audrey talked through the chain-link fence to Tommy.

"You know that pretty swamp close by? It's full of fish, all different kinds. You know how they know?"

He didn't.

"They poison little patches of it. They put out nets and then drop the poison in. It settles in the gills of the fish and suffocates them. The fish pop up to the surface and then they drag them out and classify and weigh and measure each one."

"Who?" Tommy said.

"They do it a couple times a year to see if there's as many different kinds and as many as before. That's how they count things. That's their attitude. They act as though they care about stuff, but they don't. They're just pretending."

Tommy told her that his father didn't want her to come over to the house, that he wasn't supposed to talk to her anymore.

"The Dad's back, is he," Audrey said. "What it is is that he thinks he can start over. That's pathetic."

"What are we going to do?" Tommy said.

"You shouldn't listen to him," Audrey said. "Why are you listening to him? We're the last generation, there's something else we're listening to."

They were silent for a while, listening. The other children had gone inside.

"What is it," Tommy asked.

"You'll recognize it when you hear it. Something will happen, something unusual that we were always prepared for. The Dad's life has already taken a turn for the worse, it's obvious. It's like he's a stranger now, walking down the wrong road. Do you see what I mean? Or it's his life that's like the stranger, standing real still. A stranger standing alongside a dark road, waiting for him to pass."

It appeared his father was able to keep Audrey away. Tommy wouldn't have thought it was possible. He knew his father was powerless, but Audrey wasn't coming around. Walter moved through the house in his dark, oiled boots, fixing things. He painted the kitchen, restacked the woodpile. He replaced the pipe above the ceiling in Tommy's room. It had long been accepted that this could not be done, but now it was and it did not leak. The bucket was used now to take ashes from the woodstove. Walter, Jr., had a job in the gym he worked out in. He had long, hard muscles, a distracted air. He worried about girls, about money. He wanted an apartment of his own, in town.

Tommy lived alone with his father. "Talk to me, Son," Walter said. "I love you."

Tommy said nothing. His father disgusted him a little. He was trying to start over. It was pathetic.

Tommy only saw Audrey on school days, at recess. He waited by the fence for her in the vitreous, intractable light of the southern afternoon.

"I had a boy tell me once my nipples were like bowls of Wheaties," Audrey said.

"When?" Tommy said. "No."

"That's a simile. Similes are a crock. There's no more time for similes. There used to be that kind of time, but no more. You shouldn't see what you're seeing thinking it looks like something else. They haven't left us with much but the things that are left should be seen as they are."

Some days she did not come by. Then he would see her waiting at the fence, or she would appear suddenly while he was waiting there. But then days passed, more days than there had been before.

Days with Walter saying, "We need each other, Son. We're not over this yet. We have to help each other. I need your help."

It was suppertime. They were sitting at a table over the last of a meal Walter had put together.

"I want Audrey back," Tommy said.

"Audrey?" Walter looked surprised. "Walter, Jr., heard about what happened to Audrey. She made her bed, as they say, now she's got to lie in it." He looked at Tommy, then looked away, dismayed.

"Who wants you?" Tommy said. "Nobody."

Walter rubbed his head with his hands. He looked around the room, at some milk that Tommy had spilled on the floor. The house was empty except for them. There were no animals around, nothing. It was all beyond what was possible, he knew.

In the night, Tommy heard his father moving around, bumping into things, moaning. A glass fell. He heard it breaking for what seemed a long time. The air in the house felt close, sour. He pushed open his bedroom window and felt the air fluttering warmly against his skin. Down along the river, the water popped and smacked against the muddy bank. It was close to the season when he and Audrey could go to the tower where all the birds were. He could feel it in the air. Audrey would come for him from wherever she was, from wherever they had made her go, and they would go to the tower and find the little warbler bird. Then they would know that it still existed because they had found it dead there. He and Audrey would be the ones who would find it. They were the last generation, the ones who would see everything for the last time. That's what the last generation does.

Honored Guest

SHE HAD BEEN HAVING A ROUGH TIME OF IT AND THOUGHT about suicide sometimes, but suicide was so corny in the eleventh grade and you had to be careful about this because two of her class-mates had committed suicide the year before and between them they left twenty-four suicide notes and had become just a joke. They had left the notes everywhere and they were full of misspellings and pre-tensions. Theirs had been a false show. Then this year a girl had taken an overdose of Tylenol, which of course did nothing at all, but word of it got out and when she came back to school her locker had been broken into and was jammed full of Tylenol. Like, you moron. Under the circumstances, it was amazing that Helen thought of suicide at all. It was seriously not cool. You only made a fool of yourself. And the parents of these people were mocked too. They were considered to be suicide-enhancing, evil and weak, and they were ignored and barely tolerated. This was a small town. Helen didn't want to make life any harder on her mother than it already was.

Her mother was dying and she wanted to die at home, which Helen could understand, she understood it perfectly, she'd say, but actually she understood it less well than that and it had become clear it wasn't even what needed to be understood. Nothing needed to be understood.

There was a little brass bell on her mother's bedside table. It was the same little brass bell that had been placed at Helen's command when she had been a little girl, sick with some harmless little kid's illness. She had just to reach out her hand and ring the bell and her mother would come or even her father. Her mother never used the bell now and kept it there as sort of a joke, actually. Her mother was not utterly confined to bed. She moved around a bit at night and placed herself, or was placed by others, in other rooms during the day. Occasionally one of the women who had been hired to care for her would even take her for a drive, out to see the icicles or go to the bank window. Her mother's name was Lenore and sometimes in the night she would call out this name, her own, "Lenore!" in a strong, urgent voice, and Helen in her own room would shudder and cry a little.

This had been going on for a while. In the summer Lenore had been diagnosed and condemned but she kept bouncing back, as the doctors put it, until recently. The daisies that bloomed in the fall down by the storm-split elm had come and gone, even the little kids at Halloween. Thanksgiving had passed without comment and it would be Christmas soon. Lenore was ignoring it. The boxes of balls and lights were in the cellar, buried deep. Helen had made the horrible mistake of asking her what she wanted for Christmas one night and Lenore had said, "Are you stupid?" Then she said, "Oh, I don't mean to be so impatient, it's the medicine, my voice doesn't even sound right. Does my voice sound right? Get me something you'll want later. A piece of jewelry or something. Do you want the money for it?" She meant this sincerely.

At the beginning they had talked eagerly like equals. This was more important than a wedding, this preparation. They even laughed like girls remembering things together. They remembered when Helen was a little girl before the divorce and they were all driving somewhere and Helen's father was stopped for speeding and Lenore wanted her picture taken with the policeman and Helen had taken it. "Wasn't that mean!" Lenore said to Helen.

When Lenore died, Helen would go down to Florida and live with her father. "I've never had the slightest desire to visit Florida," Lenore said. "You can have it."

At the beginning death was giving them the opportunity to be interesting. This was something special. There was only one crack at this. But then they lost sight of it somehow. It became a lesser thing, more terrible. Its meaning crumbled. They began waiting for it. Terrible, terrible. Lenore had friends but they called now, they didn't come over so much. "Don't come over," Lenore would tell them, "it wears me out." Little things started to go wrong with the house, leaks and lights. The bulb in the kitchen would flutter when the water was turned on. Helen grew fat for some reason. The dog, their dog, began to change. He grew shy. "Do you think he's acting funny," Lenore asked Helen.

She did not tell Helen that the dog had begun growling at her. It was a secret growl; he never did it in front of anyone else. He had taken to carrying one of her slippers around with him. He was almost never without it. He cherished her slipper.

"Do you remember when I put Grecian Formula on his muzzle because he turned gray so young?" Lenore said. "He was only about a year old and began to turn gray? The things I used to do. The way I spent my time."

But now she did not know what to do with time at all. It seemed more expectant than ever. One couldn't satisfy it, one could never do enough for it.

She was so uneasy.

Lenore had a dream in which she wasn't dying at all. Someone else had died. People had told her this over and over again. And now they were getting tired of reminding her, impatient.

She had a dream of eating bread and dying. Two large loaves. Pounds of it, still warm from the oven. She ate it all, she was so hungry, starving! But then she died. It was the bread. It was too hot, was the explanation. There were people in her room but she was not among them.

When she woke, she could feel the hot, gummy, almost liquid bread in her throat, scalding it. She lay in bed on her side, her dark eyes open. It was four o'clock in the morning. She swung her legs to the floor. The dog growled at her. He slept in her room with her slipper but he growled as she went past him. Sometimes self-pity would rise within her and she would stare at the dog, tears in her eyes, listening to him growl. The more she stared, the more sustained was his soft growl.

She had a dream about a tattoo. This was a pleasant dream. She was walking away and she had the most beautiful tattoo covering her shoulders and back, even the backs of her legs. It was unspeakably fine.

Helen had a dream that her mother wanted a tattoo. She wanted to be tattooed all over, a full custom bodysuit, but no one would do it. Helen woke up protesting this, grunting and cold. She had kicked off her blankets. She pulled them up and curled tightly beneath them. There was a boy at school who had gotten a tattoo and now they wouldn't let him play basketball.

In the morning Lenore said, "Would you get a tattoo with me? We could do this together. I don't think it's creepy," she added. "I think you'll be glad later. A pretty one, just small somewhere. What do you think?"

The more she considered it, the more it seemed the perfect thing to do. What else could be done? She'd already given Helen her wedding ring.

"I'll get him to come over here, to the house. I'll arrange it," Lenore said. Helen couldn't defend herself against this notion. She still felt sleepy, she was always sleepy. There was something wrong with her mother's idea but not much.

Then Lenore could not arrange it. When Helen returned from school, her mother said, "It can't be done. I'm so upset and I've lost interest so I'll give you the short version. I called . . . I must have made twenty calls. At last I got someone to speak to me. His name was Smokin' Joe and he was a hundred miles away but sounded as though he'd do it. And I asked him if there was any place he didn't tattoo, and he said faces, dicks and hands."

"Mom!" Helen said. Her face reddened.

"And I asked him if there was any*one* he wouldn't tattoo, and he said drunks and the dying. So that was that."

"But you didn't have to tell him. You won't have to tell him," Helen said.

"That's true," Lenore said dispiritedly. Then she looked angrily at Helen. "Are you crazy? Sometimes I think you're crazy!"

"Mom!" Helen said, crying. "I want you to do what you want."

"This was my idea, mine!" Lenore said. The dog gave a high, nervous bark. "Oh dear," Lenore said, "I'm speaking too loudly." She smiled at him as if to say how clever both of them were to realize this.

That night Lenore could not sleep. There were no dreams, nothing. High clouds swept slowly past the window. She got up and went into the living room, to the desk there. She looked with distaste at all the objects in this room. There wasn't one thing here she'd want to take with her to the grave, not one. The dog had shuffled out of the bedroom with her and now lay at her feet, the slipper in his mouth, a red one with a little bow. She wanted to make note of a few things, clarify some things. She took out a piece of paper. The furnace turned on and she heard something moving behind the walls. "Enjoy it while you can," she said. She sat at the desk, her back very straight, waiting for something. After a while she looked at the dog. "Give me that," she said. "Give me that slipper." He growled but did not leave her side. She took a pen and wrote on the paper, *When I go, the dog goes. Promise me this.* She left it out for Helen.

Then she thought, That dog is the dumbest one I've ever had. I don't want him with me. She was amazed she could still think like this. She tore up the piece of paper. "Lenore!" she cried, and wrung her hands. She wanted herself. Her mind ran stumbling, panting, through dark twisted woods.

When Helen got up she would ask her to make some toast. Toast would taste good. Helen would press the *Good Morning* letters on the bread. It was a gadget, like a cookie cutter. When the bread was toasted, the words were pressed down into it and you dribbled honey into them.

In the morning Helen did this carefully, as she always had. They sat together at the kitchen table and ate the toast. Sleet struck the windows. Helen looked at her toast dreamily, the letters golden against the almost black. They both liked their toast almost black.

Lenore felt peaceful. But it was a cruelty to feel peaceful, a cruelty to Helen.

"Turn on the radio," Lenore said, "and find out if they're going to cancel school." If Helen stayed home today she would talk to her. Important things would be said. Things that would still matter years and years from now.

Callers on a talk show were speaking about wolves. "There should be wolf control," someone said, "not wolf worship."

"Oh, I hate these people," Helen said.

"Are you a wolf worshiper," her mother asked. "Watch out."

"I believe they have the right to live too," Helen said fervently. Then she was sorry. Everything she said was wrong. She moved the dial on the radio. School would not be canceled. They never canceled it.

"There's a stain on that blouse," her mother said. "Why do your clothes always look so dingy? You should buy some new clothes."

"I don't want any new clothes," Helen said.

"You can't wear mine, that's not the way to think. I've got to get rid of them. Maybe that's what I'll do today. I'll go through them with Jean. It's Jean who comes today, isn't it?"

"I don't want your clothes!"

"Why not? Not even the sweaters?"

Helen's mouth trembled.

"Oh, what are we going to do!" Lenore said. She clawed at her cheeks. The dog barked.

"Mom, Mom," Helen said.

"We've got to talk, I want to talk," Lenore said. What would happen to Helen, her little girl …

Helen saw the stain her mother had noticed on the blouse. Where had it come from? It had just appeared. She would change if she had time.

"When I die, I'm going to forget you," Lenore began. This was so obvious, this wasn't what she meant. "The dead just forget you. The most important things, all the loving things, everything we … " She closed her eyes, then opened them with effort. "I want to put on some lipstick today," she said. "If I don't, tell me when you come home."

Helen left just in time to catch the bus. Some of her classmates stood by the curb, hooded, hunched. It was bitter out.

In the house, Lenore looked at the dog. There were only so many dogs in a person's life and this was the last one in hers. She'd like to kick him. But he had changed when she'd gotten sick, he hadn't been like this before. He was bewildered. He didn't like it—death—either. She felt sorry for him. She went back into her bedroom and he followed her with the slipper.

At nine, the first in a number of nurse's aides and companions arrived. By three it was growing dark again. Helen returned before four.

"The dog needs a walk," her mother said.

"It's so icy out, Mom, he'll cut the pads of his feet."

"He needs to go out!" her mother screamed. She wore a little lipstick and sat in a chair wringing her hands.

Helen found the leash and coaxed the dog to the door. He looked out uneasily into the cold, wet blackness. They moved out into it a few yards to a bush he had killed long before and he dribbled a few drops of urine onto it. They walked a little farther, across the dully shining yard toward the street. It was still, windless. The air made a hissing sound. "Come on," Helen said, "don't you want to do something?" The dog walked stoically along. Helen's eyes began to water with the cold. Her mother had said, "I want Verdi played at the service, Scriabin, no hymns." Helen had sent away for some recordings. How else could it be accomplished, the Verdi, the Scriabin ... Once she had called her father and said, "What should we do for Mom?"

"Where have you been!" her mother said when they got back. "My god, I thought you'd been hit by a truck."

They ate supper, macaroni and cheese, something one of the women had prepared. Lenore ate without speaking and then looked at the empty plate.

"Do you want some more, Mom," Helen asked.

"One of those girls that comes, she says she'll take the dog," Lenore said.

Helen swallowed. "I think it would be good," she said.

"That's it, then. She'll take him tomorrow."

"Is she just going to see how it works out or what?"

"No, she wants him. She lives in an iffy neighborhood and the dog, you know, can be impressive when he wants. I think better now than later. He's only five, five next month." She knew the dog's birthday. She laughed at this.

The next day, when Helen came home from school the dog was gone. His bowls were gone from the corner near the sink.

"At least I have my slipper back," Lenore said. She had it in her hand, the red slipper.

Helen was doing her homework. She was a funny kid, Lenore thought, there she was doing her homework.

"It's almost over for me," Lenore said. "I'm at the end of my life."

Helen looked up. "Mom," she said.

"I can't believe it."

"I'm a nihilist," Helen said. "That's what I'm going to be."

"You can't think you're going to be a nihilist," her mother said. "Are you laughing at me? Don't you dare laugh at me. I'm still your mother." She shook her fist.

"Mom, Mom," Helen said, "I'm not laughing." She began to cry.

"Don't cry," Lenore said dully.

Helen looked down at her textbook. She had underlined everything on one page. Everything! Stupid ... She'd be stupid in Florida too, she thought. She could think about Florida only by being here with her mother. Otherwise Florida didn't really exist.

Lenore said, "God is nothing. OK? That's Meister Eckhart. But whatever is not God is nothing and ought to be accounted as nothing. OK? That's someone else."

Helen didn't speak.

"I wasn't born yesterday," her mother said. "That's why I know these things. I wasn't even born last night." She laughed. It was snowing again. It had been snowing freshly for hours. First sleet, then colder, then this snow.

"Helen," her mother said, "would you get me a snowball? Go out and make me one and bring it back."

Helen got up and went outside as though hypnotized. Sometimes she behaved like this, as though she were an unwilling yet efficient instrument. She could have thoughts and not think them. She was protected, at the same time she was helping her mother do her job, the job being this peculiar business.

The snow was damp and lovely. Huge flakes softly struck her face and felt like living things. She went past the bush the dog had liked, pushed her hands deeply into the snow and made a snowball for her mother, perfect as an orange.

Lenore studied this. "This is good snow, isn't it?" she said. "Perfect snow." She packed it tighter and threw it across the room at Helen. It hit her squarely in the chest.

"Oh!" Lenore exclaimed.

"That hurt, Mom," Helen said.

"Oh, you . . ." Lenore said. "Get me another."

"No!" Helen said. The thing had felt like a rock. Her breasts hurt. Her mother was grinning avidly at her.

"Get two, come on," her mother said. "We'll have a snowball fight in the house. Why not!"

"No!" Helen said. "This is . . . you're just pretending . . ."

Lenore looked at her. She pulled her bathrobe tighter around herself. "I'm going to go to bed," she said.

"Do you want me to make some tea?" Helen said. "Let me make some tea."

"Tea, tea," Lenore mimicked. "What will you drink in Florida? You'll drink iced tea."

That night Lenore dreamed she was on a boat with others. A white boat in clear, lovely water. They were moving quickly but there was a banging sound, arrhythmic, incessant, sad, it was sad. It's the banger, they said, the fish too big for the box, that's what we call them. Let it go, Lenore begged. Too late now, they said, too late for it now.

"Lenore!" she cried. She went into Helen's room. Helen slept with the light on, her radio playing softly, books scattered on her bed.

"Sleep with me," her mother said.

Helen shrank back. "I can't, please," she said.

"My god, you won't lie down with me!" her mother said. She had things from Helen's childhood still—little nightgowns, coloring books, valentines.

"All right, all right," Helen said. Her eyes were wild, she looked blinded.

"No, all right, forget it," Lenore said. She shook her head from side to side, panting. Helen's room was almost bare. There were no pictures, no pretty things, not even a mirror. Plastic was stapled to the window frames to keep out the cold. When had this happened? Lenore wondered. Tomorrow, she thought. She shouldn't try to say anything at night. Words at night were feral things. She limped back to her room. Her feet were swollen, discolored, water oozed from them. She would hide them. But where would she hide them? She sat up in bed, the pillows heaped behind her back, and watched them. They became remote, indecipherable.

It became morning again. *Mother . . . Earth . . .* said someone on the radio.

"An egg," Helen asked. "Do you want an egg this morning?"

"You should get your hair cut today," Lenore said. "Go to the beauty parlor."

"Oh, Mom, it's all right."

"Get it trimmed or something. It needs something."

"But nobody will be here with you," Helen said. "You'll be home by yourself."

"Go after school. I can take care of myself for an hour. Something wouldn't happen in an hour, do you think?" Lenore felt sly saying this. Then she said, "I want you to look pretty, to feel good about yourself."

"I really hate those places," Helen said.

"Can't you do anything for me!" Lenore said.

Helen got off the bus at a shopping mall on the way back from school. "I don't have a reservation," she told the woman at the desk.

"You mean an appointment," the woman said. "You don't have an appointment."

She was taken immediately to a chair in front of a long mirror. The women in the chairs beside her were all looking into the mirror while their hairdressers stared into it too and cut their hair. Everyone was chatting and relaxed, but Helen didn't know how to do this, even this, this simple thing.

Sometimes Helen dreamed that she was her own daughter. She was free, self-absorbed, unfamiliar. Helen took up very little of her thoughts. But she could not pretend this.

She looked at the woman beside her, who had long wet hair and was smoking a cigarette. Above her shoe was a black parole anklet.

"These things don't work at all," the woman said. "I could take the damn thing off but I think it's kind of stylish. Often I do take the damn thing off and it's in one place and I'm in another. *Quite* another."

"What did you do?" Helen asked.

"I didn't do anything!" the woman bawled. Then she laughed. She dropped her cigarette in the cup of coffee she was holding.

The washing, the cutting, the drying, all this took a long time. Her hairdresser was an Asian named Mickey. "How old do you think I am," Mickey asked.

"Twenty," Helen said. She did not look at her, or herself, in the mirror. She kept her eyes slightly unfocused, the way a dog would.

"I'm thirty-five," Mickey said delightedly. "I am one-eighteenth Ainu. Do you know anything about the Ainu?"

Helen knew it wasn't necessary to reply to this. Someone several chairs away said in disbelief, "She's naming the baby *what?*"

"The Ainu are an aboriginal people of north Japan. Up until a little while ago they used to kill a bear in a sacred ritual each year. The anthropologists were wild about this ritual and were disappointed when they quit, but here goes, I will share it with you. At the end of each winter they'd catch a bear cub and give it to a woman to nurse. Wow, that's something! After it was weaned, it was given wonderful food and petted and played with. It was caged, but in all other respects it was treated as an honored guest. But the day always came when the leader of the village would come and tell the bear sorrowfully that it must be killed though they loved it dearly. This was this long oration, this part. Then everyone dragged the bear from its cage with ropes, tied it to a stake, shot it with blunt arrows that merely tortured it, then scissored its neck between two poles where it slowly strangled, after which they skinned it, decapitated it and offered the severed head some of its own flesh. What do you think, do you think they knew what they were doing?"

"Was there something more to it than that?" Helen said. "Did something come after that?" She really was a serious girl. Her head burned from the hair dryer Mickey was wielding dramatically.

"These are my people!" Mickey said, ignoring her. "You've come a long way, baby! Maine or Bust!" She sounded bitter. She turned off the dryer, removed Helen's smock and with a little brush whisked her shoulders. "Ask for Mickey another time," she said. "That's me. Happy Holidays."

Helen paid and walked out into the cold. The cold felt delicious on her head. "An honored guest," she said aloud. To live was like being an honored guest. The thought was outside her, large and calm. Then you were no longer an honored guest. The thought turned away from her and faded.

Her mother was watching television with the sound off when Helen got home. "That's a nice haircut," her mother said. "Now don't touch it, don't pull at it like that for god's sake. It's pretty. You're pretty."

It was a ghastly haircut, really. Helen's large ears seemed to float, no longer quite attached to her head. Lenore gazed quietly at her.

"Mom," Helen said, "do you know there's a patron saint of television?"

Lenore thought this was hysterical.

"It's true," Helen said. "St. Clare."

Lenore wondered how long it would take for Helen's hair to grow back.

Later they were eating ice cream. They were both in their nightgowns. Helen was reading a Russian novel. She loved Russian novels. Everyone was so emotional, so tormented. They clutched their heads, they fainted, they swooned, they galloped around. The snow. Russian snow had made Maine snow puny to Helen, meaningless.

"This ice cream tastes bad," her mother said. "It tastes like bleach or something." Some foul odor crept up her throat. Helen continued to read. Anyway, what were they doing eating ice cream in the middle of winter? Lenore wondered. It was laziness. Something was creeping quietly all through her. She'd like to jump out of her skin, she really would.

"You now," she said, "I believe that if Jesus walked into this house this minute, you wouldn't even raise your eyes."

Helen bit her lip and reluctantly put down the book. "Oh, Mom," she said.

"And maybe you'd be right. I bet he'd lack charisma. I'd bet my last dollar on it. The only reason he was charismatic before was that those people lived in a prerational time."

"Jesus isn't going to walk in here, Mom, come on," Helen said.

"Well, something is, something big. You'd better be ready for it." She was angry. "You've got the harder road," she said finally. "You've got to behave in a way you won't be afraid to remember, but you know what my road is? My road is the *new* road."

Like everyone, Lenore had a dread of being alone in the world, forgotten by God, overlooked. There were billions upon billions of people, after all, it wasn't out of the question.

"The new road?" Helen asked.

"Oh, there's nothing new about it," Lenore said, annoyed. She stroked her face with her hands. She shouldn't be doing this to Helen, her little Helen. But Helen was so docile. She wasn't fighting this! You had to fight.

"Go back to what you were doing," Lenore said. "You were reading, you were concentrating. I wish I could concentrate. My mind just goes from one thing to another. Do you know what I was thinking of, did I ever tell you this? When I was still well, before I went to the doctor? I was in a department store looking at a coat and I must have stepped in front of this woman who was looking at coats too. I had no idea . . . and she just started to stare at me. I was very aware of it but I ignored it for a long time, I even moved away. But she followed me, still staring. Until I finally looked at her. She still stared but now she was looking through me, *through* me, and she began talking to someone, resuming some conversation with whoever was with her, and all the while she was staring at me to show how insignificant I was, how utterly insignificant . . ." Lenore leaned toward Helen but then drew back, dizzy. "And I felt cursed. I felt as though she'd cursed me."

"What a weirdo," Helen said.

"I wonder where she picked that up," Lenore said. "I'd like to see her again. I'd like to murder her."

"I would too," Helen said. "I really would."

"No, murder's too good for that one," Lenore said. "Murder's for the elect. I think of murder . . . sometimes I think I wish someone would murder me. Out of the blue, without warning, for no reason. I wouldn't believe it was happening. It would be like not dying at all."

Helen sat in her nightgown. She felt cold. People had written books about death. No one knew what they were talking about, of course.

"Oh, I'm tired of talk," Lenore said. "I don't want to talk anymore. I'm tired of thinking about it. Why do we have to think about it all the time! One of those philosophers said that Death was the Big Thinker. It thinks the instant that was your life, right down to the bottom of it."

"Which one," Helen asked.

"Which one what?"

"Which philosopher?"

"I can't recall," Lenore said. Sometimes Helen amused her, she really amused her.

Lenore didn't dream that night. She lay in bed panting. She wasn't ready but there was nothing left to be done. The day before the girl had washed and dried the bedsheets and before she put them on again she had ironed them. Ironed them! They were just delicious, still delicious. It was the girl who loved to iron. She'd iron anything. What's-her-name. Lenore got up and moved through the rooms of the house uncertainly. She could hardly keep her balance. Then she went down into the cellar. Her heart was pounding, it felt wet and small in her chest. She looked at the oil gauge on the furnace. It was a little over one-quarter full. She wasn't going to order any more, she'd just see what happened. She barely had the strength to get back upstairs. She turned on the little lamp that was on the breakfast table and sat in her chair there, waiting for Helen. She saw dog hairs on the floor, gathering together, drifting across the tiles.

Helen felt sick but she would drag herself to school. Her throat was sore. She heated up honey in a pan and sipped it with a spoon.

"I'm going to just stay put today," Lenore said.

"That's good, Mom, just take it easy. You've been doing too much." Helen's forehead shone with sweat. She buttoned up her sweater with trembling fingers.

"Do you have a cold?" her mother said. "Where did you get a cold? Stay home. The nurse who's coming this afternoon, she can take a look at you and write a prescription. Look at you, you're sweating. You've probably got a fever." She wanted to weep for her little Helen.

"I have a test today, Mom," Helen said.

"A test," Lenore marveled. She laughed. "Take them now but don't take them later, they don't do you any good later."

Helen wiped at her face with a dish towel.

"My god, a dish towel!" Lenore said. "What's wrong with you? My god, what's to become of you!"

Startled, Helen dropped the towel. She almost expected to see her face on it. That was what had alarmed her mother so, that Helen had wiped off her own face. Anyone knew better than to do that . . . She felt faint. She was thinking of the test, of taking it in a few hours. She took a fresh dish towel from a drawer and put it on the rack.

"What if I die today?" Lenore said suddenly. "I want you to be with me. My god, I don't want to be alone."

"All this week there are tests," Helen said.

"Why don't I wait, then?" Lenore said.

Tears ran down Helen's cheeks. She stood there stubbornly, looking at her mother.

"You were always able to turn them on and off," Lenore said, "just like a faucet. Crocodile tears." But with a moan she clutched her. Then she pulled away. "We have to wash these things," she said. "We can't just leave them in the sink." She seized the smudged glass she'd used to swallow her pills and rinsed it in running water. She held it up to the window and it slipped from her fingers and smashed against the sill. It was dirty and whole, she thought, and now it is clean and broken. This seemed to her profound.

"Don't touch it!" she screamed. "Leave it for Barbara. Is that her name, Barbara?" Strangers, they were all strangers. "She never knows what to do when she comes."

"I have to go, Mom," Helen said.

"You do, of course you do," her mother said. She patted Helen's cheeks clumsily. "You're so hot, you're sick."

"I love you," Helen said.

"I love you too," Lenore said. Then she watched her walk down the street toward the corner. The day was growing lighter. The mornings kept coming, she didn't like it.

On the bus, the driver said to Helen, "I lost my mother when I was your age. You've just got to hang in there."

Helen walked toward the rear of the bus and sat down. She shut her eyes. A girl behind her snapped her gum and said, " 'Hang in there.' What an idiot."

The bus pounded down the snow-packed streets.

The girl with the gum had been the one who told Helen how ashes came back. Her uncle had died and his ashes had come in a red shellacked box. It looked cheap but it had cost fifty-five dollars and there was an envelope taped to the box with his name typed on it beneath a glassine window as though he was being addressed to himself. This girl considered herself to be somewhat of an authority on how these things were handled, for she had also lost a couple of grandparents and knew how these things were done as far south as Boston.

Congress

MIRIAM WAS LIVING WITH A MAN NAMED JACK DEWAYNE, who taught a course in forensic anthropology at the state university. It was the only program in the country that offered a certificate in forensic anthropology, as far as anyone knew, and his students adored him. They called themselves Deweenies and wore skull-and-crossbones T-shirts to class. People were mad for Jack in this town. Once, in a grocery store, when Miriam stood gazing into a bin of limes, a woman came up to her and said, "Your Jack is a wonderful, wonderful man."

"Oh, thanks," Miriam said.

"My son Ricky disappeared four years ago and some skeletal remains were found at the beginning of this year. Scattered, broken, lots of bones missing, not much to go on, a real jumble. The officials told me they probably weren't Ricky's but your Jack told me they were, and with compassion he showed me how he reached that conclusion." The woman waited. In her cart was a big bag of birdseed and a bottle of vodka. "If it weren't for Jack, my Ricky's body would probably be unnamed still," she said.

"Well, thank you very much," Miriam said.

She never knew what to say to Jack's fans. As for them, they didn't understand Miriam at all. Why her of all people? With his hunger for life, Jack could have chosen better, they felt. Miriam lacked charm, they felt. She was gloomy. Even Jack found her gloomy occasionally.

Mornings, out in the garden, she would, at times, read aloud from one of her many overdue library books. Dew as radiant as angel spit glittered on the petals of Jack's roses. Jack was quite the gardener. Miriam thought she knew why he particularly favored roses. The inside of a rose does not at all correspond to its exterior beauty. If one tears off all the petals of the corolla, all that remains is a sordid-looking tuft. Roses would be right up Jack's alley, all right.

"Here's something for you, Jack," Miriam said. "You'll appreciate this. Beckett described tears as 'liquefied brain.'"

"God, Miriam," Jack said. "Why are you sharing that with me? Look at this day, it's a beautiful day! Stop pumping out the cesspit! Leave the cesspit alone!"

Then the phone would ring and Jack would begin his daily business of reconstructing the previous lives of hair and teeth when they had been possessed by someone. A detective a thousand miles away would send him a box of pitted bones and within days Jack would be saying, "This is a white male between the ages of twenty-five and thirty who didn't do drugs and who was tall, healthy and trusting. Too trusting, clearly."

Or a hand would be found in the stomach of a shark hauled up by a party boat off the Gulf Coast of Florida and Jack would be flown off to examine it. He would return deeply tanned and refreshed, with a crisp new haircut, saying, "The shark was most certainly attracted to the rings on this hand. This is a teen's hand. She was small, perhaps even a legal midget, and well nourished. She was a loner, adventurous, not well educated and probably unemployed. Odds are the rings were stolen. She would certainly have done herself a favor by passing up the temptation of those rings."

Miriam hated it when Jack was judgmental, and Jack was judgmental a great deal. She herself stole on occasion, mostly sheets. For some reason, it was easy to steal sheets. As a girl she had wanted to become a witty, lively and irresistible woman, skilled in repartee and in arguments on controversial subjects, but it hadn't turned out that way. She had become a woman who was still waiting for her calling.

Jack had no idea that Miriam stole sheets and more. He liked Miriam. He liked her bones. She had fine bones and he loved tracing them at night beneath her warm, smooth skin, her jawbone, collarbone, pelvic bone. It wasn't anything that consumed him, but he just liked her was all, usually. And he liked his work. He liked wrapping things up and dealing with those whom the missing had left behind. He was neither doctor nor priest; he was the forensic anthropologist, and he alone could give these people peace. They wanted to know, they had to know. Was that tibia in the swamp Denny's? Denny, we long to claim you ... Were those little bits and pieces they got when they dragged the lake Lucile's even though she was supposed to be in Manhattan? She had told us she was going to be in Manhattan, there was never any talk about a lake ... Bill had gone on a day hike years ago with his little white dog and now at last something had been found in a ravine ... Pookie had toddled away from the Airstream on the Fourth of July just as we were setting up the grill, she would be so much older now, a little girl instead of a baby, and it would be so good just to know, if only we could know ...

And Jack would give them his gift, the incontrovertible and almost unspeakable news. That's her, that's them. No need to worry anymore, it is finished, you are free. No one could help these people who were weary of waiting and sick of hope like Jack could.

Miriam had a fondness for people who vanished, though she had never known any personally. But if she had a loved one who vanished, she would prefer to believe that they had fallen in love with distance, a great distance. She certainly wouldn't long to be told they were dead.

One day, one of Jack's students, an ardent hunter, a gangly blue-eyed boy named Carl who wore camouflage pants and a black shirt winter and summer, presented him with four cured deer feet. "I thought you'd like to make a lamp," Carl said.

Miriam was in the garden. She had taken to stealing distressed plants from nurseries and people's yards and planting them in an un-used corner of the lot, far from Jack's roses. They remained distressed, however—in shock, she felt.

"It would make a nice lamp," Carl said. "You can make all kinds of things. With a big buck's forelegs you can make an outdoor thermom-eter. Looks good with snowflakes on it."

"A lamp," Jack said. He appeared delighted. Jack got along well with his students. He didn't sleep with the girls and he treated the boys as equals. He put his hands around the tops of the deer feet and splayed them out some.

"You might want to fiddle around with the height," Carl said. "You can make great stuff with antlers, too. Chandeliers, candelabras. You can use antlers to frame just about anything."

"We have lamps," Miriam said. She was holding a wan perennial she had liberated from a supermarket.

"Gosh, this appeals to me, though, Miriam."

"I bet you'd be good at this sort of thing, sir," Carl said. "I did one once and it was very relaxing." He glanced at Miriam, squeezed his eyes almost shut and smiled.

"It will be a novelty item, all right," Jack said. "I think it will be fun."

"Maybe you'd like to go hunting sometime with me, sir," Carl said. "We could go bow hunting for muleys together."

"You should resist the urge to do this, Jack, really," Miriam said. The thought of a lamp made of animal legs in her life and *turned on* caused a violent feeling of panic within her.

But Jack wanted to make a lamp. He needed another hobby, he argued. Hobbies were healthy, and he might even take Carl up on his bow-hunting offer. Why didn't she get herself a hobby like baking or watching football? he suggested. He finished the lamp in a weekend and set it on an antique jelly cabinet in the sunroom. He'd had a little trouble trimming the legs to the same height. They might not have ended up being exactly the same height. Miriam, expecting to be repulsed by the thing, was enthralled instead. It had a dark blue shade and a gold-colored cord and a sixty-watt bulb. A brighter bulb would be pushing it, Jack said. Miriam could not resist the allure of the little lamp. She often found herself sitting beside it, staring at it, the harsh brown hairs, the dainty pasterns, the polished black hooves, all fastened together with a brass gimp band in a space the size of a dinner plate. It was anarchy, the little lamp, its legs snugly bunched. It was whirl, it was hole, it was the first far drums. She sometimes worried that she would start talking to it. This happened to some people, she knew, they felt they had to talk. She read that Luther Burbank spoke to cactus reassuringly when he wanted to create a spineless variety and that they stabbed him repeatedly; he had to pull thousands of spines from his hands but didn't care. He continued to speak calmly and patiently; he never got mad, he persisted.

"Miriam," Jack said, "that is not meant to be a reading light. It's an accent light. You're going to ruin your eyes."

Miriam had once channeled her considerable imagination into sex, which Jack had long appreciated, but now it spilled everywhere and lay lightly on everything like water on a lake. It alarmed him a little. Perhaps, during semester break, they should take a trip together. To witness something strange with each other might be just the ticket. At the same time, he felt unaccountably nervous about traveling with Miriam.

The days were radiant but it was almost fall and a daytime coolness reached out and touched everything. Miriam's restlessness was gone. It was Jack who was restless.

"I'm going to take up bow hunting, Miriam," he said. "Carl seems to think I'd be a natural at it."

Miriam did not object to this as she might once have. Nevertheless, she could not keep herself from waiting anxiously beside the lamp for Jack's return from his excursions with Carl. She was in a peculiar sort of readiness, and not for anything in particular, either. For weeks Jack went hunting, and for weeks he did not mind that he did not return with a former animal.

"It's the expectation and the challenge. That's what counts," he said. He and Carl would stand in the kitchen sharing a little whiskey. Carl's skin was clean as a baby's and he smelled cleanly if somewhat aberrantly of cold cream and celery. "The season's young, sir," he said.

But eventually Jack's lack of success began to vex him. Miriam and the lamp continued to wait solemnly for his empty-handed return. He grew irritable. Sometimes he would forget to wash off his camouflage paint, and he slept poorly. Then, late one afternoon when Jack was out in the woods, he fell asleep in his stand and toppled out of a tree, critically wounding himself with his own arrow, which passed through his eye and into his head like a knife thrust into a cantaloupe. A large portion of his brain lost its rosy hue and turned gray as a rodent's coat. A month later, he could walk with difficulty and move one arm. He had some vision out of his remaining eye and he could hear but not speak. He emerged from rehab with a face as expressionless as a frosted cake. He was something that had suffered a premature burial, something accounted for but not present. Miriam was certain that he was aware of the morbid irony in this.

The lamp was a great comfort to Miriam in the weeks following the accident. Carl was of less comfort. Whenever she saw him in the hospital's halls, he was wailing and grinding his teeth. But the crooked, dainty deer-foot lamp was calm. They spent most nights together reading quietly. The lamp had eclectic reading tastes. It would cast its light on anything, actually. It liked the stories of Poe. The night before Jack was to return home, they read a little book in which animals offered their prayers to God—the mouse, the bear, the turtle and so on—and this is perhaps where the lamp and Miriam had their first disagreement. Miriam liked the little verses. But the lamp felt that though the author clearly meant well, the prayers were cloying and confused thought with existence. The lamp had witnessed a smattering of Kierkegaard and felt strongly that thought should never be confused with existence. Being in such a condition of peculiar and altered existence itself, the lamp felt some things unequivocally. Miriam often wanted to think about that other life, when the parts knew the whole, when the legs ran and rested and moved through woods washed by flowers, but the lamp did not want to reflect upon those times.

Jack came back and Carl moved in with them. He had sold everything he owned except his big Chevy truck and wanted only to nurse Jack for the rest of his life. Jack's good eye often teared, and he indicated both discomfort and agreement with a whistling hiss. Even so, he didn't seem all that glad to see Miriam. As for herself, she felt that she had driven to a grave and gotten out of the car with the engine left running. Carl slept for a time in Jack's study, but one night when Miriam couldn't sleep and was sitting in the living room with the lamp, she saw him go into their room and shut the door. And that became the arrangement. Carl stayed with Jack day and night.

One of the first things Carl wanted to do was to take a trip. He believed that the doleful visits from the other students tired Jack and that the familiar house and grounds didn't stimulate him properly. While Miriam didn't think highly of Carl's ideas, this one didn't seem too bad. She was ready to leave. After all, Jack had already left in his fashion and it seemed pointless to stay in his house. They all three would sit together in the big roomy cab on the wide cherry-red custom seat of Carl's truck and tour the Southwest. The only thing she didn't like was that the lamp would have to travel in the back with the luggage.

"Nothing's going to happen to it," Carl said. "Look at dogs. Dogs ride around in the backs of trucks all the time. They love it."

"Thousands of dogs die each year from being pitched out of the backs of pickups," Miriam said.

Jack remained in the room with them while they debated the statistical probability of this. He was gaunt and his head was scarred, and he tended to resemble, if left to his own devices, a large white appliance. But Carl was always buying him things and making small alterations to his appearance. This day he was wearing pressed khakis, a crisp madras shirt, big black glasses and a black Stetson hat. Carl was young and guilty and crazy in love. He patted Jack's wrists as he talked, not wanting to upset him.

Finally, continuing to assert that he had never heard of a dog falling out of a pickup truck, Carl agreed to buy a camper shell and enclose the back. He packed two small bags for himself and Jack while Miriam got a cardboard carton and arranged her clothes around the lamp. Her plan was to unplug whatever lamp was in whatever motel room they stayed in and plug this one in. Clearly, that would be the high point of its day.

They took to the road that night and didn't stop driving until daylight disclosed that the landscape had changed considerably. There was a great deal of broken glass and huge cactus everywhere. Organ-pipe, saguaro, barrel cactus and prickly pear. Strange and stern shapes, far stiller than trees, less friendly and willing to serve. They seemed to be waiting for further transition, another awesome shift of the earth's plates, an enormous occurrence. The sun bathed each spine, it sharpened the smashed bottles and threw itself through the large delicate ears of car-crushed jackrabbits. They saw few people and no animals except dead ones. The land was vast and still and there seemed to be considerable resentment toward the nonhuman creatures who struggled to inhabit it. Dead coyotes and hawks were nailed to fence posts and the road was hammered with the remains of lizards and snakes. Miriam was glad that the lamp was covered and did not have to suffer these sights.

The first night they stopped at a motel, with a Chinese restaurant and lounge adjoining. Miriam ordered moo goo gai pan for dinner, something she had not had since she was a child, and an orange soda. Carl fed Jack some select tidbits from an appetizer platter with a pair of chopsticks. After they ate Miriam wandered into the lounge, but there was only a cat vigorously cleaning itself and staring at her with its legs splayed over its head. She picked up a couple of worn paperback books from the exchange table in the office and went back to her room.

Through the walls she could hear Carl singing to Jack as he ran the bathwater. He would shampoo Jack's hair, scrub his nails and talk about the future ... Miriam turned on the lamp and examined one of the books. It concerned desert plants but many of the pages were missing and someone had spilled wine on the pictures. She did learn, however, that cactus are descended from roses. They were late arrivals, adapters, part of a new climate. She felt like that, felt very much a late arrival, it was her personality. She had adapted readily to being in love, and then adapted to not being in love anymore. And the new climate was, well, this situation. She put the book about cactus down.

The other book was about hunting zebras in Africa. *I shot him right up his big fat fanny*, the author wrote. She had read this before she knew what she was doing and felt terrible about it, but the lamp held steady until she finally turned it off and got into bed.

The next day they drove. They stopped at hot springs and ghost towns. They stopped on an Indian reservation and Carl bought Jack colored sand in a bottle. They stopped at a Dairy Queen and Miriam drove while Carl spooned blueberry Blizzard into Jack's mouth. They admired the desert, the peculiar growths, the odd pale colors. They passed through a canyon of large, solitary boulders. There was a sign threatening fine and imprisonment for defacing the rocks but the boulders were covered with paint, spelling out people's names, mostly. The shapes of the rocks resembled nothing though the words made them look like toilet doors in a truck stop. On the other side of the canyon was a small town with two museums, a brick hotel, a gas station and a large bar called the Horny Toad. Miriam had the feeling that the truck's engine had stopped running.

"Truck's stopped," Carl said.

They coasted to the side of the road and Carl fiddled with the ignition.

"Alternator's shot, I bet," he said. He took Jack's sunglasses off, wiped them with a handkerchief and carefully hooked them back over Jack's ears. Underneath her elbow, the metal of the door was heating up.

"You check into the hotel," Carl directed her. "Jack and I will walk down to the garage. He likes garages."

Carl helped Miriam get their luggage from the back and carried it into the hotel's lobby. She arranged for two unadjoining rooms. They were the last rooms left, even though the hotel and town appeared deserted. The museums were closed and everyone was at the bar, the manager told her. One of the museums displayed only a petrified wedding cake, a petrified cat, some rocks and old clothes. It was typical and not worth going into, he confided. But people came from far and wide to see the other museum and speak to the taxidermist on duty. He was surprised that they had come here without having the museum as their destination. The taxidermist was a genius. He couldn't make an animal look dead if he wanted to.

"He can even do reptiles and combine them in artistic and instructive groups," the manager said.

"This museum is full of dead animals?" Miriam said.

"Sure," the manager said. "It's a wildlife museum."

Miriam's room was in the back of the hotel over the kitchen and smelled like the inside of a lunch box, but it wasn't unpleasant. She rearranged the furniture, plugged in the lamp and gazed out the single window at the bar, a long, dark structure that seemed, the longer she stared at it, to be almost heaving with the muffled sound of voices. This was the Horny Toad. She decided to go there.

Miriam had always felt that she was the kind of person who somehow quenched in the least exacting stranger any desire for conversation with her. This, however, was not the case at the Toad. People turned to her immediately and began to speak. They had bright, restless faces, seemed starved for affection and were in full conversational mode. A number of children were present. Everyone was wildly stimulated.

A young woman with lank, thinning hair touched Miriam with a small dry hand. "I'm Priscilla Dickman and I'm an ex-agoraphobic," she said. "Can I buy you a drink?"

"Yes," Miriam said, startled. People were waving, smiling.

"I used to be so afraid of losing control," Priscilla said. "I was afraid of going insane, embarrassing myself. I was afraid of getting sick or doing something frightening or dying. It's hard to believe, isn't it?"

She went off to the bar, saying she would return with gimlets. Miriam was immediately joined by an elderly couple wearing jeans, satin shirts and large, identical concha belts. Their names were Vern and Irene. They had spent all day at the museum and were happy and tired.

"My favorite is the javelina family," Irene said. "Those babies were adorable."

"Ugly animals," Vern said. "Bizarre. But they've always been Irene's favorite."

"Not last year," Irene said. "Last year it was the bears, I think. Vern says that Life is just one thing but it takes different forms to amuse itself."

"That's what I say, but I don't believe it," Vern said, winking broadly at Miriam.

"Vern likes the ground squirrels."

Vern agreed. "Isn't much of a display, but I like what I hear about them. That state-of-torpor thing. When the going gets rough, boom, right into a state of torpor. They don't need anything. A single breath every three minutes."

Irene didn't seem as fascinated as her husband by the state of torpor. "Have you gone yet, dear," she asked Miriam. "Have you asked the taxidermist your question?"

"No, I haven't," Miriam said. She accepted a glass from Priscilla, who had returned with a tray of drinks. "I'm Priscilla Dickman," she said to the old couple, "and I'm an ex-agoraphobic."

"He doesn't answer everybody," Vern said.

"He answers the children sometimes, but they don't know what they're saying," Irene said fretfully. "I think children should be allowed only in the petting zoo."

A gaunt, grave boy named Alec arrived and identified himself as a tree hugger. He was with a girl named Argon.

"When I got old enough to know sort of what I wanted?" Argon said, "I decided I wanted either a tree hugger or a car guy. I'd narrowed it down to that. At my first demonstration, I lay in the road with some other people in a park where they were going to bulldoze two-hundred-year-old trees for a picnic area. We had attracted quite a crowd of onlooking picnickers. When the cops came and carried me off, a little girl said, 'Why are they taking the pretty one away, Mommy?' and I was hooked. I just loved demonstrating after that, always hoping to overhear those words again. But I never did."

"We all get older, dear," Irene said.

"Car guys are kind of interesting," Argon said. "They can be really hypnotic, but only when they're talking about cars, actually."

Sometime later, Alec was still in the midst of a long story about Indian environmentalists in the Himalayas. The tree-hugging movement started long ago, he'd been telling them, when the maharaja of Jodhpur wanted to cut down trees for yet another palace and a woman named Amrita Devi resisted his axmen by hugging a tree and uttering the now well-known statement "A chopped head is cheaper than a felled tree" before she was dismembered. Then her three daughters took her place and they, too, were dismembered. Then 359 additional villagers were dismembered before the maharaja called it off.

"And it really worked," Alec said, gnawing on his thumbnail. "That whole area is full of militant conservationists now. They have a fair there every year." He gnawed furiously at his nail. "And on the supposed spot where the first lady died, no grass grows. Not a single blade. They've got it cordoned off." He struggled for a moment with a piece of separated nail between his teeth, at last freed it, examined it for a moment, then flicked it to the floor.

"You know, Alec," Argon said, "I've never liked that story. It just misses the mark as far as I'm concerned." She turned to Miriam. "Tree huggers tend sometimes not to have both feet on the ground. I want to be a spiritual and ecological warrior but I want both feet on the ground too."

Miriam looked at the white curving nail on the dirty floor. Jack wouldn't have had much to go on with that. Even Jack. Who were these people? They were all so desperate. You couldn't attribute their behavior to alcohol alone.

Other people gathered around the table, all talking about their experiences in the museum, all expressing awe at the exhibits, the mountain lions, the wading birds, the herds of elk and the exotics, particularly the exotics. They had come from far away to see this. Many of them returned, year after year.

"It's impossible to leave the place unmoved," a woman said.

"My favorite is the wood ibis on a stump in a lonely swamp," Priscilla said cautiously. "It couldn't be more properly delineated."

"That's a gorgeous specimen, all right. Not too many of those left," someone said.

" . . . so much better than a zoo. Zoos are so depressing. I hear the animals are committing suicide in Detroit. Hurling themselves into moats and drowning."

"I don't think other cities have that problem so much. Just Detroit."

"Even so. Zoos—"

"Oh, absolutely, this is so much nicer."

"Shoot to kill but not to mangle," Vern said.

"A lot of hunters just can't get that part down," Irene said. "And then they think they can bring those creatures here! To him!"

"I have my questions all prepared for tomorrow," Argon said. "I'm going to ask him about the eyes. Where do you get the eyes, I'm going to ask."

"A child got there ahead of you on that one, I'm afraid," Irene said. "Some little Goldilocks in a baseball hat."

"Oh, no!" Argon exclaimed. "What did he say?"

"He said he got the eyes from a supply house."

"I'm sure he would have expressed it differently to me," Argon said.

Alec, gnawing on his other thumb, looked helplessly at her.

"I just hate that," somebody said. "Someone else gets to ask your question, and you never get to the bottom of it."

"Excuse me," Miriam said quietly to Irene, "but why are you all here?"

"We're here with those we love because something big is going to happen here, we think," Irene said. "We want to be here for it. Then we'll have been here."

"You never know," Vern said. "Next year at this time, we might all have ridden over the skyline."

"But we're not ready to ride over the skyline yet," Irene said, patting his hand.

The lights in the Toad flickered, went out, then came back on again more weakly.

"It's closing time," several people said at once.

They all filed out into the night. Many were staying in campers and tents pitched around the museum, while others were staying in the hotel.

"I wouldn't want to pass my days in Detroit either," a voice said.

"I was using terror as an analgesic," Priscilla was explaining to no one, as far as Miriam could see. "And now I'm not."

Back in the room, Miriam sat with the lamp for some time. The legs were dusty so she wiped them down with a damp towel. She was thinking of getting different shades for it. Shade of the week. Even if she slurred her words when she thought, the lamp was able to follow her. There were tenses that human speech had yet to discover, and the lamp was able to incorporate these in its understanding as well. Miriam was excited about going to the museum in the morning. She planned on being there the moment the doors opened. The lamp had no interest in seeing the taxidermist. It was beyond that. They read a short, sad story about a brown dog whose faith in his master proved to be terribly misplaced, and spent a rather fitful night.

The next morning Miriam joined Jack and Carl in their room for breakfast.

"We've just finished brushing our teeth," Carl said. Jack's glasses were off and he regarded Miriam skittishly out of his good eye. She poured the coffee while Carl buttered the toast and Jack peeled the backing off Band-Aids and stuck them on things. He preferred children's adhesive bandages with spaceships and cartoon characters on them to the flesh-colored ones. He plastered some on Miriam's hands.

"He likes you!" Carl exclaimed.

They drank their coffee in silence. A fan whined in the room.

"Truck should be ready today," Carl said.

"Have you ever been in love before?" Miriam asked him.

"No," Carl said.

"Well, you're handling it very well, I think."

"No problem," Carl said.

Miriam held her cup. She pretended there was one more sip in it when there wasn't. "Why don't we all go to the museum?" she said. "That's what people do when they're here."

"I've heard about that," Carl said. "And I would say that a museum like that, and the people who run it—well, it's deeply into denial on every level. That's what I'd say. And Jack here, all his life he was the great verifier—weren't you, Jack? And still are, by golly." Jack cleared his throat and Carl gazed at him happily. "We don't want to go into a place like that," Carl said.

Miriam felt ashamed and determined. "I'll go over there for just an hour or two," she said.

There were many people in line ahead of her, although she didn't see any of her acquaintances from the night before. The museum was massive, with wide cement columns and curving walls of tinted glass. She could dimly make out static, shaggy arrangements within. The first room she entered was a replica of a famous basketball player's den in California. There were fifteen hundred wolf muzzles on the wall. A small bronze tablet said that Wilt Chamberlain had bought a whole year's worth of wolves from an Alaskan bounty hunter. It said he wanted the room to have an unequivocally masculine look. Miriam heard one man say hoarsely to another, "He got that, by god." The next few rooms were reproductions of big-game hunters' studies and full of heads and horns and antlers. In the restaurant, a group of giraffes were arranged behind the tables as though in the act of chewing grass, the large lashed eyes in their angular Victorian faces content. In the petting area, children toddled among the animals, pulling their tails and shaking their paws. Miriam stepped quickly past flocks and herds and prides of creatures to stand in a glaring space before a polar bear and two cubs.

"Say hi to the polar bear," a man said to his child.

"Hi!" the child said.

"She's protecting her newborn cubs, that's why she's snarling like that," the man said.

"It's dead," Miriam remarked. "The whole little family."

"Hi, polar bear," the child crooned. "Hi, hi, hi."

"What's the matter with you?" the father demanded of Miriam. "People like you make me sick."

Miriam threw out her hand and slapped his jaw. He dropped the child's hand and she slapped him again even harder, then hurried from the room.

She wandered among the crowds. The museum was lit dimly and flute music played. The effect was that of a funeral parlor or a dignified cocktail lounge. All the animals were arranged in a state of extreme and hopeless awareness. Wings raised, jaws open, hindquarters bunched. All recaptured from death to appear at the brink of departure.

"They're glorious, aren't they?" a woman exclaimed.

"Tasteful," someone said.

"None of these animals died a natural death, though," a pale young man said. "That's what troubles me a little."

"These are trophy animals," his companion said. "It would be unnatural for them to die a natural death. It would be disgusting. It would be like Marilyn Monroe or something. James Dean, for example."

"It troubled me just a little. I'm all right now."

"That's not how things work, honey," his companion said.

Miriam threaded through a line of people waiting to see the taxidermist. He was seated in a glass room. Beside him was a small locked room filled with skins and false bodies. There were all kinds of shapes, white and smooth.

The taxidermist sat behind a desk on which there were various tools—scissors and forceps, calipers and stuffing rods. A tiny, brilliantly colored bird lay on a blotter. Behind him was a large nonhuman shape on which progress appeared to have slowed. It looked as though it had been in this stage of the process for a long time. The taxidermist was listening to a question that was being asked.

"I'm a poet," a man with a shovel-shaped face said, "and I recently accompanied two ornithologists into the jungles of Peru to discover heretofore unknown birds. I found the process of finding, collecting, identifying, examining and skinning hundreds of specimens for use in taxonomic studies tedious. I became disappointed. In other words, I found the labor of turning rare birds into specimens mundane. Isn't your work a bit mundane as well?"

"You're mundane," the taxidermist said. His voice was loud and seemed to possess a lot of chilled space around it. It was like an astronaut's voice.

He fixed his eyes on Miriam, then waved and gestured for her to come around to the side of the glass room. He pulled down a long black shade on which were the words *The Taxidermist Will Be Right Back*.

"I saw and heard everything back there," he said to Miriam. "There are monitors and microphones all over this place. I like a woman with spirit. I find that beliefs about reality affect people's actions to an enormous degree, don't you? Have you read Marguerite Porete's *Mirror of Simple Annihilated Souls?*"

Miriam shook her head. It sounded like something the lamp would like. She would try to acquire it.

"Really? I'm surprised. Well-known broad. She was burned at the stake, but an enormous crowd was converted to her favor after witnessing her attitude toward death."

"What was her attitude?" Miriam said.

"I don't know exactly. Thirteenth century. The records are muzzy. I guess she went out without a lot of racket about it. Women have been trying to figure out how to be strong for a long while. It's harder for a woman to find out than it is for a man. Not crying about stuff doesn't seem to be enough."

Miriam said nothing. Back in the room, the lamp was hovering over *Moby-Dick*. It would be deeply involved in it by now, slamming down Melville like water. The shapeless maw of the undifferentiating sea! God as indifferent, insentient Being, composed of an infinitude of deaths! Nature. Gliding ... bewitching ... majestic ... capable of universal catastrophe! The lamp was eating it up.

"I've been here for ten years," the taxidermist said. "I built this place up from nothing. The guy before me had nothing but a few ratty displays. Medallions were his specialty. Things have to look dead on a medallion, that's the whole point. But when I finished with something it looked alive. You could almost hear it breathe. But of course it wasn't breathing. Ha! It was best when I was working on it, that's when it really existed, but when I stopped ... uhhh," he said. "I've done as much as I can. I've reached my oubliette. Do you know what I'm saying?"

"I do," Miriam said.

"Oh," he said, "I'm crazy about the word *oubliette*. That word says it all."

"It's true," she said.

"You're perfect," he said. "I want to retire, and I want you to take my place."

"I couldn't possibly," Miriam said.

"No stuffing would be required. I've done all that, we're beyond that. You'd just be answering questions."

"I don't know anything about questions," Miriam said.

"The only thing you have to know is that you can answer them any way you want. The questions are pretty much the same, so you'll go nuts if you don't change the answers."

"I'll think about it," Miriam said. But actually she was thinking about the lamp. The odd thing was she had never been in love with an animal. She had just skipped that cross-species eroticism and gone right beyond it to altered parts. There was something wrong with that, she thought. It was so hopeless. Well, love was hopeless . . .

"I have certain responsibilities," Miriam said. "I have a lamp."

"That's a wonderful touch!" the taxidermist said. "And when things are slow you'll have all the animals too. There are over a thousand of them here, you know, and some of them are pretty darn rare. I think you'll be making up lots of stories about them."

It seemed a pretty good arrangement for the lamp. Miriam made up her mind. "All right," she said.

"You'll have a following in no time," the taxidermist said. "I'll finish up with these people and you can start in the morning."

There was still a long line of people waiting to get into the museum. Miriam passed them on her way out.

"I've been back five times," a bald woman was saying to her friend. "I think you'll find it's almost a quasi-religious experience."

"Oh, I think everything should be like that," her friend said.

Carl's big truck was no longer at the garage. Miriam gazed around but the truck did not reappear and probably, as far as she was concerned, never would. For most people, and apparently Carl and Jack were two of them, a breakdown meant that it was just a matter of time before they were back on the road again. She walked over to the hotel and up the stairs to their room. The door was open and the beds were stripped. The big pillows without their pretty covers looked like flayed things. A thin maid in a pink uniform was changing the channel on a television set. Something was being described by the announcer as *a plume of effluent surrounded by seagulls* . . .

The maid noticed her and said, "San Diego, a sewer pipe broke. A single pipe for one point four million people. A million four, what do they expect."

Miriam continued down the corridor and opened the door quietly to her own room. She looked at the lamp. The lamp looked back at her as though it had no idea who she was. Miriam knew that look. She'd always felt it was full of promise. Nothing could happen anywhere was the truth of it. And the lamp was burning with this. Burning!

Marabou

THE FUNERAL OF ANNE'S SON, HARRY, HAD NOT GONE smoothly. Other burials were taking place at the same hour, including that of a popular singer several hundred yards away whose mourner fans carried on loudly under a lurid striped tent. Still more fans pressed against the cemetery's wrought-iron gates, screaming and eating potato chips. Anne had been distracted. She gazed at the other service in disbelief, thinking of the singer's songs that she had heard now and then on the radio.

Her own group, Harry's friends, was subdued. They were pale, young, and all wore sunglasses. Most of them were classmates from the prep school he had graduated from two years before, and all were addicts, or former addicts of some sort. Anne couldn't tell the difference between those who were recovering and those who were still hard at it. She was sure there was a difference, of course, and it only appeared there wasn't. They all had a manner. There were about twenty of them, boys and girls, strikingly alike in black. Later she took them all out to a restaurant. "Death . . . by none art thou understood," one boy kept saying. "Henry Vaughan."

They were all bright enough, Anne supposed. After a while he stopped saying it. They had calamari, duck, champagne, everything. They were on the second floor of the restaurant and had the place to themselves. They stayed for hours. By the time they left, one girl was saying earnestly, "You know a word I like is *interplanetary*."

Then she brought them back to the house, although she locked Harry's rooms. Young people were sentimentalists, consumers. She didn't want them carrying off Harry's things, his ties and tapes, anything at all. They sat in the kitchen. They were beginning to act a little peculiar, Anne thought. They didn't talk about Harry much, though one of them remembered a time when Harry was driving and he stopped at all the green lights and proceeded on the red. They all acted as though they'd been there. This seemed a fine thing to remember about Harry. Then someone, a floppy-haired boy who looked frightened, remembered something else, but it turned out this was associated with a boy named Pete who wasn't even present.

At about one o'clock in the morning, Anne said that when she and Harry were in Africa, during the very first evening at the hotel in Victoria Falls, he claimed he'd seen a pangolin, a peculiar anteater-like animal. He described it, and that's clearly what it was, but a very rare thing, an impossible thing for him to have seen, really, and no one in the group they would be traveling with believed him. He had been wandering around the hotel grounds by himself, so there were no other witnesses. The group went on to discuss the falls. Everyone could verify the impression the falls made. So many hundreds of millions of gallons of water went over each minute or something, and there was a drop of more than 350 feet. Even so, everyone was quite aware it wasn't like that, no one was satisfied with that. The sound of the falls was like silence, total amplified silence, the sight of it exclusionary. And all that could be done was to look at it, this astonishing thing, Victoria Falls, then eventually stop looking and go on to something else.

The next day Harry had distinguished himself further by exclaiming over a marabou stork, and someone in the group told him that marabous were gruesome things, scavengers, "morbidity distilled," in the words of this fussy little person, and certainly nothing to get excited about when there were hundreds of beautiful and strange creatures in Africa that one could enjoy and identify and point out to the others. Imagine, Anne said, going to an immense new continent and being corrected as to one's feelings, one's perceptions, in such a strange place. And it was not as though everything was known. Take the wild dogs, for example. Attitudes had changed utterly about the worth of wild dogs . . .

Abruptly, she stopped. She had been silent much of the evening and felt that this outburst had not gone over particularly well. Harry's friends were making margaritas. One of them had gone out and just returned with more tequila. They were watching her uncomfortably, as though they felt she should fluff up her stories on Harry a bit.

Finally one of them said, "I didn't know Harry had been to Africa."

This surprised her. The trip to Africa hadn't been a triumph, exactly, but it hadn't been a disaster either and could very well have been worse. They had been gone a month, and this was very recently. But it didn't matter. She would probably never see these children again.

They sat around the large kitchen. They were becoming more and more strange to her. She wondered what they were all waiting for. One of them was trying to find salt. Was there no salt? He opened a cupboard and peered inside, bringing out a novelty set, a plastic couple, Amish or something; she supposed the man was pepper, the woman salt. They were all watching him as he turned the things over and shook them against his cupped hand. Anne never cooked, never used anything in this kitchen, she and Harry ate out, so these things were barely familiar to her. Then, with what was really quite a normal gesture, the boy unscrewed the head off the little woman and poured the salt inside onto a saucer.

Someone shrieked in terror. It was the floppy-haired boy; he was yelling, horrified. Anne was confused for an instant. Was Harry dying again? Was Harry all right? The boy was howling, his eyes rolling in his head. The others looked at him dully. One of the girls giggled. "Uh-oh," she said.

Two of the boys were trying to quiet him. They all looked like Harry, even the boy who was screaming.

"You'd better take him to the emergency room," Anne said.

"Maybe if he just gets a little air, walks around, gets some air," another boy said.

"You'd all better go now," Anne said.

IT WAS NOT YET DAWN, STILL VERY DARK. ANNE SAT THERE ALONE in the bright kitchen in her black dress. There was a run in her stocking. The dinner in the restaurant had cost almost a thousand dollars, and Harry probably wouldn't even have liked it. She hadn't liked it. She wanted to behave differently now, for Harry's sake. He hadn't been perfect, Harry, he'd been a very troubled boy, a very misunderstood boy, but she had never let him go, never, until now. She knew that he couldn't be aware of that, that she now had let him go. She knew that between them, from now on, she alone would be the one who realized things. She wasn't going to deceive herself in that regard. Even so, she knew she wasn't thinking clearly about this.

After some time, she got up and packed a duffel bag for Africa, exactly as she had done that time before. The bag and its contents could weigh no more than twenty-two pounds. When she was finished, she put it in the hallway by the door. Outside it was still dark, as dark as it had been hours ago, though this scarcely seemed possible.

Perhaps she would go back to Africa.

There was a knock on the door. Anne looked at it, startled, a thick door with locks. Then she opened it. A girl was standing there, not the *interplanetary* one but another, who had particularly relished the dinner. She had been standing there smoking for a while before she knocked. Several cigarette butts were ground into the high-gloss cerulean of the porch.

"May I come in?" the girl asked.

"Why, no," Anne said. "No, you may not."

"Please," the girl said.

Anne shut the door.

She went into the kitchen and threw the two parts of the saltshaker into the trash. She tossed the small lady's companion in as well. Harry had once said to her, "Look, this is amazing, I don't know how this could have happened but I have these spikes in my head. They must have been there for a while, but I swear, I swear to you, I just noticed them. But I got them out! On the left side. But on the right side it's more difficult because they're in a sort of helmet, and the helmet is fused to my head, see? Can you help me?"

She had helped him then. She had stroked his hair with her fingers for a long, long time. She had been very careful, very thorough. But that had been a unique situation. Usually, she couldn't help him.

There was a sound at the door again, a determined knocking. Anne walked to it quickly and opened it. There were several of Harry's friends there, not just the girl but not all of them either.

"You don't have to be so rude," one of them said.

They were angry. They had lost Harry, she thought, and they missed him.

"We loved Harry too, you know," one of them said. His tie was loose, and his breath was sweet and dry, like sand.

"I want to rest now," Anne said. "I must get some rest."

"Rest," one of them said in a soft, scornful voice. He glanced at the others. They ignored him.

"Tell us another story about Harry," one of them said. "We didn't get the first one."

"Are you frightening me?" Anne said. She smiled. "I mean, are you trying to frighten me?"

"I think Harry saw that thing, but I don't think he was ever there. Is that what you meant?" one of them said with some effort. He turned and then, as though he were dancing, moved down the steps and knelt on the ground, where he lowered his head and began spitting up quietly.

"Harry will always be us," one of them said. "You better get used to it. You better get your stories straight."

"Good night," Anne said.

"Good night, *please*," they said, and Anne shut the door.

She turned off all the lights and sat in the darkness of her house. Before long, as she knew it would, the phone began to ring. It rang and rang, but she didn't have to answer it. She wouldn't do it. It would never be that once, again, when she'd learned that Harry died, no matter how much she knew in her heart that the past was but the present in that future to which it belonged.

The Visiting Privilege

DONNA CAME AS A VISITOR IN HER LONG BLACK COAT. IT WAS spring but still cool, and she never wore light colors, she was no buttercup. She was visiting her friend Cynthia, who was in Pond House for depression. Donna never had a drink before she visited Cynthia. She shunned her habitual excesses and arrived sober and aware, with an exquisite sinking feeling. She thought that Pond House was an unfortunate name, ponds being stagnant, artificial and small. This wasn't just her opinion. A pond was indeed an artificially confined body of water, she argued, but Cynthia thought Pond was probably the name of the hospital wing's benefactor. Cynthia had three roommates, a woman in her sixties and two obese teenagers. Donna liked to pretend that the old woman was her mother. Hi, she'd say, you look great today, what a pretty sweatshirt.

Donna had been visiting Cynthia for about a week now. She could scarcely imagine what she had done with herself before Cynthia had the grace to get herself committed to Pond House. She liked everything about it but particularly sitting in Cynthia's room, speaking quietly with her while the others listened. They didn't even pretend not to listen, the others. Sometimes she and Cynthia would stroll down to the lounge and get a snack from the fridge. In the lounge, goofy helium balloons in the shapes of objects or food but with human features were tied to the furniture with ribbon. They bobbed there opposite the nurses' station, and people would bat them as they passed by. Cynthia thought the balloons would be deeply disturbing to anyone who was already disturbed, yet in fact everyone considered them amusing. None of the people at Pond House were supposed to be seriously ill, at least on Floor Three. On Floor Four it was another matter. But here they were supposed to be sort of ruefully aware of their situations, and were encouraged to believe that they could possibly be helped. Cynthia had come here because she had picked up the habit of committing destructive and selfish acts, the most recent being the torching of her boyfriend's car, a black Corvette. The boyfriend was married but Cynthia strongly suspected he was gay. He drove her crazy. "He's a taker and not a giver, Donna," she told Donna earnestly.

She said she was so discouraged that everything seemed vaguely yellow to her, that she saw everything through a veil of yellow.

"That was in an article I read," Donna said excitedly. "The yellow part."

"You know, Donna," Cynthia said, "you're part of my problem."

When Cynthia got like this, Donna would excuse herself and go away for a while. Or she would go back to the room and talk with the old woman. She got a kick out of being extraordinarily friendly to her. Once she brought her gum, another time a jar of night cream. She ignored the obese teenagers, but one afternoon one of them deliberately bumped into her as she walked down the hall. The girl's flesh was hard and she smelled of coconut. She thrust her face close to Donna's. Her pores were large and clean and Donna could see the contacts resting on the corneas of her eyes.

"I'm passionate, intense and filled with private reverie, and so is my friend," the girl said, "so don't slime us like you do." Then she punched Donna viciously on the arm. Donna felt like crying but she was only a visitor. She didn't have to come here so frequently; she was really coming here too much, sometimes two and three times a day.

There were group meetings twice a week and Donna always tried to be present for these, although she was not permitted to attend them. Sometimes, however, if she stood just outside the door, the nurses and psychologists didn't notice her right away. Cynthia and the fat teenagers and the old lady and a half dozen others would sit around a large table and say anything they wanted to.

"I DREAMED THAT I THREW UP A FOX," ONE OF THE FAT GIRLS SAID. Really, Donna couldn't tell them apart.

"I shit something that looked like an onion once," a man said. "It just kept coming out of me. I pulled it out of myself with my own hands. I thought it was the Devil, but it was a worm. A gift from Central America."

"That is so disgusting," the other fat girl said, "That is the most—"

"Hey!" the man said. "Get yourself a life, woman."

The worm thing caused the old lady to request to be excused. Donna walked back to the room with her, and they sat down on her bed.

"Feel my heart," the old lady said. "It's pounding. I wasn't brought up that way."

The old lady liked to play cards, and she and Donna often used an old soiled deck that had pictures of colorful fish on it. Donna pretended she was in the cabin of a boat on a short, safe trip to a lovely island. The old woman was a mysterious opponent, not at all what she seemed. Donna had, in fact, been told by the nurses that she was considerably more impaired than she appeared to be. Beyond the window of the cabin were high waves, pursuing and accompanying them. The waves were an essential part of the world the boat required, but they bore malice toward the boat, that much was obvious.

"What kind of fish are these," Donna asked.

"These are reef residents," the old lady said.

They played a variation of Spit in the Ocean. Donna had had no idea that there were so many variations of this humble game.

The two fat girls came in and lay down on their beds. The old lady was really opening up to Donna. She was telling her about her husband and her little house.

"After my husband died, I was afraid someone might come in and . . ." She passed her finger across her throat. "I bought one of those men. Safe-T-Man II, the New Generation. You know, the ones that look as though they're six feet tall but can be folded up and put in a little tote bag? I put him in the car or I put him in my husband's easy chair right in front of the window. He had all kinds of clothes. He had a leather coat. He had a baseball cap."

"Where is he now," Donna asked.

"He's in his little tote bag. Actually, he frightened me a little, Safe-T-Man. I think I ordered him too dark or something. I never did get used to him."

"That's racist," one of the fat girls said.

"Yeah, what a racist remark," the other one said.

"I bet he wonders what happened to me," the old lady said. "I bet my car does too. One minute you're on the open road, one excitement after another, the next you're in a dark garage. I'm not afraid of dying, but I don't want to die old."

She was quite old already, of course, but the fat girls did not challenge her on this. Cynthia came into the room, eating a piece of fruit, a nectarine or something.

"The first thing I'm going to do when I get out of here is go home and make Festive Chicken," the old woman said. "I hope you'll all be my guests for dinner."

The fat girls and Cynthia stared at her.

"I'd love to," Donna said. "What is Festive Chicken? Can I bring anything? Wine? A salad?"

"It requires toothpicks," the old woman said. "You bake it with toothpicks but then you take the toothpicks out."

"It sounds wonderful," Donna said.

Cynthia rolled her eyes. "Would you give it a rest," she said to Donna.

"I'm tired now," the old woman said sweetly. "I'm tired of playing cards." She put the cards back in the box but it didn't have reef residents on it. It had a picture of a drab, many-spired European city, the very opposite of a reef resident.

"These don't belong in this box!" she cried. "It's the first time I've noticed this. Would you go to my house and bring back the other deck of cards?" she asked Donna.

"Sure," Donna said.

"My house is a little strange," the old woman said.

"What do you mean?"

"I bet it is," one of the fat girls said.

"I love my little house," the old woman said anxiously. "I want to get back to it as soon as I can."

She gave Donna the address and a key from her pocketbook. That evening, when visiting hours were over, Donna drove to the house, which was boxy and tidy with a crushed-rock yard and a dead nestling in the driveway. The house didn't seem that strange to Donna. One would be desperate to get out of it, certainly. There were lots of things that were meant to be plugged into wall outlets but none of them were.

She found the cards almost immediately, in the kitchen. There were the colorful fish on the cover of the box and the deck inside had the image of the foreign city. Idly, she opened the refrigerator, which was full of ketchup, nothing but bottles of ketchup, each one partially used. Donna had an urge to top off some bottles from others, to reduce the unseemly number, but with not much effort she resisted this.

On the drive back to her apartment she stopped at a restaurant and had several drinks in the bar. The bartender's name was Lucy. She had just returned from a vacation. She had spent forty-five minutes swimming with dolphins. The dolphin that had persisted in keeping Lucy company had had an immense boner.

"He kept gliding past me, gliding past," Lucy said, moving her hand through the air. "I kept worrying about the little kids. They're always bringing in these little kids who have only weeks to live due to one thing or another. I would think it would be pretty undesirable for them to experience a dolphin with a boner."

"But the dolphins know better than that, don't they?" Donna said.

"It's not all that relaxing to swim with them, actually," the bartender said. "They like some people better than others, and the ones that get ignored feel like shit. You know, out of the Gaia loop."

People in the restaurant kept requesting exotic drinks that Lucy had to look up in her *Bartender's Bible*. After a while, Donna went home.

The next afternoon she swept into Pond House in her long black coat bearing a bunch of daffodils as a gift in general.

Cynthia was in the lounge in a big chintz slipcovered chair reading *Anna Karenina*.

"Should you be reading that," Donna asked.

Cynthia wouldn't talk to her.

Donna found the old lady and gave her the deck of cards.

"I'm so relieved," the old lady said. "That could have been such a problem, such a problem. Would you do me another favor? Would you get my dog and bring him to me here?"

Donna was enthusiastic about this. "Do you have a dog? Where is he?"

"He's in my house."

"Is anyone feeding him?" Donna said. "Does he have water?" She had found her vocation, she was sure of it. She could do this forever. She felt like a long-distance swimmer in that place long-distance swimmers go in their heads when they're good.

"Nooooooo," the old woman said. "He doesn't need water." She, too, looked delighted. She and Donna beamed at each other. "He's a good dog, a watchdog."

"I didn't see him when I was there," Donna admitted.

"He wasn't watching you," the old lady said.

"What breed of dog is he," Donna asked.

She suddenly looked concerned. "He's something you plug in."

"Oh," Donna said, disappointed. "I think I did notice him." He looked like a stereo speaker. She thought they'd been talking more along the lines of Cerberus, the dog that guarded the gates of hell. Those Greeks! It wasn't that you couldn't get in, it was that you couldn't get out. And that honey-cake business ... Actually, she had never grasped the honey-cake business.

"He detects intruders up to thirty feet and he barks. He can detect them through glass, brick, wood and cement. The closer they get, the louder and faster he barks. He's just a little individual but he sounds ferocious. I always liked him better than Safe-T-Man. I got them at the same time."

"But he'd be barking all the time here," Donna said. "You have to consider that," she added.

"He can be quiet," the woman said. "He can be good."

"I'll get him for you then," Donna said as though she had just made a difficult decision.

As she was leaving Pond House she passed a man dressed all in red yelling into the telephone. There was a pay phone at the very heart of Floor Three and it was always in use. "What were you born with, an ax in your hand?" he shouted.

Donna returned the next day with the old lady's dog, which she carried in a smart brown and white Bendel shopping bag she'd been saving. She arrived just about the time the group meeting was coming to a close. Lingering near the door, she saw the fat teenagers and Cynthia's round neat head with its fashionable haircut. A male patient she hadn't seen before was saying, "Hey, if it looks, walks, talks, smells and feels like the anima, then it is the anima." Donna thought this very funny and somewhat obscene. "Miss!" someone called to her. "You are not allowed in these meetings!" She went back to Cynthia's room and sat on her bed. The old woman's bed was stripped down to the ticking. She sat and looked at it vacantly.

When Cynthia came in, she said, "Donna, that old lady died, honest to god. We were all sitting around after dinner eating our goddamn Jell-O and she just tipped over."

"I have something she wanted here," Donna said, raising the bag. "This is hers, it's from her house."

"Get rid of it," Cynthia said. "Listen, act quickly and positively." She began to cry.

Donna thought her friend's response somewhat peculiar, but that was probably why she was in Pond House.

As the day wore on, it was disclosed that the woman had no family. There was no one.

"There wouldn't have been any Festive Chicken either," Cynthia said, "that's for sure." She had her old mouth back on her, Donna noticed.

There was discussion in the room about what had happened. The old lady had been eating the Jell-O. She hadn't said a word. She'd expressed no dismay.

"She was clueless," one of the fat girls said.

"Were you two friends before or did that happen here," Donna asked them.

They looked at her with hatred. "She's a nut fucker, I think," one of them said.

They looked so much alike Donna couldn't be sure which of them had struck her in the hallway. She thought of them as Dum and Dee. She pretended she was a docent leading tours. The neuroses of these two, Dum and Dee, are so normal they're of little concern to us, she would say, indicating the fat girls. Then she pretended they were her jailers over whom she held indisputable moral sway.

The barking-dog alarm had not worked at the old lady's house. It was a simple enough thing, with few adjustments that could be made to it; its function would either be realized or it wouldn't, and it wasn't. Donna had gone outside into the street and walked slowly back toward the house, avoiding the nestling. Then she had run, waving her arms. There had been no barking at all, only the sound of her own feet on the crushed-rock yard. It had not worked in her own apartment either. It had not even felt warm.

Poor old soul, Donna thought.

Night was flickering at the corners of the hospital. There was the smell of potatoes, the sound of wheels bringing the supper trays. They always made the visitors leave around this time.

"Cynthia," Donna said. "I'll see you tomorrow."

"Why?" Cynthia said.

At home, Donna pretended she was on a train with no ticket, eluding the conductor as it sped toward some destination on gleaming rails. She made herself a drink. She almost finished it, then freshened it a bit. The phone rang and it was Cynthia. She was delighted it was Cynthia.

"You will not believe this, Donna," Cynthia said. "You know that new guy, the really annoying one? Well, at dinner he was saying that when women attempt suicide they often don't succeed, but with men they do it on the first go-round. He said that simple statistic says it all about the difference between men and women. He said that men are doers and that women are deceivers and flirts, and Holly just threw back her chair and—"

"Who's Holly," Donna asked.

"My roommate, for god's sake, the one who hates you. She attacked this guy. She gouged out one of his eyes with a spoon."

"She gouged it *out?*"

"I didn't think it could be done, but boy, she knew how to do it."

"I wonder if that could have been me," Donna said.

"Oh, I think so. It's bedlam in here." Cynthia laughed wildly. "I want to leave, Donna, though I don't feel any better. But I could leave, you know. I could just walk right out of here."

"Really?" Donna said. She thought, When I get out of here, I'm going to be gone.

"But I think I should feel better. I lack goals. I need goals."

Maybe it wasn't such a good idea, Cynthia using the phone. Donna preferred sitting quietly with her in Pond House, offering to get her little things she had expressed no desire for, reflecting about Dennis, her married man who hadn't come by to see her even once. Of course he was probably still annoyed about his car, although he had filed no charges.

Cynthia kept talking, pretty much about her life, the details of which Donna had heard before and which were no more riveting this time. She'd had a difficult time of it, starting in childhood. She had been an intense little thing but was thwarted, thwarted. Donna walked around with the phone to her ear, making another drink, crushing an ant or two that ventured onto the countertop, staring out the window at the dark only to realize that she wasn't seeing the dark, merely a darkened image of herself and the objects behind her. She sipped her drink and turned toward some picture postcards she'd taped to one of the cupboards. Some of them had been up for years. One was of a city, a cheerless and civilized city similar to the one on the old woman's playing cards.

Cynthia was saying, "I just can't accept so much, you know, Donna, and I feel, I really feel this, that my capacity to adapt to what *is* has been exceeded. I—"

"Cynthia," Donna said. "We're all alone in a meaningless world. That's it. OK?"

"That's so easy for you to say!" Cynthia screamed.

There was a loud crack as the connection was broken.

Donna had no recollection who had sent her the postcard or from where. She couldn't think what had prompted her to display it, either. The city held no allure for her. She had no intention of taking it down and looking at it more closely.

Later, she lay in bed trying to find sleep by recounting the ranks of poker hands. Royal flush, straight flush, four of a kind, full house ... A voice kept saying in her head, *Out or In. Huh? Which will it be?* Then it was dawn. She showered and dressed and hurried to Pond House, where she had coffee in the cafeteria. Her eyes darted around, falling on everything, glittering. There was her coat, hanging on a hook next to her table. The coat suddenly seemed preposterous to her. Honestly, what must she look like in that coat?

Up on Floor Three, Cynthia wasn't in her room but one fat girl was, her face red and her eyes swollen from crying.

"I just lost my friend," the fat girl said.

"You're not Holly, then," Donna said.

"I wish I was," the fat girl said. "I wish I was Holly." She lay there on her bed, crying loudly.

Donna looked out the window at the street below. You couldn't open the windows. A tree outside was struggling to burst into bloom but had been compromised heavily by the parking area. Big chunks of its bark had been torn away by poorly parked cars. When she was a child, visiting Florida, she'd seen a palm tree burst into flames. It was beautiful! Then rats as long as her downy child's arm had rushed down the trunk. Later, she learned that it was not unusual for a palm tree to do this on occasion, given the proper circumstances. This tree didn't want to do anything like that, though. It couldn't. It struggled along quietly.

She turned from the window and left the room, where the fat girl continued sobbing. She walked down the corridor, humming a little. She pretended she was a virus, wandering without aim through someone's body. She found Cynthia in the lounge, painting her long and perfect nails.

Cynthia regarded her sourly. "I really wish you wouldn't visit me anymore," she said.

A nurse appeared from nowhere like they did. "Who are you visiting?" she said to Donna.

Cynthia looked at her little bottle of nail polish and tightened the cap.

"You have to be visiting someone," the nurse said.

"She's not visiting me," Cynthia muttered.

"What?" the nurse said.

"She's not visiting me," Cynthia said loudly.

After some remonstrance, Donna found herself being steered away from Cynthia and down the hallway to the elevator. "That's it," the nurse said. "You've lost your privileges here." Donna was alone in the elevator as it went down. On the ground floor some people got on and the elevator went up again. On Floor Three they got off. Donna went back down. She walked through the parking lot to her car.

She would come back tomorrow and avoid Cynthia and the nurse, too. For now, she had to decide which route to take home. It was how they made roads these days; there were five or six ways to get to the same place. On the highway she ran into construction almost immediately. There was always construction. Cans and cones, those bright orange arrows blinking, and she had to merge. She inched over, trying to merge. They wouldn't let her in! She pushed into the line of cars. Then she realized she was part of a funeral procession. Their lights were on. She was part of a cortege, of an anguished throng. Should she turn on her lights to show sympathy, to apologize? She put on her sunglasses. People didn't turn their lights on in broad daylight just for funerals, though. They turned them on for all sorts of things. Remembering somebody or something. Actually, showing you remembered somebody or something, which was different. People were urged to put them on for safety too. *Lights on for Safety*. But this was a funeral, no doubt about it.

After what seemed an eternity, the road opened up again and Donna turned the car sharply into the other lane. In moments she had left the procession far behind.

On her own street she parked and walked quickly toward her door. She felt an unpleasant excitement. It was midmorning, and as always the neighborhood was quiet. Who knew what people did here? She never saw anyone on this street.

Then a dog began to bark, quite alarmingly. As she walked on, the rapid cry grew louder, more frantic. It was the poor old soul's dog, Donna thought, the gray machine, somehow operative again, resuming its purpose. She *knew*. But it sounded so real, so remarkably real, and the disorder she felt was so remarkably real as well that she hesitated. She could not go forward. Then, she couldn't go back.

Substance

WALTER GOT THE SILK PAJAMAS CLEARLY WORN. DIANNE got the candlesticks. Tim got the two lilac bushes, one French purple, the other white—an alarming gift, lilacs being so evocative of the depth and dumbness of death's kingdom that they made Tim cry. They were large and had to be removed with a backhoe, which did not please the landlord, who didn't get anything, although he didn't have to return the last month's deposit either. Lucretia got the Manhattan glasses. They were delicate, with a scroll of flowers etched just beneath the rim. There were four of them. Andrew got the wristwatch. Betsy got the barbells. Jack got a fairly useless silver bowl. Angus got the photo basket. Louise got the dog.

Louise would have preferred anything to the dog, right down to the barbells. Nothing at all would have pleased her even more. It was believed that the animal had been witness to the suicide. The dog had either seen the enactment or come into the room shortly afterward. He might have been in the kitchen eating his chow or he might have been sitting on the porch, taking in the entire performance. He was a quiet, medium-size dog. He wasn't the kind who would have run for help. He wasn't one of those dogs who would have attempted to prevent the removal of the body from the house.

Louise took the dog immediately to a kennel and boarded it. She couldn't imagine why she, of all people, had been given the dog. But in the note Elliot had left he had clearly stated, *And to Louise my dog, Broom.* The worst of it was that none of them remembered Elliot's having a dog. They had never seen it before, but now suddenly there was a dog in the picture.

"He said he was thinking of getting a dog sometime," Jack said.

"But wouldn't he have said 'I got a dog'? He never said that," Dianne said.

"He must have just gotten it. Maybe he got it the day before. Or even that morning, maybe," Angus said.

This alarmed Louise.

"I'm sure he never thought you'd keep it," Lucretia said.

This alarmed her even more.

"Oh, I don't know!" Lucretia said. "I just wanted to make you feel better."

Louise was racking up expenses at the kennel. The dog weighed under thirty-five pounds but that still meant fourteen dollars a day. If he had weighed between fifty and a hundred, it would have been twenty dollars, and after that it went up again. Louise didn't have all that much money. She worked at a florist's and sometimes at an auto-glass tinting establishment, cutting and ironing on the darkest film allowable by law, which at twenty percent was less than most people wanted but all they were going to get. Her own car had confetti glitter on the rear window. It was like fireworks going off in the darkness of her glass.

She was sitting alone in a bar one evening after work worrying about the money it was costing to board the dog, who had been at the kennel for a week and a half. Louise had her friends, of course, and she saw them practically constantly, but sometimes she liked to be alone. Occasionally, she even took trips by herself, accompanied only by strangers, cruises or camping trips to difficult places where she was invariably lonely and misunderstood. These trips reminded her of last evenings, one of those that occur over and over in one's life, and she thought of them as good training. She had learned a lot from them. More than enough by now, probably.

In the bar was a long fish tank that served as a wall separating it from the restaurant beyond. Louise had never been in this place before and would not select it again. She didn't like to look at the fish, one of which was trailing a cloud of mucus behind it. In the restaurant beyond the fish she saw an older man deep in conversation with a party or parties outside her vision. He had moist, closely cut hair and a Band-Aid high up on his temple. A line of blood extended several inches down from the Band-Aid. Louise became engrossed in watching him chatting and smiling and sawing away at his steak or whatever it was. But she looked away for a moment and when she looked back the blood was gone. He must have wiped it off with a napkin, perhaps dipped in his water glass. Someone in the party he was with was fond of him or even possibly more than fond and told him about the blood. That was Louise's first thought, though it had certainly taken them long enough to mention it.

The next morning she went to the kennel. A girl brought the dog out. It had yellowish wavy fur.

"Is that the right one?" Louise asked. The girl looked at her expressionlessly and cracked her gum. "It's really not mine," Louise explained. "It belongs to a friend."

The dog crouched miserably on the floor in the backseat of Louise's car. It didn't even lie down.

"You're going to get sick down there," Louise said. The dog was clearly not habituated to riding in cars, and had no sense of the happiness it could bring.

After a week, she had discerned no habits. The dog didn't seem morose, merely withdrawn. She began calling it Broom with a certain amount of reluctance.

Every other week, there would be a party at one of their houses, though it wasn't Louise's turn just yet. Rent was cheap, so they all lived in these big ruined houses. She went over to Jack's and everyone was already there, drinking gimlets and looking at a rat Jack had caught beneath the sink on one of his glue traps.

"I'm not going to use these things again," Jack said. "They're depressing."

"I use them," Walter said, "but I never get any rats."

"You're not putting them in the right places," Jack said.

The rat watched them in a sort of theatrical manner.

One of the twins, Wilbur, got up and opened a window. He picked up the trap and sailed it with its rat accompanist into the street to fall amid the passing traffic.

"I usually take it down to the Dumpster," Jack said.

Wilbur and his twin, Daisy, were the only ones who said they remembered Broom. They said he hadn't eaten from a bowl but off a Columbia University dinner plate. But in their far-out nods Wilbur and Daisy could picture almost anything. They spent most of their time lovingly shooting each other up. They had not been acknowledged in the note as gift recipients, although of course they didn't care. They insisted that matters would not have taken such a dreary turn had they been able to introduce Elliot to the great Heroisch, the potent, powerful, large and appealing Heroisch. The twins were so innocent they got on everyone's nerves. They loved throwing up on junk. A joy develops, they'd say, a real joy. It's not like throwing up at all.

They all had their big, quietly rotting houses, even the twins. Louise had a solarium in hers that leaked badly. In the rear was an overgrown yard with a birdhouse nailed to each tree. Some trees had more than one. The previous tenants must have been demented, Louise thought. How could they imagine that birds want to live like that?

At Jack's they drank, but lightly except for Dianne, who was drinking far too much recently. She'd said, "I began to wonder if it was worthwhile to undertake what I was doing at the moment. Pick a moment, any moment. I began to wonder. If I only had today and not tomorrow, would it be worthwhile to undertake what I was doing at the moment? I addressed myself to that very worthwhile question and I had to admit, well, no."

But no one tried to interfere with Dianne. They were getting over the death of their friend Elliot—each in his or her own way, was the understanding.

"It takes four full seasons to get over a death," Angus said. "Spring and summer, winter and fall."

"Fall and winter," Andrew said.

Everyone was annoyed with Angus because he had taken all the photos out of the flat woven basket where they'd always been kept and arranged them in albums, ordered by years or occasions. This pleased no one. It wasn't the same. The effect was different. Everything had looked like a gala before. Now none of it did.

They talked about the things Elliot had given them. They could not understand what he had been attempting to say. All his other possessions had been trucked away and stored. A brother was supposed to come for them. He was sick or lived in Turkey or some goddamn place, who cared. In any case, he hadn't shown up here yet.

Louise didn't think it was right that she had been given something alive. None of the others had. She made this point frequently but no one had an explanation for it.

The twins had been reading Pablo Neruda and had come across the line *Death also goes through the world dressed as a broom*, but they weren't going to tell Louise that. *Dressed* didn't seem right anyway, maybe it was the translation. But Neruda was a giant among pygmies, his mind impeccable. They were going to keep their mouths shut.

More than a month passed. Louise was working full-time in the florist's shop. She liked working there, at the long cutting table, wearing an apricot-colored smock among the unnatural blooms. A woman came in one day just before closing. She wanted to send a dozen roses to a young veterinarian assistant.

"My dog bit her when she tried to lift him for an X-ray," the woman said. "I'm so embarrassed."

Louise had never been interested in the reasons people bought flowers. "I don't like dogs," Louise said.

"Really?" the woman said. "I don't know where I'd be without my Buckie."

"You wouldn't be in here buying these roses," Louise said.

Another season insinuated itself. It was Tim's turn to give a party but things were not going well for him. The lilacs had not survived transplanting. They would never come back. Tim had done his best, but that wasn't good enough. He had also had an unhappy experience with a pair of swans. He had been following their fortunes ever since he had witnessed them mating in a marsh beside the highway. "They twined their necks like heraldry afterwards," he said. "Heraldry." But after weeks of guarding the nest the male disappeared, and a week later the female vanished. Tim had watched them so arduously, and suddenly they were gone. He was sure someone had murdered them. "Remember the lied about the swan?" he asked.

"Leda and the swan?" Angus volunteered.

"The German song," Tim said impatiently. "The lied," he said, upset.

It was about a swan who so loved a hunter by the marsh that she became a woman and married him and had three children. Then one night the king of the swans called to her to come back or else he would die, so slowly she turned into a swan again, slowly opened her wide white wings and left her husband and her children ...

"Her wide white wings," Tim said, weeping.

Lucretia gave a party out of turn. Everyone came except Dianne and Tim. Walter asked Louise about the dog.

"Old Broom," Louise answered. "Poor Broom." The dog was not demanding. It was modest in its requirements. It could square itself off like a package in a chair, it could actually *resemble* a package, but that was about it. Everyone half expected that Broom would have disappeared by now, run away.

"Listen," Lucretia said. "I'll tell you. One of those glasses I was given got a little chip on the rim and I found myself going to a jeweler's and getting an estimate for filing it down. It cost seventy-five dollars and I paid for it, but I'm not picking it up. I didn't even give them the right telephone number. I decided, enough's enough."

Walter confessed that he had thrown away the silk pajamas immediately, without a modicum of ceremony.

"None of it makes a bit of sense," Betsy said. "What would I want with barbells? I took those barbells down to the park and left them by the softball field. You're a saint, Louise. I could see you maybe not wanting to take it to the pound, but I always thought, She's going to take it to a no-kill facility."

"What do you mean," Louise asked.

"A no-kill facility. Isn't that self-explanatory?"

"Well, no," Louise said, "not really. I mean it doesn't sound all that great somehow."

"Most places keep unwanted pets for two weeks and then, if they're not adopted, they put them to sleep."

"Put them to sleep," Louise said. She didn't know anybody said that anymore and here was her friend Betsy saying it. It sounded like something you'd do with a small child in a pretty room while it was still light out.

"And these people never do. I've just heard about these places, I've never seen one. I don't think there are many of them, but they are around."

"I don't like the sound of it either," Andrew said, "oddly enough."

"You know that woman came into the florist's the other day to buy roses and I said to her, 'Oh no! Has Buckie bitten someone again?'" Louise said.

Her friends looked at her.

"And she said, 'I don't know what you're talking about.'" Louise laughed. "She was pretending she wasn't the same person."

Louise always wanted to talk about Broom with the others until they actually wanted to discuss him, then she didn't want to anymore.

Early one evening after work, Louise was sitting on the front steps of her house when a van pulled up across the street and a man got out. Louise was startled to see him walk over to her. He was deeply tanned with a ragged haircut. The collar of his shirt was too big for him.

"How do you do, Louise?" he said. "I'm Elliot's brother."

Louise cast herself back, remembering Elliot. She found him with more difficulty than usual, but then she had him, Elliot, she could see him. It was still him, exactly. Powerful Elliot. She said to the man, "You don't look at all like Elliot."

He seemed to be waiting for her to say more. When she didn't, he said, "I've been ill and out of the country. I couldn't travel, but I got here as soon as I was able. Elliot and I had quarreled. You can't imagine the pettiness of our quarrel, it was over nothing. We hadn't spoken for two years. I will never forgive myself." He paused. "I heard that he had a dog and that you have it now and it might be something of a burden to you. I'd like to have the dog. I'd like to buy it."

"I couldn't do that," Louise said simply.

"I insist on paying you something."

"No, it's impossible. I won't give the dog up," Louise said. He could be a vivisector for all she knew.

"It would mean a great deal to me," he said, his mouth trembling. "My brother's dog."

Louise shook her head.

"I can't believe this," he muttered.

"Believe what?" Louise said, looking at Elliot's brother, if that's who he was, although there was no reason to doubt him, not really.

He spoke again, patiently, as if she had utterly misunderstood his situation and the seriousness of his request. His guilt was almost holy, he was on a holy quest. He had determined that this was what must be done, the only thing that remained possible now to do.

"We were so close," he said. "He was my little brother. I taught him how to ski, how to drive. We went to the same college. I'd always protected him, he looked up to me, then there was this stupid, senseless quarrel. Now he's gone forever and I'm all ruined inside, it's destroyed me." He rubbed his chest as if something within him really was harrowed. "If I could care now for something he had cared for, then I would have something of my brother, of my brother's love."

"I don't mean to sound rude," Louise said, "but we've all been dealing with this for some time now and you suddenly appear, having been ill and out of the country both at the same time. Both at the same time," she repeated. "It's just so unnecessary now, your appearance. It's possible to come around too late."

"That's not true," he said. He was sallow beneath his tan. "Your friends, Elliot's friends, said they were sure you'd appreciate the opportunity, that they were sure you wouldn't mind, that in fact you'd be relieved and delighted."

"That just shows how little we comprehend one another," Louise said. "Even when we try," she added. "Have you ever had a dog before?" Louise was just curious. She didn't mean to lead him on, but as soon as she said this, she feared she'd given him hope.

"Oh yes," he said eagerly. "As boys we always had dogs."

"They'd die and you'd get another?"

"That's a queer way of putting it."

"Look," Louise said, "your brother had this dog for about three minutes." She felt she was exonerating Elliot.

"Three minutes," he said, bewildered.

"I said about three minutes. You should get a dog and pretend it was your brother's and care for it tenderly and that will be that." Louise was not going to get up and go inside the house and lock the door against him. She would wait him out. "There's nothing more to discuss," she said.

He turned from her sadly. There were several youths peering into his van. "Get away from there!" he cried, and hurried toward them.

It was Walter's turn to give a party. He had a fire in the fireplace although it wasn't at all cold. Still, it was very pleasant, everyone said so.

"I ordered half a cord of wood but it wasn't split, it was just logs," Walter said, "and one of the logs had a chain partly embedded in it, like a dog chain. The tree had started to grow right over the chain."

"Wow," Daisy said. "I don't think so."

"Sometimes," Wilbur said, "certain concepts, it's better not to air them."

The twins held each other's hands and looked into the fire.

"Who would have thought that Elliot would have such a dreary brother," Angus said. "I wouldn't have given him the dog either."

"Still, I'm amazed you didn't, Louise," Jack said.

"I guess he got all the things we actually remembered Elliot having," Andrew said. "I remember a rather nice ship's clock, for instance. That wristwatch I was given, who'd ever seen that before?"

"Elliot wasn't in his right mind," Betsy said. "We keep forgetting that. He wasn't thinking clearly. If you're thinking clearly, you don't take your own life."

Again, Louise marveled at her friend's way of phrasing things. To take your own life was to take control of it, to take possession of it, to give it a shape by occupying it. But Elliot's life still had no shape, even though it had been completed.

"I want to confess something," Andrew said. "I tossed that watch." He had crammed it into an overflowing Goodwill bin in the parking lot of a shopping mall. He described the experience of pushing the watch into an open-throated, softly bulging sack as an extremely unpleasant one. Everyone knew the Goodwill bin and its mute congregation of displaced things, some too large to have been slipped inside, all those things waiting to be revisited in this life, waiting to be used again.

That evening everyone drank too much and later dreamed vivid dreams. The twins dreamed they were in the middle of a highway, trying to cross, trying to cross. Angus dreamed he was in a coffee shop where a kindly but inefficient waitress who looked like his mother was directing him to a table that wasn't there. Lucretia dreamed she was carving *Kindertotenlieder* as sung by Kathleen Ferrier out of a block of wood with a chain saw. That's quite good, someone was saying. It's only a copy, Lucretia demurred. Walter dreamed he was kneeling at the communion rail in the silk pajamas. The cup was coming toward him but had become a thermometer to be placed beneath the tongues of the devout, and by the time it reached him it was a dipstick from a car's engine that a mechanic was wiping with a filthy cloth.

Louise had had the dog for five months now. When she realized how much time had passed, she thought: Seven more months to go. In seven months we'll know more.

Someone was putting a house up behind Louise's house. The yard had been bladed and most of the trees taken down. The banal framework of a house stood there. When Louise gave a party, everyone was shocked at the change.

"I thought that yard went with this house," Jack said.

"Well, I guess not," Louise said.

"All those little birdhouses are gone," Lucretia said. "People put them inside now, you know, as a decorative accent. They paint them in these already fading, flaking colors and put them around."

"They're safer inside," Angus said.

"That thing is going to be huge, Louise," Betsy said. "It's going to loom over you."

They talked for a while about what she could plant to block it out.

"Nothing will grow in time," Betsy said.

"In time for what?" Walter said.

"Everything takes so long to grow. My god, Louise," Betsy said, "you'd better just move."

"Louise," the twins said, "if you die are you going to leave us anything?" They were sitting on the sofa eating pretzels. Outside, the wind was blowing hard but there were no trees anymore to indicate this with their tossing branches. A door blew open, though, banging.

Louise was going to move. She didn't want that house going up behind her. Within a week, she had found another place. Walter and Lucretia helped her move. He had a truck and they transferred all the furniture in one trip. They transferred Broom too, with his dog bed and his dish for water and his dish for food. Then Louise packed her car with what remained, right up to the roof. Even so, she had thrown away a lot of things. She was simplifying and purifying her life, keeping only her nicest, most singular things. Louise swept the old house clean, glad to be leaving. She looked with satisfaction at the empty rooms, the stark windows and their newly ugly vistas. She slammed the door and headed for her car but it wasn't where she'd left it. She stared at the place where the car had been. But it had vanished, been stolen, and everything was gone. The sun was bright, still shining on the place where it had been.

It was Betsy's turn to have a party. They told theft stories—they all had them—and tried to cheer Louise up. She had already bought another car with the insurance money. It wasn't as appealing but she liked it in a different way. She liked it because she didn't like it that much, wasn't as girlishly pleased with it as she had been with the other one.

"You can get all new clothes," Lucretia said. "You can go on a spree. That favorite dress of yours had a spot on it anyway, kind of on the back."

"It did not," Louise said. "I got that spot out. I loved that dress."

"I bet you can't even remember everything you packed in the car," Jack said.

"My pearls," Louise said sadly.

"Christmas is coming," Angus said. But he always said that, as if he were going to buy everyone wonderful gifts, only ones of their most perfect desiring. But all he bought was champagne and cookies that they would drink and eat.

"My grandmother's silver tea service."

"Louise, you know you never used that and never would even once in your life," Lucretia said. "It didn't have a place."

"But it's gone," Louise said. It was gone, of course, but there was something else, something worse. She had made all these choices. She had discarded this and retained that and it hadn't mattered.

"Things are ephemeral," Daisy said.

"And an illusion," Wilbur said.

"Well, which is it?" Jack demanded, annoyed.

Everyone was a little embarrassed. Seldom did anyone respond to the twins.

"I'll tell you one thing," Jack said. "I sold that crazy bowl of Elliot's to an antique store."

None of them could think about Elliot without being thwarted by the mystery of the things he'd given them. His behavior had been inexplicable. It was all inexplicable.

"Oh, I can't think about it anymore!" Louise cried. They were all drinking margaritas out of silly glasses.

"How is Broom," Andrew asked delicately.

"Oh, I've rather gotten used to Broom," Louise said.

Lucretia looked at her unhappily. Louise had lost her sparkle, Lucretia thought.

Louise settled quickly into her new house. It was bigger than the other one, and more ordinary. Broom didn't know which room to disappear into. He had tried them all and couldn't decide. He would try the most unlikely places. Sometimes she would come across him on the fifth step of a narrow back staircase. What an odd place to be! Wherever he was he looked uncomfortable. Still, she was sure Elliot would not have wanted her to surrender the animal so easily. Of course she would never know Elliot's thoughts. She herself could only think—and she was sure she was like many others in this regard, it was her connection with others, really—that life would have been far different under other circumstances, and yet here it wasn't, after all.

Charity

THEY HAD BEEN TOLD ABOUT IT BY A POLICE OFFICER EATING a tamale at a cafe near the Arizona–New Mexico border.

"I just went out there in all that white sand and got me a dune and went up on it and looked and looked and just let it sink in, and I never saw anything like it, never felt anything like it. I think I could stay out there in that white sand for a real long time and I don't know exactly why."

"It doesn't sound like something you'd want to do too often," Richard said. The policeman frowned. Then he ignored them.

Back in the car, Janice wanted to go there immediately. They were having a look at the Southwest on their way to Santa Fe. They were both wearing khaki suits, and Richard had a hand-painted tie he had paid a great deal of money for around his neck.

They drove to the White Sands National Monument, paid the admission and went in. The park ranger said, "We invite you to get out of your car and explore a bit, climb a dune for a better view of the endless sea of sand all around you."

They drove slowly along a loop road. Everything was white and orderly. It was as if the dunes had a sense of mission.

"Do you want to get out?" Richard said. "I'll wait in the car."

Janice felt that she was still capable of awe and transfiguration and was uncomfortable when, together with Richard, she felt not much of anything. She was distracted by the knowledge that they were on a loop road. She studied the dunes without hope. As they were leaving, they saw something small and translucent, like a lizard, stagger beneath their wheels, and they both remarked on that.

"I don't know what that policeman was talking about," Richard said.

"He was trying to express something spiritual."

"Don't you get tired of that out here? Everything's sacred and mysterious and for the initiated only. Even the cops are after illumination. It wears me out, to be quite honest."

She wished she had gotten out of the car. She hadn't even gotten out of the car. She was wearing high heels. "Let's go back," she said. "Let's try it again."

"Janice," Richard said.

After some miles he said, "I forgot to take a leak back there."

"Really!" she exclaimed.

"I'm going to pull into this rest stop."

"To take a leak! How good!" she said. She fixed an enthralled expression upon him.

Outside, the heat was breathtaking and the desert had a slightly lavender cast. People were standing under a ramada, speaking loudly about family members who smoked like chimneys and lived into their nineties. Farther away, someone was calling to a small dog. "Peaches," the woman called, "you come here now." The dog seemed sincere in its unfamiliarity with the name Peaches. This was clearly a name the dog felt did not indicate its true nature, and it was not going to respond to it.

The road led past the toilets and ramadas through a portion of landscape where every form of plant life was explained with signs, then back out onto the highway. Janice walked along it toward a group of vending machines. She loved vending-machine coffee. She felt it had an unusual taste and wasn't for everyone. While waiting for the cardboard cup to sling itself down and fill with the uncanny liquid, she noticed a chalky purple van parked nearby. Two beautiful children stood beside it with their arms folded, looking around as though they had a certain amount of authority. They were rather dirty and blond and striking. A man and woman were rummaging around inside the open van. Both the man and the boy were barefoot and shirtless. The woman, who had long, careless hair, said something to the girl, who climbed inside just as the man triumphantly produced what appeared to be an empty pizza box. Janice could hardly take her eyes off them. She finished the coffee, which was now cold and tasted even more peculiar, and returned to Richard and their rental car, which had a small scratch on the hood that she had taken great pains to point out to the agency so they would not be held responsible for it. The grille had collected a number of butterflies. Without speaking, she got in and shut the door. She'd like to tell Richard how much she refrained from saying to him, but actually she refrained from saying very little.

As they passed the van, the man raised the scrap of box on which was now printed in crayon PLEASE: NEED GAS MONEY.

The colon in this plea touched Janice deeply. "Richard," she said, "we must give that family some money."

The man held the sign close to his chest, just above an appendectomy scar, as the children looked stonily into space.

"Richard!" she said.

"Oh, please, Janice," he said. "Honestly."

"Go back," she said.

They had reached the highway, and Richard accelerated. "Why do you always want to go back. We're not going back. Why don't you do things the first time?"

She gasped at the unfairness of this remark. She considered rearing back and hammering at the windshield with her high-heeled shoes. "I want to give that poor family some gas money," she said.

"Someone will give them money."

"But I want it to be us!"

Richard drove faster.

"Look," she said reasonably, "what if you were in the hospital and you needed a new liver and the doctor finally came in and he said, 'I have good news, the hospital has found a liver for you.' Wouldn't you be grateful?"

"I would," Richard said thoughtfully.

"Someone would have given you a second chance."

"It would be a dead person," Richard said, still thoughtful. "It would have to have been."

"I wish I were driving," she said.

"Well, you're not."

Janice moaned. "I hate you," she said. "I do."

"Let's just get to Santa Fe," Richard said. "It's a civilized town. It will have a civilizing effect on us."

"That tie makes you look stupid," she said.

"I know," he said. He wrenched the knot free, rolled down the window and threw the tie out.

"What are you doing!" Janice cried. The tie was of genuine cellulose acetate and had been painted in the forties. It depicted a Plains Indian brave standing before a pueblo. That the scene was incorrect, that it had been conceived in utter ignorance, made it more expensive and, they were told, more valuable in the long run. But now there was no long run. The tie was toast. She shifted in her seat and stared breathlessly into the distance ahead. She thought of the little family with grave compassion.

"I'm afraid I have to stop again. For gas," he said.

He was pitiless, she thought. A moral aborigine. She hugged herself.

They rolled off an exit into a town that stretched a single block deep for miles along the highway and pulled into a gas station mocked up to look like a trading post, with a corral beside it filled with old, big-finned cars. Richard got out and pumped gas. Then he cleaned the windshield, grinning at her through the glass.

She did not know him, she thought. She was really no more acquainted with who he was than she was familiar with the cold dark-matter theory, say.

He tapped on the glass. "Want to come inside?" he said. "Shot glasses, velvet paintings, lacquered scorpions?"

He was a snob, she thought.

He sighed and walked away, patting the breast pocket of his jacket for his wallet. Janice moved across the seat quickly, grasped the wheel and drove off in a great rattle and shriek of sand. She was back at the rest stop in fifteen minutes. The children had climbed the van's ladder and were lying on the roof. The woman was nowhere visible. The man was still rigidly holding the sign. Janice pulled up beside him.

"How you doing?" he said. He had bright, pale eyes.

"I want to give you twenty dollars," Janice said. She opened her purse and was disturbed to find she had only two fifty-dollar bills.

"Rose!" the man yelled, lowering the sign. He had a long, smooth torso, except for the appendectomy scar.

The woman emerged from the van and regarded Janice coolly.

"Yes?" she said.

"I saw your sign," Janice said, confused.

The children rose languidly from the roof and looked down at her.

"We have to travel seventy miles to our home and get these children in school tomorrow," Rose said formally. "What we do, what our policy is, is we drive to the nearest gas station and at that point you give us the amount you've decided on. That way you'll be assured that we're using it for gas and gas only."

Janice was grateful for the rules they had worked out.

"People will give you money at a rest stop whereas they wouldn't at a gas station," the man said. "It's just human nature. They're more at peace with themselves in rest stops."

Introductions were made. The man's name was Leo. The children were Zorro and ZoeBella. Janice identified herself too.

"Skinny Puppy's my gang name," Zorro said, "but use it at your peril."

"Gang name my ass," Leo said. "He doesn't know anything about gangs. He signed a lowrider last week. Practically got us killed."

"I didn't know I was signing," Zorro said. "I just had my hand out the window."

"Bastard about run us off the highway," Leo said.

Janice realized that she was gazing at them openly, a little stupidly. She suggested that they drive to the gas station so they could all be on their way.

"Can I go with you," Rose asked. "I would like to feel like a human being, if only for a few miles."

"Lemme too!" Zorro cried. He opened the back door of Janice's car, tumbled over the front seat and snuggled against her. "Mnnnn, you smell fine," he said.

"I don't know where he picks that shit up from," Rose muttered. "Certainly not from his father. Get out of that vehicle now!" she screamed.

The child flipped backward over the seat and out the door and jumped into the van. ZoeBella, who had not uttered a word, climbed in beside him.

Janice invited Rose to ride with her to the gas station, which Leo seemed to be familiar with. She felt blessed with social responsibility. She was doing well. It would be over soon, and she would be able to look back on this in the future. Richard had only one mental key and it didn't open all locks, she had always felt this about Richard. And she had lots of mental keys, she thought gratefully, and that's why she was moving so freely through a world that welcomed her.

Leo started the van with difficulty. Blue smoke poured from the tailpipe.

"That doesn't look good," Janice noted.

"Rings, seals, valves, you name it," Rose said.

The van gained the highway and wobbled off ahead of them. Smoke appeared to be rising from the wheels as well. The sky was cloudless and sharply blue, and the smoke floundered upward into it.

"Some people like the sky out here," Rose volunteered, "but I prefer the sky over New York City. Now that's sky. The big buildings push it back so it's far, far overhead. It looks wilder that way."

Janice agreed, thinking that this was a highly original remark. She felt splendid about herself. She looked at Rose warmly.

"That Zorro smudged your seat," Rose said, regarding a dusty footprint on the car's upholstery.

Janice waved this concern away. "Such beautiful children," she said. "And such unusual names."

"God knows I didn't want to call him Zorro, but his father insisted. Those two aren't from the same stock. ZoeBella's dad, Warren, was blind. I hope that you, like many others, aren't under the misperception that blind people are good people. It just isn't so. Blind people don't feel that they have to interact with others at all. They contribute nothing to a conversation. He had a wonderful dog, though, Mountain. Mountain came to Lamaze class with us. Lamaze encourages you to focus on something other than birth and I focused on Mountain week after week, but when it was finally time to have ZoeBella they wouldn't let Mountain into the delivery room. A violation of infection-control procedures, they said. Well, I freaked, and I think the whole thing messed ZoeBella up too. Here I went the whole pregnancy with no cigarettes or liquor and then they won't let the goddamn dog into the delivery room. It was a very, very difficult birth and Warren, the bastard, was no help at all. But we sued the hospital for not letting us have Mountain in there, and they settled out of court. Warren was long gone by then, but that money did us for four years, Leo and Zorro too. What an inspiration that was. I wish I could come up with another one that good. Have you ever fucked a blind man?"

"Why, no," Janice said. "No, I haven't."

"Do it before you die, girl," Rose said. "There's nothing like it."

Janice nodded.

"But don't stick around afterwards. Get your cookies out of there," Rose advised.

Janice nodded again. She was beginning to worry somewhat about Richard's mood when she retrieved him. The van weaved smoldering before them. Janice felt a little queasy watching it. By the time they reached the exit, Janice found that she was gripping the steering wheel tightly. The van turned not in to the gas station where Janice had left Richard but into one across the street, where it clattered to a stop.

"Makes you want a cocktail just looking at that heap, doesn't it?" Rose said.

"I'd like to give you fifty dollars, if you don't mind," Janice said. "I think you probably need some oil too. Wouldn't you like some oil? To make it home safely?"

"Oh, you could drop a bundle into that thing," Rose said. "It's a suck-hole." She accepted the bill slowly from Janice's fingers. "Thank you," she said slowly. She seemed absorbed in some involuted ritual. She didn't respect the money, it was clear, but she respected the person who gave her the money. Was that it? Janice wondered. Why was she giving her so much money anyway? Her own behavior was becoming increasingly suspect.

Rose got out of the car, stretched and ambled toward her family. Janice drove across the street. The trading post was locked tight. Four spotted dogs with heads the size of gallon buckets regarded her avidly from the car corral.

"Richard!" she called. The dogs went into an uproar. They raced around the enclosure, baying with the thrill of duty, upsetting their water dishes. Janice drove slowly in circles in the area of the trading post, then pulled out into the street and came to the end of town. The town simply stopped at an enormous Road Runner statue, beyond which were many thousands of acres of grazing land with not a single creature grazing. She stopped the car near the statue and got out, taking tiny sips of the superheated air, afraid to breathe too deeply. An elderly couple approached and asked if she would take a picture of them with their camera.

"Doesn't it have one of those timers?" Janice said. "Can't you place it on a rock, set the timer and let it take its own picture?"

The old couple looked puzzled and began to tremble.

"OK. Forgive me," Janice said. "I'm sorry. Give it here."

"Be sure to get it all in," the woman said. "You have to back up."

Janice backed up and raised the camera to her eye. There they were.

"You have to step back some still," the woman said.

Janice moved farther back and clipped the side of her shoe against a trash can.

"That must be why they put that receptacle there," the woman said.

"The receptacle marks the spot!" her withered companion shouted.

"Smile if you want to," Janice said. "Done. Got it." She had not taken the picture. She would not. It was a defensible right.

"Thank you so much," the old man said.

"Most kind of you," the woman said, "once you agreed."

Janice returned to the car on her broken heel and drove back through the town, honking her horn frequently. Not only was Richard annoying he could actually be hazardous. His behavior was hazardous, she thought. She circled the pumps of the deserted trading post once again. The big-headed dogs were lying on their stomachs, sharing something fuscous and eviscerated. She drove across the street. Rose and the children were sitting on the ground on a bedsheet. The van was on a lift inside the garage.

"Are you looking for someone," Rose asked.

"No," Janice said. "I don't look as though I am, do I?"

"You look hungry, then, or something," Rose said.

"I'm hungry," Zorro said. "Jesus I am."

"Are those horse?" ZoeBella said, pointing at Janice's shoes.

Janice was startled to hear her voice, which was soft and solemn. "What?" she said.

"Your shoes, are they horse?"

"I don't know. They're leather of some sort. That would be awful, I guess, if they were, wouldn't it?"

"You seem uncertain," ZoeBella said quietly.

Leo came up to them, wiping his greasy hands on his pants. Stripes of grease ran down his chest and there was oil in his hair. "We got a little problem but it can be fixed," he said. "Man here's going to let me use his tools. Why don't you women and children get something to eat?" he said expansively. "Sit in a nice air-conditioned restaurant and get something nice to eat."

Rose was particular about the restaurant. She wanted it dark, with booths, no salad bar, no view of the outside. They got into Janice's car and drove up the street again. Zorro was sent into several establishments to determine their suitability. He had put on a T-shirt that said BAN LEGHOLD TRAPS. A number of birds and animals crippled and quite conceivably dead were arranged colorfully around a frightful black iron trap.

"He loves that shirt, but I don't think he gets it," Rose confided to Janice.

"You should bury that shirt, with Zorro in it," ZoeBella said quietly.

Janice continued to scan the street for Richard. She saw no one who even remotely resembled him, not that she would have settled for that, of course.

"You sure you're not looking for someone," Rose asked.

"Not at all," Janice said. "I'm just trying to be aware of my surroundings."

ZoeBella leaned over the front seat and said softly, "I think that policeman behind us wants you to pull over."

"Yes!" Zorro said. "There go the misery lights!"

Janice was told by the officer that she had drifted through a stop sign. He very much resembled the officer she and Richard had encountered at breakfast. While he was writing out the ticket, which was for two hundred dollars, Rose asked him which eating establishment he would recommend, and he recommended the one they were parked in front of.

"This kind of event calls for a cocktail," Rose said to Janice. "It always does."

Inside, Janice felt disoriented. ZoeBella placed her small hand in Janice's and led her to a booth. They sat holding hands opposite Zorro, whose T-shirt featured prominently in the darkness. Janice ordered a double gin with ice and Rose specified an imported bottled beer, then ordered turkey plates for everyone.

"Turkey plate's always the best," she said.

ZoeBella did not release Janice's hand even after the food arrived. The children ate as though starved.

"Do you believe in God?" ZoeBella murmured.

Janice was trying to locate a hair that had found its way onto her tongue.

Rose said, "When I was ZoeBella's age, every time I thought of God I saw him as something in a black Speedo bathing suit and I saw myself sitting on his lap, but this perception was drummed out of me. Just drummed out. Now whenever the name comes up I don't think anything."

"I think of God as a magician," ZoeBella whispered, looking closely at Janice. "A rich magician who has a great many sheep who he hypnotizes so he won't have to pay for shepherds or fences to keep them from running away. The sheep know that eventually the magician wants to kill them because he wants their flesh and their skin. So first the magician hypnotizes them into thinking they're immortal and that no harm is being done to them when they get skinned, that on the contrary it will be very good for them and even pleasant. Then he hypnotizes them into thinking the magician is their good master who loves them. Then he hypnotizes them into thinking they're not sheep at all. And after all this, they never run away but quietly wait until the magician requires their flesh and their skin."

ZoeBella's skin was very pale and her eyes were large and blue. "Goodness," Janice said, perturbed. Only a piece of bread was going to find this hair, she decided. She pushed one into her mouth.

Zorro said, "I think of God—"

His mother yanked his arm sharply. "We don't want to hear that again," she said.

Zorro collected everyone's forks and put them in the pocket of his shorts.

"We always need forks," Rose explained to Janice. "I don't know what happens to them at our house."

The children ordered large butterscotch sundaes and polished them off within minutes. ZoeBella ate delicately but with lightning speed. She had released Janice's hand to better wield the long spoon, but when she finished she tucked her hand in Janice's once again.

"I hope I'm at school tomorrow," she said in her almost inaudible voice. "If I'm not at school tomorrow I don't know what I'll do." She arranged her face in an expression of horror.

Janice couldn't imagine a child like ZoeBella thriving at school, but she squeezed the child's sticky hand. The magician and the sheep had caused her to feel a little unwell and considerably undirected, though she now knew what she would do. She would take Rose and the children to their home. She was sure that the situation with Leo and the van had not improved and she was eager to finish what she had begun. Otherwise, how would she be able to think about it? She wouldn't be able to think about it. They lived in a town that wasn't exactly on the way to Santa Fe, but she could still make it to Santa Fe before dark if they left immediately. Richard had made reservations at a hotel there. There would possibly be a message waiting, or even Richard himself. If there wasn't, if he wasn't, then when she arrived she would be the message. One's life after all is the message, isn't it, the way one lives one's life, the good one carries out?

"I can see you're thinking," ZoeBella said in a quiet, disappointed voice.

Back at the garage, Leo was agreeable to Janice's idea. "I believe I'm going to be here for days," he said. He kissed the children and shook Janice's hand. In the car again, Janice remarked that Leo seemed like a good man.

"He's all right," Rose said. "Whenever he gets drunk he threatens to kill the kids' rabbits, but he hasn't done it yet."

They drove in silence for a while. When they got to their home, Janice was not going to go inside. She would be invited, but under no circumstance would she go inside. She didn't want to go so far as to enter that home even in her thoughts. She would leave them at their own threshold and be gone.

"What's your credit card look like," Zorro asked. "Is it black with a mountain on it and an eagle and a big orange sun? Because if it is, you left it back there by the cash register. I saw it when I got the toothpicks."

"Zorro sees credit cards everywhere," Rose said. "I've told him never never pick them up. He's got a shrewd eye, and I want him to have a shrewd eye, but my feeling is that he could go from shrewd to dishonest real quick."

"I'm not going back," Janice said.

No one contested this. They were on a narrow blacktop road streaking urgently through the desert. In the distance, a man was riding a horse.

"There is a horse," ZoeBella said reverently.

Then Zorro saw the snake on the edge of the asphalt.

"Look at him!" he screamed. "Look at the size of that sucker! He's a miracle, you can't just pass him by!"

He grabbed the wheel and turned it toward the snake, but Janice wrenched it back and slammed on the brakes. The car shot off the road, not quite clearing a stony wash, and with a snapping of axles it crumpled against a patch pocket of wildflowers—primrose and sand verbena and, as ZoeBella pointed out quietly later, sacred datura, a plant of which every part was poisonous.

"Is everyone all right?" Rose said. "All in one piece? That's the important thing, nothing else matters."

"I just wanted that snake so bad," Zorro said.

"He's always after his dad to hit things for him," Rose said. "You're in somebody else's vehicle, Zorro! You are a guest in another person's car!"

They got out of the car with difficulty and looked at it. It was clearly a total wreck. The key had snapped off in the ignition, so Janice couldn't even unlock the trunk to retrieve her suitcase.

ZoeBella touched Janice's hand. "I'm glad you didn't run over the snake," she whispered.

"I have a terrible headache," Janice said.

"You bumped your head pretty bad," Rose agreed. "I saw a motel back there. Why don't we get a room and declare this day over."

There was only one room available at the motel, and there was a lone, large bed, which pretty much filled it. The other rooms were unoccupied, according to the Indian girl in the office, but each possessed a unique incapacity disqualifying it from use. A clogged drain, a charred carpet, a cracked toilet, a staved-in door. Fleas.

Zorro soared from the door to the bed and began bouncing on it. "Skinny Puppy enters the ring!" he shouted. He crouched and weaved, jabbing the air. Rose swatted him away.

"You lie down," she instructed Janice. "I'll take the kids over to the cafe so you can rest. They've got cocktails, I noticed. Do you want me to bring you back a cocktail?"

"I think I'll just lie down," Janice said.

"Don't do anything until you've rested a bit," Rose said.

"Don't look in the mirror or anything," ZoeBella urged her softly.

"You look white as a sheet," Rose said. "Maybe we should stay with you just until you get your color back."

"I don't feel at all well," Janice said. She crept across the bed and lay on her back. She didn't want to close her eyes.

"Scooch over just a little bit," Rose said, "more to the middle so we can all fit."

They all lay on the bed. After a few moments someone began to snore. Janice wouldn't want to bet her last fifty that it wasn't her.

Anodyne

MY MOTHER BEGAN GOING TO GUN CLASSES IN FEBRUARY. SHE quit the yoga. As I understand it, yoga is concentration. You choose an object of attention and you concentrate on it. It might be, but need not be, the deity. This is how it was explained to me. The deity is different now than it used to be; it can be anything, pretty much anything at all. But even so, my mother let the yoga go and went on to what was called a .38—a little black gun with a long barrel—at a pistol range in the city. Classes were Tuesday and Thursday evenings from five to seven. That was an hour and a half of class and half an hour of shooting time. I would go with her and afterward we would go to the Arizona Inn and have tea and share a club sandwich. Then we would go home, which was just as we had left it. The dogs were there and the sugar machine was in the corner. We left it out because we had to use it twice a day. I knew how to read it and clean it. My mother and I both had diabetes and that is not something you can be cured of, not ever. In another corner was the Christmas tree. We liked to keep it up, although we had agreed not to replace any of the bulbs that burned out. At the same time we were not waiting until every bulb went dark before we took the tree down, either. We were going to be flexible about it, not superstitious. My grandmother had twelve orange-juice glasses. A gypsy told her fortune and said she'd live until the last of the twelve glasses broke. The gypsy had no way of knowing that my grandmother had twelve orange-juice glasses! When I knew my grandmother, she had seven left. She had four left when she died. The longest my mother and I ever left the tree up was Easter once when it came early.

This is Tucson, Arizona, a high desert valley. Around us are mountains, and one mountain is so high there is snow in the winter. People drive up and make snowmen and put them in the backs of their trucks and on the hoods of their cars and drive back down again, seeing how long they will last. My mother and I have done that, made a little snowman and put him on the hood of the car. There are animals up there that don't know that the animals below them in the desert even exist. They might as well be in different galaxies. The mountain is 9,157 feet tall, and 6,768 feet above the city. Numbers interest me and have since the second grade. My father weighed 100 pounds when he died. Each foot of a saguaro cactus weighs 100 pounds, and that's mostly water. My father weighed no more than one cactus foot. I weigh 68 pounds, my mother weighs 116, the dogs weigh 80 each. I do my mother's checkbook. Each month, according to the bank, I am accurate to the penny.

The man who taught the class and owned the firing range was called the Marksman. He called his business the Pistol Institute. There were five people attending the class in addition to my mother, three women and two men. They did not speak to one another or exchange names because no one wanted to make friends. My mother had had a friend in yoga class, Suzanne. She was disturbed that my mother had dropped the yoga and was going to the institute, and she said she was going to throw the I Ching and find out what it was, exactly, my mother thought she was doing. If she did, we never heard the results.

My mother was not the kind of person who lived each day by objecting to it, day after day. She was not. And I do not mean to suggest that the sugar machine was as large as the Christmas tree. It's about the size of my father's wallet, which my mother now uses as her own.

When my father died, my mother felt that it was important that I not suffer a failure to recover from his death and she took me to a psychiatrist. I was supposed to have twenty-five minutes a week with the psychiatrist, but I was never in his office for more than twenty. Once he used some of that time to tell me he was dyslexic and that the beauty of words meant nothing to him, nothing, though he appreciated and even enjoyed their meanings. I told him one of our dogs is epileptic and I had read that in the first moments of an epileptic attack some people felt such happiness that they would be willing to give up their life to keep it, and he said he doubted that a dog would want to give up its life for happiness. I told him dead people are very disappointed when you visit them and they discover you're still flesh and blood, but that they're not angry, only sad. He dismissed this completely, without commenting on it or even making a note. I suppose he's used to people trying things out on him.

My mother did not confide in me but I felt that she was unhappy that February. We stopped the ritual of giving each other our needles in the morning before breakfast. I now gave myself my injections and she her own. I missed the other way, but she had changed the policy and that was that. She still kissed me good morning and good night and took the dogs for long walks in the desert and fed the wild birds. I told her I'd read that you shouldn't feed the birds in winter, that it fattened up the wrong kind of bird. The good birds left and came back, left and came back, but the bad ones stayed and were strengthened by the habits of people like my mother. I told her this to be unpleasant because I missed the needles together, but it didn't matter. She said she didn't care. She had changed her policy about the needles, not the birds.

The Pistol Institute was in a shopping mall where all the other buildings were empty and for lease. It had glass all across the front and you could look right into it, at the little round tables where people sat and watched the shooters and at the long display case where the guns were waiting for someone to know them, to want them. When you were inside you couldn't see out, because the glass was dark. It seemed to me the reverse of what it should be, but it was the Marksman's place so it was his decision. Off to the right as you entered was the classroom and over its door was the sign BE AWARE OF WHO CAN DO UNTO YOU. No one asked what this meant, to my knowledge, and I wasn't about to ask. I did not ask questions. I had started off doing this deliberately sometime before but by now I did it naturally. Off to the left behind a wall of clear glass was the firing range. The shooters wore ear protectors and stood at an angle in little compartments firing at targets on wires that could be brought up close or sent farther away by pressing a button. The target showed the torso of a man with large square shoulders and a large square head. In the left-hand corner of the target was a box in which the same figure was much reduced. This was the area you wanted to hit when you were good. It wasn't tedious to watch the shooters, but it wasn't that interesting either. I preferred to sit as close as possible to the closed door of the classroom and listen to the Marksman address the class.

The Marksman stressed awareness and responsibility and the importance of accuracy and power and speed and commitment and attitude. He said that having a gun was like having a pet or a child. He said there was nothing embarrassing about carrying a gun into public places. You can carry a weapon into any establishment except those that serve liquor, unless you're requested not to by the operator of that establishment. No one else can tell you, only the operator. Embarrassment is not carrying a gun, the Marksman said. Embarrassment is being a victim, naked, in a bloody lump, gazed upon by strangers. That's embarrassment, he said.

The Marksman told horrible stories about individuals and their unexpected fates. He told stories about doors that were opened a crack when they had been closed before. He told stories about tailgating vehicles. He told a story about the minivan mugger, the man who hid under cars and slashed women's Achilles tendons so they couldn't run away. He said that the attitude you have toward others is important. Do not give them the benefit of the doubt. Give them the benefit of the doubt and you could already be dead or dying. The distinction between dead and dying was an awful one and I often went into the bathroom, the one marked DOES, and washed my hands and dried them, holding and turning them for a long time under the hot-air dryer. The Marksman told the story about the barefoot, bare-chested madman with the machete on the steps of the capitol in Phoenix. This was his favorite story, illustrating as it did the difference between killing power and stopping power. The madman strode forward for sixteen seconds after he had been warned and his chest blown out. You could see daylight through his chest. You could see the gum wrappers on the marble steps behind him right through his chest. But for sixteen seconds he kept coming, wielding his machete, and in those sixteen seconds he annihilated four individuals. My mother kept taking the classes, so I heard this story more than once.

My mother decided that she wanted to know the Marksman socially and invited him to dinner along with the others in the class. We decided on a buffet-style arrangement, the plates and silverware stacked off to the side. This way, if no one came, we wouldn't feel humiliated. The table had not been set. No one came except the Marksman. Not the fat lady who had her own pistol and a purple holster for it, not the bald man or the two college girls, not the other man with the tattoo of a toucan on his arm. The Marksman was a thin man in tight clothes and he wore a gold chain and had a small mustache. Sometimes he favored bloused shirts but that night he was wearing a jacket. I sat with him in the living room while my mother was in the kitchen. The dogs came in and looked at him. Then they jumped up onto the sofa and curled up and looked at him.

"You allow those dogs every license, I see," he said.

I wanted to say something but had no idea what it was.

He asked me if I'd been to Disneyland.

"No," I said.

"How about the other one, the one in Florida?"

I said that I hadn't.

"Where are you from," he asked me.

"Here," I said.

"I'm from San Antonio," he said. "Have you ever been to San Antonio?"

"No," I said.

"There's a big river there, a big attraction, that runs right past all the shops and restaurants and that's all lit up with fairy lights," the Marksman said. "Tourists take cruises on it and stroll beside it. They promenade," he said in a careful voice. "Once a year, they pump the whole thing out, the whole damn river, and clean it and then put the water back in again. They scrub the bottom like it was a bathtub and fill it up again. What do you think about that?"

My hands were damp. I was beginning to worry about this, but my mother always said there was nothing more useless than dreading something you weren't understanding.

"People have lost their interest in reality," the Marksman said.

THE CLASSES CONTINUED AT THE INSTITUTE. THE OLD GROUP left and a new one with the same silent demeanor took its place. I stayed close to the door and listened. The Marksman said never to point the muzzle of a gun at something you weren't willing to destroy. He said that with practice you're often just repeating a mistake. He stressed caution and respect, response and readiness and alertness. When class was over, everyone filed out to choose a handgun and buy a box of ammunition, then strode to their appointed cubicle.

My mother did not extend any more dinner invitations to the group, although the Marksman came every Friday. It became the custom. I knew my mother did not exactly want him in our life, because she already was making fun of his manner of speaking, but she wanted him somehow. There are many people who have artificial friendships like this that become quite fulfilling, I'm sure. I tried to imagine him living with us. The used targets papering the rooms, his bloused shirts hanging on the clothesline, his enormous black truck in the driveway. I imagined him trying to turn my father's room into a safe room, for the Marksman spoke often about the necessity of having one of these in every house. The requirements were a solid-core door, a dead bolt, a wireless telephone and a gun, and this was the place you should immediately go to when a threat presented itself, a madman or a fiend or merely someone who, for whatever reason, wanted to kill you and cease your life forever. My father had died in his room, but the way I understood it, with very few modifications it could be made into a safe room of the Marksman's specifications.

The psychiatrist had said that my father had been fortunate to have his room, in his own home with his own family—that is, my mother and myself and the dogs. I did not disagree with this.

I liked the Marksman's truck. One Friday night when we were eating dinner I told him so.

"That's because you're an American girl," the Marksman said. "Something in the American spirit likes great size and a failure to be subtle. Nothing satisfies this better than a truck."

The Marksman usually ignored me, but would address me if I spoke to him directly. With my mother he was courteous. I think he liked her. She did not like him, and I didn't know what she was doing. She had not become a very good shot, either.

My mother and father loved each other. He had been big and strong before he got sick. He had favorite meals and movies and places. He even had a favorite towel. It was a towel I'd had with big old-fashioned trains on it. He said he liked it because whenever he dried himself he felt he was going somewhere, but when he got sick he couldn't wash himself or dry himself or feed himself. When he was very sick my mother had to be careful about washing him or his skin would come off on the cloth. He liked to talk, but then he became too weak to talk. My mother said my father's mind was strong and healthy, so we read to him and talked to him, even though I grew to hate the thought of it. This hidden mind in my father's body.

The Marksman had been coming over for several weeks when he appeared one evening with a cake in a box for dessert. I told him that we couldn't have dessert, that we had the sugar. It had never come up before.

"What do you do on your birthday without cake?" he said.

"I have cake on my birthday," I said.

He didn't ask me when my birthday was.

I wanted to show him how I used the sugar machine, but didn't want to tell him about it. I took the lancet, which was in a plastic cylinder and cocked with a spring, and touched it against my finger to get a drop of blood. I squeezed the single drop onto the very center of the paper tab and put it into the machine. My mother was outside, in the back of the house, putting out fruit for the birds, halves of oranges and apples. I looked at the screen of the machine, acting more interested than I actually was, as it counted down and then made the readout. A hundred and twenty-four, it said.

"I'm all right," I said.

"You're an American girl," the Marksman said, watching me.

"What are you doing?" my mother said.

"I'm all right," I said. "Nothing."

I took the pitcher of water off the dining table and busied myself by pouring some into the saucer of the Christmas tree stand. The tree wasn't taking water anymore. The room was sucking up the water, not the tree. But it looked all right. It was still green.

"Do you want to learn to shoot," the Marksman asked me.

"Goodness no," my mother said. "Isn't there a law against that or something? She's just a child."

"No law," the Marksman said. "The law allows you certain rights— you, me, her, everybody."

I wondered if he was going to say I could be a natural, but he didn't.

"No," my mother said. "Absolutely not."

I didn't say anything. I knew I would not always be with my mother.

I went to the psychiatrist longer than my mother and I went to the institute. We stopped going and the Marksman stopped coming over for dinner. The last time I went to the psychiatrist there was a new girl in the waiting room. There had always been a little girl about my age and now there was this new one, an older one. We were all girls there. It was a coincidence, is my understanding, that there were no boys. The littlest one was cute. She had a pretty heart-shaped mouth and she carried a toy, a pink and purple dinosaur that she was always trying to give away. You could tell she liked it, that she'd had it probably since she was born, it was all worn smooth and gnawed in spots. Once I got there and she had another toy, a rabbit wearing an apron, and I thought that someone had actually been awful enough to take the dinosaur when she offered it. But it showed up with her again and she was back to trying to give it not just to me but to anyone who came into the waiting room. That seemed to be the little girl's problem, or at least one of them.

The new girl told us that she was there because her hair was thinning and making her ugly. It looked all right to me, but she said it was thinning and that she had to spend an hour each day lying upside down with her head on the floor to stimulate its growth. She said she had to keep the hairs in the sink after she washed it and the hairs in the brush and the hairs on her pillows. She said she'd left some uncollected hairs on a blouse that her mother had put in the laundry, and when she found out about it she'd become so upset that she did something she couldn't even talk about. The other girl, the one my age, said that our aim should be to get psychopharmacological treatment instead of psychotherapy, because otherwise it was a waste of time, but that's what she always said.

I was the last of us to see the psychiatrist that afternoon. When my time was almost up he said, "You're a smart girl, so tell me, what's your preference, the manifest world or the unmanifest one?"

It was like he was asking me which flavor of ice cream I liked. I thought for a moment, then went to the dictionary he kept on a stand and looked the word up.

"The manifest one," I said, and there was not much he could do about that.

ACK

WE WERE VISITING FRIENDS OF MINE ON NANTUCKET. OVER the years they've become more solitary. They're quite a bit older than we are, lean, intelligent and carelessly stylish. They drink too much. And I drink too much when I visit them. Sometimes we'd just eat cereal for supper; other times we'd be subjected to an entire stuffed fish and afterward a tray of Grape-Nuts pudding. Their house is old and uncomfortable, with a small yard that's dark with hydrangeas in August. This was August. I told my wife not to expect dinner from my erratic friends, Betty and Bruce. We would have a few drinks, then return to the inn where we were staying and have a late supper. Only one other guest was expected this evening, a local woman who had ten daughters.

"What an awful lot," my wife said.

"I'm sure we'll hear about them," I said.

"I suppose so," Bruce said, struggling to open an institutional-size jar of mayonnaise that had been set on a weathered picnic table in the yard.

"She's unlikely to talk about much else with that many," my wife said. "Are any of them strange?"

"One's dead, I believe," our host said, still struggling with the jar. " 'Whatsoever thy hand findeth to do, do it with all thy might . . .' " he said, addressing his own exertions.

"Let me give that a try," I said, but Bruce had finally broken the plastic seal.

"I meant *strange* as in intellectually or emotionally or physically challenged," my wife said. She had already decided to dislike this poor mother.

Bruce dipped a slice of wilted carrot into the jar. "I really like mayonnaise. Do you, Paula? I can't remember."

"Bruce, you know very well it's Pauline," Betty said.

"I'm addicted to mayonnaise, practically," Bruce said.

My wife smiled and shook her head. If she had resolved to become relaxed in that moment it would be a great relief, for Bruce had been kind to me and there was no need for tension between them. Pauline prefers to be in control of our life and our friendships. She's a handsome woman, canny and direct, never unreasonable. I suppose some might find her cold but I am in thrall to her because I had almost been crushed by life. I had some rough years before Pauline, years I only just managed to live through. I might as well have been stumbling around in one of those great whiteouts that occur in the far north where it is impossible to distinguish between a small object nearby and a large object a long way off. In whiteouts there is no certainty and every instinct is betrayed—even the birds fly into the ground, believing it to be air, and perish. I strained to see and could not, and torn by strange sorrows and shames I twice attempted suicide. But then a calm overtook me, as though my mind had taken pity on me and called off the hopeless search I had undertaken. I was thirty-two then. I met Pauline the following year and she accepted me, broken and wearied as I was, with an assurance that further strengthened me. We have a lovely home outside Washington. She wants a child, which I am resisting.

We were all smiling at the mayonnaise jar as though it were one of the sweet night's treasures when a bell jangled on a rusted chain wrapped around the garden gate. We had engaged the same bell an hour before. A woman appeared, thinner than I expected, almost gaunt, and shabbily dressed. She seemed a typical wellborn island eccentric, and looked at us boldly and disinterestedly . . . It was difficult to determine her age and thus impossible to guess at the ages of her many daughters. My first impression was that none of them had accompanied her.

"Starky! Have a drink, my girl!" Bruce said in greeting.

She embraced him, resting her cheek for a moment in his hair, which was long and reached the collar of his checkered shirt. She breathed in the smell of his hair much as I had and found it, I could imagine, sour but strangely satisfying. She then turned to Betty and kissed, as I had, her soft warm cheek.

She had brought a gift of candles, which Betty found holders for. The candles were lit and Pauline admired the pleasant effect, for with nightfall the hydrangeas had cast an almost debilitating gloom over the little garden. It did not trouble me that we had brought nothing. We had considered a pie but the prices had offended us. It was foolish to spend so much money on a pie.

"Guinivere," Bruce called. "We're so glad you came!"

A figure moved awkwardly toward us and sat down heavily. It was a young woman with a flat round face. Everything about her seemed round. Her mouth at rest was small and round.

"Look at all that mayonnaise," Starky said. "Bruce remembered it's a favorite of yours."

"I like maraschino cherries now," the girl said.

"Yes, she's gone on to cherries," her mother said.

"I have jars of them awaiting fall's Manhattans," Bruce assured her. "Retrieve them from the pantry, dear. They're in the cabinet by the waffle iron."

"Guinivere is a pretty name," my wife said.

"She was instrumental in saving the whales last week," her mother said. "The first time, not when they beached themselves again. The photographer was there from the paper but he always excludes Guinivere, she doesn't photograph well."

Every year brings the summertime tragedy of schools of whales grounding on the shore. It's their fidelity to one another that dooms them, as well as their memories of earlier safe passage. They return to a once navigable inlet and find it a deadly maze of unfamiliar shoals. The sound of their voices—the clicks and cries quite audible to their would-be rescuers—is heartbreaking, apparently.

Pauline pointed out that those sounds would seem like that only to sympathetic ears. It was simply a matter of our changing attitudes toward them, she argued. Nantucket's wealth was built on the harpooning of the great whales. Had they not cried out then with the same anguished song?

Starky murmured liltingly, "*Je t'aimerai toujours bien que je ne t'aie jamais aimé.*"

It was impossible to tell if she possessed an engaging voice or not, the song, or rather this fragment, being so brief. It was quite irrelevant, in my opinion, to the topic of whales.

Pauline frowned." 'I will always love you though I never loved you'? Is that it? Certainly isn't much, is it?"

"One of Starky's daughters has a wonderful voice," Betty said, looking around distractedly.

Pauline nudged me as if to say, Here it's beginning and now we'll have to hear about all of them, even the dead one. She then continued resolutely, "As a statement of devotion, I mean. But perhaps it was taken out of context?"

"Everything's context," Bruce said, "or is as I grow older."

Guinivere returned with a bottle of cherries and munched them one by one, dipping her fingers with increasing difficulty into the narrow jar.

"Those aren't good for you," Pauline said.

The girl tipped the liquid from the jar onto the flagstones and retrieved the last of the cherries.

"They're very bad for you," Pauline counseled. "They're not good for anyone."

The girl ignored her.

"Guinivere has a job," Betty said. "She works at the library. She puts all the books back in their proper places—don't you, Guinivere?"

"Someone has to do the lovely things," Bruce said.

"And someone does the ugly things too," Guinivere said without humor. "In Amarillo, Texas, more cattle have been slaughtered than any other place in the world. They make nuclear bombs in Amarillo as well."

"You must read the books then," Pauline said, "as you put them back on the shelves?" Her efforts at engagement with this unfortunate child were making me uncomfortable. She wanted a child, but of course a lovely one. She had no doubt it would be lovely. Would even a bird build its nest if it did not have the instinct for confidence in the world?

"I have a joke," Guinivere said. "It's for him." She pointed at me. "They name roads for people like you." She paused. "One Way," she said, and she smiled a round smile. She was much older than I initially thought.

"You're such a chatterbox tonight," her mother said. "You must let others speak."

Guinivere immediately fell silent, and for a moment we all were silent.

"I'm going to get more ice," Pauline announced.

"Thank you!" Bruce said. "And more ingredients for the rickeys all around, if you please."

Starky rose to accompany her into the house, which I knew would vex Pauline as she wanted only to remove herself for a while from a group I'm sure she found most unpromising.

"You look good, my boy," Bruce said.

"Thank you, it's Pauline," I said. Betty's look was skeptical. "I've found there's a trick to knowing where you are," I said. "It's knowing where you were five minutes ago."

"Why, you were here!" Betty said.

"I know where you were long before five minutes ago," Bruce said.

"Yes, you do," I agreed. "And if that man, that man you knew, came into the garden right now and sat down with us, I wouldn't recognize him."

"You wouldn't know what to say to him," Bruce asked.

"I could be of no help to him."

"Those were dark times for you."

I shrugged. I had once wanted to kill myself and now I did not. The thoughts I harbored then lack all reality for me.

Quiet voices from the street drifted toward us. The tourists were "laning," a refined way of saying they were peering into the lamplit and formal rooms of other people's houses and commenting on the furnishings, the paintings, the flower arrangements and so on.

My thoughts returned to the whales and their deaths. They were small pilot whales, not the massive sperm whales Pauline had made reference to, the taking of which had made this island renowned. The pilot whales hadn't wished to kill themselves, of course. But one was in distress, the one first to realize the gravity of the situation, the dangerous imminence of an unendurable stranding, and the others were caught up in the same incomprehension. In the end they had no choice but to go where the dying one was going.

Or that's how I'd put it. A marine biologist would know far better than I.

Pauline returned carrying a tray with an assortment of bottles and a plastic bowl of melting ice. "Starky is on the phone," she announced.

"It's probably her real-estate agent," Bruce said. "She told me he might be contacting her tonight. She's selling her home, the one where she raised all her girls."

"I'm sure she'll get whatever he's asking," Pauline said. "People are mad for this place, aren't they? They'll pay any price to say they have a home here."

The night was growing colder. Bruce had brought out several old sweaters, and I pulled one over my head. It fit well enough—a murrey cashmere riddled with moth holes.

Betty placed her tanned and deeply wrinkled hand on mine. The veins were so close to the surface I wondered that they didn't alarm her whenever they caught her eye. She had to look at them sometimes.

"We are all of us unique, aren't we? And misunderstood," she said.

"No," I replied, not unkindly, for I was devoted to Betty, though I was beginning to wonder if she wasn't becoming a bit foolish with age. The world does not distinguish one grief from another. It is the temptation to believe otherwise that keeps us in chains. "We are not as dissimilar from one another as we prefer to think," I said.

The rickeys were not as refreshing as they had been earlier, perhaps because of the ice.

Starky reappeared, as gaunt and unexceptional as before and giving no explanation for what had become a prolonged absence.

"Oh, do begin now," Betty said.

"Begin what?" Pauline asked.

"Without further preamble?" Starky said.

"Or delay," Bruce said.

"What must this place be like in the winter!" Pauline muttered.

We all laughed, none more forgivingly than Starky, who then began to describe her children.

"My first daughter is neither bold nor innovative but feels a tenderness toward all things. When she was young she was understandably avaricious out of puzzlement and boredom, but experience has made her meek and devoted. She is loyal to my needs and outwardly appears to be the most praiseworthy of my children. She ensures that my lucky dress is always freshly cleaned and pressed and waiting for me on its cloth-covered hanger. Despite such conscientiousness, I feel most distanced from this child and might neglect her utterly were she not the first.

"My second daughter is the traveler of the family even though she seldom rises from her bed. One need only show her the shell of a queen conch or a paperweight with its glass enclosing a Welsh thistle and she is swimming in the Bahamas or tramping the British Isles, though this only in her mind for she is far too excitable and shy to make the actual journey. She prepares for her adventures by anticipating the worst, and when this does not occur she delights in her good fortune. Some who know her find her pitiful but I believe she has saved herself by her ingenuity. The bruises she shows me on her thin arms and legs, even on her dear face, incurred in the course of these travels, evoke my every sympathy."

"How preposterous," Pauline whispered to me.

"My third daughter," Starky continued, pausing to sip her drink, "is plain and compliant with great physical stamina. In fact it is by her strength that she attempts to atone for everything. She is sentimental and nostalgic, which is understandable for given her nature her future will be little different from her past. She is not lazy, on the contrary she labors hard and conscientiously, but her work is taken for granted. She is hopeful and trusts everyone, leaving herself open to betrayal. She pores over my trinkets, believing they have special import for her. She often cries out for me in the night. She fears death more than I do, more, perhaps, than any of us here."

"Bless her heart," Betty said.

"Does she?" Pauline asked. "But there's no way of judging that, is there? I mean, how can you even presume—"

"I wish you'd continue," Betty said to Starky.

"Yes," Bruce said. "Mustn't get stalled on that one."

"My fourth daughter is a singer, an exquisite mezzo-soprano. Her voice was a great gift, she hasn't had a single lesson. Even when it became clear that she was extraordinary we decided against formal training, which would only have perverted her voice's singularity and freshness. Sing, I urged her always. Sing! For your voice will desert you one day without warning."

"Mommy," Guinivere said—startling me, for I had forgotten her completely.

"Do sing for us, Guinivere," Betty said. "We so love it when you sing."

"Yes, go ahead," her mother said.

The girl's round mouth grew rounder still and after a moment in which, I suppose, she composed herself, she sang in the most thrilling voice:

> If there had anywhere appeared in space
> Another place of refuge, where to flee,
> Our hearts had taken refuge in that place,
> And not with Thee.
>
> . . . .
>
> And only when we found in earth and air,
> In heaven or hell, that such might nowhere be—
> That we could not flee from Thee anywhere,
> We fled to Thee.

"How sweet," Pauline allowed.

"Is that Trench?" Bruce asked. "I'm not as keen as I used to be in identifying those old English hymnists."

Guinivere rose and said something urgently to Betty.

"Go behind the bushes, dear," Betty said. "It's quite all right."

"Behind the bushes!" Pauline appeared scandalized. "She's a grown woman!"

"Our house rather frightens Guinivere," Betty said.

"Perhaps there are ghosts," Pauline said. She giggled and whispered in my ear, "Don't tell me the Vineyard wouldn't be better than this."

"I don't know about ghosts," Betty said, "but in any old house you can be sure things happened, cruel and desperate things."

When Guinivere had disappeared behind the large lavender globes of the hydrangeas, her mother said quietly, "Her voice is in decline."

"I find that difficult to believe," I said, though of course I am no expert. "Her voice is splendid."

Starky said calmly, "She is like a great tree in winter whose roots are cut, only mimicking what the other trees can promise—the life to come."

Guinivere returned and took her place. She could not be persuaded to sing again. We were all sitting on old metal chairs, rusted from years of the island's heavy, almost unremitting fog, but not so badly that they marked one's clothes. I believe Bruce and Betty stored them in the cellar during the winter.

"My fifth daughter," Starky resumed to my dismay, "is the one I personally taught about time. I did her no service for she is my most melancholy child. She is unable to give value to things and never surrenders herself to comforting distractions. Alternatives are meaningless to her. She is a hounded girl, desolate, a captive, seeking in silence some language that might serve her. Faith would allow her some relief but she resists the slavishness of spirit that faith would entail. No, for her faith is out of the question."

Bruce gestured for me to make fresh drinks for all. I wanted further drink badly, indeed I had almost taken Pauline's glass and drained it as my own. I made the drinks quickly, without the niceties of sugar or lime and with the last of the ice.

"My sixth daughter is dead," Starky said. "She ran the brief race prescribed to her and now her race is done."

"She has a lovely stone," Betty said.

"She wanted a stone," Starky said. "I had to assure her over and over that there would be a stone."

"Well, it's lovely," Betty said.

"She found the peace which the world cannot give," Starky said, quite unnecessarily, I thought.

Pauline stared at her, then turned to me and said, "What could she possibly mean? How could she know what the poor thing found?"

I wanted to calm her though I knew she was more angry than anxious. Only hours before this mad evening had begun we were sitting quite contentedly alone on the moors, or what on this island they refer to as moors. We had wasted the morning, we'd agreed then, but not the afternoon. We could not see the sea, though we were aware of it because of course it was all around us. Love's bright mother from the ocean sprung, the Greeks believed.

"I can't bear this another moment," Pauline said, rising to her feet. "Why do you expect to be so indulged? Why did you have so many? Where is the father? Who is the father? The children are freakish, at least as you present them. Why do you put them on such cruel display? Why are their efforts so feeble and familiar? Why are you not more concerned? This is not how friends spend a sociable evening. Why didn't you tell a real story, not even once? How could you believe we would even be interested? No, I can't endure this any longer."

And with this she hurried out, unerringly I must say, through the dark garden, across the uneven flagstone. It took me several minutes to deliver my apologies and good-byes, but even so I left in such haste that it was not until I was well down the street that I realized I was still wearing Bruce's old sweater. I would mail it to him in the morning before we boarded the ferry. I wondered if Betty and Bruce would store the old chairs when the days grew bitter and if, assuming they did, the effort would be made to bring them out again in the spring.

It must have been quite late for the streets were deserted. I hoped that a walk, at my own pace in the light chill fog, would clear my head. Starky had seemed amused by Pauline's outburst and Betty and Bruce unperturbed, while Guinivere had not raised her head, either then or at my own departure. Indeed, she appeared to be practically in a stupor. Her mother might have been correct. The effort she was making could not be sustained much longer.

I walked slowly down the cobblestoned main street, turning left at the museum where earlier in the day Pauline and I had spent less than an hour for it was a dispiriting place, cheerfully staffed by volunteer docents but displaying the most grotesque weapons and tools of eighteenth-century whaling—knives and spades and chisels, harpoons and lances and fluke chains. Antique drawings and prints accompanied by descriptive commentary filled the walls. One sentence concerning the end of the flensing process, which took place alongside the ships, remains with me: *Finally the body was cast off and allowed to float away.* Most disturbingly put, I felt, the word *allowed* being particularly horrible.

Pauline had been quite right about the whales. Had they not cried out in the days of their destruction with exquisite and anguished song? Yet their pursuers wanted only to extinguish them. Indeed, man had reveled in the fine red mist that rose and then fell, as though from heaven, from the great collapsing hearts to herald the harried and bewildered creatures' deaths.

The inn where we had taken lodging was now in sight. I thought once again of the debt I owe Pauline and wondered if, in time, she would leave this life before me. It is proof of her success with me that I could entertain such a thought. One of us will be first, in any case, and until then we have each other.

The Other Week

"T HE FIRE DEPARTMENT CHARGED US THREE HUNDRED AND seventy-five dollars to relocate that snake," Francine said.

"Must have missed that one," Freddie said. "Fire department was here? Big red truck and everything?"

"There was a rattlesnake on the patio and I called the fire department and they had a long . . . it was some sort of hooked pole, and they got the snake in a box and released it somewhere and it shouldn't have cost anything because that's one of the services they provide to their subscribers, which is why everyone knows to call the fire department when a snake shows up on the patio. But we're not one of their subscribers, Freddie. I was informed of this after the fact. We have not paid their bill and their service is not included in our property taxes, which we likewise have not paid."

"Must've been taking a tub."

"The charge is excessive, don't you think? They were here for five minutes."

"Why didn't you just smack the thing with a hoe?"

"It's very civilized of the fire department to effect live removal. Why aren't we one of their subscribers, Freddie? If the house started to burn down, they'd respond but it would cost us twenty-five thousand dollars an hour. That's what they told me when I called to complain."

"The house isn't going to burn down."

"Freddie, why aren't you paying our bills?"

"No money," he said.

It was October in the desert and quite still, so still that Francine could hear their aged sheltie drinking from the bidet in the pool house. He was forbidden to do this. Francine narrowed her eyes and smiled at her husband. "What happened to our money?"

"It goes, Francine. Money goes. I haven't worked in almost three years. Surely you've noticed."

"I have, yes."

"No money coming in, and you were sick for a year. That took its toll."

"They never figured out what that was all about," Francine admitted.

"No insurance. Seventeen doctors. You slept eighteen hours a day. All you ate was blueberries and wheatgrass."

"Well, that couldn't have cost much."

"Like a goddamn mud hen."

"Freddie!"

"Seventeen doctors. No insurance. Car costs alone shunting you around to doctors cost more than four thousand that year, not including regular maintenance, filters, shocks and the like. Should've rotated the tires but I was trying to keep costs down."

"There was something wrong with my blood or something," Francine protested.

"Bought you an armload of coral bracelets. Supposed to be good for melancholia. Never wore them. Never gave 'em a chance."

"They pinched," Francine said.

"Even stole aspirin for you. Stole aspirin every chance I got."

"That was very resourceful."

"Oh, be sarcastic, see where that gets you. There's no point in discussing it further. We're broke."

The sheltie limped out into the sun, sated. He barked hoarsely, then stopped. He was becoming more and more uncertain as to his duties.

Francine went to the kitchen for a glass of water. She searched the refrigerator until she found a lemon, a small shriveled one from which she had some difficulty coaxing a bit of zestful juice. The refrigerator was full of meat. Freddie did the shopping and had overfamiliarized himself with the meat department.

"Broke," Francine said. He couldn't be serious. They had a house, two cars. They had a *gardener*. She returned to the living room and sat down opposite her husband. He was wearing a white formal shirt with the linkless cuffs rolled up, black shorts and large black sunglasses. His gaze was directed toward an empty hummingbird feeder.

"It's bats that drain that thing at night," Freddie said. "You don't have hummingbirds at all, Francine. You've got lesser long-nosed bats. They arrive in groups of six. One feeds while the others circle in an orderly fashion awaiting their turn. I enjoyed watching them of an evening. Can't even afford sugar water for the poor bastards anymore."

"What do you propose to do about our finances, Freddie?"

"Ride it out. Let the days roll on. You had your year of sleeping eighteen hours a day."

"But that was a long time ago!" Once she had been the type of person who didn't take much between drinks, as they say, but the marathon sleeping—it actually had been closer to twenty hours a day, Freddie always was a poor judge of time—had knocked the commitment to the sauce right out of her.

"Seventeen doctors. No insurance. Never found out what it was."

"I pictured myself then very much like a particular doll I had as a little girl," Francine mused. "She was a doll with a soft cloth body and a hard plastic head. She had blue eyes and painted curls, not real curls. The best part was that she had eyelids with black lashes of probably horsehair, and when you laid the doll on its back those hard little eyelids would roll down and Dolly would be asleep. Have I ever told you that's how I pictured myself?"

"Many, many times," Freddie said.

Dusk arrived. A dead-bolt gold. Francine maintained an offended silence as vermilion clouds streamed westward and vanished, never again to be seen by human eyes. Freddie made drinks for them both. Then he made dinner, which they took separately. A bit less meat humming in the refrigerator now. Francine retired to the bedroom and turned on the television. The sheltie staggered in and circled his little rug for long minutes before collapsing on it with a burp. He smelled a little, the poor dear.

FREDDIE IN SEERSUCKER PAJAMAS LAY DOWN BESIDE HER IN THE bed. He settled himself, then placed his hand in the vicinity of her thigh. A light blanket and a sheet separated his hand from the thigh itself. He raised his hand and slipped it beneath the blanket. But there was still the sheet. He worked his hand under the fabric until he finally got to her skin, which he patted.

They were watching a film that was vicious and self-satisfied, tedious and predictable, when in a scene that did not serve particularly to further the plot a dead actor was introduced to digitally interact with a living one.

The dead actor was acting away. "Look at that!" Francine said.

The scene didn't last long, it was just some cleverness. The dead actor seemed awkward but professional. Still, this wasn't the scene he had contracted for. Watching, Francine knew a lot more than he did about his situation, but under the circumstances he was connecting pretty well with others.

"What are you getting so upset about?" Freddie said.

"Space and time," she said. "Those used to be the requirements. Space and time or you couldn't get into the nightclub. Our senses establish the conditions for the world we see. Kant said our senses were like the nightclub doorman who only let people in who were sensibly dressed, and the criterion for being properly dressed or respectably dressed, whatever, was that things had to be covered up in space and time."

"Who said this?"

"Kant."

Freddie removed his hand from her thigh. "Something's been lost in your translation of that one, Francine. Why does one want to get into the nightclub anyway? Or that nightclub rather than another one?"

"We're the nightclub!" she said. "We're each our own nightclub! And the nightclub might want other patrons. Other patrons might be absolutely necessary for the nightclub to succeed!"

"I think it's a little late for us to be discussing Kant with such earnestness," Freddie said.

"You mean a little late at night or a little late in life?"

He nodded, meaning both.

She snatched the blanket off the bed and walked through the darkened house to the patio. It was long past the hour when people in the neighborhood used the outside. It was a big concern among Francine's acquaintances, who were always vowing to utilize the outside more, but after a certain hour they stopped worrying about it. To many of Francine's acquaintances, the outside was the only flagellator their consciences would ever know.

She wrapped herself in the blanket and lay on the chaise longue. She was very uncomfortable, but when she lay on it in the daytime she never was. Finally she managed to wander into sleep, a condition for which she was losing her knack. When she woke it was glaring day and the gardener's face was hanging over hers. His name was Dennis, and he'd been in their employ for years. She had never been stared at so thoroughly. She frowned and he drew back and stood behind her. He placed his fingers lightly on her forehead and ran them down her neck, then dragged them up again and rubbed her temples. The day was all around her. The refulgent day, she thought. His hand floated to just above her collarbone and she felt an excruciating pain as his thumb dug into the tendon there and scoured it. She screamed and struggled upright.

"That shouldn't hurt," he said mildly. "It's because you're so tense."

She hurried into the house and quickly dressed. There was no coffee. She required coffee, and there was none. The house was silent. Both Freddie and the sheltie were gone. He sometimes took the dog for a walk, which Francine had thought was kind before she learned that their destination was usually a small park on a dry riverbed frequented by emaciated and tactically brilliant coyotes. There had been several instances when a coyote had materialized and carried off some pet absorbed in peeing, frolicking or quarreling with its own kind and thus inattentive to personal safety. Francine had accused Freddie of being irresponsible, but he insisted that these attacks were rare. More important was the *possibility* of attack, which gave distinction to an otherwise vapid suburban experience and provided a coherence and camaraderie among a group of people who socially, politically and economically had little in common. They were a fine bunch of people, Freddie assured her, and they shared a considerable pool of knowledge regarding various canine personality problems—fear-biting, abandonment issues and hallucinations among them—as well as such physical disorders as mange, anal impaction and incontinence, to name only a few.

Francine searched hopelessly for coffee. Outside, Dennis had scooped up a large snake between the tines of a rake and was dropping it over the wall that separated their lot from the Benchleys'. It looked quite like the snake the fire department had recently removed. Dennis was being helpful but she would have to dismiss him. He would simply have to retreat to his life's ambition, which he had once told her was to run a security-cactus ranch. There he would cultivate hybrids specific to sites, creating fast-growing, murderously flowering walls with giant devil's-claw spines that could scoop an intruder's throat out in a heartbeat.

She went outside. "Dennis," she began.

He turned toward her, not a young man. He had deep lines in his narrow face, running from his eyes to the corners of his mouth. They were not unattractive. If a woman dared to have lines like that she would naturally be considered freakish.

"Rattlesnakes don't have anyplace to go anymore," Dennis said.

The snake, deposited in a flower bed maintained by the Benchleys at a cost of great aggravation, set off in the direction of a large rock Francine knew to be fraudulent. It weighed little more than an egg carton and concealed a spare house key for the maid.

"Dennis, I'm afraid we must terminate your services. We haven't the money to pay you."

Dennis shrugged. "Nobody's paid me for coming on a year."

"Freddie hasn't been paying you?"

"Told me six months ago you didn't have any money. I come here because you remind me of Darla. When I first saw you I said to myself, Why, she's the spit and image of Darla, taking the years into account."

"Spitting image," Francine said. "What on earth does that mean?"

"I'll talk any way you want me to. You want me to talk less formal? I'm just so happy we're talking at last, like the more than friends we were meant to be."

"This is of no interest to me, but who is Darla?"

"Darla was my nanny when I was eight years old. She was ten years older than me."

Francine was shocked. A nanny! Though she did not want to believe herself a snob.

"Darla liked snakes."

"I don't *like*—"

"She had lots of stories about snakes. She told me, for instance, that the Mayans practiced frontal deplanation in newborn children so their heads would look like a rattlesnake's head. They bound up the newborn's soft little skull with weights. They believed snakes were sacred and that people with rattlesnake skulls would be more intelligent and creative. This had a positive, motivating psychological force on them. They became freer, more aware, bright and unusual. And I remember saying to Darla when she told me this that I wished someone had the imagination and foresight to do that to me when I was first born because I wouldn't mind having a deeply ridged, crenellated head. And Darla said it was too bad but that knowing my parents, which of course she did very well, it would never have happened were they given the opportunity for a thousand years, they still wouldn't have done it. They were very conservative. Not like Darla. Darla could leap up as high as her own shoulders from a standing position. Darla rocked! We lived in St. Louis, and once a year Darla and I would come out here to the desert, each spring for three years, and spend a week at a dude ranch and shoot bottles and ride mules and sleep in bunk beds. The corral is where Galore is now."

"Is that a new town?"

"Barbeques Galore is there."

"Oh," Francine said. She found this quite funny but decided to say in her most gracious manner, "Change can be quite overwhelming at times."

"That's right, that's right," Dennis said. "And then we'd come back to St. Louis and Darla would go off on another week of vacation but without me, and as you might imagine I resented that other week very much because I loved Darla. And then Darla had to have an operation."

"Wait," Francine said. "An operation?"

Dennis nodded. "She had to go under the anesthesia. And when a person goes under the anesthesia they're never the same when they come back up. You've got another person you're dealing with then. It makes just the smallest difference, but it's permanent. The change only happens once. That is, you might have to go under the anesthesia again for one reason or another and there'd be no change. Change don't build on that first change."

"Why did she have to have an operation?" Francine wondered.

"I was never told why," Dennis said, "so that's not important."

She shouldn't have been jumping as high as her own shoulders, perhaps, Francine thought.

"We still talked about snakes and made pineapple upside-down cake and swam and rode bicycles and I was still in love with her and then she took her other week again, which I begrudged her as usual, and when she came back she died."

"I'll be darned!" Francine exclaimed. She really was trying to follow this unformed history. It would cost her nothing to be polite. They owed him money and he had done a good job. Not a remarkable job, but a good one. Also, he was a human being who had suffered a loss, even if this had been by her estimation almost thirty years ago. The shock had clearly addled him. It must have come exactly at the wrong time. A moment either side of it and he would've been perfectly all right. She hoped they hadn't had an open casket.

"My parents permitted me to put a piece of broken glass in the coffin because Darla and I collected pieces of broken glass. It was one of the many collections we maintained. My parents didn't want there to be any confusion in my mind. They wanted me to realize that this time Darla was gone for good. Still, I had difficulty with the concept. It was a little beyond me."

"An open casket can sometimes backfire," Francine said.

"What?"

Darla sounded like a good-hearted girl, energetic, inventive, a nice kid, called too soon from life's parade or banquet, whatever it was. She couldn't imagine anyone being further from the idea of Darla than herself.

"I don't know what I would have done if I hadn't found you," Dennis said.

"You haven't found me!" Francine said, alarmed.

"I'm not saying you *are* Darla. Jeesh, I'm not crazy. I'm just wondering if you wouldn't like to go out some night and talk like we used to."

"I was never Darla."

"Jeesh," Dennis said. "I'm not saying you were Darla and now you're not, I'm not crazy. But I was thinking we'd go out in the desert and build a little fire. Darla loved those fires so! I could bring the wood we'd need to get it started in the motorcycle's saddlebags. In less than fifty miles we could be in the desert. Fat Boy could get us there in an hour."

"We are in the desert."

"You know they don't know what this is now where we are."

He was missing a tooth, far back, only noticeable in the way that hardly noticeable things are.

"You've seen my Harley. Haven't you just wanted to climb on Fat Boy and *go*? That bike gets so many compliments. If I ever wanted to sell, the ad would read *Consistent compliments*, but I'll never sell. Or maybe you'd want to go somewhere else. I'll take you anywhere you want. I got another pair of jeans, newer jeans. What? My hearing's not so good. After Darla died I stuck knives in my ears. You know how they say you shouldn't put anything smaller than your elbow in your ear? It was in honor of Darla because I loved her voice so much and never wanted to hear another's. I probably hear better than I should but I miss some of the mumble. You were mumbling there, not making yourself clear."

"The only place I'm going now, Dennis, is inside my home. I don't feel well."

"You don't look as good as you do sometimes. You got a headache? Darla used to have the cruelest headaches. I'd soak cloths in cool vinegar and put them on her head."

She probably had tumors the size of goose eggs in that head, Francine thought. Any operation was bound to be futile.

"OK, you go on inside," Dennis said. "Close the blinds. Put on this music I'm going to give you. Put this in your tape player. Take whatever's in there and throw it away. You'll never care for it again." He unbuttoned the pocket of his denim shirt and removed a plastic baggie containing a tape. "It's Darla playing the piano. It was in the lodge at the dude ranch right where Galore is, as I've told you. We didn't have a piano in St. Louis. This is pure Darla. She was so talented! When you hear this you'll recognize everything for the first time."

"Music can't do that."

"It can't?" He pressed the tape into her hand. "Since when?"

THERE WAS STILL NO COFFEE. SHE WASN'T GOING TO WASTE HER time looking for coffee when there wasn't any. A moth was floating in the sheltie's water bowl. This was one of those recurrent things. She went into the bedroom and lay down on the unmade bed. She wanted to sleep. She could no longer fall asleep! Insomnia, of course, was far worse than just being awake. She thought longingly of those two stages—the hypnogogic and the hypnopompic, although she could never declare with confidence which was which once she'd been informed of their existence—on either side of sleep, the going into and the coming out when the conscious and the subconscious were shifting dominance, when for an instant the minds were in perfect balance, neither holding dominion. But she couldn't sleep, she lacked her escorts, the hypnopompic and the hypnogogic, who of late had been acting more like unfriendly guards.

The sun was slipping into the afternoon, exposing the dirtiness of the windows, which she never cleaned in the hope of dissuading doves from crashing into the glass. The doves flew undissuaded. The many blurred impressions of their bodies depressed her but she was convinced that sparkling windows would be even more inviting to them as they attempted to thread through the houses in their evening plunge from the foothills to the valley below.

She had removed the tape from the dusty little bag and played it. It was a formal exercise—familiar, pleasant, ordinary. It didn't cast a spell or create a mood. It was not the kind of music that tore hungrily at her. It did not appeal to her at all. Much of the tape was empty of all but hum and hiss. The playing had simply stopped and had not resumed again. There was no applause, no exclamations of approval, no sense of an audience being present, least of all an impressionable child. Darla had certainly taken that kid for a ride. Had she confounded everyone she met in her brief life or only him? Probably him alone. Francine didn't think Dennis even knew this Darla very well, not really. He had a collection of queer memories—a girl leaping in place to what avail—of no more value than bits of broken glass. He had nothing. Darla inhabited his world more than he did, for she infused it, doing what the dead would like to do but in most cases couldn't, which in Francine's opinion was a very good thing. As far as she was concerned, though, Darla, her quenched double, was a disappointment.

She played the tape again and it sounded even less interesting than before and briefer as well. She didn't know what was missing, it had just become, was becoming, more compressed. She began to play it once more, then thought better of it. She ejected it from the machine and put it back in the baggie. Locating a pencil, she tore an envelope in half—another unpaid bill!—and wrote:

Dear Dennis. We appreciate the work you've done. Good luck in
raising security cactus! Good-bye and all best.

Her sentiments were not at all sincere but such were the means by which one expressed participation in the world.

Dennis was scrubbing the swimming pool tiles with a pumice stone.

"Here's your tape back," Francine said.

"It's something, isn't it," Dennis said.

"I found it a little repetitive."

"Yes, yes, those final chords can never be forgotten quickly enough." He seemed pleased.

"Dennis, I'm curious about a number of things."

"Darla was curious."

"You are from St. Louis and Darla is buried there?"

He nodded. "My family once owned half of St. Louis but they don't anymore."

"It seems a lot to be responsible for," she agreed. "But my point is, with you treasuring the memory of Darla so, I would think you would find her more present back there."

Dennis opened his mouth in a wide grimace. "Sorry," he said. "Darla always told me I eat too fast. Sometimes I can't catch my breath. I just had lunch."

"You could visit her grave and such," Francine went on relentlessly.

"That would be unhealthy, wouldn't it?" Dennis said. "Besides, Darla never liked St. Louis. She didn't care for vernacular landscapes. You couldn't see the stars in St. Louis. Darla liked a pretty night. No one liked a pretty night more than that girl did."

"She sounds like an exceptional young woman," Francine said dryly.

"She was beautiful and smart and kind and generous."

"I don't see her, Dennis! I can't picture her at all!"

"And when she looked at you, she did it with her whole heart. You existed when she looked at you. You were . . ." He appeared to be short of breath again.

"I'm not a particularly nice person, Dennis. I've had to admit that to myself, and I'll admit it to you as well. I might have been nice once but I get by the best I can now. I don't even know how you'd look at someone, anything, with your whole heart. Why, you'd wear yourself out. You'd become nothing but a cinder. Now, it sounds as though you had a very fortunate childhood until you didn't. It's what I always think when I see cows grazing in the fields or standing in those pleasant little streams that wind through the fields or finding shade beneath the occasional tree, that they have a very nice life until they don't. An extreme analogy, perhaps—well, yes, forget that analogy, but you have to move on, Dennis."

"What?" Dennis said.

"Now I want you to read the note I've given you. And I really must find Freddie. He and the sheltie have been gone for an unusually long while."

Francine walked briskly through the patio to the garage. The door was open and Freddie's large dour Mercedes was gone, leaving only "her" car, an unreliable convertible she professed to adore. She would go to the dog park. She stepped into the convertible, turned on the ignition and studied the gauges. It was very low on fuel.

At the gas station, the attendant inside said, "What would you do if this wasn't a real twenty-dollar bill, backed by the United States government?"

"What would I do?"

"Yeah!" The girl had unnaturally black hair and a broad unwinning smile.

"Of course it's real. Do you think I'm trying to pass off a counterfeit?"

"I'm not going to take it," the girl said. "I'm using my discretion. Nobody uses money anymore."

"It's a perfectly good bill," Francine said. "Don't you have a pen or a light or something that you pass over these things?"

"I'm using my discretion."

Francine was about to continue her protests but realized this would only prolong the girl's happiness. She returned to her car, annoyed but not so shaken that she failed to offer the moribund palm on the pump island her customary sympathy.

There was no dearth of gas stations. She sacrificed the entire twenty to the gluttonous little car. Then, after driving for miles and making several incorrect turns, she arrived at the dubious park. When she and Freddie had first moved to Arizona they took a rafting trip and everyone on it got sick. The guide hadn't lost enthusiasm for his troubled industry, however. "Nobody likes to get sick from a little bacteria!" he said. "But you're on the river! Some folks only dream of doing this!" This was another river, though, or had been.

A half dozen dogs rushed up to her. One had a faded pink ribbon attached somehow to the crown of its head, but none of them had collars. She tried to befriend them with what Freddie referred to as her birthday-party voice, though they seemed a wary lot and disinterested in false forms of etiquette. She wondered which one of them had the hallucinations and what he thought was going on around him right then. She waded through the pack and approached a group of people sitting on a cluster of concrete picnic tables.

"Has a man with a sheltie been here today?"

"The sheltie," a woman said. "Congratulations!"

"I'm sorry?" Francine said.

"No need to be. It was a dignified departure, wasn't it, Bev?"

"As dignified as they come," Bev said. "We all almost missed it."

"I find it so much more convincing to just see how things happen rather than to observe how we, as humans, make them happen," a man said.

"Yeah, but we still almost missed it," Bev said, "even you." She winked at Francine. "He thinks too much," she confided.

"A swift closure," another man said. "One of the best we've seen."

Francine began to cry.

"What's this, what's this," someone said fretfully.

Francine returned to the car and drove aimlessly, crying, around the sprawling city. "Poor old dear," she cried. "Poor old dear." But I might have misunderstood those people completely, she thought. What had they said, anyway? She stopped crying. When it was almost dark she pulled up to a restaurant where she and Freddie had dined when they did such things. She went into the restroom and washed her face and hands. Then she opened her purse and studied it for a long moment before removing a hairbrush. She pulled the brush through her hair for a while and then replaced it. Slowly she closed the handbag, which as usual made a decisive click.

In the dining room, the maître d' greeted her. "Ahh," he said non-committally. She was seated at a good table. When the waiter appeared she said, "I'm starving. Bring me anything, but I have no money. Tomorrow I can come back with the money." She was a different person now. She felt like a different person saying this.

The waiter went away. Nothing happened. She watched the waiters and the maître d' observing her. On the wall beside her was a large framed photograph of a saguaro that had fallen on a Cadillac Brougham in the parking lot and smashed it badly. Save for such references, one hardly knew one was in the desert anymore.

People came into the restaurant and were seated. They made their selections, were served and then left, all in an orderly fashion. A glass of water had been placed before Francine when she first sat down and she had drunk that but the glass had not been refilled.

She left before they flipped the chairs and brought out the vacuum cleaner. When she arrived home the garage door was still open and Freddie's Mercedes was not there. There would probably be a reminder in their mailbox the following morning that subdivision rules prohibited garage interiors from being unnecessarily exposed. No one likes to look at someone else's storage, they would be reminded. Francine very much did not want to go into the house and face once more, and alone, the humming refrigerator and the moth floating in the sheltie's water dish. Given Freddie's continued absence, she would probably have to call the police. But she did not want to call the police after her experience with the fire department. She considered both of these official agencies and their concept of correctness of little use to her. She eased the car into gear—it sounded as though something was wrong with the transmission again—and drove off once more into the dully glowing web of the city, lowering the roof and then raising it again. Finally she left the roof down, though no stars were visible. The lights of the city seemed to be extinguishing them by the week.

Stopped at a light at a large intersection, she saw the Barbeques Galore store. The vast parking area covered several acres and was dotted with dilapidated campers, for the store was not closed for the evening but had gone out of business, providing welcome habitat for the aimless throngs coursing through the land.

She turned in and, threading her car among the vehicles, heard the murmur of voices and saw the silhouettes of figures moving behind flimsily curtained windows. Some trucks had metal maps of the country affixed to the rear, the shapes of the states colored in where the people had been. Dangling from the windshield mirrors were amulets of all kinds, crosses, beads, chains. On the dashboards were cups, maps, coins and crumpled papers, even a tortoise nibbling on a piece of lettuce. And there, swooping in a graceful arc on the darkened margin of the place, Galore, the ineradicable locus of what had been his happiness, was Dennis on his waxed and violet Fat Boy. He hadn't seen her yet, of that she was sure. But if she went to him, what could be the harm? For he was no more than a child in his yearnings, and his Darla was just an exuberant young girl who could never dream she didn't have a life before her.

Hammer

ANGELA HAD ONLY ONE CHILD, A DAUGHTER WHO ABHORRED her. Darleen was now sixteen years old, a junior in boarding school who excelled in all her courses. Her dislike of Angela had become pronounced around the age of eleven, increasing in theatricality and studied venom until it leveled off in her thirteenth year, the year she went off to Mount Hastings.

Darleen's father had died in a scuba accident when she was but an infant. He had held his breath coming up the last twenty feet of an otherwise deep and successful dive. An absolute no-no. One did not hold one's breath on the ascent to the light no matter how eager one was to return. He had been instructed in that, as had Angela and everyone else in the resort training course they'd been taking. While he'd been recklessly rising Angela had still been fooling around down in the depths, interesting herself in a rock that was in the process of being dismantled or constructed—it was hard to tell which—by colorful wrasses.

Angela had known few men after her impetuous young husband, whose name had been Bruce. She lived in the house she had returned to as a widow in the town she'd always lived in. Despite the dislike her daughter felt toward her, Angela was devoted to Darleen and awaited the day when their estrangement would be over, for surely that day would come. At the same time she feared that something would break then in Darleen, never to be made good again.

Ever since the girl insisted on going off to boarding school, Angela had worked as a masseuse in an old spa on the outskirts of town. She found the work distasteful and yet persisted in it, kneading and pummeling, rapping and slapping, the trusting hides presented to her. The old bodies became delusionarily flattered and freshened beneath her cool hands. Still, she was not as popular as the other masseuses. She spoke little and had no regulars. In her white cubicle on a white wooden table beside the high white-sheeted table was an envelope with her name written on it, a reminder that a gratuity would be appreciated. Seldom did it contain anything at the end of the day, though once an extraordinarily long and vigorously curling eyebrow hair had been deposited there.

On a cold morning in late February, Angela had a single appointment. She knew the woman, a wealthy and opinionated patron of the arts who was dedicated to social inclusion, moral betterment, sculpture in the parks and dance. She smiled at Angela thinly, disappointed that she was not being served by Margaret, everyone's favorite. Outside the sky was dark, almost cyclonic, but inside a warm, optimistic light bathed everything. There was an orange on the table that really ought to be thrown out, and Angela left the room for a moment to dispose of it.

Midway through the session, just as Angela's tape was about to end—it was Schweitzer playing Bach's Fugue in G Minor, and she was dreamily placing the shaggy-haired theologian thumping away on an organ in the jungle, pulling out all the stops in a green and unreconciled jungle, which he was not doing at all of course—she snapped her prosperous client's wrist bone, and before the ambulance arrived she'd been fired.

"I have no choice, Angela," the manager said.

"What if the others signed a petition to keep me on," Angela asked.

"They wouldn't do that, Angela. They wouldn't trouble themselves, you know that."

"Oh, it doesn't matter," Angela said.

"Of course it doesn't," he said.

Angela did not return home that night. Instead, she drove to the coast several hours away and boarded a ferry that served a number of weedy, unremarkable islands popular with the very rich, who maintained large and hidden homes there. In the tiny lounge of the ferry, people were talking about a dog that had fallen overboard during the previous night's crossing and had not yet been found. It was a chocolate-colored Lab named Turner. The owners, a young couple just married, were practically keening with distress, according to the purser. Angela stared at the water with the four other passengers. Occasionally, the ferry's searchlight would cast a broad beam over the waves.

Angela checked into the inn closest to the ferry slip on the first island. She had come here before in times of distress, usually when she was trying to stop drinking. The following day, in her old wool coat and with a borrowed scarf over her head, she walked along the beach. The few people she encountered referred to the drizzle as mizzle, which had been more or less constant since New Year's Day. Angela's thoughts floated beside her. The vigorous eyebrow hair in the envelope appeared more than once, seemingly determined to show its jurisdiction over her most recent months. It had quite attached itself to Angela, though only in spirit, for she certainly hadn't kept the damn thing.

When she boarded the ferry the next morning, people were talking about the brown Lab that had been rescued the night before, on the boat's last run. He'd actually slipped below the waves just before they'd gotten a flotation ring around him. He was an instant from being gone but they'd hauled him in, and he'd smiled the way Labs do, pulling back his lips in a black, rubbery grin. After he'd been warmed and fed, the distraught couple had been called, and when the ferry returned to the mainland the three of them were reunited. But the couple said it wasn't Turner. In their minds they had endured with Turner the weight of the stinging sea, the whipping of the starless dark, the bewilderment and despair that this animal too must surely have suffered. But this was not their Turner, and they were not going to take him home with them.

"I never saw a dog looked more like another dog in my life," the cashier in the galley was saying. "That Turner came in here three days ago with those people and he ate a fried-egg sandwich."

The couple apparently had been heckled off the boat.

"They weren't crying anymore," the cashier said. "They were stubborn about it, they'd made up their minds. It was the captain took the dog."

Angela pressed herself against the rail and looked at the water much as she had earlier, waiting for something to appear. This time she would be the first to glimpse it. There! she imagined herself calling out to the others. Though it was unlikely now. No, it would never happen now.

She drove home, detouring through the grounds of the old spa, which looked as ruined and complacent as it had when it was a big part of Angela's life. Smoke rose from one of the chimneys. The fireplace in the game room frequently harbored a meager fire. The immense moribund pines, dying because of the town's controversial road-salting practices, loomed protectively over the winding narrow road.

The phone was ringing as she opened the door. It was Darleen, who announced that she was arriving the next day for a brief visit.

"It would be thoughtful of you if you canceled your appointments at that vile place you work so we could spend some time together," Darleen said.

"What would you like to do?" Angela said.

"I thought I'd help you put in a garden, Mummy."

"I don't have a garden, dear. There was never ... I mean nothing's changed much since you were here last."

"I know the conditions under which you live, Mummy. I was just being annoying."

"How is school?"

"They've completed the new library, and we're allowed two days off from classes to move the books from the old institution down the hill to the new institution. We are to be utilized as a merry and willing human chain. I resist being so utilized. I'm here to learn."

"So you're coming here instead," Angela said.

There was silence.

"Which is wonderful," Angela said. "Really wonderful."

"I'm hanging up, Mummy. You can continue with your inanities if you wish."

That night Angela had a dream. She was in a furniture store and the salesman was speaking about the wood of a bed she was looking at. Angela was not really interested in the bed and had no intention of buying it but she had been staring at it for some time. No wonder the salesman thinks I'm interested in it, she thought in her dream, I keep walking around and around it. "Now some people," the salesman said, "they look at a thousand-year-old tree and they say, 'So?' They don't respect it, you know? Thing's just growing out of the ground. But to cut to the detail, this bed comes to you from Indonesia fresh from a managed forest, what they call a managed forest, and it hasn't been treated yet so you've got to care for it. You've got to oil it at least once a year. It's like it's still alive. The molecules are still stretching and expanding.

I admit it's not like a fine piece of furniture that your grandmother might have taken pride in and cared for because it isn't a fine piece of furniture, it's hacked out by simple Malay Archipelago artisans for export. With fairly crude tools. Now some people like this situation, it's just what they want. They want to feel they're doing their part by providing a commitment, a commitment to life, a thwarted life, not just to an inert tyrannical object like the kind your forebears served. And this baby's cheap. Of course the timber industry is out of control worldwide, and this price hardly reflects the real costs entailed—the *invisible* costs, you might say. But the opportunity you have right here is to acquire something that's alive even when it's dead, do you hear what I'm saying?"

The salesman had a head that looked like a medicine ball. How heavy that must be, Angela thought. When it began to resemble something more like a brown dog's head, she woke up.

DARLEEN ARRIVED WITH SOMEONE SHE INTRODUCED AS DEKE, her assistant and guide, a man with graying, slicked-back hair. He wore a leather shirt and extremely tight-fitting leather pants that suggested no knob. Angela couldn't help but notice this. Darleen had dyed her hair white and it sprang above her pale face like a web composed of bristles and points. She had not, however, adorned her face with rings or studs, as was so much the fashion among the young. The rings always seemed to presuppose some sort of leash to Angela. She was pleased that Darleen had not succumbed to convention.

"Slippery out," the man said.

Upon arrival he requested a bath. His bathing was noisy and prolonged, and when he emerged from Angela's bathroom the immediate premises smelled fruity and foul. "Bag?" he said to Darleen.

"I put it in the kitchen."

Angela heard him opening and shutting drawers, criticizing the color scheme—green and red or "rhubarb"—and bemoaning the dearth of protein. There was then the sound of a bottle being uncorked. He appeared with a single water goblet filled to the brim with wine. "Glasses look as if they were washed on the inside only," he complained. "Knives badly in need of sharpening." He stood before them, sipping the wine appreciatively. Angela's eyes reluctantly strayed to his remarkable leather pants.

"Can't see nothing for seeing something else," Deke muttered.

"Dear . . ." Angela began.

"I want to marry him, Mummy, I'll spend years if necessary nursing him back to health. I want a large wedding in an English garden with a champagne fountain." She chewed on her fingers and laughed.

Angela decided to ignore the subject and the presence of Deke, assistant and guide, for the moment. "Is everything going well at school? Tell me about school."

"We finished our studies of archaic cultures with the Aztecs. As everywhere else in the world, the Aztec elite had more varied ideas about their gods than the common people."

"Don't you go believing that now!" Deke exclaimed.

"Religious thinking among the elite developed into a real philosophy that stressed the relative nature of all things," Darleen continued briskly. "Such a philosophy can only develop in a sophisticated environment."

She then lapsed into silence. Deke said he was going to take a peek around if it didn't disaccommodate anyone.

"What will you be doing this summer?" Angela asked after a while. "Will you be a nanny again for the Marksons?"

"I hardly think so." Darleen gazed at her critically. At some point in boarding school she had learned how to enlarge her eyes and make them glassy at will, like some carnivore about to attack.

"I was on the island just yesterday but I didn't walk as far as their house."

"Am I supposed to find that interesting?" Darleen sighed. "In another class we're reading Dante. Do you know why he called it a comedy?" She raised a gnawed paw to prevent her mother from replying, although Angela had no intention of interrupting her. "Because it progresses from a dark beginning to redemption and hope."

"What translation are you using?"

"Oh, for god's sake, Binyon. Laurence Binyon. What do you care? That's not the point I wish to make. My point is that Dante's imagination was primarily visual. In his time people didn't dream, they had visions. And these visions had meaning. We only have dreams and dreams are haphazard and undisciplined, the meager vestige of a once great method of immediate knowing." She gnawed on her fingers again. "You see visions today and you're considered abnormal, uncouth."

Deke hurried past them back into the kitchen, where he poured more wine.

"This ain't much of an establishment if you pardon my saying so," he said to Angela. "No steaks in the freezer, no ice cream, sound system inadequate, music fit only to disinform the listener, no point in hearing it twice, towels thin, washcloths worn and most suspect, bed lumpy, poor recycling practices, few spare lightbulbs on hand, fire extinguishers out of date, no playing cards, clocks not set properly—"

"I like them a little fast," Angela conceded. It was all true. He was in no way exaggerating.

"Potted violets on windowsill in very poor condition, worst case of powdery mildew I ever saw. I could go on."

"I remember those violets," Darleen said. "Those violets are from my childhood."

"Now that's just plain wrong," Angela protested.

"Suffering the same fate regardless," Darleen said.

"You got a considerable amount of canned goods, however. Can I take some back to my friends?" Deke's hair was still wet, but already scurf was bedecking his thin shoulders like fresh snow.

"See, Mummy, even though a person has no future to speak of, he can take a moment to think of others. He can trust even in the blackest part of night that the daylight is not going to forget to come back for him."

"She's a talker, isn't she," Deke said.

"That surprises me, actually," Angela confessed. "It really does." She was brooding about that daylight-coming-back business. You couldn't think that way about daylight, that's why the ancients were always so hysterical. It was just too mental, too neurasthenic. Certain things just couldn't forget to come back. And when they finally didn't, it wasn't because they *forgot*. They did it with deliberation.

Deke had casually resumed his litany of the inadequacies of Angela's method of living. "Carpeting not particularly clean—gritty, in fact. No handy cold-care tissues available, no Proust."

"You're the biggest show-off I've ever known for someone who a couple hours ago was begging outside the bus station," Darleen said.

"Selling newspapers," Deke said.

"They were giveaway papers," Darleen said. "They were supposed to be free." She turned to her mother. "I was kind of not looking forward to us being together. I needed a respite from you at first. So I gave this one money to come here with me."

"You want it back?" From a slit pocket in his shirt he extracted a bill, then proceeded to unfold Benjamin Franklin's enormous head.

"Yes, she does," Angela said. "Of course she does." She sent Darleen a hundred dollars every month for, the word they had agreed upon was *incidentals*, and she certainly did not want her to waste the money in this fashion. "I send you a hundred—"

"Big goddamn deal," Darleen said. "My roommate gets two hundred each month from her parents, which they earn by collecting cans and bottles. The Garcias search the streets and alleys thirteen hours a day for cans and bottles. It's their goddamn job. Fifteen thousand cans pay their rent each month and another six thousand nets their little scholar Isabelle two hundred bucks, and I can inform you that Isabelle—who's the biggest goddamn fraud I've ever met—spends it on fancy underwear. The Garcias are tiny, selfless, worn-out *saints* walking the earth, I've seen 'em, and Isabelle buys *lingerie*." She waved the proffered bill away. "What's gone is gone," she said, and laughed.

Deke refolded the bill and placed it back in his shirt. "She's probably referring to an unfortunate erotic crisis I underwent recently. Otherwise, given its more general application, I would say that she doesn't subscribe to the gone-is-gone theory one bit."

Darleen scowled at him. "This is not the appropriate moment."

Deke sniffed loudly, rotated his arms and clasped his hands together. "Cold in here too. Not cozy. Only thing of interest is this old painting. Where'd you get this? Quite out of place. An odd choice, I'd say."

It was a large oil of beavers and their home on a lake, painted the century before. It was not in a frame but affixed to the wall by nails. Angela looked at it, resting her chin in her hand thoughtfully. The colors of the landscape were deep and lustrous. The water was a fervent, rumpled barren of green, the trees along the curving shore like cloaked messengers. Everything seemed fresh and clean with kind portent, even the sky. God had poured his being in equal measure to all creatures, Angela thought solemnly, to each as much as it could receive. Beavers were peculiar and reclusive, but that was their nature. They were not frivolous beings. They behaved responsibly and gravely and with great fidelity. Here they were involved in the process of constructing their house, carrying branches and twigs and so forth in their jaws and on their great paddle-like tails, though the structure was already large and in Angela's view extremely accomplished, a mansion, in fact, the floors of which were carpeted with boughs of softest evergreen, the windows curving out over the water like balconies for the enjoyment of the air.

"Mummy stole that painting," Darleen said.

"Well, good for you!" Deke said. Clearly, Angela had been elevated in his regard.

"Some years ago, Mummy used to be quite the drinker," Darleen said.

"Is that so!" Deke exclaimed, more delighted still. "Why'd you give it up?"

The painting had been in a roadhouse she once frequented. Sitting and drinking, pretty much alone in that unpopular place, she would watch the painting with all her heart. Slowly her heavy heart would turn light and she would feel it pulling away as though it wasn't responsible for her anymore, freeing her to slip beneath the glittering skein of water into the lovely clear beaver world of woven light, where everything was wild and orderly and real. A radiant inhuman world of speechless grace. This was where she spent her time when she could. These were delicate moments, however, and further weak cocktails never prolonged them. Further cocktails, actually, no matter how responsibly weak, only propelled her to the infelicitous surface again. The artist, the bastard, had probably trapped and drowned the beavers and thrust rods through their poor bodies to arrange them in life-assuming positions, as Audubon had done with birds, the bastard, and Stubbs had done with horses, the bastard, to make his handsome portraits.

"Your mother isn't very forthcoming with the details, is she?" Deke said.

"I would wake up weeping," Angela said. "Tears would be streaming down my face."

"You quit, and now they don't anymore," Deke asked suspiciously.

Angela stared at him.

"Doesn't seem much to give up the drink for, a few tears. How long's it been since you've cried now?"

"Oh, years," Angela said.

"And now her heart's a little ice-filled crack. Isn't it, Mummy?" Darleen said.

"Why don't you leave your mother alone for a while," Deke said. "Look at you. You're a vicious little being, like one of those thylacines."

"The Tasmanian wolf is extinct," Darleen said. "Don't show off so goddamn much."

"Their prey was sheeps," Deke said. "But the sheeps won out in the end. They always do."

"Sheeps," Darleen snickered.

"A vicious little being you are," Deke repeated mildly. He regarded the painting once more. "I got a friend knew a guy who lived with a beaver in the Adirondacks. Every time my friend would go visit him, that beaver would be there with its own big beaver house made of sticks and such right against this guy's cabin. He'd rescued this beaver and they had a really good relationship. You broke bread with my friend's friend and you'd break bread with that beaver."

"Mummy, when do you plan on serving supper?" Darleen said. "She never has food in this house," she said to Deke.

"She's got a number of vegetables ready to go. Vegetables are good for you," he said without much conviction.

At dinner, Angela felt impelled to ask him about his circumstances.

"This is what I got to say to that remark. I don't know if you read much, but there's a story by Anton Chekhov called 'Gooseberries.' And in this story one of the characters says in conversation that there should be a man with a hammer reminding every happy, contented individual that they're not going to be happy forever. This man with a hammer should be banging on the door of the happy individual's house or something to that effect."

"You think you're the man with the hammer?" Angela said.

Deke smiled at her modestly.

"Mummy is certainly not happy," Darlene said.

"If I recall that story correctly," Angela said, "the point being made about the man with the hammer is that there is no such person." Angela had attended boarding school herself. She remembered almost everything she had been alerted to then and very little afterward.

"You're so negative, Mummy. You dispute anything anyone has to say." Darleen crouched over the table with her fist wrapped around a fork, not eating.

"The man with the hammer that I recall is in another story, not by Chekhov at all. In 'A Mother's Tale' the circumstances couldn't be more—"

"Don't be tiresome, Mummy," Darleen said.

"Why don't you leave your mother alone, the poor woman," Deke said. "This is an ordinary woman here. Where's the challenge? Why do you hate her so much? Your hate's misplaced, I'd say."

"Why do I hate Mummy?"

"Not at all clear. Whoa, though, whoa, I got a question for Angela. You ever confess under questioning from this child that you had considered, if only for an instant when she was but the size of a thumb inside you, not having this particular one at all, maybe a later one?"

"No," Angela said.

Deke nodded. "That's nice," he said. He picked at his potato. "This is a little overcooked," he said.

"I just want to check on something," Darleen said. She disappeared into what had been her bedroom. It had ugly wallpaper in a dense tweedy pattern that would make anyone feel as though they were trapped under a basket. Darleen had selected it at the age of eight. Angela didn't use the room for storage. Technically, it was still Darleen's bedroom.

"Dinner was OK, actually OK," Deke said pleasantly. "Glad you didn't go the fowl route. You ever had goose? There's this wealthy woman in town and she's got this perturberance about nuisance geese. They're Canada geese but they're not from Canada, she says, and she's got the town to agree to capture and slaughter them and feed them to the poor. If you have any influence, would you tell that old girl we don't like those geese? The flavor is off. They're golf-course geese and full of insecticides and effluent and such."

"Betty Bishop!" Angela exclaimed. "Why, I just broke her wrist!"

"Good for—" Deke began, then stopped.

"It was an accident, but what a coincidence!"

"I guess you wouldn't have the influence I seek, then," Deke said, sniffing. "You ever get the air ducts in this place cleaned? Should be cleaned annually. Dust, fungi, bacteria—you're cohabiting with continually recirculating pollutants here."

Darleen returned. "Where's my little fish?" she demanded.

"Well, it, oh goodness, it's been years," Angela said.

"Is that my fish's bowl in the kitchen filled with pennies and shit?"

"I saw that," Deke said. "Clearly a fishbowl, now much reduced in circumstances."

"I had a little fish throughout my childhood," Darleen explained to him. "I said 'Good morning' to it in the morning and 'Good night' to it at night."

Deke stretched out his long, black-wrapped legs.

"For years and years I had this little fish," Darleen said. "But it wasn't the same fish! I'd pretend I hadn't noticed there was something awfully wrong with fishie sometimes before I went to school, and she would pretend she hadn't slipped the deceased down the drain and run out and bought another one before my return."

"Oh, I knew you knew," Angela said.

"If it had been the same fish, you two would have lacked the means to communicate with each other at all," Deke suggested.

"Mummy, I want to be serious now. Do you know why I'm here? I'm here because Daddy Bruce requested that I come. That's why I'm here."

For an instant, Angela had no idea who Daddy Bruce was. Then her heart pitched about quite wildly. Darleen had neglected to put her eyes in full deployment and she gazed at her mother with alarming sincerity.

"I was studying one night. I'd been up for hours and hours. It was very late and he just appeared, in my mind, not corporeally, and he said, 'Honey, this is Daddy Bruce. I don't want you cutting yourself off from your mom and me anymore. Your mom's a painful thing to apprehend but you've got to try. She's living her life like a clock does, just counting the hours. You can take a clock from room to room, from place to place, but all it does is count the hours.'"

"He never talked like that!" Angela exclaimed. "He was just a boy!"

"Well, that's what happens pretty quick," Deke said. "They all get to sounding the same. It's characteristic of death's drear uniformity. Most difficult to be pluralistic when you're dead."

"He said he never loved you and he's sorry about that now."

Angela's heart was pounding hard and insistently, distracting her a little, making a great obtrusive show of itself. Be aware of me, it was pounding, be aware.

"He said if he had to do it all over, he still wouldn't love you and you still wouldn't know it."

"It don't seem as if this Bruce is giving Angela much of a second chance here," Deke said.

"Daddy Bruce wanted to assure you that—"

"Tell him not to worry about it," Angela said. There were worse things, she supposed, than being told you had never been loved by a dead man.

Deke giggled. "What else he have to say? Did he suggest you were studying too hard?"

"He would hardly have bothered to come all the way from the other world to tell me that," Darleen said.

"I suspect there's only one thing to know about that other world," Deke opined. "You don't go to it when you're dead. That other world exists only when you're in this one."

"Yes, that's right," Angela said. She took a deep, uncertain breath.

"That might be correct," Darleen said, gnawing on her hands again. "The dead are part of our community, just like those in prison."

"Ever visit the prison gift shop?" Deke said. "Can't be more than ten miles from here. They sell cutting boards, boot scrapers, consoles for entertainment centers. The ladies knit those toilet-seat covers, toaster covers. Nice things. Reasonable. They won't let the real bad ones contribute anything, though. They want to sell products, not freak collector items. It's like that tree used to be outside the First Congregational Church. That big old copper beech they cut down because they said it was a suicide magnet? Wouldn't use the wood for nothing either, and that was good wood. Threw it in the landfill. Tree was implicated in only four deaths. Drew in two unhappy couples was all. Wouldn't think they'd rip out a three-hundred-year-old tree for that, but down it went. And now they've got a little sapling there no bigger around than a baseball bat."

Angela dismayed herself by laughing.

"That's right," Deke giggled. "If a young person gets it in his mind now passing that spot, he's got to *wait*."

"I should have suspected you two would get along," Darleen said sourly.

"You sick?" Deke asked Angela. "Is that why you don't care so much? Some undiagnosed cancer?"

"She's never been sick a day in her life," Darleen said. "She has the constitution of a horse."

"Horses are actually quite delicate," Deke said. "Lots can go wrong with a horse, naturally, and then you can make additional things go wrong, should you wish, if it's in your interests."

"Deke worked a few summers in Saratoga," Darleen said. She suddenly looked weary.

"A sick horse is a dead horse, pretty much," Deke said. "I'm going to uncork that other bottle now." From the kitchen, Angela heard him excoriating the rust on the gas jets, the lime buildup around the sink fixtures, the poorly applied adhesive wallpaper meant to suggest crazed Italian tiles. Goblet once again brimming, he did not resume his place at the table but walked over to the painting. "I can see why you felt you had to have this," he said. "At first it appears to be realistically coherent and pleasantly decorative, but the viewer shortly becomes aware of a sense of melancholy, of disturbing presentiment."

Angela wondered if it was possible to desire a drink any more than she did at this moment. It couldn't be.

"You clearly got an affinity with unknowing, unprepared creatures," Deke went on.

"Deke used to be an art critic," Darleen said.

He waved one hand dismissively. "Just for the prison newsletter."

"Yeah, Deke attended prison for two years," Darleen said.

"I began my thesis there," Deke said. "'Others: Do They Exist?' But I never completed it. I was a couple of hundred pages into it when I had to admit to myself that it wasn't genuine breakthrough thinking."

Angela rose to her feet suddenly and tried to embrace Darleen. The girl was all stubborn bone. Her clothes smelled musty, and a stinging chemical odor rose from her spiky hair. She pulled away easily from Angela's grasp.

"Whoa, whoa, whoa there," Deke said.

Darleen laughed. "Daddy Bruce better get here quick. Wake you up."

"I have to . . . I have to . . . "

They looked at her.

"It's late and I have to go to work tomorrow," she said, ashamed.

"You said you'd take the day off!" Darleen cried.

"Take the day off, it don't fit when you put it on again," Deke said. "Attention here, I'm taking the fishbowl and going out for more wine. Liquor store has one of those change machines. Those things are fun, you ever seen one work?"

"Don't leave!" Angela and Darleen exclaimed together.

"At a dangerously low level," he said, raising the bottle.

No one could argue that it was otherwise.

"Just stay a little while longer," Darleen said.

Deke pursed his lips and pressed his hands to his leather shirt. "I might commence to pace," he said. He grimly poured himself the last of the wine.

"There was a strange thing that happened the other night," Angela began. "I was on a boat, the ferry that goes to the islands. There'd been the most remarkable coincidence—"

"A coincidence is something that's going to happen and does," Deke said. "You got a fondness for the word, I notice."

"Oh, Mummy is so seldom precise," Darleen said. "When I was small, she would tell me I had my father's eyes. Then one day I finally said, 'I do not have his eyes. He was not an organ donor to my knowledge. A little frigging precision in language would be welcome,' I said."

Deke looked at her impatiently, then stood as though yanked up by a rope. "You girls hold off on the Daddy Bruce business until I get back. That's dangerous business. You don't want to go too far with that without an impartial yet expert observer present."

He left without further farewell bearing the fishbowl, the door shutting softly behind him.

Angela laughed. "I think we disappointed him."

The room felt stifling. She opened a window, beyond which was a storm window, a so-called combination window, adaptable to the seasons. She fumbled with the aluminum catches and pushed it up. The cold clutched her, then darted past. She turned and looked at her daughter. "I love you," she said.

"Mummy, Mummy." Darleen sighed. Then, tolerantly, "The new headmaster has a white cockatoo that likes to be rocked like a baby."

"Do tell me about it, please," Angela said.

"Stupid bird," Darleen said cheerfully.

SEVERAL YEARS LATER, ANGELA WAS DYING IN THE TOWN'S HOSpital, in a room where many before her had passed. She had known none of them, but this room they had in common, and the old business engaged in there. Darleen had been summoned but would not arrive in time. Angela was fifty-five years old. She had not gotten out as early as she might have, certainly, but now she had firmly grasped death's tether.

"Passed that little sapling tree on the way here," Deke said. "Still being permitted to grow in the churchyard. Too new yet to cast a shadow, but it had better mind its manners, no?"

Angela wanted to laugh, even now. What a night that had been!

"Most enjoyable evening," Deke agreed.

The new little nurse said, "It sounded like, 'Did you bring the hammer?' "

The other nurse said, "You'll wear yourself out trying to make sense of no sense." She didn't care for this one. She was awfully eager and still being evaluated. It was quite possible that ultimately she wouldn't get the job.

Fortune

IT WAS THE PARENTS! WHEN WOULD THE PARENTS STOP COMING? They'd been coming for months, since Christmas, since *before* Christmas, since the Burning of the Devil festivities on the seventh. June's mother and her second husband had arrived, missing Howard's parents by only a few days, for they had come down specifically for his twenty-second birthday. Caroline's father had come down for Valentine's Day with his new wife and their fairly new infant to show her to Caroline, as though she cared. Abby's parents were still in town, having arrived for Semana Santa—Holy Week, which was now just past—and James's parents would be showing up any day now from Roatán, off Honduras, where they had been diving. And each set of parents had a new child with them. There was Emily and Morgan and Parker and Bailey and Henry, not one of them over the age of six. It was a phenomenon.

The parents were generous when they visited. June's mother's new husband chartered a plane and flew them all to Tikal. They climbed Pyramid IV and watched the sunrise, even baby Morgan in her tiny safari ensemble. And even though June's mother's new husband had rented rooms for them at the Jungle Lodge, one night they'd slept out among the ruins in hammocks. Everyone knew this was the desired, anecdotal thing to do, sleeping out among the ruins beneath the bats during a full moon, which it happened to be that night. June's mother and her new husband had expensive cameras and they took pictures of everything, they were delighted with everything. They were already planning on returning to Antigua in July for the Parade of the Heads to see the *gigantes* and the *cabezudos* weaving down the streets beneath the fireworks and whistling rockets.

When Howard's parents came, the father, a prominent throat specialist, rented horses for everyone and they had ridden to one of the lakes for a picnic. Even baby Bailey made the trip, wrapped in his mother's arms with one tiny hand clinging to the pommel. The whole group of them, eight in all, trotting like a cavalry through the poor little towns on these big-assed horses, leaving behind piles of green-flecked dung. Where had they gotten such healthy horses? It was embarrassing. "*Buenos días!*" Howard's parents said to anything that moved. It was amazing they hadn't been stoned.

Caroline's father appeared with darling Emily, a redhead, and his lively new redheaded wife, who wore a ring in her navel and was only two years older than Caroline. There had actually been something of an incident when everyone had been invited for lunch in the garden of the Hotel Antigua. There were some hummingbirds in the hibiscus bush near them, green and purple ones, the size of mice. One veered toward Emily in her high chair, no doubt encouraged by the feathery brilliance of her hair, and her attentive mother smacked it sharply with a guidebook she was holding. The bird spun to the ground in a buzzing heap.

They all shrank back from it a little.

"Gee, Penny," Caroline said.

"It was coming right at the baby," Penny said. "It almost flew into her."

"Hummers can be exceptionally aggressive," Howard said, smirking.

"Maybe it's just stunned," June said. "Maybe if we put it under a bush."

James took a linen napkin from the table and placed it over the bird, which was still whirring like a windup toy. Darling Emily bounced in the high chair and clapped her hands. She wore a sweet little dress embroidered with ducks. James walked beyond the table and was about to lay the hummingbird down.

"Farther," June said. "A farther bush."

He came back with the napkin and put it on the table.

"James," Abby said, "is that blood?"

He picked it up again and refolded it.

"Maybe we should have eaten it," Howard said. "You know, so as not to waste it. We should find its nest and eat that too. The Chinese eat nests."

Penny frowned at him. "I *am* sorry," she said. She dabbed at the plate of fruit she had been feeding Emily. "What is this, guava? Or papaya? One of them upsets her tummy."

Another pitcher of margaritas appeared from somewhere. It was a very well-run place. Gardeners swept the walks quietly with palm fronds tied to sticks. One of the swimming pools had the heads of a hundred ivory-colored roses floating in the deep end.

"You're great kids," Caroline's father said. "Really, you're terrific kids." Clearly, his spirits had taken more of a beating from the hummingbird incident than his wife's. "You're fine kids. Caroline, you have fine friends," he said.

All the visiting parents liked to pretend that the young people were charming. It was funny seeing this, each of them pretending this in their own way. The children were exhausted by the parents' vigor, they felt wearied by their presence. They were repelled by the parents' dedicated interest in them, they were astonished. Will we ever be *this* blind, do you think? they'd say. No, they agreed, they could not imagine themselves being this blind . . .

They were all starting off in their twenties. Each had come separately to this colonial town in the bowl-shaped valley beneath the three volcanoes and found one another here. Each of them remembered their first solitary days in town and then the speed with which they became involved in a life with the others, their friends. And they still wondered how this had been accomplished, and how much of it they had each been responsible for. They felt that here their lives were now beginning.

At the same time, they felt it was possible that their actual lives were still waiting for them, and that they involved different people. This was something they found themselves thinking about more and more, usually with unhappiness, as the parents kept coming.

Holy Week and its enormous, numbing spectacle was over for another year. The great obligation was over. The great *anda* borne by the penitents had been stored. The dyed sawdust and fresh flowers that had covered the streets in elaborate designs before being mangled by the penitents' feet had been swept away. Everyone loved Good Friday—betrayal and trial and cruelty still having the power to captivate—but Easter was a letdown. The promise of Easter was the same old promise. The town was hot and quiet, and everyone was still a little drunk.

Abby and June were having breakfast at one of the cafes that faced the park. The fountain was not operative this morning. Usually water plashed from the stone nipples of a trio of heroically sculpted women, but today they stood inactive, though still with their mysteriously withdrawn expressions as they held their lovely breasts. Workmen in boots rooted around in the water beneath them.

"I think your parents are cute," June said. "They're not like Howard's. Poor Howard."

"I spent ten to two with them yesterday," Abby said. "Then I took them to the market and my mother would say about anything, 'Is this the best price you can give me? Is this the best you can do?' In English, of course, slowly, in English. Candles, bananas, those tiny bags of confetti, everything . . . She bought me lightbulbs, she insisted. 'You have all these dead lightbulbs,' she said, and I said, 'Mom, we can buy these in the store, we don't have to be bargaining for them in the market.' Then I had to spend six to nine with them too, back at the hotel. And that Parker! He had to run across the cobblestones, and of course he falls down and practically tears off his kneecap. Finally, I cracked. I said, 'I've got to have a day off. I can't have another meal with you for a while, I just can't,' and my father said, 'We aren't taking out taxes.' "

June laughed, but then she said, "What did he mean?"

"Maybe he said withholding," Abby said. "It was a joke. Like I thought it was a job, my being with them."

"Oh, that's funny," June said. "That's what I mean. They're not that bad."

"I can't believe they adopted that child and then named him Parker," Abby said. "Where did that name come from? My mother reminded me that I had promised to take him tonight so they could go out to dinner by themselves."

"When my mother was here and I was with her at the bank?" June said earnestly. "And I was sitting there looking at my mother in line to get money? I had an epiphany."

"Really," Abby said.

"It was . . . my mother will always love me."

"That's an epiphany?" Abby said.

"It wasn't a thought. It was like . . ." June trailed off. "Your mother will always love you too, forever, no matter what."

"Isn't that amazing?" Abby said. "Really, it's amazing, if it's true."

A young Guatemalan boy wearing filthy green shorts with a broken zipper and a Chicago Bulls T-shirt came into the cafe holding three glass Shangri-La bottles by the neck. Then they saw Caroline walking by with her brown long-legged dog on a rope leash.

"Caroline!" they cried together.

She joined them, dragging the dog in with her. He had been neutered not long before, and he had a plastic basket on his head so he wouldn't rip his stitches out. The stitches should have been taken out by now and the basket removed, but Caroline was putting it off even though the Indians laughed rudely at the sight of them. Neither Abby nor June would have been capable of walking a dog around town with a basket on its head.

"Can't we take that off the poor thing?" Abby said.

"I know, I know, but then he bites his fleas," Caroline said. "I've got to give him a bath first."

The dog smacked the basket against the table leg and lay down with a thump. He was an odd little dog with large dewclaws and a strangely malformed mouth. Caroline had bought him in the market for two quetzales, about thirty-five cents. She took excellent care of him in a somewhat unbalanced fashion and was always trying to improve him. Caroline was an artist, she had always been an artist, things just came to her sometimes. She was thin, almost ascetic-looking, and had a temper.

Abby continued to look at the dog, at its long fawn-colored legs that seemed so breakable. Pets made Abby feel discouraged. In the run-down motel where they all rented rooms by the month, the guardian had an aged, arthritic parrot who was brought out on a stick every morning and left to hobble around on a broken bench beneath some banana trees until dusk. Sometimes June would gently spray him with water from the hose, which seemed to neither distress nor delight him, so Abby didn't know why she bothered. The motel also housed some members of a street band, who were seldom there, and a morose man with a bulging vein in his forehead that appeared to beat incessantly. He made a living from his fortune birds—three yellow canaries in a bam-

boo cage that would tell your future by selecting a small rolled piece
of paper from a pinewood box. The tiny prophets' names were Profeta, Planeta and Justicio, and they seemed untroubled. The motel was
not far from the *parque central* and was next to one of the town's many
ruined cathedrals, the rubble from one of the collapsed walls making
up part of the courtyard. The rooms were small, dark and cold, but
each had a perfect view of Agua, the most beautiful of the volcanoes.

The Guatemalan child, having been paid for the bottles, was threading his way back through the tables. He paused and gazed beseechingly
at June's pancake, which she had barely touched. Abby had not eaten
hers either and was using the plate more or less as an ashtray.

"June," Caroline said.

June looked at the boy. "Sure, sure," she said. He plucked up the pancake with slender fingers and hurried outside. He crossed the street
and stared at June as he ate.

"Is he scowling at us?" June said. "I mean, what is it exactly that one
is supposed to do?"

The others would often tease June for being so grave about everything. She wore oversize American clothes, a plaid shirt and brown
shorts, and a woven necklace that her mother had bought her during
her visit. June had wanted the necklace badly and had led her mother
to the store, which was frequently closed, more than once. She affected
ragged black and blond hair, which she made sticky with shaving cream.

"Imagine him and Parker as playmates," Caroline said. "Little playmates."

"That is so radical," Abby said.

The boy finished the pancake, then turned modestly away from
them to urinate.

"Oh, gaaa," June said.

"My mother is finally beginning to notice the public urination,"
Abby said. "'You know, honey,' she said, 'this is a lovely town, but so
much public urination goes on. I don't think I've ever seen so much
public urination. You walk through the park and men are urinating
behind pieces of cardboard. Boys are urinating on flowers. We went to
look at some churches and were poking around the courtyard and an
old man was urinating on a pile of sand. When he finished he flapped
his hands at us. He scolded us! He said we were not supposed to be in

the courtyard, we could only be in the church. He was the ostiary or something, or thought he was . . . '" Abby was mimicking her mother's nasal, bemused manner of speech.

"They're still here, your parents?" Caroline said.

"Oh god, yes," Abby said. "I have to watch Parker tonight so they can go out. It's their anniversary."

"We'll all watch him," Caroline said. "We'll sit around in a circle and blow smoke at him or something. Howard will ask him his opinion of death."

"That is getting so old," Abby said. "It's like an old bar trick or something."

"Morgan's been the darlingest," Caroline said to June. "Don't you just love her?"

June blushed. "Do you know what my mother told me? She said she had always been emotionally indifferent to my father, from the very first, but now she had found happiness and she hoped that I would find such happiness."

"Oh," Caroline said. "It's like a little blessing she gave you, isn't it? That's so nice."

"I love watching June blush," Abby said. "Really, June, you are so funny."

Then she and Caroline talked about how they wished they had a car they could share. Then they began talking about how James claimed to have stolen a car in Texas and driven it through Mexico into Guatemala, where he'd sold it for a great deal of money in the capital. This was a difficult, virtually impossible feat and the story had always elicited considerable admiration. James also claimed that once, prior to stealing the car, he had been arrested in California for underage drinking, and that as part of his sentencing he was forced to attend the autopsy of a drunk driver. He described how they had sawed off the top of the dead man's head.

"I think he made up that stuff about the cadaver," Abby said.

"I didn't believe that for one minute," Caroline said.

"I don't know about that car from Texas either," Abby said. "He's so enthusiastic about that experience, he probably didn't have it."

"What are you thinking, June," Abby asked.

"I was thinking I have no sense of direction," June said. "I can't remember the names of flowers or ruins or saints. And I can't keep a journal. Any journal I keep sucks." She was thinking of Edith Holden's precious Edwardian journal with all the lovely drawings. The one she had in prep school. Edith Holden had died tragically young, drowning in the Thames while collecting horse chestnut buds, the twit.

The bill arrived and June began to go over it painstakingly. "Excuse me, pardon me. *Perdóneme?*" she called to the waitress. "But no one here ordered the *huevos revueltos.*"

"Oh, just pay for it," Abby said. "All that stuff is fifty cents or something, isn't it? I'll pay for it."

"No, it's my turn," June said, counting out some coins. They then got up with a great scraping of chairs on the ugly tiles.

On the street, the dog strained toward a mound of burned plastic in the gutter and managed to acquire something repellent before Caroline hauled him away.

"He is so dim," she said. "I thought fixing him would make him smarter."

"That is so funny," Abby said.

They reached the heavy scarred wooden doors of their compound. They pushed them open and Caroline unknotted the rope from the dog's collar. He leapt into the air and ran around the courtyard three times at remarkable speed before a bougainvillea stump snagged the basket and sent him sprawling. The parrot dropped the piece of mango he'd been toying with and crouched against the gnawed slats of his bench. The parrot's name was Nevertheless as far as anyone could translate it. The dog didn't have a name.

The fortune birds were not up yet. Customarily they rested until noon in their cage, beneath a clean dish towel. For them Easter Week was one of the biggest weeks of the year. They had told a thousand fortunes. Their director, the man with the staggeringly large vein, was sitting at a card table in a corner of the courtyard writing new fortunes in an elegant script on blue pieces of paper. He wrote swiftly, without reflection or emotion. James and Howard were playing Hacky Sack on the grass with a tiny stitched ball that said I ♥ JESUS on it. They had bought it from some evangelicals who did massage. The boys had been so dumped the night before, clutching their glasses of *aguardiente*, that they could hardly find their mouths. Now here they were, sleek and quick.

June blushed when she saw James, for she had drunk a great deal of *aguardiente* last night as well and recalled asking him, "Do you think I have a personality?"

"No," he had said.

"A personality," she persisted.

"Why would you want one? You're fine."

"But I should," June said.

"Look at my wallet," he said. It was a long leather wallet clipped by a chain to his belt. "There was a whole bin of these on sale at the airport and the merchant said that each wallet had its own personality because it was natural material and the lines and colors and imperfections made each one unique."

"That's sick," June had said.

"Personality is secondary to predicament," James had said.

She was attracted to James, to his deep-set eyes and perfect skin, but none of them were lovers. That would have spoiled everything. Love was a compromise, they felt. They were not like their parents, who were always in love and who just went on and on with life, changing partners, acquiring new children, abandoning past interests and assuming new ones, always in love with someone or something.

It was almost noon. The boys continued to play Hacky Sack, thrusting out their long feet.

"I'm going to wash the dog," Caroline announced. "After which we shall remove the basket." She produced some special soap she had bought at the market. It came in a small box that had the drawing of an insect on it.

"It doesn't really look like a flea, though," Abby noted.

"They intended it to look like a flea," Caroline said confidently.

They captured the dog and poured a bucket of water over his wiry coat. The soap made a quick brown lather and almost instantly, motionless black fleas appeared.

"Look at those fleas," Abby said. "They're enormous."

"This soap must be lethal," June said.

The guardian and his family came out to watch the dog being

bathed. The parrot watched, too, swaying excitedly. The dog stood passively, his head bent, the basket touching the ground.

They rinsed and scrubbed, then rinsed again. There were fewer fleas at the end but there were never no fleas at all.

"Shouldn't we have gloves?" June asked.

"The fortune dog," Caroline said. "Divination by fleas." She picked them off. "This is not good," she said. "This is not good. This is not good either."

Then there was the ceremony of removing the basket, which was attached to the dog's collar with thick, dirty tape. Finally the basket was wrenched off. The dog's head looked somewhat smaller than anyone remembered.

"He really is unsatisfactory, isn't he?" Caroline said. "He needs something. What do you think, June?"

"Maybe a bandanna," June said.

"Oh, I hate bandannas on dogs," Caroline said. "The vet said he had too many teeth in his mouth. A couple of them should be pulled. And see all those warts on his head? They keep growing back."

The dog squatted on his haunches and stared at them. He had probably never been meant for this life. He was just not consubstantial with this life.

One of the reasons Caroline had acquired the dog was to practice concern. They all felt that sometimes it was necessary to practice the more subtle emotions.

The dog suddenly widened his eyes as though in delighted recall, shot up and sideways and danced away to his favorite spot in the compound, the smoldering refuse pile in one of the stalls that once stabled horses, rooting about for only an instant before finding something ragged and foul that he settled down to eat. At the same time, the owner of the fortune birds capped his pen, rose from his chair, rolled his shoulders, crouched slightly to fart and removed the cloth from the little birds' cage. Immediately the birds began to sing.

It was a lovely day. White clouds streamed past Agua, but so low that its dark cone was visible against the bright blue sky.

"I want to do something today," Abby said. "Don't you?"

From a distance Agua was magnificent, but they had all climbed it once and found it disappointing.

Abby looked at her watch. She said, "If I got this wet, I'd die."

"Let's climb Fuego," Howard said, giving the Hacky Sack a final, unraveling kick.

"It's too late," Abby said. "We'd have to start earlier than this." Fuego, the live volcano, was no higher than Agua but the ascent was more difficult. The third volcano, Acatenango, commanded little interest though surely it had its dignity, dangers and charms.

"Never too late to climb Fuego," James said. "The hot one, the mean one."

"Oh, that damn Fuego," Caroline said.

They had never climbed it, although they had set out to do so more than once. They would stay up all night and dawn would bring with it the desire to climb Fuego. They would take a taxi to Alotenango, a poor town surrounded by dark coffee trees, from which the ascent began. They would climb for a while, floundering through the greasy ash. Rocky furrows ran alongside the trail like empty rivers and sometimes became the trail. The furrow would sometimes vanish and a faint path through the ash would begin again above them. Some paths were marked by rocks painted NO! for though they looked like a reasonable choice they were not. The rocks bore the name of a hiking club, the members of which they had never seen. They'd never seen anyone climbing, although once they saw a dead colt with a braided mane.

They had always turned back after a few hours, because what was the point, really, of climbing Fuego?

"I think nature's kind of senseless, actually," Caroline said. "I mean real nature. I don't get it."

The hours passed. It was midafternoon when the cage holding the fortune birds was strapped to the motorbike for the trip to the plaza.

"We should do those birds sometime," Abby said. "I can't believe they're right here with us and we've never had them tell our fortune."

"I'd want Planeta to tell mine," June said. "The one with the black eyes."

"They all have black eyes," Caroline said.

"I mean black rings around the eyes," June said.

"This earth is my home for life," James said. "Do you ever think that?"

"That is unacceptable," Howard said.

"I don't think Profeta looks that well," Caroline said. "She doesn't look as yellow. Her beak looks like it's peeling."

Caroline's dog had danced over to the motorcycle and was nosing the cage.

"Get that cur away from here or I'll break its goddamn back," the man with the remarkable vein said in startlingly clear English. The birds chirped on, hopping about in their tiny, airy cage, the bars of which were woven with pale, wilted flowers, the floor of which was covered with the shredded faces of movie stars from shiny magazines.

Caroline hurried over and hauled the dog away. No one remarked on the outburst, recalling that it had happened before.

Shortly after the birds' departure on the black motorbike, Abby's parents arrived at the gate with young Parker and two string bags filled with food.

"Oh, I can't believe it," Abby murmured to Caroline. "So soon?"

"I'm sorry we're early," Abby's mother said, "but we went on a ruin run. We managed eight ruins today, which must be some sort of record, and when we got back to the room we discovered that we'd been robbed. Isn't that something!"

The three of them, even Parker, seemed almost enchanted that they'd been robbed, as if this were just another aspect of an exciting life. "They took nothing of real value," Abby's mother said. And that, too, added to the enjoyment of it all.

There was a little something on Abby's mother's nose that perhaps had been in her nose and somehow gotten out and around onto the side of it. All of them looked at it politely. With a small adjustment in her gaze, June looked at Parker and the large white bandage he wore insouciantly on one knee. She narrowed her eyes and the child receded into some blurry future, permitting the present to be inhabited by herself and her friends, which was proper.

Abby's mother set down the bags. "There's all kinds of stuff in here," she said. "I thought you could have a picnic supper."

"That is so sweet!" Caroline said.

"What did they take?" Abby asked.

"It was so stupid of me," her mother said. "I have so much trouble locking that door. I think it's locked but it's just stuck, so the room wasn't even locked. They took this jade necklace I'd just bought. It was still wrapped in tissue. It wasn't that expensive, but the thing was I'd bought it for you. Then I thought I'd keep it, because I didn't think it was really you, and then it got stolen. It serves me right, doesn't it?"

"That's really ironic, Mom," Abby said.

June asked Abby's mother which of the ruins had been her favorite.

"I loved the convent Las Capuchinas," Abby's mother said.

"Oh, I love Las Capuchinas too!" June exclaimed, as though everyone didn't say their favorite ruin was Las Capuchinas.

"What do you think actually went on there, on that subfloor?" Abby's mother wondered. "I have three guidebooks and they all suggest something different. It was either a pantry, or for laundry, or for torture."

"You have four guidebooks," Abby's father said.

"I think it's all a matter of wild conjecture." Abby's mother raised her hand and brushed the inconsequential thing off her face. "There were twenty-five nuns, right? Twenty-four? And they were never allowed to leave except when there was an earthquake."

"I like those creepy mannequins at prayer in their cells," Caroline said.

"Don't you just want to know everything?" Abby's mother exclaimed suddenly. "Just think of all the information children Parker's age will have access to, and so quickly!"

"What's your favorite ruin," June asked Abby's father.

"I don't have one," he said. "My favorite meal was the steak at Las Antorchas."

"I can't believe we're going back to Las Antorchas," Abby's mother said. "Honey," she said to Abby, "I'm sorry we're so early but we'll be back early. I just want to get this anniversary dinner over with."

"I don't want to stay here," Parker announced. "I want to stay with you." His hair was firmly combed. He wore madras shorts and a short-sleeved button-down shirt, dressed in a manner that small children often are for an event they are not really going to attend.

"Parker, look at that parrot!" Abby's mother said.

He studied the parrot, which was staggering across the grass to retrieve a bit of melon. "I don't like it, there's something wrong with it," he said. "I don't like that dog, either." The dog had been straining toward them soundlessly on its rope all the while, panting wildly.

"Well, just stay away from the dog," Abby's mother said. "Play with your trucks." She whispered to Abby, "We're just going to slip away now." They left and Parker sat down on the grass, dropping his head rather dramatically into his hands.

Howard went into his room and brought out an almost full bottle of Jägermeister. There was still the possibility, which they all embraced, that the liquor was made with opium. This had not been utterly discounted. "Hey, Parker," he said. "Would you like a drink?"

Parker raised his head. "I like iced tea," he said. "The kind you get at home, at the store, in a bottle. My favorite is Best Health's All Natural Gourmet Iced Tea with Lemon, and you wouldn't have that in a million years."

"He's into iced teas," Caroline said. "Isn't that scandalous."

"There's one that tastes kind of like fish," Parker said. "Sort of like rusty fish. But not right away. Just a little afterwards."

"They actually make an iced tea like that?" Howard said. "Cool."

"That is so radical," Abby said.

They drank the Jägermeister, ignoring Parker. The mosquitoes arrived. The parrot was coaxed onto a broom handle by the guardian's wife and taken in. Howard lit the paper trash and scraps of wood in the fire pit, a short, shallow trench he tended every evening. He was a big, meticulous young man. Each day he would set off with a burlap bag and scavenge for his fire pit. He kept the fire calm, he was very particular about it.

"What are you thinking, June," James asked.

"Do the Chinese really eat nests?" she said.

"Just those of a certain bird, a kind of swift," Howard said. "The swift builds the nests out of its own saliva and the stuff hardens."

"You're kidding!" Caroline said. "Those damn Chinese."

June blushed.

"Oh, what are you thinking *now*, June?" Abby said. "You're so funny."

June had had a dream where a boy was kissing her by spitting in her mouth. He just didn't *know*, she thought. It was awful, but in the dream she was unalarmed, as though this was the way it had to be done. "I was thinking about picnics. Didn't you used to have the best picnics when you were little?"

"You're too nostalgic, June," Caroline said. "Nostalgia nauseates me. I lack the nostalgic gene, thank god."

"Why do you ask her what she's thinking?" Parker demanded.

"Why, because it's a game," James said. "Because she'll tell us and nobody else ever does."

"I wouldn't tell my thoughts," Parker said. "They're mine."

"But you don't have any thoughts," James said. "You're too little."

"I do too," Parker said. He was angry. He had broken one of his trucks. It was not by accident that he'd broken it, but even so.

"Well, what's one of them?" James said.

After a moment Parker said, "I like ants."

"Ants are great!" Howard said. "Ants live for a long time. I read about this guy, this ant specialist who kept this queen ant and watched her for twenty-nine years. She laid eggs until she died."

"Eggs?" Parker said.

"Occasionally she allowed herself the luxury of eating one of them," Howard said. "This guy just watched his ant. What do you think? You want to do stuff like that?"

The sky was full of stars and they were beneath them, contained as if in a well.

"I'm sleepy," Parker said.

"We should have the picnic," June said. "What about the picnic?"

"What's it feel like to be adopted, Parker?" Howard asked. "You can hear me from over there, can't you?" He sprinkled out the last of the Jägermeister into their glasses. The bottle's arcane label had a stag's head, over which there was a cross.

"I was chosen by Mommy and Ralph," Parker said.

"Ralph!" Abby laughed. "Why don't you call him 'Daddy'?"

"Daddy," Parker said reluctantly.

"Why don't you call Mommy 'Joanne'?" Abby said.

"They got to *choose* me," Parker insisted.

"When you take a dump, do you save it in the bowl for Ralph to see before you flush it down?" Howard asked. "That's what I remember. The prominent throat specialist had to see mine and tell me it was good or it didn't go away. It *stayed* until the prominent throat specialist came home."

"Poor Howard," Caroline said. "That's what you remember?"

"Fondly," Howard said.

The guardian and his family were hammering away in the corrugated shed attached to their kitchen. Each night there was the sound of grinding and hammering. They made door knockers, June thought. But no one knew for certain. Those pretty door knockers in the shape of a lady's hand.

They began discussing, mostly for Parker's benefit, the rumors of a gringo ring that trafficked in the organs of Guatemalan children. This rumor had been around for years.

"There's a factory where the organs are processed," James said. "It's behind the video bar in Panajachel. It's just that everyone's too stoned to see it."

The gringo entrepreneurs didn't take the whole kid, they recounted loudly. Except in the beginning, of course. They took just a kidney or some tissue or an eye, which left the rest of the kid to get along as best he could, which usually wasn't very well.

"Parker," Howard said, "I hope Mommy and Ralph were sincere tonight as to their whereabouts. I hope they're not, in fact, kidnapping little Guatemalan children so they can have parts on hand for you, should any of your own parts fail. They could land in big trouble, Parker."

"I think he's asleep," James said.

"Wake up!" Howard roared. But Parker slept. Howard moodily raked his fire and then announced he was leaving to get some beer.

"I'll go with you," Abby said.

June would never have gone off alone with Howard. There was something cold and clandestine about him.

"What are you thinking, June?" James said after what seemed like a long while with Abby not yet back with Howard.

"I was thinking about that great, swaying float and how quiet everyone was when it passed."

"The *anda*," Caroline said. "The Anda de La Merced."

"That thing weighs three and a half tons," James said.

"It really was impressive, wasn't it?" June said.

"Well, duh," Caroline said. But she smiled at June as she said this.

"The drumrolls are still in my head," James said. "They provide the necessary cadences. The men probably couldn't bear it forward without those cadences being maintained."

"I can still hear the drumrolls too," June said gratefully.

"What's the word for the men who carry it?" James wondered. "I should keep a glossary."

"*Cucuruchos,*" Caroline said. "One of them looked just like that cute dishwasher at the pizza place. I'm sure it was him."

"Look who we found!" Howard called from the gates.

It was the bottle boy from that morning, the one who'd eaten June's pancake.

"He was just outside," Abby said, "the beggar boy. Howard wanted him to share our picnic."

"He is not a beggar," Howard said. "His eyes lack the proper cringe. He is my brother, come to visit. That Bailey brat you met before was the false son and brother. A substitute substituted. Soul and body alike are often substituted." He was very drunk.

The boy was shivering. His shirt was torn and he wore a small silver cross around his neck. The shirt had not been torn that morning, June didn't think.

"Where's Parker's sweater?" Abby demanded. "I'm giving it to this one, that's what I'm going to do." She dug a red cable-knit sweater from Parker's bag and pulled it over the bottle boy's dark head, then pushed his arms through the sleeves. "I hope I don't get fleas now," she said.

Parker was sitting up and rubbing his eyes.

"Give him a sandwich," Caroline demanded.

Abby gave the bottle boy a sandwich thick with ham and cheese. He ate it slowly, watching them. Howard smoothed his fire with a stick. They drank beer.

"This is good," June said.

"It's the same kind we always drink," James said. "It's from Cuba."

They stood or sat drinking beer while the boy slowly ate the sandwich and watched them.

"I've been thinking about this for a while," Howard said. He threw his empty bottle down and pushed the sandals from his feet. "I have."

He made fists of his hands, rolled his eyes upward and quickly walked the length of the fire pit.

"I don't believe it," Caroline said.

He turned and walked the fire again. "Cool moss," he screamed. "You think *cool moss*." He sank to the ground laughing, unharmed.

"You're loco," James said.

"Feel my feet, feel them," Howard said. "I ask you, are they hot?"

Caroline boldly touched the soles of his feet and pronounced them not warm at all. They were clammy, in fact.

"It doesn't have anything to do with belief," Howard said. "But if you have doubts, you burn. It's an evolutionary stimulant. I am now evolutionarily advanced."

"That is a fire that should so be put out right now," Abby said.

"I want to walk," Parker said. "I'm gonna walk." He stood and made small fists.

Abby yanked him toward her and slapped his bottom. "You are going to bed!" Abby said.

The fire winked radiantly at them all. Howard was laughing. He was deeply, coldly happy, and the revulsion June felt for him shocked her. She looked at Caroline uneasily.

"I do not believe this," Caroline said.

The Guatemalan boy had been collecting the empty bottles strewn about. He held them against his chest, against the bright red sweater. Then he put them down and, smiling furtively at Howard, stepped onto the fire. He screamed at once. Howard pulled him back, the boy screaming thinly. "You're all right, man, you're all right," he said, pouring beer over the boy's feet. "You were distracted and doubtful, man, and when you're D and D, you burn. *No tenga miedo. No es nada.*" He held the boy's feet and crooned *No es nada* to him mournfully, but he looked pleased.

Whimpering, the boy reached blindly for his bottles and clutched them once more to his chest.

"Get him out of here," Caroline said. "Give him the rest of the food. Give him the whole damn basket." She ran to the gates and opened them. "*Váyase! Váyase!*" she yelled at him.

As the boy stumbled out, he almost collided with the fortune birds being escorted home on their motorbike. The man of the remarkable vein steadied him with a snarl and then, regarding them all grimly, pushed the motorbike across the courtyard.

June ran up to him, digging coins from her pocket. "My fortune," she said, "*por favor.*"

"In the morning," he said distinctly.

June looked closely at the tiny prophets clinging wearily to the bars of their cage, at their tiny breasts and dull feathers. Only a few rolled papers tied with rough string were on the bottom of the cage.

"More in the morning," he said. "Better for you."

"No," June said. "I need it now. Morning no good. *No está bien,*" she said cautiously. "That one, Planeta, I want her to do it."

"*Importa poco.*"

"What?" June said.

"It makes little difference."

"Planeta," she insisted. She pointed to the little one with the dark, opaque eyes that looked as though they'd been ringed in crayon.

"That is Justicio," he said. "Justicio," he sang softly, "Justicio . . ."

The bird dropped to the soiled floor of the cage and seized a tiny scroll as if it were a seed of much importance, one that could nourish it throughout the night. June pressed her fingers to the crookedly woven bars, almost expecting to receive a slight shock. The bird knocked the paper against her fingers. Once. Twice. She took it and the bird fluttered upward to its perch, where it crouched like a clump of earth.

"Oh, June," Abby called. "What does it say?"

She turned toward her friends and walked slowly toward them, unrolling the paper. The writing was florid and crowded. There were many unfamiliar words. Caroline knew the language best, then Howard. What a mistake this had been! She would need time to study it and there was no time. Everyone was looking at her.

"Oh, it's just silly," she said, and threw it in the fire, where it burned sluggishly. No one attempted to retrieve it.

"God, isn't it late, where are my parents?" Abby said, yawning. "I want to go to bed."

June sat with them all a little while longer before going to her room. She lay on her bed discouraged, uncomfortably, listlessly awake. She heard a wailing from far away, but when she listened closely she could not hear it. She listened avidly now. Nothing. She could not recall the cadence of the drums. She had lied to James about that. But she could picture the *anda* being borne down the streets. That she would remember. It was fascinating to have seen the designs so meticulously created and then the *anda* passing, being borne on, swaying, and in its wake the designs smeared, crushed, a scattered wonder. And that part, the after, had been fascinating too.

But she didn't really believe it was fascinating. It wasn't good to deceive yourself. She thought about Howard, hating him and his cold grin. He was fleshy, did he not know that? Fleshier than most. He was not attractive. That was a lie, what Howard had done. It could hardly be anything else. She thought of the mannequins praying in their cell. A lie, too, but one that was funny. Things had to be funny.

IN THE MORNING, CAROLINE'S DOG WAS GONE AGAIN. THE ROPE had been knotted any number of times; it was always breaking. And when it broke, the dog would escape from the courtyard and, barking with joy, run through the streets. Caroline said that when it disappeared for good, it would be time to go. She had heard somewhere that angels tell you when it's time to leave a place by leaving just before you. June thought she had heard that too. Something like that.

Bromeliads

JONES'S GRANDCHILD IS EIGHT DAYS OLD. JONES AND HIS WIFE have not been sent a picture of the baby and although they have spoken with their daughter several times on the telephone they do not have a very good idea of what the child looks like. It seems very difficult to describe a new baby. Jones has seen quite a few new babies in his years of serving a congregation and he has held them and gazed into their eyes. These experiences, however, cannot help him picture *this* child, his only grandchild, this harmonious and sweet thought that he carries green and graceful in his mind.

Jones and his wife had no idea that their daughter was going to have a baby. They had seen her six months ago and she had mentioned nothing about a baby. Several days after the birth, her husband had called them with the news.

Jones lies awake in the night, troubled by this. His wife twists restlessly beside him. She has been having great difficulty sleeping lately. Sleep is full of impossible chores, unending labors. She is so tired but her body cannot find any rest. She feels cold. She gets up and goes into the bathroom and runs hot water over her hands. She pats her cheeks with the hot water. While she is in the bathroom, Jones goes down to the kitchen and boils water for two cups of tea. He makes up a tray of tea and lemon peel and peanut butter cookies. He and his wife sit in bed and sip the tea. She does not feel so cold now. She feels better. They talk about the baby. Their daughter has told them that she has a nice mouth and pale brown hair.

"Pale brown," Jones says enthusiastically.

His wife wants very much to travel down and see the baby even though the trip is more than a thousand miles. She wants to leave as soon as possible, the next day. She is insistent about this.

· · ·

JONES WALKS WITH HIS DAUGHTER IN THE WOODS BEHIND HER
small house. She is pointing out the various species of bromeliads that
flourish there. The study of bromeliads is his daughter's most recent
enthusiasm. She is a thin, hasty, troubling girl with exact and joy-
less passions. She lopes silently ahead of Jones through the dappled
lemon-smelling woods. The trees twist upward. Only the tops of them
are green. She is wearing a faded brief bikini, and there are bruises on
her legs and splashes of paint on the bikini. There is a cast to the flesh,
a slender delicate mossy line on her flat stomach, extending down from
the navel. It is a wistful, insubstantial line.

The baby is napping back in the little cypress cottage that Jones's
daughter and her husband are renting. Jones's wife is napping too.
Earlier that morning Jones had gone to the supermarket and bought
food for his wife that was rich in iron. Perhaps she is tired because of
an iron deficiency. Jones had gone through the aisles, pushing a cart.
There was an arrangement in front of the handle that could be pushed
back into a seat, two spaces through which a child could put his legs.
Many children were in the store, transported in these carts. Some of
them smiled at Jones with their small prim teeth. Jones had bought
eggs, green vegetables, liver, molasses and nuts. When he returned,
his wife had wanted nothing. She sat in her slip on a cot in the baby's
room.

Jones fanned his face with a road map. "I'd like to treat us all to a
strawberry soda later," he said.

"Oh, that would be very refreshing," his wife replied. "That would be
very nice, but right now I think I'd just like to watch the baby while she
sleeps." She had moved her lips in a gesture for Jones.

Jones had kissed her forehead and gone outside. His daughter is
walking there, padding through the rich mulch of oak leaves with her
bare feet.

"*Neoregelia spectabilis*," his daughter says. "*Aechmea fulgens.*" There are
hundreds of bromeliads, some growing in the crotches of trees, others
clinging epiphytically to one another, massed across the ground. His
daughter identifies them all. "*Hohenbergia stellata*," she says. They are

thick glossy plants with extraordinary flowers. Their rosettes of leaves are filled with water.

"Perhaps Mother should drink some of this," she says, waggling her finger in the cups of a heavily clustered bromeliad. The water is brown and acrid. Jones stares at his daughter. She shrugs. "They call it tea," she says. Her face is remote and bony. "I don't know," she says, and begins gnawing on her nails.

The sunlight falls down through the branches of the cedars and the live oaks as though through measured slats in a greenhouse.

"Bromeliads are fascinating," she says. "They live on nothing. Just the air and the wind. The rain brings dust and bird excrement to feed them. Leaves from trees fall into their cups and break down into nutrients. They must be one of God's favorites. One doesn't have to do anything for them. They require no care whatsoever."

Jones was saddened by her words.

Jones's daughter is preparing dinner. She darts from kitchen to porch, nursing the baby as she lays out the silverware. The cottage is dark and hot. Everyone is very hot. The dog drinks continually from a large bowl set on the floor. Jones fills it when it is empty and the dog continues to drink. Jones stands in the kitchen, by the refrigerator, filling a glass with ice cubes. His daughter is at the stove, stirring the white sauce with a whisk. The baby has fallen asleep, her cheek riding on her mother's tanned breast, her mouth a lacy bubble of milk. Jones would like to hug them both, his daughter and her child. He does. The baby wakens with a squeak.

"Daddy," Jones's daughter says. She hunches her shoulders. Her lower lip is split and burned by the sun. She has brushed her brown hair straight back from her forehead and a rim of skin just below the hairline is burned raw too. Jones stands beside her.

"It's too hot in the kitchen, Daddy, please," she says.

Jones walks to the porch with the glass of ice and gives it to his wife. She has a craving for ice. She chews it most of the day. "What is it that my body wants?" she asks, her teeth grinding the ice.

Jones's son-in-law arrives with a bottle of gin and makes everyone a gin and tonic with fresh limes from a tree that is visible from the house. The tree is in fruit and blossom at the same time.

"Isn't that peculiar?" Jones remarks.

"It's wonderful!" his wife says. "I understand that. It's beautiful!"

For a moment, Jones fears that she will cry.

JONES'S DAUGHTER HAS PREPARED A VERY NICE MEAL. THE SUN has vanished, leaving the sky cerise. Jones's wife wears a gay yellow silk blouse. It is the shade of the tropical south, of the summer sundown, a color that brings no light. They all prepare to sit down. Jones's son-in-law looks concernedly at his hands.

"Excuse me," he says, "I must wash my hands." He is blond, affable. He recognizes everyone in some way. There is in him a polite and not too inaccurate recognition of everything. He is a somnolent, affectionate young man.

Jones and his wife and daughter sit down at the table.

"Every time he has to take a leak, he gives me that crap about his hands," Jones's daughter says. "Every time. It drives me crazy."

Her hands knock angrily against the plates. Her husband returns. She won't look at his face. Her eyes are fixed somewhere on his chest. She thrusts her face forward as though she is going to fall against his chest.

Jones's wife says, "I hope you take photographs of the baby. There can never be enough pictures. When one looks back, there are hardly any pictures at all."

THE NIGHT BEFORE JONES AND HIS WIFE ARE TO RETURN HOME, he wakes abruptly from a sound sleep. He hastily puts on his bathrobe and moves through the strange room. He senses that he has fallen into this room, into, even, his life. He feels very much the weight of this moment, which seems without resolution. He is in the present, perfectly reconciled to the future but cut off from the past. It is the present that Jones has fallen into.

He walks to the baby's crib and she is fine, she's sleeping. Jones moves a chair up beside the crib. The baby wakes when the morning comes. She begins to cry. Jones's daughter does not come into the room. She has been gone from them now for hours.

Jones can no longer think about his daughter with any confidence.

His head sweats. The sweat runs down his cheeks. *In things extreme, and scattering bright . . .* a line from Donne, those are the words that murmur in his mind. There are no other words in his mind.

A LETTER FROM JONES'S DAUGHTER ARRIVES SEVERAL DAYS LATER. His daughter writes, *I am not well but I will get better if I can only have some time.* She does not mention the baby.

Everyone agrees that Jones and his wife should care for the baby. She is weaned easily. She is a healthy, good baby.

Jones's son-in-law is very apologetic. He folds his hands behind his back and bends slightly when he looks at the baby. He hums softly, abstractly, a visiting relative.

MONTHS PASS. THE BABY IS FIVE MONTHS OLD NOW. SHE IS WEAR-ing bright blue overalls and a red turtleneck shirt. She is sitting on the floor and wants to take off one of her shoes. She struggles with the shoe. She cannot think of requesting or demanding assistance in this. She tugs and tugs.

Jones and the baby sit with Jones's wife in the hospital. It seems there is something wrong with her blood. She is not in a ward. She is just here for tests and she is in a stylish wing where she is allowed to wear her own clothes and even make a cup of tea on the hot plate. She bends now and unties the baby's shoe and holds it in her hand. The baby isn't wearing socks. Jones had just done a washing and none of the socks was dry.

Jones wiggles the baby's largest toe. "That's Crandlehurst," he says. He invents silly names for the baby's toes.

The baby looks severely at the toe and then stops looking at it without moving her eyes. Jones cannot think of names for all the baby's toes. No fond and foolish names flower in his brain. No room! His brain, instead, hums hotly with weeds, the weedy metaphors of doctors. *The white cells may be compared to the defending foot soldiers who engage the attacking enemy in mortal hand-to-hand combat and either destroy them or are themselves destroyed.*

Jones presses his finger as unobtrusively as possible against his temple. He looks at the carpeting. It is redder than the baby's jersey, red as a valentine.

Jones tells his wife how nice she looks. She is wearing a dress that he likes, one about which he has happy memories. It is very warm in the hospital. She has entered this hospital and is in another season. Outside it is winter. But the memory is one of summer, his wife in this dress with tanned pretty arms. Jones can share this with her. He shares his heart with her, all that there is. As Rilke said . . . where was it where Rilke said *Like a piece of bread that has to suffice for two?* His heart, Jones's love. He looks at the dress. It is a trim blue and white check, slightly faded.

It is summer. They are in a little cottage, on holiday. There is a straw rug on the floor, in a petal pattern through which the sand falls. When the rug is lifted, the design remains, perfectly, in the sand. There is a row of raisins on the porch sill for the catbirds.

Jones remembers. In the mornings, the grass seems polished with a jeweler's cloth. And Jones's wife is in this dress, rubbing the face of their daughter with the hem of this dress. Yet it cannot be this dress, surely, everything was too long ago . . .

But now the visiting hours are over. A buzzer goes off in each of the rooms. Jones and the baby return home. Jones undresses her and then dresses her again for bed. He stays in her room long after she has fallen asleep. Then he goes downstairs and builds a fire in the fireplace and searches through the bookshelves for his collection of Rilke's work. The poems have been translated but the essays have not. He takes out his German grammar and begins to search for the phrase that came to him so magically earlier in the evening. Jones enjoys the feel of the grammar. He enjoys the words of another language. He needs another language, other words. He is so weary of the words he has. He enjoys the search. Is not everything the search? An hour later he comes across the passage. It is not as Jones had thought, not as he expected. Rilke is speaking not of women but of *Dinge*. He is speaking not of lovers and life, but of dolls and death. Each word rises to Jones's lips. *Was it not with a thing that you first shared your little heart, like a piece of bread that had to suffice for two? Was it not with a thing that you experienced, through it, through its existence,*

through its anyhow appearance, through its final smashing or enigmatic depar-
ture, all that is human, right into the depths of death?

JONES'S WIFE HAD BROUGHT THE BABY A TOY FROM THE HOSPITAL
gift shop. It is a soft, stuffed blue elephant, eight inches high. Inside it is
a music box that plays "The Carousel Waltz." While the waltz plays, the
elephant's trunk rotates slowly. It is a pretty toy. Jones's wife is happy
she has finally found something here that she can give the baby. For
the last several days she has walked down the corridor to the gift shop.
Every day, like a bird, in the warmest, strongest hour of the day, she has
ventured out. When at last she saw something she wanted to buy, she
felt relieved, unambiguous. She is in control, a woman buying a toy for
her grandchild. There have been so many tests. She has been here for
days; they will not release her. They do not know what is wrong, but
it is not the worst! The first tests have been negative. It is bad but it is
not the worst. What can the worst have been? She no longer needs to
fear it.

She returns this day with the toy, panting a little, the veins on either
side of her eyes throbbing. She sits on her bed quietly. The veins seem
to hover outside her head. They are out and they want to get in. They
are coiled there, almost visible, knotted, stiff, a mess, tangled like a
cheap garden hose. These veins, this problem, is something she could
take care of, something she is certainly capable of correcting, of making
tidy and functional again, if only she had the strength. She feels calmer
now. The noises in her face have stopped. She looks at the toy elephant.
The girl who runs the gift shop has put it in a bag. A brown paper bag,
crumpled as though it has been used over and over again.

Jones's wife wraps the toy in tissue paper and waits for the evening
visiting hours. Jones and the baby arrive. The baby smiles at her new
plaything. She is not surprised. She is too little. She raises her face to
the overhead light and closes her eyes.

NEW STORIES

Brass

MOTHER COMES BACK ONE EVENING AND SHE STARTS UP AT supper about feng shui, how our house isn't organized for a happy life, how the front door should never line up with the back door like ours does—never. One of her colleagues in Parks and Recreation told her that.

"They're all dipshits down there," I said.

And the boy said, talking with his mouth full like he always does, "That's why you're not supposed to have a crucifix in the bedroom. Is a cross the same as a crucifix?" he says.

I could see the meat with the ketchup on it in his mouth. "No," I said. "A crucifix is a cross with the body on it."

"A cross is OK, then," he said. "And a crucifix is OK as long as the eyes aren't open. You don't want that in the bedroom."

Usually nobody said anything at supper but sometimes it would go all haywire like this. I went into the backyard for a cigarette. I've got a velvet mesquite back there and two saguaros. All of this was here when I bought the place in 1972. The saguaros don't have arms on them yet. A saguaro has to be seventy-five years old before it puts out an arm.

Another night, I come out of my shop in the garage for supper and he appears without a hair on his head. Not on his arms either.

"Jesus," I say. "What have you done now?"

"This is how you foil the drug testers," he says.

"You aren't ingesting drugs, are you," I ask.

"Nah," he says. "It's just unconstitutional to take a sample from a man's head, from a hair. I'm protesting the unconstitutionality of it."

As a little kid when he wanted to curse but didn't dare or probably didn't even know how, he'd say, "Babies!" It was pretty damn cute. "Oh, babies!" he'd say. I don't know where he got that from.

Did he respect his mother? I'd say yes. I mean, he didn't pay much attention to her.

I FIXED CLOCKS IN THE GARAGE FOR A WHILE BUT THEN I STOPPED serving the public, who were never, ever satisfied. So it's just a personal hobby, taking apart clocks and watches and putting them back together again. There was a Frenchman centuries ago, a watchmaker, who created a life-size mechanical duck. It could move its head, flap its wings, even eat from a bowl of grain. Then it could even shit out the compacted grain. It was all gears and springs. More than four hundred parts moved each wing. They call things like that automatons.

The boy says, "Can you learn about ducks by studying mechanical ducks?"

"Of course not," I say. No wonder his teachers don't like him, I think.

"It's not a dumb question," he says, "given where we are today, studying all these computer systems and simulations and making all these performance assessments that are no more than abstractions we try to apply to the real world. Real people are complex. A real situation can't be broken down into abstractions. I don't support nuclear power because there's no place to bury nuclear waste," he says. "Nuclear power cannot be separated from nuclear waste."

I think, This boy just needs to get laid, but I say, "Why are you worrying about nuclear waste, you should just go out and get a job and keep it, make some money for yourself." But I don't have a job and haven't for years, so my words ring somewhat hollow. Mother's job is sufficient for us. There's a preacher says a family of four can live handsomely on fifty thousand dollars a year before taxes and if they make more they should give that amount away to others. And we're just a family of three. Do they still call people like us a nuclear family?

WE WENT TO NEW YORK CITY ONCE. TO THIS DAY I DON'T KNOW why she insisted on it. "Why don't we go to the Grand Canyon?" I said, but she wanted to do something different. We'd seen the Grand Canyon. She wanted to go to that restaurant, Windows on the World, was it? And she wanted to take in some musical theater. That's exactly how she put it, "I want to take in some musical theater." She's had a job for years with P & R, working with heavy machinery, loppers and saws and stuff, and first thing at LaGuardia she falls on the stairs and sprains her ankle. It's all she can do to hobble from bed to bathroom in the crummy little hotel room we have. So I'm supposed to be showing the boy New York City. He was around nine. We had just emerged from a subway, the boy and I, totally disoriented, and this Mexican guy passes by and grunts at me and lifts his chin at this woman standing beside us waiting for the light to change and she's blind with dark glasses and a cane, clearly blind, and the guy's saying, without speaking—Do your duty, man, I'm going the other way.

The blind don't grab on to you like you'd think or clutch your hand. She just put her finger on my jacket with the lightest touch.

"There's a big grate here," I say, thinking the last thing we needed was for her to get her stick snapped off in one of the holes in the grate. We cross the street and she angles herself to cross another one and I say, "Do you want us to stay with you for this one as well?" and she says, "Thank you very much, but only if you're going in this direction, of course." She had the lightest, nicest, most refined voice. It was surprising. And then the boy bawls out, "We don't know where we are and we don't know where we're going!" And she says, still in that lovely voice, "Oh, now you're beginning to frighten me." Well, I was furious at him, very, very furious. We ushered the lady across the street and then I dragged him back down into the subway and we went back uptown to the hotel and we stayed there for two days. I was the only one who went out and that was just for crackers and Coke. The boy kept saying, "I'm sorry, Daddy, I'm sorry." That was what he'd do. He'd do something, give somebody he shouldn't some lip and then back right down. We didn't see anything of New York City and that was the last time we left Arizona.

I GO INTO THE BIRD-FOOD STORE FOR SUET. I'VE GOT SOME SUET feeders I made. The cheaper stuff you buy in the big-box places and the hardware stores isn't rendered and can spoil. Most people don't know this. They're the same ones still putting that red-dye shit in the hummingbird feeders. Every time I go in there someone's asking what they've got that will keep the doves away. I don't want the doves. How can I get rid of the doves? And the clerk's fussing around trying to sell them some contraption made from recycled materials for fifty bucks that only birds who feed upside down can get at. So I say, one customer to another, "A Taser. Try a Taser." And they look at me sort of interested until I finally say, "I'm kidding."

HE FOUND A DOG OUT BY THE RAYTHEON PLANT AND BROUGHT her home. She looked like a puppy but who knows. Her teeth weren't particularly white. He called her Vega.

"What the hell does that mean?" I say. "How did you come up with that?"

"It's Arabic," he says.

"You're just asking for trouble, aren't you?" I say. "Why would you give a dog an Arab's name? It doesn't even sound Arabic, it sounds Spanish. What's it in Spanish?"

"Open plain," he says.

"That's some stupid name for a dog," I say. "Open plain."

I called her Amy. He stopped caring for her after a few weeks anyway and I fed her and trained her a bit. I had the time, not working. And you've got to have time, god knows, with the training exercises.

Sit . . . good girl . . . down . . . no! Stay . . . good girl. Twenty minutes twice a day. You're never supposed to repeat a command.

We got all the way up to Day Fifteen, which is pretty much the end of it. That's when you get them to sit and stay and you disappear and say hello to an imaginary person at the door and you come back and then disappear again and talk to people who aren't there. That was amusing to me because no one ever came to our door, which was the way I preferred it. Sometimes the boy would have a friend over, but not often. Kids, they're in a different lane. Slow. They move slow, they talk slow. Everything slows down.

THE BOY SAYS, "WHAT'S THE POINT OF TRAINING THAT DOG? She's not even good-looking."

It's true, Amy wouldn't turn any heads. And I say to him, "What do you know about good-looking?" Clean up that goddamn acne, boy, I wanted to say, for I can be petty with him at times, but I didn't.

"A man doesn't have to be good-looking," he says. "He's just got to have presence, he's got to be in command."

"Absolutely," I say. "You're really in command at all the fast-food joints you keep getting fired from." He'd been fired from one for eating salad back in the kitchen with his fingers, right out of one of those bowls big as an engine block. His *fingers*.

"It'd have been the same if I used a fork," he says.

Then the next place he'd told the manager she was sitting on her brains.

"I like Amy," he says. "I was the one who found her, remember?"

Backing right down like he always did.

SOMETIMES MOTHER WANTS TO MAKE SOMETHING SPECIAL FOR dinner, like a soup. She asks me to go to Safeway and get a can of coconut milk and some cilantro. I can't imagine a worse-sounding soup but if she's willing to make dinner, I'll eat it. I'm not about to make dinner. So Amy and I drive over to the Safeway. The Brownies are out front at a little table selling cookies. They've always got somebody out front selling something, even original oil paintings. Sometimes even politicians set up shop there. So I bought a box of cookies. You'd have to be some sort of wicked not to buy cookies when confronted by a little Brownie. Of course I can't find the damn coconut milk and I'm wandering around until some kid says, "Can I help you, sir?" and then ushers me smugly to the proper shelf. I'm going through the checkout and the checker says, "Do you need any help out with this, sir?"

All the way back to the truck, I mutter, "Do you need any help out with this, sir, do you need any help out with this, sir?"

They're all automatons.

HE TOOK A POETRY CLASS AT THE COMMUNITY COLLEGE. "THAT'S lovely," I say. "It's quite beyond lovely," I say, sarcastic.

"We're studying Rimbaud," he says. "He was French, too, like your watchmaker, the one who made the duck. Isn't that interesting?"

"Why is that interesting?" I say.

"Listen to this," he says. He opens up this little paperback book and he's highlighted these lines in blue Magic Marker. He says, "*For I is someone else. If brass wakes up a trumpet, it isn't to blame. To me this is evident: I give a stroke of the bow: the symphony begins to stir in the depths.*"

"That ain't even grammatical," I say.

"*For I is someone else,*" he says somberly. "*If brass wakes up a trumpet it isn't to blame.*" Then he smirks at me. He's been working on this smirk.

"Now that's the translation," he says. "But for class I'm going to translate the translation."

"Somebody should translate you," I say.

"No one's going to be able to translate me," he says.

HE SAID SOME OLD WOMAN CAME IN TO TUTOR THEM SOMETIMES and she smelled like laundry.

"Laundry," I said. "Clean laundry, I hope."

"Yeah, yeah, yeah," he said.

"You shouldn't need tutoring now, should you? You're in college, community college, you've been going there for years."

"She's one of those do-gooders. I told her about Rimbaud and she said he was the first modernist."

"What the hell's that mean?"

"The beginning of the way we are? He was a savage dreamer, Rimbaud."

And he delivers that smirk.

"Daddy," he says, "you don't think I can do anything."

"I'm not going to engage you on that one," I say. "You'll make your mark or you won't."

"What you're wanting to do is stop time," he says, "and that's dangerous."

"I don't want to stop time," I say. "Time don't stop because I'm working on a broken watch."

But he looks at me as though he thinks it does. "I see things in parts, too," he says.

"Don't you need to be wearing a cleaner shirt?"

"Do you think I do?"

"That one's filthy. I've been looking at it for days."

"Are you thinking other stuff when you think that?"

"God almighty," I say. "Just go put on a fresh T-shirt."

"When I think something it rethinks it for me," he says.

"WE'VE GOT TO BE TOLERANT," MOTHER SAYS TO ME. "YOU'RE NOT a tolerant man and that hurts, that shows."

"Tolerant," I say. I don't know when I got into the habit of repeating a single word. Just picking it out of her conversation.

"He might be neuroatypical, that's what Tom says."

They all annoy the hell out of me over at P & R but Tom takes the cake. He's so fat I don't know how he can tie his goddamn shoes.

"Tom says neurodiversity might be more crucial for the human race than biodiversity."

"Tom's handling too much weed killer," I say. "He's not a friend of the earth." Which reminds me of something the boy lobbed at us the other night about Albert Einstein's last words. He's staring off to the side of us as we're sitting in what he loves to refer to emphatically as the *living* room and he says, "Albert Einstein's last words were: *Is the earth friendly?*"

I say, "I doubt that."

"Yeah, yeah, yeah," he says. "It's true. I think of what I'm going to have for last words sometimes."

"Let's hear 'em," I say.

"It's not going to be a question."

"I can't imagine your last words being a question," I say.

He glances up at me and decides to be pleased. Usually he won't look right at a person. He says eye contact is counterproductive to comprehension and communication. He's got any number of ways to justify himself, that's for sure.

Mother continues to go on about Tom and Jimmy and Christina and their theories about the boy, whom they've never met but think they know from her going on and on about him, I guess. She's got quite a little socializing network going on for her down at the park. She had a chance to work over at Sweetwater, the marsh they've built out by the sewer treatment plant. She would have made more money but said she'd be lonely with new people. She didn't want to leave her friends. She don't like change.

"Neurotypical," I say. "Kindly tell me what the hell TomTom's talking about." I call him that because two normal-size men could fit in his bulk.

"Neuro-*a*-typical," she says.

"Oh, goodness, pardon me," I say. "And why exactly are you discussing our family with those dipshits? Our family is no concern of theirs. TomTom's living with one of those women that looks like a man, isn't he? Let him worry about the atypicality of that."

"She's sweet," Mother says. "And anyway, Tom wasn't saying anything bad about him. He was just trying to make me feel better. I told my friends about them not letting him back in those classes he was taking."

"I don't want you talking to them about the boy," I say. "And I want to remind you, you're the one who wanted one, not me. Just one, you said. One and done."

"YOU'RE THE LOW-HANGING FRUIT," HE SAYS TO ME AND MOTHER. She just purses her lips and pushes her fork around a serving of store-bought pie.

"And I suppose you're not," I say. "You're the high-hanging fruit."

You've just got to find him hilarious sometimes.

"They've used up what's easy, like you. They've just used you up. But now they're going to have to deal with the likes of me. And there's no formula."

"The likes of you," I say.

He stands up so fast he knocks his glass of milk off the table. But then he catches it. It was flying laterally for an instant and damn if he didn't catch it. But then he storms out of the house and Mother tears up. Then the phone rings and it's one of those robo-calls you can't shut off until they've said their piece.

. . .

IT WAS AROUND ELEVEN IN THE MORNING. A BEAUTIFUL DESERT day. You forget how pretty the sky can still be. Mother was over at the park fixing a sprinkler system for the fortieth time. I think they break them deliberate so they'll have something to do. I'm in my shop thinking like I frequently do that the third cup of coffee tastes funny and then all hell breaks loose. People banging on the door and screaming and shouting and I even hear a helicopter overhead. And I say, "Stay, Amy, stay, stay," and walk out of the garage and there's law officers out there screaming, "sumabitch, sumabitch" and "the congresswoman" and "sumabitch" again, even the women, all of them in uniform and with guns, and I think whatever I was thinking a minute ago is the last peaceful thought I will ever have. Though sometimes now I try to pretend he's still in the house, in his room with the door closed. I pretend he's still living with us and eating with us and getting by with us. But of course he's not and he isn't.

No, we were never afraid of him. Afraid of Jared?

The Girls

THE GIRLS WERE SEARCHING ARLEEN'S ROOM AND HAD JUST come upon her journal. The girls were thirty-one and thirty-two. Arleen was of a dowdy unspecific age, their parents' houseguest. She had arrived with the family's city pastor, an Episcopal priest, who had been in a depression for a number of months because his lover had died. The priest spent most of his time in the garden wearing only a bright red banana sling, his flabby body turning a magnificent somber brown. The girls were certain their parents regretted inviting him, for he was not at all amusing, the way he frequently could be, in the pulpit.

Arleen was presently occupied with washing her long hair in the shower down the hall. It had taken the girls many clandestine visits to her room to find anything of interest. The journal was in the zippered pocket of her open suitcase.

"I know I looked here before."

"She must move it around."

"Should we start at the beginning or with the last entry? That would be last night, I suppose."

"That was the Owl Walk. She went on the Owl Walk with Mommy and came back and said, so seriously, 'No owls.'"

The girls found that hysterical.

The sound of water on the curtain ceased and the girls hurried downstairs. They made tea and curled up on the sofa with their cats. There were two cats living and two cats dead. The dead cats were Roland and Georgia O'Keeffe, their cremains in elaborate colorful urns on the mantelpiece. The ceramic feet on Roland's urn were rabbits, the ones on Georgia O'Keeffe's, mice. The urns had been conceived and created by the girls.

"Good morning, Arleen," they said together when she appeared, her hair wadded wetly on her back. She peered at them and smiled shyly. The back of her blouse was soaked because of the sack of hair. She wore khaki shorts. They were the weird kind to which leggings could be buttoned to create a pair of trousers.

"I was hoping," Arleen said, "that the kitty litter box could be taken out of the bathroom?"

The girls and the cats stared at her.

"It smells," Arleen said.

"It *smells?*" the girls said.

There was silence. "I took a lovely long walk early this morning," Arleen said. "I bicycled out to the moors and then I walked. It began to rain, quite hard, and then it suddenly stopped and was beautiful."

The girls mimed extreme wonder at this remarkable experience.

"It reminded me of something I read once about the English moors and the month of April," Arleen said. *"April, who laughs her girlish laughter and a moment after weeps her girlish tears is apt to be a mature hysteric on the moors."* She looked at them, smiling quickly, then dipped her head. She had a big ragged part in her hair that made the girls almost dizzy.

"April is far behind us, Arleen," one of the girls said. "It's June now. You've been here almost two weeks."

Arleen nodded. "It's been very good for Father Snow."

"What is *your* home like," the other asked. They'd found one couldn't be too obvious with Arleen.

"It has stairs," Arleen mused. "Very steep stairs. Sometimes I don't go out, because coming back there would be the stairs, and often when I am out, I don't return because of the stairs. Otherwise it's quite adequate."

"Are you fearful of crime?" the girls said. They widened their eyes.

"No," Arleen said. She had very much the manner of someone waiting to be dismissed. The girls loved it. They spooned honey into their tea.

"Did you have a nice birthday, Arleen?" one asked.

It had been announced several evenings before by Father Snow that it was Arleen's birthday. The girls had remarked that birthdays were more or less an idiotic American institution regarded with some wonder by the rest of the world. Arleen had blushed. The girls had said that they did not sanction birthdays but that they adored Christmas. Last year they had given Mommy and Daddy adagio dance lessons and a needlepoint book, the pages depicting scenes from their life together—Mommy and Daddy and the girls.

No one had given Arleen anything on her birthday but she and Father Snow had taken the opportunity to present their house present—a silver-plated cocktail shaker engraved with Mommy's and Daddy's initials.

"We were looking for something suitable but not insufferably dull," Father Snow said.

"No, no, you shouldn't have," Mommy said.

"We have ten of those!" one of the girls said, and they rushed to haul them out of the pantry, even the dented and tarnished ones. The cocktail shaker had proved to be a most popular house present over the years.

"I had a lovely birthday," Arleen said. She looked at her wrist and scratched it. "Is Father Snow outside?"

The girls pointed toward the garden. They had long pale shapely arms.

Arleen nodded vaguely and turned to leave, stumbling a bit on the sill.

Between themselves, the girls referred to Father Snow as Father Ice, an irony that gave them satisfaction, for his fat sorrow elicited considerable indignation in them. Where was his faith? He didn't have the faith to fill a banana sling. Where was his calm demeanor? It had fled from him. He was the furthest thing from ice they could imagine, the furthest from their admiration of ice, the lacy sheaths, the glare, the brilliance and hardness of ice. There had never been enough of it in their lives. A little, but not much.

Cuddling and kissing the living cats, the girls walked to the kitchen window and looked out into the garden. Arleen was on the ground at Father Ice's feet, her head flung back, drying her hair. Father Ice was talking with his eyes shut, tears streaming down his cheeks.

What a pair! the girls thought. They kissed the cats' stomachs. Father Ice's mouth was flapping away. His lover, a gaunt young man named Donny, had cooked for Father Ice and pressed his vestments. Father Ice had broken down at dinner the previous night over a plate of barbecued butterflied lamb, recalling, it could only be assumed, the manner in which Donny had once prepared this dish. He had just recovered from having broken down an hour earlier at cocktails.

The girls, through the glass, watched Arleen closely.

"She's in love with him, can you believe it? That is not just friendship."

"That kind of love is so safe."

The girls had never been in love. They did not plan on marrying. They would go to the dance clubs and perch on stools, in their little red dresses, their little black ones and white ones, darling and provocative tight little dresses, and they would toss their hair and laugh as they gazed into each other's eyes. There were always men around. Men were drawn to them but one would not be courted without the other, even for amusement—they would not be separated. They were like Siamese twins. They were not Siamese twins, of course, they weren't twins at all, nor were they even born on the same day a year apart, which was why they didn't care for birthdays. Men did not mind the fact that they would not be separated. It excited them agreeably, in fact. They didn't believe they didn't stand a chance in the long run.

The girls dropped the cats and moved away from the window, retiring to the large glassed-in porch on the south side of the house to work on their constructions. These were attractive assemblages, neither morbid nor violent nor sexually repressed as was so common with these objects, but tasteful, cold and peculiar. One of the several young men who were fascinated by the girls made the beautiful partitioned boxes in which selections were placed. One of them contained a snip of lace from Mommy's wedding dress. They hadn't asked her for it, but she hadn't recognized it when she saw it either. There were many things of that nature in the boxes.

They heard Mommy's voice. She was saying, "Now how would you describe the sound it made? An asthmatic squeal is what the bird book said though I wouldn't describe it like that. It certainly didn't sound like an asthmatic squeal to me."

Arleen muttered something in reply. She had apparently come back into the house. It was a three-story nineteenth-century house with fish-scale shingles and wide golden floorboards. It was a wonderful house. Mommy and Daddy almost always had houseguests in the summer. The girls didn't like it, it was as though Mommy and Daddy didn't want to be alone with them in these loveliest of months. The houseguests didn't stay long, usually no more than a week, but no sooner did they depart than others would arrive. The girls found few of them remarkable. There had been one young woman who held their interest for a weekend by drawing in pencil dozens of semi-Gothic, semi-Saracenic buildings, clearly intended to be visions of the starved or the drugged. They watched her closely, thinking her tremendously chic and fraudulent, and were disappointed when she left abruptly, taking, for it was never seen again, one of Mommy's Hermès beach towels, the one with the Lorraine cross.

Most of the guests never returned, but Father Snow had been invited several times. Priests were freeloaders, in the girls' opinion, and although Father Snow could give a good performance in the right surroundings—they had observed this at high holidays—he was no exception. They had not encountered Arleen before. At first, certainly, she had not appeared to be a problem. She was shy, deferential and plain. She wore red sneakers, the left one slit, she admitted, to accommodate a bunion. She did have lovely auburn hair. The one story she told concerned her hair. She had lovely hair as a child as well and had worn it in a long braid. She had cut it off one morning and given it to a man she had a crush on, a married man, a post office employee or some such thing. It had not been returned and the man had moved away. The girls loved that story. It was so droll it was practically retarded.

The girls heard Mommy's voice again and cocked their heads. She was planning the marketing. If Arleen would like to go into town they could get flowers and liquor and food as well and Arleen could give her opinion about a sweater Mommy was considering buying. Daddy said that when you look death in the eye you want to do it as calmly as a stroller looks into a shop window. But Mommy never looked into shop windows like that. She looked into them with excitement and distress. Sometimes what Daddy said didn't take Mommy into account.

"Girls!" Mommy called.

The girls put aside their constructions and glided into the kitchen, where Mommy was putting away the tea things.

"Arleen said she saw the cats playing with a mockingbird earlier. She said they had snapped its legs clean off."

"*Clean off?*" the girls repeated, marveling at the infelicitous phrasing.

Mommy nodded. She was wearing a lovely floral dressing gown and silk slippers just like the girls.

"Those weren't our cats," one of the girls said, "our cats are sweet cats, old stay-at-home cats, they play with store-bought toys only," knowing full well that even this early in the summer the cats had slaughtered no fewer than a dozen songbirds by visible count, that they were efficient and ruthless and that the way in which they so naturally expressed their essential nature was something the girls admired very much.

"Are you aware," Arleen said, "that domestic cats kill four point four million birds every year in this country alone?"

"Awful," Mommy said faintly.

"Mommy, Mommy, Mommy, don't you listen to such dreadful things. Such dreadful things don't happen in our garden," the other girl said, hugging her, pretending to hang off her, clutching at her soft waist with her narrow hands, prattling on until Mommy made a smile.

"On a lighter note," the girls then announced, glaring at Arleen, "we are going to the beach."

There they spent the remainder of the day, nude and much admired, glistening with frequently applied oil. They talked about Mommy and Daddy. This they did not usually do, preferring to keep them inside themselves in a definite and distinct way, not touching them with words not even inside words, but just holding them inside—trapped, as it were—and aware of them quite clearly without thinking about them, fooling around with them in this fashion.

But Mommy and Daddy were changing. In the girls' eyes, they seemed to be actually crumbling. This was of concern. Daddy was smoking and drinking more and surrendering himself to bleak pronouncements. He was sometimes gruff with them as though they were not everything to him! And Mommy's enchantment with life seemed to be waning. They were behaving uncertainly, and it was harder for them to be discriminating. Daddy had wanted to burn like a hot fire, and he had not. Clearly, he had not. Something was hastening toward him, and Mommy too, at once hastening but slowly, cloaked in the minutes and months.

The girls returned home subdued, coming through the garden and passing beneath the rose arbor where the bird's nest was concealed prettily among the climbing canes. The girls grimaced at it, knowing it contained two rotting eggs, having investigated it some days before. They had not informed Mommy of the nest's pulpy contents and they never would, of course.

In the kitchen there was a message for them, written in Mommy's rounded hand on heavy stationery.

Father Snow and Arleen have gone downtown for ice-cream cones. Daddy and I are taking our naps.

The girls skipped upstairs and into Father Snow's room. There was nothing there but two black round stones on the table by the single bed.

"He doesn't think that's him and Donny, does he?"

"How ghastly."

In Arleen's room, they immediately went to the suitcase but couldn't find the journal. The journal was missing again, it was nowhere. Then they found it. But they had been absorbed to such a degree in their search that they scarcely noticed Arleen standing in the doorway. She was a smudgy thing, round-shouldered, carrying a whale-shaped purse, a wretched souvenir of this perfect island.

Then she was gone.

"Well, that was considerate of her."

"It *is* our house."

But just as they opened the book, which had a disgusting pink and rawly fibrous cover, Arleen appeared again and spoke the words as they appeared on the first page.

"*Headaches . . . Palpitations . . . Isolated . . . Guilt . . .* And that's a sketch of a photograph your mother showed me. It's you and your parents when you were little girls."

The girls peered at it, at a loss. The woman had no talent whatsoever. On impulse, they bent forward and sniffed it.

"Your mother thinks of her heart as a speeding car," Arleen said. "Too big, too fast, out of control, no one at the wheel. And her head too, also speeding . . . Farther on, there are accounts of some of her dreams."

"She didn't tell you her dreams!" The girls didn't believe it for a moment, that Mommy would tell this *troll* her dreams.

Arleen gently tugged her journal from their hands, smiled thinly at them, and left.

The girls sat for several moments in a perturbed silence. Later, in their own room, which constituted the entire third floor and was exotic and theatrical, they bathed and dressed and put up their hair. It was now dusk, and the downstairs parlor where they were all to gather for cocktails was filled with a golden light.

The girls tiptoed down the stairs. Daddy was telling Father Snow about a former houseguest who claimed he could get out of his body anytime he wanted to and turn around and look at it. The girls remembered *that* weekend. They rolled their eyes.

"I never believed him," Mommy said. "But then it's a very subjective matter, I would think."

"Must have gotten a taste for it," Father Snow said.

"I never would, I don't think," Mommy said.

This was regarded as amusing by all. The girls were scandalized by the friendship between Mommy and Daddy and this weird duo. They couldn't bear it for another night.

"Oh, girls, you look lovely!" Mommy exclaimed.

Father Snow was stirring martinis. He wore a jacket and tie. Arleen was wearing . . . something dreadful. The drinks in their crystal glasses were passed around. Father Snow liked to offer a small prayer before the cocktail hour began. To the girls it was merely one of his excruciatingly annoying habits. Prayer is a means of getting rid of some of our own ignorance about ourselves, Father Snow had always said. Mommy and Daddy and Arleen bowed their heads. The girls, as they always did, looked around the room. At the mirrors, the embroidered footstool, the good Chinese rug, the little brass clocks, the wallpaper of rose madder. They adored it, all this was theirs.

"A toast," Father Snow said, "a toast to those not with us tonight." He looked at them unhappily. "We all have to do this at once," he said. They all took a sip of their drinks.

"Was Donny your first best boy?" one of the girls asked brightly.

"I wish I could snap out of this," Father Snow said.

"Maybe you're in the wrong line of work," the other girl said with concern.

"I am thinking of resigning my parish," Father Snow said, chewing on an olive, "and dealing with people on a one-to-one basis. Seeing them through. One by one."

Daddy remarked that he and Mommy were with him one hundred percent on that.

"Poor Donny," Father Snow said. "He led a fairly incoherent existence and then he died."

"But that's because he was so typical," one of the girls said. "And there is nothing wrong with that, absolutely nothing. But what was the matter with his teeth? He had like a high-water mark on his teeth." The girls found the ensuing awkward moment quite satisfying.

Father Snow blinked. "I love him very much."

The girls sighed. He seemed to them like a mollusk at that moment. He was hardly worth the effort.

"Mommy," one said, "tell the story about the night Daddy proposed."

"Oh," Mommy said, "yes. He knelt before me and said, 'Let's merely see each other every day for the rest of our lives.'" She passed Arleen a cracker with a bit of foul and expensive cheese daubed on top of it. This was declined. "Almost thirty-five years ago now."

"Tell the whole story," the girl squealed. "We love the story. Tell how Daddy ran over that man who was standing beside his disabled car on the highway that winter night, but Daddy didn't stop even though he knew he'd very likely killed him because you were going to a concert. It was the night Daddy was going to propose to you and he didn't want your life together compromised or delayed. You had your life before you!"

Father Snow visibly paled.

"It was Janáček's 'Fairy Tale' that evening," Mommy said. "Debussy and Beethoven were also on the program."

Father Snow looked very ill at ease. Mommy reached out and squeezed his hand. "If this happened," Mommy said, "you'd be able to accept it, wouldn't you? If it had happened, you'd understand."

Father Snow squeezed back. "Only if it had," he said.

"That story has not been previously aired in public," Daddy said.

The girls closed their eyes and hummed a little. They loved the story—the night, the waves of snow descending, the elegant evening clothes, the nonexistent girls, some stranger sacrificed.

Father Snow drained his drink. "I'm going to make another batch of these if I may," he said. He extricated his hand from Mommy's and dumped more gin in the shaker, swirled it once and poured, without ceremony. Some situations simply did not allow for the sacralization of the ordinary, which he otherwise made every effort to observe.

He swallowed and groped for Mommy's hand again, recoiling slightly when he found it.

"Do you think we could do something about it?" Mommy said tentatively. "Is it possible after all these years?"

"Repent?" he said, his voice cracking. "Repent," he said.

Mommy looked at him with some annoyance. "Is that all? I've always thought that was a rather common thing to do." She wanted to offer more cheese to all but her hand was trapped. "I do feel sorry," she said. "We do."

"But the word is misunderstood!" Father Snow said. "The word translated throughout the New Testament as *repentance* is, in the Greek, *meta-noia*, which means change of mind. *Meta* means transference, as in *metaphor*—transference of meaning. Transformation."

"Repent," Mommy said. "So unhelpful. So common, really."

"The English word *repentance* is derived from the Latin *poenitare*, which merely means to feel sorry, suggesting a change in the heart rather than in the mind. *Poenitare* is a most inadequate word that doesn't reflect the challenge involved," Father Snow said excitedly.

"We've had a good life," Daddy said, smoking. "Full. Can't take that away from us."

Father Snow looked at his drink. The moment of exhilaration had passed. He was now merely drunk and again missing Donny. "Very difficult. Another way of thinking, a different approach to everything in life . . ." he said uncertainly.

The cats came into the room and leapt up onto Arleen's lap. The cats would do this to people they sensed hated them, and this amused the girls. But Arleen stroked them, first the one, then the other. From one's side she plucked a bloodsucker the size of a swollen dime. She held it between her fingers, a fat full thing with tiny waving legs, and dropped it in the dish Daddy was using as an ashtray. From behind the ear of the second cat, Arleen snapped off another. Its removal occasioned a slight clicking sound. She dropped it beside the other one. The things stumbled around in the ashes in the little china dish. The attractive floral pattern that was so Mommy, that Mommy admired on all her china, was totally obscured. In this pretty room, this formal room with the silk shades, the portraits of ancestors and the lark beneath the bell jar.

"That's disgusting, Arleen," one of the girls said. They had no doubt that she had produced them fraudulently. Their pets, their darlings, could not possibly be harboring such things. "Are you a magician? Isn't that unchristian?"

"No, no," Arleen said, ducking her head shyly. "I'm hardly a magician, I'm an adviser, a companion."

"Arleen's no amateur," Father Snow said.

"A companion?" the girls said.

"The woman can listen to anything and come to a swift decision," Father Snow said. "I rely more on the ritual stuff. Words. Blah, blah, blah."

Arleen turned to Mommy. "You should get rid of them."

"The cats?" Mommy said. "Oh, I know, sometimes they *spray*."

"No, the girls," Arleen said. "High time for them to be gone."

The girls gaped at her.

"Your mother's not well, you're killing her," Arleen said simply.

Mommy looked at them. She looked as though she didn't know what to think. Daddy rested his burning cigarette in the dish, then ground it out and lit another. The ashes moved with continuing, even renewed, effort.

Mommy quickly spread more cheese on the crackers, wads of it, a bit more than was nice, actually. She stood up to pass the plate, tottering a bit.

"Oh, do sit down," one of the girls said, exasperated.

She did, abruptly, looking puzzled.

Father Snow said, "Clarissa, are you all right?" for Clarissa was Mommy's name.

"Dear?" Daddy said.

She smiled slyly and gave a little grunt. It was all so not like Mommy. She swayed and slid to the floor not at all gracefully, entangling herself in the cord of a lamp and striking her head on the lintel of the fireplace.

The girls clutched each other and cried out.

Arleen moved to cradle Clarissa's head, and Father Snow, with surprising sureness, crouched beside them both. He had quite regained his composure, as though for the moment he had put the old dead behind him and was moving on to the requirements of the quickening new.

Revenant

CLIFF'S FATHER HAD MADE ALL THE ARRANGEMENTS FOR HIS own funeral and when he died his lawyer called and informed Cliff of the time and place, a small church graveyard on an island that held no associations for Cliff or, as far as he knew, his father, though the two of them had been estranged for some time.

"The stone's not ready yet. Deer Isle marble. No name, no dates, just the words *And you, what do you seek?*"

Cliff said nothing.

"It's certainly different," the lawyer offered. "That might be what's taking them so long."

It was winter then. He was twenty-eight. For a year he had been working in the city at a publishing house, one of the best, and spending the weekends with a woman and her two-year-old son in a little house in Connecticut that her grandmother had left her. Her own parents had died some time before. She had no one either. Well, she had the child.

The island lay in a frigid haze. Only two ferry runs a day were scheduled at that time of year—one left at nine in the morning and returned to the mainland immediately, and the other left the island at four in the afternoon. The crossing took forty minutes.

Cliff drove into the hold, which was brightly lit with yellow bulbs. The light made everything colder. There were two new SUVs and a truck loaded with lumber and pipe. Cliff was wearing a suit and fine shoes with thin socks; he had dressed carefully for the occasion. He had a coat and gloves but they were more formal than warm. He should have dressed more warmly. He would have brought something to read but again he thought, My father has died. He did not want to be reading. The service would be at exactly twelve o'clock and would probably last no more than fifteen minutes. He had been told there was an inn near the ferry dock that served food, but the island did not do much to accommodate the casual visitor. There was no town. There was a golf course and a Coast Guard station and the beaches were rocky and mostly private. It was an island of estates invisible down winding roads.

He tried to picture a woman at the graveside, a beautiful weeping stranger. He hoped for this, expecting some disclosure still about a life, his father's, that was so unknown to him.

When the ferry began to move, he got out of the car and went up to the cabin. The steel of the floor was painted blue and the oak benches were highly varnished. There were four passengers and an enormous dark dog, a Newfoundland. There was a handsome elderly couple, the truck driver and, sitting with the dog, a young woman about twenty. They all looked at him briefly except for the truck driver, who was holding a paper cup of coffee but appeared to be sleeping. The girl was reading, and the jacket of the book she was holding said starkly *The Poems of Yeats*. After a few moments she put the book down and glanced at him.

"'The Cap and Bells,' that's a nice one," he said.

She smiled at him tightly and picked the book up again.

He had always liked poetry.

He sat quietly on one of the varnished benches. No one spoke but they seemed comfortable, at ease. He did not feel at ease. He thought for a moment that if they knew his situation they would be kind to him. Then he felt ashamed.

It was black outside the windows. The crossing to the island was smooth and he tried to remain aware of it.

Something struck the window. He stared, but saw nothing. The others, too, looked at the window. Even the huge dog raised its head, which looked warm and moist and trembled slightly, like something baking. When he had been a child, someone had told him that every dog's heart was the same size, it didn't matter how big the dog was. This had troubled him for years. He had never owned a dog himself.

He closed his eyes and not long after heard the engine slow. He rose and went outside. He could see the dock ahead, the battered boards of the cradle shining greasily beneath a single large light. He went down and sat in his car. He found the directions the pastor had given him to the church and studied them again. They were not complicated. The pastor had not known his father but was in receipt of the cremains.

A deckhand appeared and pulled the gates of the hold back. The sound of the engine rose as the ferry slowed and rocked against the boards. Cliff watched the docking procedure carefully. When the deckhand gestured to him, he realized he had been dreading this, leaving the ferry first, driving ahead of the others up the road.

The car clattered over the steel plates and plunged up the road, skidding a little. The other vehicles followed. Within a few moments he had passed the darkened inn and, a mile later, the church and its attendant graveyard. Still, they followed. He should have turned toward the church, since it was the reason he was here, after all. He felt humiliated. The road branched and he bore to the left. The others followed, as though intent on tormenting him. Finally he saw the truck turn off. Wet trees lined the road and stone walls glittered through dead vines. One car turned down a lane but one still followed. His head felt illuminated. He saw a fox in the road and slammed on the brakes. The fox vanished and the car behind him sped by, the girl at the wheel, the huge dog filling the backseat. He pulled over and paused a moment. On the shoulder lay another fox, long crushed. But it hasn't happened after all, came the incoherent thought, and he was frightened.

CLIFF LOVED HIS WORK AS AN EDITOR. HE LOVED THE OLD OFFICES, the ruthlessness and formality of the meetings. He didn't have any authors of his own yet. He had worked on a few anthologies and guidebooks and had one historical novel on the fall list. During the week he stayed in a bed-and-breakfast brownstone in the West Eighties. His room was small, had a bright worn Turkish rug on the floor, and the bed was high and narrow. A Steiff animal collection filled one of the shelves, and a vacuum cleaner was stored in the closet. The only breakfast provided was English muffins and strawberry jam and he couldn't keep any food of his own in the refrigerator. He was always hungry. On the weekends he took the train to Connecticut and stayed with Ricky and the boy, Richard. He liked the idea of having an attractive family that he had not been responsible for creating.

One of the senior editors seemed interested in his progress, a man named Franklin Woolf, but everyone called him Loup. He was erudite and viciously funny. You want to be the last to leave the room when he's in it, one of the other junior editors warned Cliff, though he was eager to learn and knew he could learn a lot from him. Loup arranged to have him move into the midtown writing studio of one of the house's venerable authors, who had relocated temporarily to Mexico. It was full of books and had good light and a kitchen, and the bathroom was his alone. It was a far better arrangement than the brownstone. The author was working on a "volcano" of a book but everyone knew he had stopped writing, that he'd lost his nerve. Nobody went to Mexico anymore to write books. The man was finished.

ONE OF THE ASSISTANTS DIED AND MOST OF THE OFFICE ATTENDED the funeral. He was younger than Cliff, just out of Bard. He'd drowned, horsing around in some lake on a long holiday weekend, and now he was dead. Then, less than a week later, a beloved agent died from the complications diabetes often brings. That was a memorial service, and the first time Cliff heard Loup speak in such a venue. Although Cliff had not known the agent, he found Loup's words moving, even thrilling in a peculiar way. He was by far the best speaker there. Life seemed sweet and carefree and cruel, futile, almost comprehensible. He could have described to no one what Loup had said.

"Jesus," Loup muttered to him afterward, "let's go get a drink." It was three o'clock in the afternoon and they went to the Carlyle. As they were handing over their coats to be checked, Cliff saw Loup glance at the Phi Beta Kappa key he wore as a lapel pin on his coat. A diligent student, he had graduated from a midwestern college of no great reputation. He wore the pin with some secretiveness but casually, as though it didn't matter. And it did not matter, because he hadn't gone to the right school.

Loup bestowed on him the slightest of smiles. Cliff was too nervous to even get drunk. Later, when he returned to the writer's studio, he removed the pin and threw it in a drawer.

· · ·

LOUP WAS GOING THROUGH BOXES OF MANUSCRIPTS, A DOZEN OF them that had been on his desk for a month. He was now disposing of them rapidly. He would pick an even-numbered page and give it his full attention. One page could tell him everything. Sometimes the decision was made on a single line. It was all true, what writers suspected.

He called Cliff into his office and read aloud, "*I looked out the window. I could not tell which were the thoughts and which were the trees.*" He said to Cliff, "What the hell does that mean?"

"I like it," Cliff ventured. "It's not bad."

"So give her a chance. If we don't change her life, somebody else will."

LOUP AND CLIFF SWEPT INTO MEMORIAL SERVICES TOGETHER, two fine-looking men in dark coats. There were so many occasions, at least once a month, in cathedrals and supper clubs, in arboretums, in chapels, under bridges, in theaters. A dignified lament seemed almost perpetual, resting lightly over the vigor and flash of the city. There was nothing suspicious or extraordinary about the numbers, nothing particularly unnerving about the manner in which the usual course of nature was accomplished upon those taken. Surprises were not infrequent, although there were no suicides. The enemy agent appeared in its own time, arrived on its own schedule. A translator died in a domino car wreck in a dust storm on a New Mexico interstate. A poet was murdered by his wife. The founder of an old, stubbornly prestigious quarterly collapsed, having just excused himself from dinner.

And after the funeral it felt good to be drinking and talking, unfazed, strengthened, made alert by his attendance at these courteous rituals where Loup often spoke in his oblique, heretical, much-admired fashion, addressing those gathered in a courtyard holding flutes of champagne or standing barefoot in the verge of some gently receding tide or assembled in some vast prewar apartment—not every war bestows upon the time just preceding it such desirable architecture—or moteless, light-filled loft, where the faces seemed as idealized as masks, some but not many half barbaric with grief. They thought Loup was telling them they were still winning, for their hearts, though they might be cold or troubled or uncertain or even without honor, had not yet died within them. They were winning. The day belonged to them still, though tomorrow was promised to no one.

On the weekends, Ricky tried to match him drink for drink. He increasingly arrived hours later than he had promised. The neat little house felt stifling to him. The boy's face was flushed but he was sleeping, drugged with the heat, wearing only a dazzlingly white cloth diaper.

"Why don't you open some windows?" he demanded.

"I kept the house shut up to be cool," Ricky said. "Gramma did and it was always cool."

"It's like being in an oven," Cliff complained.

"I guess I wasn't thinking. I was just waiting for you."

He moved quickly through the house, noisily pushing up windows. They had to be held in place with sticks, cracked croquet mallets, the rungs of old chairs. That was how the old woman had done things. A fragrant breeze slipped in immediately from the meadow but did not mollify him.

In the morning, they sat out on a redwood deck the grandmother was having built the month she died. Cliff had tried to finish the work himself and done it badly but Ricky didn't seem to notice. She liked having breakfast on the ugly deck, which she'd made even uglier with pots of geraniums everywhere. Farther away, near the marsh, red-winged blackbirds swayed on the tips of tall grasses.

Ricky was reading the newspaper avidly, as she always did. Her morning homage to the newspaper. Finally she put it down.

"What?" she said. "You're restless."

"I have a lot of work to do."

"You could have brought it with you. I don't mind."

"I better go back early. Maybe after lunch."

"Oh," she said, disappointed. She began pinching dead stems off the geraniums.

"Those things have a helluva smell," he said.

"I like roses better but I'm not good with roses." After a moment she said, "Don't be unhappy with me, Cliff, with us."

"I'm not unhappy," he said. "Don't start that stuff."

.   .   .

ON THE FERRY, THE GIRL HAD BEEN STROKING THE DOG'S HEAD as she read. Then she raised her eyes and looked at him again. He must have been staring at her without realizing it.

"Rilke's my favorite," he said. "He wrote about dogs a great deal. He wrote about going into them, you know? He'd have been fascinated with your big fellow."

"My big fellow," she said slowly.

"It's apparently why Rilke left his wife, why he left home. Because he wasn't allowed to 'go into the dog.' Or if he did he would have to attempt to explain it, which spoiled everything. He loved easing himself into the dog, into the dog's very center, into the place from which the dog existed as a dog, the very place, he said, where God would have rested when the dog was complete, to watch him." He spoke quickly. Usually he didn't talk much. He felt a little breathless.

"I'd like to make something clear to you," she said. "Do you think that would be possible? I mean really clear."

"I'm sorry," he said. "I didn't mean to—"

"I think you understand me," she said.

After she had sped around him on the road, he drove for a time, disoriented, across the island. Then he returned to the church and the graveyard. There were a few large marble stones, pink as uncooked bacon, then some low granite pillow stones, as he'd heard them called. It was not an old cemetery. There was probably an older one somewhere on the island. He couldn't see that any earth had been freshly excavated. He hoped that they remembered, that they knew what they were doing. He got out of the car and walked toward the wrought-iron fence that enclosed the burying ground. With relief he saw some shoveled earth, some waiting earth. He returned to the car and poured a cup of coffee from the thermos he'd brought. It seemed he had known more about everything before his father's death, which had just been six days before, and now he would know less and less. He looked at the church and the graveyard and the parking lot where gulls stood hunched. On the beak of each one was a perfect red dot like a drop of blood. He couldn't understand any of it. The church had no spire. It had an architectural suggestion of a spire.

He walked toward the church and the gulls shuffled away from him and spread their wings but did not fly. The door was unlocked, so he went in, without looking at the sanctuary, and found the bathroom. When he came out he saw the pastor's office and put his hand on that door too, but it was locked. The church was as cold as the outside, maybe even colder.

He sat down self-consciously in the last pew. There was a child's mitten on the floor. Less than an hour had passed since he'd driven off the ferry. He sat in the cold. The church felt like the shell of something, something unlucky. The flowers from the Sunday service were still in their vases, browning. The silver vases, however, shone. This was Wednesday.

He could see his own breath before him and his teeth began to chatter. He nudged the child's mitten away with his foot, under the pew in front. The pews were as heavily varnished as the benches on the ferry. He stood and walked past the pastor's study into an open room full of rummage, games and glasses, shoes and clothes. On a coatrack there were a number of worn sweaters and jackets. He put his ungloved hand idly in the pocket of one of the jackets and touched cigarette butts and rubber bands. He wondered if any of his father's things were in this room. He would not have recognized them; he had last been with him two years ago and it hadn't been anywhere his father lived, just a restaurant in the city. He remembered a plate of bloody meat. Apparently the restaurant was cherished for its firm, fresh, bloody meat. The evening with his father had been all right, though he couldn't remember all that much about it.

The hand he had placed in the jacket now felt dirty, tingling, even a little numb, as if it had been bitten by poisonous insects. Cigarette butts and rubber bands and death the promised end. He went back to his car, turned on the heater and drove into the interior of the island again. He didn't see the crushed fox this time and kept going. There were moors with scrub pines, thickets and ponds. There were no houses here in what was common land, a conservancy, crisscrossed by rough trails. He drove aimlessly and slowly through the moors, then stopped on a high knoll. Some distance away he saw a vehicle creeping along with a dog trailing behind it. It was the Newfoundland. This was how the girl exercised him. The bitch, he thought. Oh, the lazy bitch. He sat slumped in his seat, despondent, hating her, following the lumbering dog with his eyes. They didn't approach him. She must have seen him there, his white car on the moors, but she was selecting trails now that took her farther and farther away. They disappeared from his sight.

The water of the distant sound looked like pavement, an empty boulevard. He must not allow the girl to ruin this island for him, this unknown place where his father would be buried forever. He had to give his father his full attention; it was absolutely essential. He looked at his watch. It was still some time before the burial. He remembered thinking then that the pastor should have invited him to his house during this interval. It would have been nice.

THE WRITER WHO COULD NOT TELL WHICH WERE THE THOUGHTS and which were the trees made quite an impression. But her agent double-crossed Cliff and her next contract was with another house. Still, Cliff was credited with having good instincts and given better opportunities. His authors respected the careful work he did while he found he admired them less and less. The best books were those uninhabited by those who wrote them.

"Fierce, tactile prose," Loup said. "That's what we want and are so seldom given.

"There's no fucking energy around anymore," Loup said. "You notice that? It's because death's energy, death's *vital* energy, is being ignored. It's not being utilized. The more and more death, the more it's wasted. People just let it evaporate. But not us. We know how to husband the source. I'm sure you are aware," Loup said, "that the soul was invented. A Greek invented it in the sixth century BC. Pindar the Greek."

"THEY TOLD ME I WAS WASHING THE DIAPERS WITH TOO MUCH bleach and that's why the baby's been cranky," Ricky said. "Do you think that could be true?"

He had so wearied of her it was like an ache in his bones.

"I've found a good sitter," she said. "It took me forever to find a really responsible one. Why don't I come along to the service for your father?"

"Why would you want to do that?"

"We never do anything important together. I hardly ever see you. Afterwards we could go out, couldn't we?"

"We'll have another drink and go out tonight. We'll go to that seafood place."

It was late afternoon and the sun was falling with haste toward the earth.

"Gramma said that when dusk falls it reminds God of the hearts of men. That's the only time he thinks of us, at dusk."

"Your grandmother was an amazing woman," Cliff said.

She looked at him uncertainly.

They would quarrel later. He was relieved it was finally over.

He had stopped at the inn before reboarding the ferry. The girl's car was in the parking lot and in the backseat, like a judge in his robes, sat the dog.

In the dining room the tables were set with white tablecloths but no one was there. People were eating and drinking in the bar. He went into the dining room, ordered a whiskey and soda and some soup and asked for bread. He was almost trembling with hunger. He ate most of the bread with his drink.

The girl materialized from the dimness of the bar and walked across the dining room to his table. She had on jeans and a tweed jacket and was wearing dark red lipstick.

"I'm sorry I was rude to you this morning," she said. "I feel badly about it. It was interesting what you were saying."

He picked up the last piece of bread in the basket and began chewing it. "The bread here isn't very good," he said.

"It's better on the weekends," she said. "Or it sometimes is." She laughed.

"Would you like a drink?" he said.

"No thank you. I just wanted to apologize. I was so awful. I'm like a different person in the morning."

She was being terribly pleasant. "Yes," he said. "You seem like a different person."

The waitress was coming across the room with the soup.

"I'll leave you in peace now," the girl said, and went back to her friends.

He ate the soup. A few minutes later the waitress returned with a fresh drink. "It's on the house," she said. He took it and ordered another. A drink someone bought for you didn't taste any different than a drink you bought yourself. No one else came into the dining room.

As he left, the girl called out good-bye to him.

"Bye-bye," he said. She meant nothing to him.

It was growing dark and he could barely make out the great patient bulk of the dog in the car next to his own. He thought about being watched from the inside. He would not want to be watched from the inside.

Now he and loup were sitting in a corner of the bar they frequented. They had been regulars here for months. Cliff had finished telling him the story of the island, his father, the girl. He had missed the service at the graveyard. He must have fallen asleep in the car or been thinking of the girl, wishing her ill and the dog too, hoping for something to enter their lives and break her heart. When he had looked at his watch it was well past noon. Even then he had done nothing until it was hours past the moment for which he had come, the committal. He continued to sit in the car with the heater running. But then he had driven back across the island and past the deserted church without even glancing at the grave site to see if the earth was smooth or still disturbed.

It was a story meant to be told in a different way, he thought reasonably, protectively.

"You can go back for the installation of the stone," Loup said. "There's always the next opportunity."

Cliff looked at him meekly but the older man was looking away, studying someone across the room, someone whom he had greeted earlier and already dismissed.

The Mission

A MR. HILL WAS DOING MY PAPERWORK.

"What will you take away from this experience," he asked me.

I looked at him, a little wildly, I guess.

"What do you think you will learn from the incarceration experience?" he said.

"I don't know," I said.

Mr. Hill wore a pink shirt and looked tired. His eyes were bloodshot.

"Have you been swimming," I asked.

"I haven't been swimming," he said frankly.

I thought of Mr. Hill doing a strenuous butterfly in a blue cool but overchlorinated pool deep in the earth beneath the Mission.

I had been in jail but a single day and night when they realized they had overlooked the wedding ring on my hand. I wasn't married anymore but couldn't get the ring off. My knuckles were swollen possibly because of the prednisone I'd been taking because I was tired, so tired. It was just a cheap gold band but I made a terrible fuss when they said they'd have to cut it off. Some of the girls had gathered around.

"They're gonna cut off her wedding ring," one muttered with amused awe.

I asked for Mr. Hill. He might tell them not to bother, I thought. I was only in for nine days.

But they couldn't find Mr. Hill or he had in the meanwhile sickened or died, I don't know.

They were determined to cut off my ring and after several attempts with a variety of implements they did. They took pictures. First the little ring was on my lumpish hand, then the poor broken thing was zipped up in a baggie for safekeeping and future retrieval. I didn't regret the mangling of the ring as much as the disclosure heard throughout the dorm that I would be there for a mere nine days. Most of the girls were serving ninety or a hundred and eighty days. One girl, Lisa, who even with my paucity of instinctual knowledge terrified me, had been here since September and it was now June.

It was Sunday evening and on Sunday evenings there was Snack, a bottle of Pepsi and a packaged cookie. Usually you had to pay for this stuff out of the machines. Two inmates with magnificent hair distributed Snack, which was allocated by bunk number. Everyone except the guards had the most astonishing hair. I didn't want to call any more attention to myself so I lined up with the others but someone had already used my number to double-dip.

"It doesn't matter," I said.

"You didn't pick up Snack already?" one of the gloriously maned girls demanded.

"It's perfectly all right," I assured her.

"Somebody take her cookie?" the other said, her eyes darkening.

"Some bitch took her cookie."

"Really, it's fine," I said. "I didn't—"

"I'm gonna find the bitch took her cookie!" She looked around with unsettling purpose.

"Please, please, please," I said.

"She don't want to get the bitch in trouble," the first one said, not altogether approvingly.

They pushed a warm soda and a cold cookie into my hands.

"You can give me them if you don't want it," the girl behind me said.

I was DUI, which was so boring in the vast scheme of things and particularly in the louche gray world of the Mission. DUIs were beneath interest and I had already experienced girls looking right through me in a practiced way even though this would change if the particulars of my case became known. I had been drinking Manhattans all afternoon for reasons that remain obscure and when returning home had driven off the road into the city's largest cemetery, demolishing seven headstones before my old Suburban stopped. If one of those girls had a friend or family member whose marker had been so desecrated, God himself wouldn't be willing to help me.

The first policeman on the scene said, "You're lucky you didn't kill somebody." Naturally, he was laughing.

This happened four months ago. I didn't go to jail right away. First they took me to a place called the Pit, where more or less endless processing is conducted. There's a water fountain and a phone. My only companion was a woman saying "Mom? Mom? Mom? Mom. Mom. Mom" into the receiver. I don't think anyone was on the other end. I think she was just trying to pass time in the Pit.

Do you know that Kafka is buried with his mother and father in Prague? Their names are on his stone. He couldn't get away from those people, not in life and not in death. I have never been to Prague but had I been and by some misfortune demolished Kafka's headstone, the rage of the people there, indeed the rage of people the world over, would not exceed that of the kinsmen of those whose rest was disturbed here in our little city's largest cemetery. The families Dominguez and Schrage and Tapia and McNeil and Byrne and Pennington ... they hated me. They howled for my ruin. I'd been told their anguish was existential and therefore without limit or promise of closure. Reparation would never be enough.

They let me go after twelve hours to deal with all the horrid things that would occupy me for years—the sentencing and community service and judgments, the lawyers and lawsuits and probation officers and trials and plea bargains and financial penalties and loss of privileges and rights. Nine days at the Mission might very well be the least of my burdens.

In the bunk next to me was a girl whose eyelids were tattooed. I had never seen anything like it. She was a vandal. She went out into nature, into state parks particularly, and hacked whatever she could to pieces. She hacked up trees and spray-painted SOMA on boulders and petroglyphs and interpretive signs. She had misread *Brave New World*, maybe in high school, I thought, but I wasn't going to mention that to her or anything else.

"Have you ever read *Brave New World*," I asked.

She turned her head in my direction, closed her eyes, and very very slowly shook her head.

"OK," I said. "Cool."

You're better off if you don't count the days in jail. Never count the days. Time served does not go Monday, Tuesday, Wednesday and so on but Monday to Tuesday, Tuesday to Wednesday, in that manner. It's longer that way, which is how they want it.

One girl said that when she got out there was a job waiting for her decorating cakes. But she did not have high hopes for the position. "You can't be real creative," she said. "It's not as creative as you'd think."

I just overhear these things, no one ever speaks to me. For example, I heard that Lisa was in for armed robbery and three of the five fathers of her children had restraining orders against her. One afternoon Lisa looked at a girl who had left her boyfriend for dead with a knife in his head as they were traveling by bus to Key West—just left him in the seat when she exited in Key Largo—and said, "Do you have anything you'd like to share?" Most of the girls kept food they'd bought from the machines in the drawers under their bunks. I was very frightened but the girl gave Lisa Snickers and Skittles and even a little bag of that Smartfood popcorn, all of which Lisa accepted in a gracious manner.

The next morning I saw Mr. Hill standing by the front station with some folders.

"Mr. Hill!" I cried.

"Hello, N. Frame," he said.

"I'm not N. Frame," I said, somewhat hurt, "unless she's to be released today."

"She is to be released today."

"Then sure I am," I said.

"No," he said, studying me with his bloodshot eyes, "I see you are not."

"Have you been swimming?" I said, trying to resume our old intimacy.

"You'd better go back to your bunk now," he said, "and tuck your shirt in."

"But it's been nine days! I know you're not supposed to count."

"Whoever told you that?" he said. "Of course you're supposed to count the days."

Not long after, the girls who distributed Snack were released and the girl who would have the job at the bakery and even Lisa. She strode away, her mighty bronze and black hair swinging.

I started counting the days.

When I counted a certain way I had not been there anywhere near nine days.

New girls arrived. They didn't need to know me either because the reality is DUIs will never be among the elite at the Mission. One of the new ones—she was just in for violating probation—managed to hang herself. No one could figure out how she got away with it. Like everyone else she had been asked a dozen times throughout the admission process if she harbored suicidal thoughts but she must have lied.

For a while afterward there were more guards, even men, boys really. The boy guards always looked uneasy. There's a shitload of girls in the bathroom, we heard one of them say anxiously. Somehow the numbers had gotten away from them. There are supposed to be only seven of us in the bathroom at any given time.

The girls gave one another facials at the picnic table in the little cement yard where we were allowed to go at erratic times. The times became even more erratic, if that was possible, after the hung girl. Her name had been Deirdre, but no one mentioned her by name. It was just too weird to call her by her name.

A facial was just squeezing blackheads and whiteheads. Even so, I was not invited to participate, neither as extractor nor as extractee. I felt so isolated and alone, though no more than usual.

My lawyer said, "You're better off where you are for the time being. The environment out here is not conducive to . . ." She paused.

"To what?"

"Conducive to your privacy, to your ability to come and go."

"I want to be able to come and go out there."

"Don't we all," the lawyer said. "I mean in the deepest sense."

From the very first I had found her annoying.

"But I didn't hurt anyone."

"A felony's a felony," she said.

I spent my days attempting to read a little pamphlet entitled *The Room*. It was about file cards and Jesus. It was pretty depressing. It was trying to provide hope but I didn't find it hopeful. Too, the problem might have been with the lighting, which was deliberately terrible. It took forever to read anything.

Then I saw Mr. Hill again. I rushed to the red line painted on the floor. He nodded for me to advance.

"Hello, N. Frame," he said.

"Hello!" I said. Thinking quickly, I added, "I am to be released today."

Then I wanted to take it back because by my calculation N. Frame had been released many days before.

"I'm afraid not," Mr. Hill said. "You're a recidivist and your time with us starts all over again."

Despite myself I thrilled to his use of the word *recidivist*, which is a lovely-sounding word.

"I'm really not N. Frame," I said. "But for my own actions I take full responsibility. I am so contrite."

He looked at me wearily.

"I am," I said.

"Nothing you do will be enough," he said. "No compensation will suffice."

"I know, I know, I know," I said.

He shifted the folders he held from one hand to the other. "Enhanced punishment," I heard in part.

"Wait, wait, wait," I said, for *enhanced* was a lovely word as well, though I believe in this context it wasn't as nice as it sounded. "Am I a recidivist or did my sentence just get worse regardless?"

Even before I finished I felt the unworthiness of my question. I retreated to my bunk and I thought of Mr. Hill returning to his residence beneath the Mission, where the light was good and where water moved as if it were alive and where possibly dozens of the pressed pink shirts I admired were in orderly rows. Our clothes smell of metal—our soap and socks and even the candy that we keep. It all smells unconsolingly of metal.

It was very late and all was quiet. There wasn't a dream moving.

The girl with the tattooed eyelids said to me, "There is no Mr. Hill."

I felt better immediately.

Her eyes were shut, of course. There was a design on her lids but I had always felt that any attempt to determine what it was would be most unwise and I feel that way still.

Another Season

HE HAD TAKEN THE BOAT FROM THE MAINLAND WHEN HE WAS still a young man and stayed on. He remembered the first night being the hardest, as they say the first night of being dead must be. But he was not newly dead, he was entering for the first time what would become his life. He slept that first night on the beach, curled behind a boat, and his dreams were no longer those of his childhood—the plastic ball enclosing a plastic lion crushed by the doctor's car as over and over the doctor's pale car arrived at the anguished house.

He woke to a stinging rain and a strong east wind. The road to town was dark with little birds, dovekies he was later told, little auks blown in from the storm. He scooped up as many as he could catch and placed them in the bushes.

"Not there, not there!" a man in yellow oilskins shouted. "They live only on water, they can't lift their bodies into flight from land!"

Together they carried dozens back to the sea but as many others died exhausted in their hands.

Later the man in oilskins said to him, "What is your name?"

"Nicodemus."

"Not Nick?"

"Nicodemus."

"He was the gentle one."

The man was long retired from some successful industry. Now he was a hobbyist, a birder. He offered to hire Nicodemus as a handyman for his own grand residence, which he would vacate after Thanksgiving. In a matter of weeks, Nicodemus knew everyone on the winter island. He fixed pumps, caulked boats, split wood. He shingled roofs with the help of the waning moon.

Still, nothing was familiar to him here, neither morning nor evening. In the southern dusk, the dark grew out of the sky like a hoof of mud dissolving in a clear pool. But on the island, dusk seemed to grow out of nothing at all. Dusk and night being a figment of fog, an exhaustion of wave, the time when blackness sank into the town as if buildings and trees were a pit to be filled.

A deer fell on the once friendly hillside, the crack of the gun sounding a playful instant later.

His benefactor died on the mainland in a traffic accident. The great stone house was sold immediately. Nicodemus stayed on, in a single-room cottage on the grounds. In the South it would have been called a shack. He became more solitary; his health was not good, but his strength never failed him, he was very strong.

The new owners' big Airedale had had surgery. Nicodemus carried the dog into the house and laid him on pillows and comforters that had been arranged on the floor by the fireplace.

"When do the stitches come out," Nicodemus asked.

"They don't take them out anymore," the new owner said. "They dissolve on their own when their work is done."

The man's wife was slouched in a wing chair reading a paperback book. She looked at the dog and said, "Poor guy, poor Blue." Then she glanced at the book again. "Lem hated the film Tarkovsky made of *Solaris*. I want to see *Stalker* again. I think it's his masterpiece. What a genius."

"Would you like a drink," the man asked Nicodemus.

He shook his head.

"I'd like a drink," the woman said. "Something fun, not just a gin and tonic."

"A martini?"

"That's not fun, that's trouble. Oh, don't bother to make me anything."

"Breakfast of Champions. That's what Kurt Vonnegut called a dry gin martini."

"Oh yes," she said, mollified. "He's a genius. When he speaks, it's genius speaking."

The dog did not recover. Within the week Nicodemus was called upon to bury him.

"I can't do it," the man said. "I loved Blue so much. I just can't see him now, do you understand?"

"Yes," Nicodemus said, though he did not.

"I don't like that man," the woman confided to her husband. "Do you know the story of that servant of Frank Lloyd Wright's? He went berserk and killed Wright's mistress and her children, others too, with a shingling ax. He served luncheon, then killed them and burned the house down as well."

"Nicodemus is not a servant," he said, laughing.

"Yes he is, he's dying to serve, that one, believe me."

Her husband laughed again and shrugged, but she had decided. She didn't like Nicodemus, his silence, his solitariness.

"I think he's illiterate too," she said. "I bet he is."

At the end of the summer, he was let go. It was all right. He found another place, a real shack this time, out by the old haulover, past the striped lighthouse that the summer residents had moved back from the eroding cliffs at enormous expense.

Fewer than a hundred people lived on the island in the winter. The library and church were closed. The hotel was boarded up and the flags put away. The numbered planks of the beach club's pier were stacked in the ballroom. There was a single fire engine but no school. Someone taught him backgammon, baffled that he didn't excel at darts. He drank bitter coffee at the grocer's store.

A scalloper opened the door and announced, "I must bring back the can of corn I bought yesterday. I thought it was pineapple."

The bakery remained open. Her specialty was still Parker House rolls.

"Maybelle come in the other day and she says she's got two husbands. 'Why, Maybelle,' I start, and she says, 'One drunk and one sober.'"

The ferry came three times a week in winter, sometimes not even that when ice choked the passage. But the winters were no longer as cold as they had been, the storms as dire. The dovekies had only that one year been blown ashore, the year he had arrived, now a long time ago.

He could no longer work as he once had. Sometimes, he couldn't catch his breath and at those times he would think, You're my breath, you belong to me. We have to work together. You need me too, he'd address his breath. But oddly, he didn't really believe his breath belonged to him. It was a strange thought that didn't trouble him particularly.

Each summer, more and more people arrived on the island with their enormous vehicles, their pretty children and roisterous pets. It was another season and each summer Nicodemus liked them a little less and they liked him a little less as well, no doubt. There were more creatures dead in the summer. Drowned dogs, car-hit cats and deer and foxes. All manner of birds, gulls, herons and songbirds bright as gold coins. One night in August, on one of his late strolls, for he no longer slept well, he came upon a flock of wild ducks that had attempted to walk across a road that bisected two ponds, a habit safe enough at certain hours and one accommodated mostly with tolerant amusement. But some vehicle had torn through them and continued on, leaving a crumpled wake of the dead and the dying.

Nicodemus picked them up and placed them beside the marsh's shores. Others he put in his jacket, attempting to calm and warm them before their inevitable deaths. This was observed by some who passed by, including Brock Tilden, the owner of a new guesthouse. He admired the thoroughness with which Nicodemus returned the unfortunate site to a relative sense of serenity, even carrying some of the birds off with him, perhaps to eat, Brock thought, for Nicodemus was known to be both odd and resourceful.

Brock was a big booster of the island and its potential. He was a gracious hotelier and many who stayed in his pleasant rooms were so charmed by his enthusiasm and helpfulness that they went on to buy or build places of their own. Brock's idealized version of the island relied heavily on the picturesque and the modestly abundant—he had organized the first daffodil festival in his gardens only that spring—and the dead animals that were increasingly littering the roads and lanes had become an aesthetic problem, demanding a solution.

He conferred with several of the other business owners and they sought out Nicodemus and presented a proposition. They would provide him with a truck, a gasoline card at the dock's pumps and two thousand dollars a year to make the island appear as though death on the minor plane were unknown to it.

"On the minor plane," Nicodemus said.

"Well, yeah, we can't do anything about the big stuff," Brock said, thinking irritably about the prep school boy suiciding by his daddy's basement table saw in June just as the season was starting, or the stockbroker all over the news who was found with an anchor line tied around his ankle. "But we can maintain a certain look that sets this place apart. Dead animals are disturbing to many people. There's also the ick factor."

"What about litter," Nicodemus asked.

"We've got people for litter. This job is yours alone. We'll put it in the beautification budget."

The truck was old but the heater worked and the clutch didn't slip. The bed was wood and had slatted sides. Nicodemus drove slowly along the roads with a red cloth hanging from the tailgate and when he saw the carcass of a dead bird or animal that had been killed due to a momentary and fatal lapse in watchfulness or timing, he would signal a stop, paddling his arm from the window, and step down to the sand-straddled road. He would always pick them up with his ungloved hands and lay them carefully in the truck. He stroked the clotted fur, arranged the stiffening limbs and curved talons, then wrapped them in scraps of sheets and towels. He put the dogs and cats he deemed to have been pets in coffins of cardboard in case they would be claimed and restored to someone's futile care. He printed descriptions on cards and posted them on the grocer's public board along with the advertisements for massages, pellet stoves and dories. If they were not claimed in two days he would bury them in the meadow ringed with pines behind his shack. It was the blackness of their eyes that touched him, the depthless dark of their eyes.

In the winter nights, the sea could have been dark fields or an endless forest of felled trees.

In his room, he ate from chipped plates and forks marked with another's initials, and kept letters that had never been for him neatly tied with string. He had a postcard of a lion in a zoo and one that spoke of a William he had never known from an Elisabeth who promised she would soon arrive. He took the letters from the dump, from the sunken spots in the ground that the flames couldn't reach. The gulls wobbled in the smoke's heat when the island's trash was burned there, and the letters smelled of orange rind and ash.

All his worn furnishings came from the dump. "What do you do with your money, Nicodemus?" they teased him. He didn't know, he had no idea where it was and didn't need it.

He was gaunt, but clean and neat. His hands became the most remarkable things about him. They were beautiful, unworn by the work he did. "You need a good pair of gloves, Nicodemus," they said. But he didn't wear gloves even on the bitterest days, when even the sandpipers' heartbreaking cries were quieted by the cold.

In the summer, the children called him the Undertaker. They would sometimes kill small things for sport and say, "The Undertaker will take care of them now."

He slept little. He didn't think he slept at all, but that was an illusion, he knew. He would think of himself as resting beneath a large black wave, just before it curled and fell, wondering: Why am I this Nicodemus? Why am I not another? When I die, will I become another? Does God love all equally? Does he love the living more than the dead?

It seemed to him that God must love the living more, but could he love the dead less, having made them so?

That summer was the hottest anyone could remember. The flowers browned against the white fences, the berries withered before they were blue. At the ends of the roads, there were dark mirages and the boats seemed to ride on glass.

One night, as he buried a shattered animal, he placed a note in its grave.

Later, he thought, I must not do that again.

HE WORE HIS WOOL SHIRT, HIS HEAVY SERGE TROUSERS, AND HE was shivering from the heat as he drove down the road. The boy who always begged to travel with him when he worked was waiting as he always was and Nicodemus, for the first time, stopped and picked him up. Everyone knew the boy. He wasn't a bad boy, but if someone asked if they liked Peter their answer would be, *Not yet.*

They found a deer first, then two raccoons, small and large, the warm wind still purling through their fur. Nicodemus stayed in the cab while the boy heaved the bodies into the back. The following day he picked the boy up again, though he could barely look at him. But after that, no more.

They found him in his shack, his beautiful hands crossed on his chest, his mouth agape in the awful manner of the dead. He was old and he'd had a strange life. It was unsustainable, really, the life he was leading at the end, the kind of work he'd devoted himself to.

They missed Nicodemus. And Peter was no more than an epigone, they agreed. Still, they had to say that the boy managed to keep the island just as clean.

Dangerous

A YEAR AFTER MY MOTHER MOVED FARTHER OUT, SHE BECAME obsessed with building a tortoise enclosure. This was in preparation for receiving a desert tortoise—*Gopherus agassizii*—or, as the Indians would say, or rather had said, *komik'c-ed*—shell with living thing inside. That's the Tohono O'odham Indians. My mother said she'd read that somewhere.

I was recently at a party and found myself talking to a linguist who told me that we had been pronouncing *komik'c-ed* incorrectly but that it meant pretty much what my mother claimed it did.

Sometimes I drink too much but mostly I don't. I go to AA meetings on occasion but I can't really bond with those people and never see them socially. They're nice enough but some of them have been sober for twenty-five or thirty years. I have a copy of the Big Book and sometimes I read around in it but it never makes me cry like Wordsworth's *Prelude*, say. I don't have *The Prelude* anymore. I misplaced it, unbelievable, but it was falling apart with my looking at it so much and I moved away too after my father died so it was probably misplaced then. My mother is a widow now for two years but she never worries about her situation or talks about it like some people would. She never let on to me or others that she was sorrowful or lonely. I'm twenty-one. It could be argued that there are worse ages to lose your father than in your twentieth year but I found it to be a difficult time, mostly because I was just old enough to try to take it in stride. Sometimes I think it would have been worse if I was eight or even twelve and I don't know why I indulge myself like that. It doesn't make me feel better and I admit I have no imaginative access to the person I was then. I can't imagine that girl at all. I certainly can't imagine having a conversation with her. My mother told me that when I was eight all I wanted to do was swim. Swim, swim, swim. Then I stopped wanting to do this. When I was twelve she said that my most cherished possession was a communication badge I'd earned in Girl Scouts. It showed a tower emitting wiggly lines.

Which is odd because communicating is not a skill I naturally or unnaturally possess. I'd prefer to think of myself as a witness, but honestly, I doubt I'm even that.

The apartment I moved into is a shithole but convenient. Bars, restaurants, automobile services galore and a Trader Joe's where you can buy pizzas fast-frozen in Italy and coconut water from Thailand, not that they're unusual anymore, it's what's come to be expected. The apartment complex is clean, inexpensive and devoid of character. We tenants just refer to it as a shithole because it's so soul-sucking. We don't really believe our souls are being destroyed of course because we feel we have more power over our situation than that. The facility has a good view of sunsets in the summer when they're not at their most legendary and it's too hot to sit outside and view them anyway.

Shortly after my father died and I moved into the shithole without even my *Prelude* to remind me of loftier, simpler and more beautiful emotions, my mother sold our house in the foothills and moved into a run-down adobe on thirty acres of land in the mountains. Is there any kind of adobe other than run-down? I think not.

After a while she began to speak frequently of a neighbor, Willie, and his water-harvesting system. He had a twenty-six-thousand-gallon belowground cistern and got all his water from roof runoff during our infrequent but intense rains. I feared Willie might be a transitional figure in my mother's life but he turned out to be an old man in a wheelchair with an old wife so cheerful she must have been on a serious drug regimen. They did have an ingenious water-collection system and I was given a tour of all the tanks and tubes and purifiers and washers and chambers that provided them with such good water and made them happy. They also kept bees and had an obese cat. The cat, or rather its alarming weight, seemed out of character for their way of life but I didn't mention it. Instead, I asked them if his name was spelled with an *ew* or an *ou*. They found this wildly amusing and later told my mother they'd liked me very much. That and a dollar fifty will get me an organic peach, I said. I don't know why my mother's enthusiasm for them irritated me so much. Soon they were gone, however, both carried off by some pulmonary infection that people get from mouse pee. A man my mother described as a survivalist later moved into their house and I was told little about him other than he didn't seem to know how to keep the system going and ended up digging a well.

It was Lewis with an *ew* that kept bringing diseased rodents into the house, is my suspicion.

From the time I was ambulatory until I was fourteen and refused to participate, every year on my birthday my father would video me going around an immense organ-pipe cactus in the city's botanical garden. The cactus is practically under lock and key now. It could never survive elsewhere, certainly. Some miscreant would shoot it full of arrows or smack holes in it with a golf club.

My father would splice the frames and speed them up so I would start off on my circuit, disappear for a moment and emerge a year older, again and again a year older, taller and less remarkable. I began as a skipping and smiling creature and gradually emerged as a slouching and scowling one. Still, my parents appeared unaware of the little film's existential horror. My mother claims that she no longer has it, that it no longer exists, and I have chosen to believe her.

On the other hand I find it difficult to believe that my father no longer exists. He lives in something I do not recognize. Or no longer recognize and never will again. There are philosophers who maintain we are not our thoughts and that we should disassociate ourselves from them at every opportunity. But without this thought, I would have no experience of the world and even less knowledge of my heart.

I've had a comfortable life. I've not been troubled or found myself an outcast or disadvantaged in any way. This too was the case with my mother and father. Lives such as ours are no longer in vogue. Since I've lived in the shithole, however, I've found that another's perception of me can sometimes be unexpected. For example, the other night I was looking at some jewelry in an unsecured case at Hacienda del Sol, waiting for my friends to arrive so we could start drinking overpriced tamarind margaritas, and this hostess stalks up to me and says, "Can I help you"... in other words, You look beyond suspicious, what are you even doing here...

She appeared a somewhat older version of one of the paramedics who arrived at the house the night my father died, though it was unlikely that anyone would go from being a paramedic to being an employee at a resort that had seen better days and was, in fact, in foreclosure. Though perhaps she had accumulated a record of not saving anyone and had lost her position as an emergency responder.

"Do I know you," I asked. Or maybe it was "Have I seen you before?" because I had never known her, even if she'd been the one to feel my father's last breath leave his body. She threw me a dismissive look and returned to her station to greet and seat a party of four, whom she'd evidently been expecting as they had planned ahead and made a reservation.

My point is that however fortunate your life or—considering the myriad grotesque ways one can depart from it—your death, it's usually strangers who have their hands on you at the end and usher you down the darkened aisle. Or rather that was one of my reflections as I waited for my friends with whom I would commence a night of serious drinking.

So my mother is out there alone, in what I swear is one of the darkest parts of the mountain, with only a rarely-in-residence survivalist for a neighbor, and she is erecting a three-hundred-square-foot protective enclosure for a reptile that isn't even endangered, though my mother claims it should be.

I don't go out there much to visit, not nearly as often as I should, I suppose, but I'm aware that the work is proceeding slowly. My mother is insisting on doing everything herself. The most strenuous part is digging the trench, which Fish and Wildlife guidelines mandate should be fourteen inches deep. The trench is then to be filled with cement and a wall no less than three feet tall built on top of it. All this is to prevent the tortoise from escaping, for this is to be an adopted tortoise, one that has been displaced by development and should not be allowed to return to a no longer hospitable environment. At the same time, everything within the enclosure should mimic its natural situation. There should be flowering trees and grasses, a water source and the beginnings of burrow excavations, facing both north and south, that the tortoise can complete.

The site my mother had chosen was several hundred yards from the adobe. Wouldn't it be easier, I asked, if she just enclosed an area using one of the house's walls? Then she wouldn't have to dig so much, it would be more of a garden, and she could bring out a table and chairs, have her coffee out there in the morning, maybe have a little fire pit for the evening—no, not a fire pit, certainly, what was I thinking? But possibly her aim should be the creation of a pleasant and meditative place that she could utilize for herself as well as for this yet unacquired tortoise.

Actually, I think a space for meditation is the last thing my mother needs. I don't even know why I mentioned it. She didn't respond to my suggestion anyway. She simply said she wasn't doing this for herself.

The earth on the mountain is volcanic and poor. Some of the stones my mother dislodges are as big as medicine balls. She uses some sort of levering tool. Still, it's dangerous work, as every part of the grieving process is if it's done correctly. Don't think I don't realize what my mother's up to.

"If you injure yourself your independent aging days might as well be over," I said. She laughed, which I hoped she would. "Where did you come across that dreadful phrase," she asked. "Someone in the shithole," I answered, and she laughed again. "Why are you punishing yourself," she said, "by living in that place?"

One of my acquaintances here is a widow too, but she's only ten years older than I am. Her husband died in one of those stupid head-on wrecks blamed by the surviving driver on the setting sun. *It blinded me!* She kept his shoes. People would visit her and there would be his running shoes in the bathroom, his boots by the couch, and if he'd been old enough for slippers they would have certainly been by the bed. They'd been in the home they had before she moved here, now sort of on display, she told me, sort of stagy. Everyone who saw them was moved to tears and she kept them out longer than she should have, she realized that. Then one day she just threw them away—they were too beat-up to give to charity—and she got rid of a lot of other things as well and moved into the shithole.

We can't keep pets here. It's one of the rules and is strictly enforced. No one cares. I mean no one tries to smuggle a pet in. They don't feel the lease violates their rights. Several years ago there was a tenant with a Great Dane who went off one morning and shot up his nursing class at the university because he'd received a bad assessment, killing his instructor and two fellow students before killing himself. There was no mention of what happened to the dog afterward, not a single mention. Information about the dog is unavailable to this day. I sometimes think of this guy who wanted to be certified as a nurse, and not only what was he thinking when he set off that morning to murder those people but what was he thinking leaving the dog behind with its dog toys and dog dishes and dog bed? What did he think was going to happen?

Tortoises spend half their life in burrows, from October into April. Should you see a tortoise outside its burrow in the winter months it's not well and veterinary assistance should be sought.

"So," I say to my mother, "have you met this tortoise?"

She said she hadn't, but had filled out all the paperwork and was on a list. She'd be contacted when the enclosure was complete.

"So you don't know how old it is or whether it's a he or a she or whether it's a special-needs tortoise with a malformed shell or a missing leg."

"I don't," my mother said.

"I would think that after going through all of this, all the woman-hours and expense, you'd want a perfect tortoise."

"Well," my mother said, "maybe I'll get one."

My mother used to be much more talkative. There used to be a lot more going on, more being said, lots of cheerful filler. Maybe that's why I go to AA as much as I do because at least people are telling stories, pathetic and predictable as they may be, and all manner of reassurances and promises are being made. When I go into my mother's little house now, I don't recognize much. There seems to be very little remaining of the life I had known, been cocooned in, you might say. I should have emerged from it in glorious certitude by now.

Often I think, and it is with a certain dismay, that I will age out of the shithole one day, for it is a young crowd who reside here briefly and then move on. The ones who stay don't remain in touch with those who leave. What would we speak of with one another? When someone vacates, the manager comes in, paints the walls, sands the floors and cleans the windows. New tenants arrive quickly—it's cheap, practically free! It's convenient! We're not crazy about them at first but we gradually enfold them. No point in playing favorites here. We're all pretty much the same.

My mother finally finished the trench. It was pretty impressive when you think it was all accomplished by her hand. Then she bought some rebar and a cement mixer and in really no time it was all filled in and ready to accept the blocks. But then matters slowed down again. It was June and the heat was beginning to build. She'd be working, covered head to toe and with a hat and welder's gloves, but gradually she'd only get a few hours in between dawn and dusk. The rest of the time I don't know what she did—waited in that little adobe for dawn and dusk, I suppose. She didn't have air-conditioning, just a rattling, inefficient swamp cooler in need of new pads.

"What she's doing doesn't sound healthy," the young widow in the shithole said. "You should take her out to dinner or something. Get her out of there. Insist on it. Or she should take up running. I should take up running, I know. And what kind of a companion is a tortoise going to be? You're not even supposed to pick them up much, are you?"

"Fish and Wildlife claim they're very personable," I said.

"Those people are morons. Didn't they want to open a hunting season on sandhill cranes?"

"I don't know," I said.

"You've probably never even seen one. But I'm from Colorado, so I have. They're very elegant and even have this elaborate dance they do. They mate for life. When one's taken and the other's left, that's loneliness—real loneliness."

She is pretty intense at times but also can be superficial—as with those shoes, which I have the grace not to mention.

Certainly my mother did not need to be taken out to dinner. People aren't much help to one another under most circumstances, is what I've found. I'm reminded of the evening I dropped in at AA and a ruddy-faced woman came up to me and said, "I hear you've lost your mother, I'm so sorry." And I said, "No, it was my father who died." And she said, "Oh, I'd heard it was your mother."

And that was it.

· · ·

IT WAS THE FOURTH OF JULY WHEN I MANAGED TO GET OUT TO MY mother's house again. The blocks had been cemented in place and were ready to be plastered and my mother had found a gate that she'd installed and painted blue. It swung inside, though, rather than outside, which I found somewhat awkward.

We were in the kitchen of the adobe eating toasted bread and some cold soup my mother had made. I had brought a bottle of wine but my mother, incredibly, did not have a corkscrew. You could barely see the enclosure from the house. It was so strange to me that she wouldn't want to be closer to it when it was finished and had its occupier, though to be truthful I could not imagine the creature inside very well or the relief that seeing it would provide.

"Mom," I said.

"I'm good," my mother said.

Her face was sun-darkened and her thinning hair looked as though it would be crisp to the touch.

"Do you ever think of heaven," she asked.

"No."

"Good." She laughed. "I wouldn't want you thinking of heaven."

We never did, did we?

I wished I were twelve again and could ask questions and pretend the answers were what I needed.

"How about divinity," she asked.

"Gosh no," I said, "that's even harder to think about, isn't it?"

She said the exciting work was about to begin—the preparation of the inner keep.

"Is that what it's called?" I wondered, and she said that's only what she called it.

I managed to get the cork out with a screwdriver. It seemed to take me forever. My mother accepted a glass of wine without comment and we resumed talking about the plants she would put in that would provide food and shade for the tortoise. I wondered what she would do when everything was complete since it was very close to being complete. Grief is dangerous work, I thought again, but when you have overcome it and it passes away, are you not left more bewildered and defenseless than ever?

I didn't know what she meant by divinity, but that strange word was not mentioned again.

"Your mother is trying to contain her grief in a beautiful garden of her own devising," the young widow said. "Or maybe it's not grief at all. Maybe it's something else, early-onset something. I'm sorry," she said, "I don't mean to simplify your mother's situation in any way. Or yours. Or even mine, for that matter. You know what grief hates? Analysis or comfort of any kind."

I believed she was wrong. Grief thrives on comfort. Comfort is the vehicle by which it can go anywhere, inhabit anything. Still, I said, "What does it love then?"

"The ones for which we grieve," she said. "The lost. Grief knows how to love them because we don't know how to do it anymore."

"That's not true," I said.

"Take Larry's shoes, for example. What did I think I was doing? I didn't know what I was doing."

"They say there are many ways to grieve," I said. "There's not any right way to do it."

I could not help but speak falsely to her, I don't know why. She sighed and shook her head. The skin around her mouth was broken out in tiny pimples but her hair was pretty, dark and glossy like a healthy animal's. She seemed younger than I, impossibly young, and I did not want to discuss such matters with her anymore. She didn't drink, which made my avoidance of her easier, but I was left with her perception of grief. I began to think of it as something substantial and assured and apart, more competent and attentive than I, and no longer mindful of me and my poor efforts.

I then began to fear that my mother would be denied the very thing she had so inexplicably sought after my father's death. She would never receive *komik'c-ed*. The program would have closed down. Even from the little I'd been told, the arrangement seemed unwieldy and misguided. The tortoise had to be microchipped and someone in an official capacity had to check on its health twice a year. There weren't public funds available for these things.

Instead, it turned out that my mother had not built the home for the as-yet-unrealized tortoise on her land. A real-estate agent came out to see if the adjacent lot would appraise out to make it worthwhile to subdivide and noted the error. The enclosure was well within her client's property line and had to be removed.

"*Appraise out*," my mother said. "Who comes up with these dreadful phrases?"

I agreed that language was becoming uglier the more it was becoming irrelevant to our needs.

My mother took on the task of dismantling everything she had accomplished. She broke up the walls and trucked away the rubble. She even dug out the filled trench. Then she rough-raked the ground and rolled some of the large stones back into place. She left the few flowering shrubs and grasses she had so recently planted, but without protection the birds and animals that are so seldom seen quickly consumed them. Such is their need.

Eventually I moved out of the shithole, though I still go to AA. I've even stopped drinking. I would say then that all is continuing here. Is it the same way there?

In the Park

RANGER PREYMAN SLIPPED THE PHOTOGRAPH INTO THE DIS-
play case. Then he sat down under the ramada and waited for
someone to approach it. He was supposed to lead the tour at eleven but
he knew from experience that he would not accumulate a group. Gaunt
and sweating in his uniform, he looked on the verge of flying apart, and
tourists instinctively avoided him. At times he actually sweated blood.
Blood vessels close to the surface of his skin ruptured into the exocrine
glands. The condition had a name. He was grateful it didn't often happen. It was the beginning of the rainy season although there had been
no rain yet. The crowds of the winter had diminished. A woman on
the bench behind him was complaining to her companion about a dog
she'd picked up at the pound. He was a beautiful dog, smart and obedi-
ent, but he was always looking for someone. He would go up to cars
and peer inside. When she took him for a walk, he was always looking,
looking. It was getting her down. He didn't appreciate his new situation, the fact that he had been saved; she was seriously considering taking him back to the pound. Preyman had noticed that people seldom
spoke about what they were experiencing at the time. They saved it for
later. He'd overheard a man on the boardwalk saying, They've built a
hotel on the Mount of Olives. I just couldn't get over that. Here it was
Florida, the Everglades, in the park.

The photograph was of an alligator with a great white heron folded
in its mouth. The bright colored feet, the long bill, everything was there,
an entire large bird. Alligators shared their water-hole homes with all
manner of creatures, until they didn't. One didn't register the bird at
first, it was just another picture of an alligator with open jaws. Then
came the awareness of the delicate collapsed presence within.

But people had become wary of looking into the display case, Preyman had found. There were too often pictures of plowed fields pressing

at the gateway to the park, of animals caught dead on the center line, of cities and trash, of the outside crawling closer. It wasn't Nature, it all lacked subtlety, possibility. None of it was equivocal enough. People preferred the equivocal, they found comfort in it. They were heartened by the news that more panthers were killed by one another than by mercury or cars. Preyman was doing them a favor with this picture. Even so, no one gave it a glance.

Eleven o'clock came and went. No one seemed desirous of Preyman's expertise, his dismal numbering of extirpated plants and declining species, his depressing accounts of water, water withheld, water diverted, water dirtied and wasted. They had already taken him off the list of rangers who led the children on informative hikes. He was incapable of telling groups of fourth graders how they could save the park. They couldn't save the park! He took off his hat and ran his shaking fingers through his soaked hair. A group of foreign tourists walked by, talking quietly. They approached the place as though it were an aspect of work, something to check off their life list—another biosphere preserve. Preyman stared past them at the photograph. He did not take pictures himself. When his mother died, there had been film in her camera and he had brought it to be developed. None of them had come out. It was the fault of someone new in the darkroom. They had apologized and offered to give him free film. It was part of the new responsibility, to admit to mistakes that had been made, to irredeemable errors. His mother had been out of her mind when she died. Out of her mind.

He unlocked the display case and removed the photograph, then, trembling, walked through the parking lot to his Jeep for a cigarette. He passed the life-size bronze statue of a panther. Two children sat on it, drinking from boxes of juice. The Jeep was parked several hundred yards away, near one of the park's canoe trails. Preyman smoked several cigarettes and fieldstripped them. His hair tingled.

One of the girls who worked in the concession pulled up in her little car. They wore plastic name tags with their home states below their first names. This was Cynthia Massachusetts.

"It's a small world ... we're all in this together ... only the species, man, can correct what the species, man, has wrought ... I am part of the web of life ... I gave blood to an Everglades mosquito ... wave a pint jar through the air, you'll come up with a quart of mosquitoes ...

reduce, recycle ... this is a park in peril ... it's worth preserving, don't you think ..." She grinned at him and put on a pair of green sunglasses. His disheveled shape was twice reflected. "It's a full moon tonight," she said. "Make your request early to be chained to the gates. Lock your car, secure your valuables and have a good one. Pete," she said, "cheer up."

Cynthia Mass got out of the car and jogged off. She was all right. So was Madeline New York and Jim Arkansas. Bruce Oregon was a pain in the butt. They were all much younger than he was.

It was quiet except for the ticking of the girl's car beside him. Farther down the row, a raven was investigating the interior of an open convertible. It picked up a pen, then dropped it. Over the parking lot was the sky that belonged only to Florida. Immense ragged clouds moved freely past. The raven selected an empty beer huggie and flew off with it. From a break in the buttonwood trees a young couple appeared, portaging a canoe. They stopped when they saw him and put the canoe down. Preyman felt they were looking at him anxiously. His mind had been utterly blank for a few moments. He rubbed his jaw and put his hat back on. "How you doing?" he said.

"I think there's something you should see," the boy said.

"And maybe get," the girl said.

"We didn't want to get it down, we thought we should report it so you could make the right kind of notes about it. It's a wood stork, a mile, maybe a mile and a half past Bear Lake, not on the water but deeper into the strand. It's hanging in a tree, tangled in a fishing line. It hasn't been dead too long."

"It's like something out of the tarot," the girl said. She had made up her mind. This was the way she would remember this.

Preyman looked at them. He was behind his sunglasses too. They were all behind their sunglasses. Someone died here last night and in great pain too, his father used to say when Preyman visited him. But it couldn't always have been true, not the night before each time he came to call, not every time, it wasn't likely. People hung on in nursing homes, it's what they did there. If you could get me a warm Coca-Cola, his father would say, it would give me great pleasure, I promise. He had been a minister and Preyman had been in awe of him and liked to listen to him. But then it had come down to just the someone dying business and the warm Coke business.

"I'll take care of it," Preyman said. What could he mean by that? The words had no possible meaning.

The boy nodded. "I could give you better directions." He began describing the place they'd beached the canoe, the trail, the distance traveled beyond the mahogany grove. Preyman shut his eyes behind his glasses.

When the boy finished, Preyman said, "Thank you very much." He opened his eyes.

"Wood storks used to nest in the park but don't anymore, is that right?" the girl said. "They're pretty rare? I read that."

"Wood storks are an indicator species," Preyman said. "They sort of function as a pressure gauge. That's actually what we use them for now, almost exclusively, a pressure gauge."

They watched him uncomfortably. Throughout all this, they had been some distance from Preyman and his Jeep. The girl rolled her shoulders. She was dressed in brown. Her bare lean legs and arms were brown from the sun and she wore a handkerchief around her neck. She bent down and picked up her end of the canoe.

Preyman smiled at them. He could still perform this vital variation on his face, he was sure of it. He stood in place a moment longer and had another cigarette. Then he climbed into the Jeep and drove away as they were tying the canoe down on the roof of an old station wagon. He drove onto the main road, then turned down an official-use road, swinging the gate shut behind him. It was wide, of crushed stone, and led to several trailers and some cannibalized swamp buggies and airboats. He stopped at the end and took out his pack, water, knife and netting. There was no trail from here to the place the boy had mentioned, but he knew how to reach it. It wasn't far. Nothing was very far. He had probably covered pretty much every foot of the park and he'd worked here only a few years. Hurricanes would sometimes make a place inaccessible but it didn't stay like that for long. It had all been touched by someone and not touched lightly. It had been piteously easy to find the rookeries. They set fire to the hammocks after they'd collected a few tree snails or orchids, to make them rarer. They set fire to the hammocks to drive out the game. They set fires to kill the deer who hosted the ticks they thought were killing the cattle they wanted to raise. Everywhere there were borrow pits and the remains of old attempts to drain. It was warm and still and quiet. After an hour of hiking, his head felt hot and his eyes burned with sweat. He would cut the creature down, bring it in, someone would take pictures and these would become part of an educational exhibit . . .

In bright illusion on the ground before him was a plastic guide to the birds, slipped from someone's pack or pocket. It was the size of a letter, the birds crowded on both sides for easy identification. He looked at it warily and did not touch it, knowing that what he was seeing had finally become only a symbol of what was now invisible. Too, he knew it wasn't actually there. His foot passed over it and it vanished.

There was a lovely poem about a kestrel by an Englishman, a lovely, lovely poem. Florida had a kestrel and it was called a killy hawk, a killy hawk.

He was deep in the hammock now and it was still quiet, darkly green with broken light. When he saw the man in the clearing he sat down with a sigh. The man was digging a fern from the deep grooved bark of an oak. He had some sort of tool, a useful little tool to do this with. It was his father quite clearly and the fern was a hand fern, it really looked like a hand with spread fingers. Preyman's father had preached for thirty years and never given the same sermon twice, though he frequently discoursed on the line *And it was night* from the Fourth Gospel. He loved the line, the immaterial night, glorious, full of promise. His father's interests were not of this world. The Greek was *en de nux*. Preyman had learned some things . . . When his father retired he had lived in a condominium building in Miami called Ambience—they'd had a laugh or two about that—and then he'd had a stroke and died in a nursing home, an innocent, which did not keep him from dying in terrible fear. His father's long hands cupped the fern now, the roots falling through his white fingers and dangling in the air. His father was dead, the fern was extinct, the last taken years before from the Everglades. Preyman felt the reassuring logic of this but then it passed over him, no more than a gust of rancid air.

I must arrest this, Preyman thought, I must arrest what this is, and he opened his mouth with a cry to do so.

Cats and Dogs

LILLIAN WAS TELLING HER DAUGHTER ABOUT THE PERIOD IN her life when she killed cats.

"I had a system going. I would bait a Havahart trap with a bit of sardine on a saucer and put it out in the yard just before retiring. In the morning, I would hurry out in my bathrobe, and if I was successful, which I almost always was, I'd place the trap with its disbelieving victim on the step at the shallow end of the swimming pool and in less than thirty seconds, maybe twenty, that would be that."

Toby was barely listening to her. She was looking at her mother's permed hair, which resembled molded plastic.

"Most of them seemed pretty blasé in the moment before I dunked them," her mother said. "As though they'd been in Havahart traps before and expected delightful and challenging futures, a refreshing change of venue, maybe the country, or even the challenges of a shopping center. My last cat, though, looked much like the first. Nothing changes them. That's their nature. I began to feel I was catching and disposing of the same cat over and over. I lost the necessary ambition. I wasn't getting anywhere, you see."

"You shouldn't keep telling that story, Mama," Toby said. "Aren't you afraid there's going to be an accounting?"

"Oh, you," her mother said vaguely. "You're just needling me."

"You want to go over and see Daddy? Let's go over and see Daddy for a while, then I have to go."

"My first stroke," her mother said. "I remember it as though it were yesterday."

"Well," Toby said, "it wasn't."

"There was a sound like cloth ripping. The thing zigged through me just like that and then I was on the floor for no one knew how long before anybody came."

It was Halloween in the twin assisted-living facilities; her mother was in one, and across the courtyard her father was in the other. Both buildings were decorated with orange and black bunting, and cardboard witches and ghosts tacked to the walls. There was a mound of plastic pumpkins by the receptionist's desk. What a place to be observing Halloween! Staff was crazy in here. That's what they called themselves. They were undoubtedly hitting the pharmacy day and night in order to maintain their gay demeanor.

"Where are you now," Lillian asked. "Whatcha up to?"

Toby sighed. "You don't know who I am, do you?"

"That is not entirely true," Lillian said. This woman before her who suddenly seemed angry was like everybody, anybody who had ever lived.

"I told you before, Mama, if you keep not knowing who I am, I'm going to stop coming here."

"You're my child," Lillian said. She hoped she didn't sound bewildered. She wanted to sound affirmative, torrentially affirmative, like a great artist.

Toby was not appeased. She felt distracted by Staff, who was spraying cobwebs from a can onto the windows.

"I sold the house today," Toby said loudly. "I just closed on it, right before I came over here."

Her mother frowned. "We've discussed that," she said. "Was it fun?"

"A young couple bought it."

"Why did a young couple buy it?"

"Let's go over and see Daddy before you drive me out of my mind."

Toby nudged the brake off the wheelchair with her sandaled foot and they proceeded down the corridor and into the courtyard. There were several benches, unoccupied, and two trees whose limbs looked smooth and severed like human stumps, with the skin drawn tightly forward and folded over into a tight tuck. Yet on the tips of these eerie branches were lovely white and still-fragrant flowers. And these trees were not at all uncommon at this latitude.

Toby had made a good profit on the house, the last one her parents had lived in together. She had capitalized on something legally exotic. Her mother and father had been in the house less than six months when they learned from a neighbor that a murder had taken place there, just one, but involving almost every room, upstairs and down, in what could only have been a long, drawn-out process. Toby took advantage of a gray area in the law and sued the real-estate agents for selling them a stigmatized property. The lawyer had been delighted by the largeness and grayness of the area. The house appeared to be making every effort to be charming and forthright, but in a court of law it was considered psychologically impacted and the real-estate company was found liable for not informing the buyers of its past. The money involved was not considerable but it was still amusing to have. After her mother's stroke and her father's tumble, Toby had put the house on the market herself with full disclosure and it sold eventually to a couple who'd had a loved one murdered (the relationship here was blurry) and required intensive counseling. Now they could accept sudden and untoward death, even reside with it. They made their money in video.

They signed all the papers at the house on the hood of the couple's car. It had been hand-painted with images of fish, following one of the customs of the town to fancifully paint old cars with complex, detailed scenes of virtually vanished worlds. The fish had inaccessible startled faces and curving silver bodies. Each scale, carefully delineated, shone. It was all carefully, glowingly done; the water was rendered crystalline. The vehicle itself, however, had bald tires, a cracked windshield and a dragging tailpipe.

"Video pays the bills," the girl said. Her name was Jennifer. "But it's our nutty money that makes life worth living. Boyfriend sells his sperm to fertility clinics. He has the highest IQ in the business, practically."

"Of course the doctors make a lot more," boyfriend said.

"I can't believe people would freak out just because this lovely home hosted a sad event," Jennifer said. "People get so unnecessarily freaked. We're on this earth with a part to play but instead of playing the part as an actor does, some people think the part is really *them* and they freak out all the time. Listen, you can hear the ocean from here."

"That's the freeway, I think," boyfriend said.

"It sounds OK, though. I mean, if they can make a freeway sound like an ocean, so much the better."

Toby had never lived in this house. It meant nothing to her. Even if she had lived in it, its sale would have been of minor significance. She didn't consider a house as a large cradle or nest. For the last several years she had moved around a number of properties her father had bought for back taxes at the courthouse when the owners could not be located; he had busied himself in his retirement by acquiring houses in this fashion. They were all dumps and Toby was in the process of disposing of them in an accelerated manner. She was at present occupying an oddity built decades before that had never been remodeled. Its roofline was angled like wings. The ceilings were crazed and water-stained, an avocado green shag covered the plywood floors, the bathroom wallpaper depicted toreadors and bulls, rather a single toreador and a single bull over and over again. The wood was biscuit-colored and flimsy, the rooms small, the foundation cracked, the malfunctioning kitchen appliances a grotesque shade of ruby. The yard was large. There had once been flower beds, all in ruin now, and a small pond was spanned by a concrete arch from which a concrete fisherperson "fished." The place was a hoot, though Toby felt it worsened her sinus condition.

This house, though, her parents' last house, was proper, formal, clean and patient, even though it was unlucky. It was aware that it was unlucky. It had been sold with all furnishings, dishware, linens, even the Oldsmobile in the garage.

"What's the first thing you're going to do," Toby asked.

They looked at her blankly.

"To the house."

"Oh, tear it down," boyfriend said. "We really wanted more of a yurt."

"He's kidding," Jennifer said.

"It's entirely up to you, of course," Toby said.

"He's kidding!"

"Maybe we'll slap some paint on the Olds, though. Coral reef."

"Pretty, pretty, *pretty*," Jennifer enthused. She carried a child's lunch box as a purse and from it she pulled a money order made out for the full purchase amount as well as three small cupcakes with orange frosting, which she distributed.

Toby swallowed hers without thinking, then said, "Oh, I . . . is there something in this?"

"Just a little celebratory weed," boyfriend said.

"Chink, chink," Jennifer said, swallowing. She flung her arms wide, almost clipping Toby with the lunch box. "I'm going to plant stuff all around here. My granddad had a wisteria vine and he said that when he went out to look at it, it would lean forward and lay its head on his shoulder, it liked him so much. That thing was *huge*. Once, when he wasn't around, I hit it with a croquet mallet. I was pissed at Granddad because he put my favorite sweater in the dryer and ruined it. It was, like, the size of a chinchilla's sweater."

"A Chihuahua's, I think," boyfriend said.

"Kids today would've taken the mallet to Granddad," Jennifer went on, "but I took it to that vine—oh, did I. It flew away in big green and purple chunks and never came back. I was such a bad girl then, a demon!"

"But then you found Jesus," boyfriend said.

"You found him?" Toby said. "Where?"

"What he means is Jesus found *me*," Jennifer said kindly, "and I take comfort now in knowing, *knowing*, that in my granddad's heaven a wisteria vine grows."

"That is so unlikely," Toby said.

"Say?"

"Unlikely," Toby said. "Doubtful. No way."

Jennifer removed her sunglasses and looked at Toby coldly.

"Maybe you should leave now," boyfriend said.

"Certainly," Toby said. She felt somewhat woozy from the cupcake. "Our transaction is complete," she said, in a simper she was aware was taking up entirely too much of her face.

"She can still pack a heck of a wallop," boyfriend warned her.

So had the sale ended on its awkward note.

Still, the cupcake had managed to whisk her in gleeful transit to the convalescent home—a distance of some twenty miles through normally aggravating traffic—before it dumped her without warning behind her mother's wheelchair on the back of which some impish Staff had affixed the sticker THIS IS NOT AN ABANDONED VEHICLE.

"Look!" Lillian cried. Her heart was beating eagerly, stupefied. "Look!" But she then realized it was no more than water from a lawn sprinkler fanning lightly back and forth across the grass.

"What!" Toby said. "You're not going to get wet. Are you afraid of getting wet?"

Lillian remembered a green umbrella, furled, in the vestibule when she had been young. She feared umbrellas. "I'm afraid of umbra … umbra … umbrellas," she said shyly.

"Don't be foolish," Toby said.

They found Robert in the reading room, alone at a large table, staring at a book on ancient Egypt. Here was her *father*, Toby thought. She waited for the next thought but nothing immediately arose.

"Hi, Daddy," Toby said. She always expected something, but what?

He ignored her and addressed his wife. "Are you aware of this Osiris?"

Lillian studied the highly illustrated page. "Well, that's not him, the one with the jackal's head, he doesn't look like that."

"She was always the smart one, your mother," Robert said. "Could always count on her."

Toby scanned the text. Sibling drowned Osiris. Then chopped up body into fourteen parts and scattered them all over the place, all over Egypt. Someone found everything except for the penis, which had been eaten by fish, then put him back together again and made him king of the underworld.

"They shouldn't have books like this lying around here," Toby said. "Here, of all places."

"Those Egyptians had to worry that their own hearts might testify against them after death," Robert said. "Isn't that something? That was one of the things those people had to worry about."

"They worried that their own hearts would turn them in?"

"That's right, Mother."

"Like they were criminals?"

"I don't understand," Toby said without curiosity.

Robert looked at her with disapproval, though he had harbored no preference for a son. They'd had Toby when they were quite along in years. She was their wan surprise.

"You're the one who said there was going to be an accounting," her mother reminded her.

"I came close to saying that," Toby admitted, "but I never did."

They sat silently around the table, the great book of Egypt open before them.

"What are you having for dinner, Daddy? What are they serving?"

"Some sort of meat you can eat with a spoon," he said moodily, "and orange sherbet. It's Halloween."

"She never liked Halloween," her mother said. "She was never formidable enough for it."

"Ahh, Mama," Toby whined.

"What's the weather out," her father asked.

"It's . . ." Toby couldn't remember. What difference did it make? The days were mostly bright as blazes, this being Florida.

"We had a good life together, didn't we, Mother?" Robert said.

This could go either way in Toby's experience, and she wasn't about to hold her breath.

"I don't think so," Lillian said. She was choosing not to be torrentially affirmative at the moment.

The reply, whatever it was, usually marked the moment when Toby would look at her watch and express dismay at the lateness of the hour. It was just a little sign she had taken to relying on.

"All right, Mama, Daddy, I'm going to leave now. Mama, why don't you have supper here with Daddy, and Staff can take you back to your own room afterwards."

"Leave me here, leave me here," her mother said. "It's perfectly all right. I'm just waiting my turn."

TOBY SAT ON THE PORCH OF THE NEXT HOUSE SHE WAS ABOUT TO unload and looked at the street. There would be no trick-or-treaters. It was a bad neighborhood and many of the kids were undoubtedly in jail. No one had infants here. Half-grown rollicking figures in baggy pants and jackets were produced, some of whom drove low, bullet-shaped cars with tricked-out axles that allowed them to bow tip and curtsy like circus horses. One of these vehicles rolled by now without performing. A man laughed and a can of beer shot through the air and struck the rotting steps. It was unopened, however, thus indicating to Toby a modicum of goodwill.

She had no admirers at present. Since leaving her parents' home at eighteen she'd experienced two brief marriages—one to a Ritalin-addicted drywaller, the next to a gaunt, gabby autodidact, brilliant and quite unhinged, who drank a pound of coffee a day, fiddled with engines and read medieval history. After their parting, he flew in a small plane he had built to Arizona and found employment as a guide in a newly discovered living cave. Daily, he berated the tourists by telling them that every breath they took was robbing the cave of its life, even though each of them had gone through three air locks and was forbidden to touch anything or take photographs. People didn't mind hearing they were well-meaning bearers of destruction, apparently. According to him, he was the most popular guide there. She was amazed to learn that people liked him. She certainly hadn't.

She sat rocking slightly in an old roof-hung swing. One chain looked just about to snap but it had looked like that for some time. A big orange moon labored up the sky.

A limousine longer than the wretched porch drew up to the house and stopped. The inhabitants were probably seeking the gin palace several blocks over, Toby reasoned. There were often singers and bands performing there. But no request for directions was forthcoming. Instead, an immense woman emerged, dressed in red and drenched in strong perfume. The limousine pulled away.

"Are you the present owner of this property," the woman asked. "I hope you are."

Toby narrowed her eyes and did not reply. The woman was her own age but striking, tremendous.

"I was a little girl in this house!" the woman announced. "This used to be the only house this side of the street. Next door there was nothing but a pretty field with a shed on it and the family the next street over would raise veal calves in that shed, it was a calf hutch. The man wouldn't let his own kids play with those calves, he didn't want them to make pets out of them and then get sad, but he let me play with them. I loved those little calves so, each one was dearer to me than the one before. On hot nights like this I'd take my sweet pillow and lay on the little bridge out back. Oh, how many wondrous nights I spent sleepless and singing my little songs of praise beneath the great wheel of heaven as I laid on that little bridge."

"You lived here," Toby said, uncharmed.

"Sister, I did. And I want to come home. I want to buy this precious property."

"I'd consider selling it," Toby said, she hoped not too eagerly. She hadn't invited the woman up on the porch and didn't think she would.

"What's your price," the marvelous woman asked. Her dress was remarkable—a divine, shrieking crimson.

Toby paused, then named a figure that made her blush, it was so unreasonably high.

"I'll pay you twenty thousand more. I have money. I'm a success. I say this in all modesty, believe me."

"It needs some work," Toby admitted reluctantly.

"We all need work, sister. We're all of us a work in progress. And no one knows in what guise the end of the familiar will arrive. We're like darling veal calves in that regard."

"So they used to farm around here," Toby said. "It certainly is different now, I don't have to tell you that."

"Nobody farmed, sister. It was just that one mean cracker who ran a calf hutch for the restaurants in Sarasota."

Toby felt corrected and did not care for it. She brushed a mosquito off her knee and said, "Is this a serious offer you're making? Because I've had some interest and I'd have to let these other parties know. Of course they don't appreciate the place as much as you do." She would concede that much to the imaginary.

"I've already agreed to your price and more, sister. I do appreciate it. And my mother and father, they appreciate it too. They're right out back there. Probably just about given up hope that I'd ever get back to them."

A moment passed and Toby said, "What do you mean 'out back there'?"

"This is our story, sister," the woman said, straightening her smooth brown shoulders and causing the red dress to strain and shine. "They were the finest people you'd ever have the luck to meet. They were Edenists, my loved ones was, they truly believed our days are spent in Eden, that Eden was here and now. They were good and they were grateful and one afternoon just this time that year they were taking a neighbor boy out for a driving lesson. They'd promised to teach this boy, Billy Crawford, how to drive in our truck so he could get his license. It was just a kindness on their part. My daddy was a builder and his tools, his boards and paints and such, were in the old truck's bed. He sat in the middle on the bench seat with Billy Crawford behind the wheel and my mother by the window appreciating the breeze. She'd go for a little ride at any opportunity. Why my daddy took Billy Crawford on as a student we'll never know. You couldn't tell that boy nothing and he never wore his glasses as he was supposed to for he was vain. He was driving, he wasn't speeding, speed was not a factor. But what he did was he ran over this fellow's dog. Knocked him down with the tires, didn't even see him, and it was a big dog. From all reports, the man who was standing beside the dog, whose dog it was, became a threatening figure right away, fearsome in his grief, for who knows how long that dog had been his only friend. He was dressed in so many rags they looked like robes and he started screaming and hammering on that truck and wouldn't be comforted or listen to reason, not that there was any reason involved, it being an accident. Billy Crawford, who might have been following my father's directive or not, put his foot back on the pedal and commenced to drive away. But the man, his name was Rockford Wiggins, clung to the truck and hauled himself into the bed, where he continued screaming and baying, and now that he had boards and cans and tools to do his hitting with he began to beat on the window that was all that separated him from them, from Billy Crawford and my dear ones. There was a can of turpentine in the back as well and it wasn't long before death triumphant placed it in Rockford Wiggins's hands. He drenched himself and all those rags were like a hundred wicks so when he set himself off with a packet of matches, the whole truck went. I was told that it looked like a parcel of hell burning, in the manner that hell is popularly pictured. Well, sister, they all of them died, burnt to the bones. And a professional reduced my dear ones further to ashes because that was getting to be the trend back then. And I took those ashes and made them into bricks, for there was no one to tell me not to and no voice was raised against it. I knew some things since my father had been a builder, as I said. It was necessary to add something—three parts sand, one part lime and clay—but now the fundaments of those bricks are my dear ones. I mortared them into the base of the little bridge we built ourselves in the days that we were Edenists. And then I had to leave, sister. I had to go out in the world and make my way and fortune."

"You're saying there're two bricks out back there that aren't just bricks," Toby said.

"I didn't mingle the ashes. If I was to do it today I would've mingled them all, poor Rockford Wiggins and bratty Billy Crawford and the big dog too."

Toby smacked at her knees. The bugs were really getting to her. "What I don't understand is how you could imagine that anyone who bought this dump would have kept things as they were." She smiled to show that she meant no offense.

The woman smiled back. It was the sort of smile the terminally ill might realize they'd been receiving as the days wore on.

"I'm just saying that you took quite a gamble," Toby said. "This isn't a graveyard. No one's under any obligation to care for what's here." Or what isn't, she might as well have added.

"My broker will call you tomorrow," the woman said.

"I'll need a few days to make arrangements."

"In three days, then," the woman said.

"You can come back in three days, then—no, better make it four," Toby said.

The woman nodded and turned. The limousine appeared like a liquid poured from the shadows. She addressed Toby once more before she stepped into it. "It's perfect here!"

Her eyes were certainly dishabituated to reality, Toby thought, if she believed this crummy locale to be perfect. She pushed herself off the swing and went into the house, opening and shutting the warped door with difficulty. She sat down at the kitchen table, an old pink Formica and chrome thing, and turned the pages of a phone book until she found a listing of demolition contractors. She copied down a number of names. She would call them all in the morning. She wanted everything torn up and down. The job would go to the one who could do the work most quickly. A great devotional emptiness swam up in her. She was doing the woman a favor. It had probably just been a prank anyway. There would be no call from a broker. She sneezed sharply from the mildew and held a tissue to her nose. Some people's behavior was simply inexplicable. They outlasted their lives or something.

The great moon was now obscured by clouds. Toby picked up a flashlight and went outside, stalking across the lost but unforgotten garden to the little bridge. She bent and studied the blocks that supported the foolish thing. No two bricks were different from the rest—all pitted, common, unparticular, of uniform size and texture.

On her knees, she held the light against them. "I don't believe you," she said.

ROBERT HAD BROUGHT THE GREAT BOOK OF EGYPT TO DINNER, and before it could be removed from his grasp had spilled milk on it. He was scolded at length. Lillian had been returned to her room and was being trussed up by Staff in preparation for her personal night. She felt compelled to speak of the cats again.

There was the trap and the pinch of food on the chipped china saucer. Never too much, not that it seemed wasteful, it just wasn't right. And the saucer—it had to be a chipped one. A perfect saucer would have conferred something else entirely. She had meant no real harm. What if everything one did mattered. Thank God, it could not.

The Bridgetender

I AM TRYING TO THINK. SOMETIMES I CATCH MYSELF SAYING JUST those words and just in my head. It seems I got to start everything in my head with something in my head saying I am trying to think. I remember how it begins but can't remember how it ends. Even though it's over now. It don't seem right that it could be over and me back where I've always been not even knowing what it was she gave me or what I should do with it.

Because the bridge is still here and the water and the shack. And though I haven't been to town since she disappeared, I imagine the town's still there too. Her fancy car is still here sitting on the beach, though it seems to be fading, sort of like a crummy photograph. It's a black car but the birds have crapped all over it and it's white now like the sand. Sometimes it hurts my eyes. The chrome catches the sun. But as I say, sometimes I can't hardly make it out at all. It ain't really a car anymore. It wouldn't take nobody anywhere.

What it is I think is that before she came I knew something was going to happen and now that she's been, I know it ain't. She didn't leave a single thing behind except that car. Not a pair of panties or a stick of gum or nothing. Once she brought over a little round tin of chicken-liver patay. Now I know I've never eaten chicken-liver patay so it must be around here somewhere, but I can't find it. My head's fuller'n a tick on a dog. Full of blood or something. And my prick lies so tame in my blue jeans, I can't hardly believe it's even gone through what it's been through.

She was like smoke the way she went away. She was like that even when she stayed. She'd cover me up, wrapping herself around me tight, tasting sweet and as cool as an ice-cream cone, smelling so good and working at loving me. Then she would just dissolve and I'd fill right up with her like a water glass. I can't recall it ending, as I say, but I know it's stopped. Black rain at four in the afternoon like it used to be. Black trees and empty sky. And the gulf running a dirty green foam where it turns into the pass.

But I can think about it beginning. So. That first morning I come back to the shack and there's a big brown dog sitting there drinking out of the toilet bowl. He'd drained it. And looked at me as though it was me and not him that had no right being there. Drained it and sat and stared at me, its jaws rolling and dripping at me. Now, I like dogs all right but I could see this one was a bum. In the Panhandle, I had two catch dogs that was something to watch. Them dogs just loved to catch. They was no-nonsense dogs. But this can licker was a bum. Somebody's pet. A poodle or something. The big kind. Before I got around to giving him a good kick, he pushed the screen door open with his paw and left.

I was so mad. And I was thinking and figuring how to get that brown dog, not even thinking then how queer it was that there should be any dog at all, because I hadn't seen a thing for six months around the bridge or on the beach except wild. And I hadn't seen another person in that time either and then as soon as I remember this, I see the girl walking along the beach with the dog.

She's in a bright bikini and long raggedy-wet hair and I remember how long it had been since I'd seen a girl in a bikini or any girl at all because my wife had left me a long while ago, even then having stopped being a girl in any way you could think of and went back to living in Lowell, Massachusetts, the place she come from and left just to plague me. Somewhere, in that town, setting on a lawn outside a factory, is or was a chair fit for a giant's ass. Forty or fifty times bigger and crazier than a proper chair. And she come from that town. And she sold off my dogs to get back to it on a one-way ticket on a bubble-topped Trailways.

I never knew her that well. She wore more clothes, jesus, you'd think she was an Eskimo. Layers and layers of them. I never knew if I got to her or not and she'd be the last to tell me. She never talked about nothing except New England. Everything was better there, she'd say. Corn, roads, Christmas decorations. The horses ain't as mean, she'd say. The bread rises better up North. Even the sun, she'd say, is nicer because it sets in a different direction. It don't fall past the house this way at home, she'd say. I was a young man then and I never cheated. I was a young man and my balls were big as oranges. And I threw it all away. She caught my stuff in her underwear.

When I think about what a honey bear I was and how polite and wonderfully whanged and how it was all wasted on a loveless woman . . . She had a tongue wide and slick as a fried egg. And never used it once. I guess that's what I was waiting on but I might just as much have hoped for striking oil in the collards patch. She said she was a respectable woman and claimed to have worked in an office in Boston. But she didn't have no respect for the man and woman relationship and she didn't have no brain. She couldn't bring things together in her head. I'd bring her head together all right if I ever see her again. I'd fold it up for her so she'd be able to carry it in her handbag. Selling the best catch dogs in the state of Florida for a bus ticket.

So. I see the girl in the bright bikini and all I can think of is the old lady. It'd been so long and all I could think of was that witch I once had or maybe never had. I spent all this time here over the water not imagining anything. I just see that when I see the girl. And I got scared. I felt as though I caught myself dying. Like you'd catch yourself doing something stupid.

I walked across the bridge and climbed up into the box and got the binoculars. They belong to the state but they're mine as long as I leave them here. And, I figure, the girl's mine as long as she keeps herself in range. She's walking down the beach, stopping every few yards and squatting down and setting out a stick. She's got a bathing suit on that's like two big Band-Aids. Promising but not too promising. She had a knife strapped around her waist and wore a big wristwatch. She also had a notebook.

It wore me out watching her. She'd squat down and write something and then spring up again so graceful like she knew someone was watching her and give the bottoms of her bikini a little flip with her finger. I watched her for a long time, but she didn't do nothing spectacular. I was real happy just watching a near-naked woman move. Every once in a while she'd go into the water and swim out a few hundred yards, that damn dog swimming beside her barking like hell, and each time when she come out it was like that bikini had shrunk a little bit more and she was falling out of it every which way all plump and bubbly white.

I watched her until she got out of sight, around a bend in the beach, and then I started looking at other things. Mess of birds in the mangroves. Mullet boats way offshore. And what I'd later know was the girl's car parked on the hard sand under some cedars. A weird-looking vehicle. I know right away it's from Europe or someplace foreign. A mean car shaped like a coffin. But it reminded me of sex too, you know, though I never seen a machine that reminded me of sex before. But that car set me to feeling things, like the girl, that I hadn't felt maybe never. Though I knew what they were. And it felt so good feeling them.

I finally put up the binoculars. Wiped them off. The glass was getting milky from all the wetness in the air. As a matter of fact, I think they was shot from my never using them, never caring for them at all. Lots of things are like that. Life you know, it begins to rot if you don't use it. Everything gets bound or rusted up. Tools especially. Gear. My tool. Ha ha.

It worried me a little about the binoculars since they belong to the state. They could hassle me about them. Like they could about the bridge. Because the bridge sure ain't being what it's supposed to be. If a boat ever wanted to come through and I had to wind this devil back I believe it would just fall apart, the whole apparatus, like one of them paste-and-paper bridges you see blowing up in war movies. But no boats come through anyhow. It just ain't a proper waterway. The channel needs to be redug or a good hurricane's gotta come through here and clean everything out. A pretty beach. Good fishing but no boats come and no people either. Something happened here years ago, I heard. A sickness or something. In the water. An attack or something coming in on the tide. Somebody died or got hurt. You know the way these things are. People remember bad news even though they might never have heard it in the first place.

So the state has let it slide. Though you never know when they'll show up and raise all sorts of hell because things ain't how they want them. But it was them and not me that built this crazy beach and it was me and not them that saw, on my first day on the job, the sign just above them rotting joists around the crank that says CAUTION WHEN INSTALLED PROPER THIS SIGN WILL NOT BE VISIBLE.

Well, it ain't my concern. And I'll tell you I never really expect the state to come and hassle me. They know they got a bargain. It takes a special man to put up with living out here. I don't think anybody will come at all. Though I'd been waiting on this girl. It sure is easy to see that now.

So. After she got out of range, I went back to the shack and took a shower. Goddamn frogs come out of the wood and sat there while I did it. Like to have broke my neck slipping on them. Put on clean clothes and cut my nails. Prettied myself up like a movie idol, then I fell asleep right in the chair in the middle of the day. Which was unusual. And when I woke up it was practically black out and the girl was there looking at me.

She was feeding cornflakes to her dog. Piece by piece. My cornflakes. She was so brown from the sun, she was shining. And she was so warm-looking that I started to sweat. Then she come over to me and darn if she didn't sit on my lap and blow in my ear. God, she was warm. It was like being baked in a biscuit.

So the first night went by and the sun come out. And my baby tickled me up with a pink bird's feather. Bright pink like it come out of a cartoon. A roseate spoonbill feather, she said, for her specialty was birds. Ha ha, I said. Because I knew where her talent was.

But she was crazy about seabirds. When she wasn't tending to me and making up inventions, she was always going on about them birds. She had a canvas bag she was always toting around and damn if inside there weren't two dead birds, perfect in every way except for their being dead. She didn't know what kind they was and she was toting them around until she could find a book that would tell her. And there were little speckled eggs in that bag too, no bigger than my thumbnail, with holes in them and all the insides gone. And other crap she picked up along the beach. And the knives. Dinky little things. She said they was for predators on land or in the sea but they couldn't do no real damage, I told her that. Do in a splinter is about all.

That girl's big pretty eyes would fill up with tears when she talked about birds. She told me to respect them because they live their lives so close to dying.

So do us all, I thought, and that was no surprise to me. It was her inventions that was a surprise and she had started in on them the first day. She never made me pretend to be things I wasn't. Only things I was. But I believe we went through a hundred changes the days she stayed with me. We didn't have costumes or nothing naturally but it was like we were playing other people doing things. Though all the time it was us. I was a gangster and she was the governor's daughter, you know, or I was a bombardier and she was the inside of the plane. Or I was a preacher, maybe Methodist, and she was a babysitter. And even her dog did it because sometimes he was like a whole other object, you know. Or like he became a feeling in the shack and quit being a dog.

She messed up time and place for me. And just with her, I felt I was loving the different women of a thousand different men. We just went on for five days with them inventions and never did the same one twice. She'd go off sometimes in her fancy car, I don't know where. I'd lie there while she was gone, not even able to move hardly nor sleep neither. Lie there with my eyes open, trying to think what was happening, listening to the sound her car made traveling over the bridge and it was like the bridge went on for miles it was the only car I'd heard traveling for so long. There were four silver pipes sticking off the end of that car. I never seen anything like it. I was trying to think, but never once did I think about her not coming back. She always come back.

On the fifth day, I went down with her to the beach. First time I been out of the shack. Hotter than a poor shotgun. No wind. We was walking over the bridge to the beach when she said, This isn't a drawbridge. It's a solid piece. There isn't any grid. And so what do you tend, I'd like to know.

Well, of course it ain't a drawbridge. Did she think I'd been here for all these years paid by the country, here every day with no vacation and never no real quitting time without knowing that the goddamn thing wasn't a drawbridge?

I didn't say nothing but just gave her a look telling her that she should tend to what she knows about and I'll tend to what I know about.

The beach was full of eggs. She kept steering me around so I wouldn't step on them. All them eggs cooking in the heat and the birds going crazy over us as we walked along. Diving down and screaming, shitting on our heads. I went down to the water to get away from them. I was still put out with the girl and wasn't paying her any mind. She was trotting up and down the beach, slaving like a field hand, writing things down in her book. Finally she run right by me and fell in the water. Tried to tease me in. Took off her suit and tossed it in my face. Skin there like the cream in a chocolate éclair. But I paid her no mind. That day was so white my eyes ached. I was floating and felt sick. All that sun, it never bothered me before. She come out and sprinkled water all over me from her hair and even that wasn't cool. It was hot as the air. I was mad because I felt she was thinking my thoughts weren't real. But then I said, Come on, I been without loving too long. Because I thought her loving would pick me up. And we went back to the shack, me with my eyes closed and my arms resting on her because it hurt so bad looking out on that day. It ain't never been that bright here before or since.

So we went back. And I was a professor and she was a dance-hall cutie. And I was a big black lake and she was a sailboat tacking over me. But that night she and that dog was gone.

There are sharks, I know. I seen them rolling out there. And the bars sometimes are tricky. They change. Fall off one day where they didn't the day before. But it don't really seem dangerous here. I just don't know where she went to. Leaving nothing except that car, which like I say is sort of fading out. Rats building their nests beneath the hood. I hear them in it when I walk close.

So it's over but I can't help but feel it's still going on somewheres. Because it hasn't seemed to have ended even though it's stopped. And I don't know what it was she gave me. Maybe she even took something away. And I don't really even know if she's dead and it's me sitting here in the pilothouse or if I was the one who's been dead all the while and she's still going on back there on the gulf with all them birds.

Souvenir

THIS IS IN ENGLAND, IN CORNWALL, AND A MORE WEIRD dreary spot could scarcely be imagined. Nevertheless, tourists were beginning to arrive in ever-increasing numbers because they had been everywhere else. The inhabitants of the place were in many respects peculiar, poor and cruel with extraordinary dark eyebrows, but the cream teas were excellent. The dogs were polite. The gulls were big, the crows enormous.

The weather was foul.

The graveyards weren't as full or as mossy as those in Wales, the lanes not as snug. The cooking not as delightful; few turnips, no leeks. Actually, the dogs, though courteous, didn't work as hard as the dogs of Wales. The ones without heads were the devil's dogs. Even the most unobservant tourist had no problem in identifying them.

Most of the ghost stories in Cornwall involved ships and drowned sailors. And these drowned people, these ghosts, were always coming back, coming back to harass the living. Or to drag a beloved into the grave with them. Sometimes they came back to smile at their mums. The stories were a little tiresome.

In the old days, ships were always going down. The people on land liked it best when fruit ships went down. Oranges floated in. Grapefruit.

In King Arthur's town in Tintagel, there was a big run-down hotel on a cliff. The drinking room there was called the Excali-Bar. It was for tourists. The locals wouldn't be caught dead in the place. A group of travelers were sitting this night in the Excali-Bar drinking Adiós Amigos—gin, brandy, white rum, red vermouth, bit of lemon juice, shake and stir.

A frightful storm lashed the windows.

The locals were in the chapel eating pancakes because it was Shrove Tuesday. In a few hours Lent would commence.

The locals didn't care for the tourists. Never had. As for the tourists, they were beginning to believe what they'd been told—that Cornish culture was nothing but ghost stories and meat pies. Not that they were here for culture. They were here for a bit of the odd, a bit of the creepy.

There were seven species of seagulls in the area. That was somewhat creepy. And a village called Lizard, an odd name indeed.

The locals had polished off their pancakes and were tidying up, preparing to play their Lenten prank. This year it fell to Paul and Paul, two old men. They staggered out of the chapel into the windy, rainy night and tottered along the cliff road to the Excali-Bar.

The travelers had stopped drinking Adiós Amigos and were now experimenting with Sheep Dip—gin, sherry and strong sweet cider, stir and strain. There were two boy hikers, several married pairs, three ladies from Ohio, a transvestite, and a French couple who sat apart (quite aware that the others were thinking ... The French ... The French eat horses but they don't eat corn). The transvestite was having a quiet holiday alone, if you could say that a transvestite was ever quite alone. The imagination it takes to be one ... It must be exhausting ...

She was dressed sensibly, sensible shoes.

Paul and Paul lurched, dripping, into the revelers' midst. They both had suffered strokes in the past. One hand on each was cold and crabbed. Their eyes were bulging and clouded.

They weren't going to tell any scary stories, not these two. Weren't going to tell this crowd about the vanishing hitchhiker or the man with half a face. Or the ones about the boiled baby's revenge and the body of water that likes to break little boys' backs. They were just going to play a few games, give these tourists something to remember. What did they think life was, a vacation?

The travelers had been playing a game of sorts before the old buzzards' arrival. They were secretly assigning zoomorphs to everyone present. Of course privately they all thought of themselves as cheetahs. There was not a single exception to this.

Paul and Paul had wide, rotting smiles. Once they had been young and vigorous. Clever. Handsome. Their lives before them. But they'd had to give it all up. It seemed to have been the deal that had been struck at birth.

The tourists made an effort to find them engaging. They so terribly wanted to be amused. They bought them beverages, having moved from Sheep Dip to Blimlets to Blue Skies by then. Blue Skies are gin, lemon juice, a dash of unflavored food coloring and half a maraschino cherry, if available. After a few Blue Skies it was clear to all that the two Pauls were the cabaret.

It all began innocently enough. They proceeded to engage their audience.

Each among them had to confess to a loss.

"I lost my skill at baking cakes," one of them ventured.

"I lost a rucksack once."

"A ring."

"My hair."

"My trigger finger." The fellow raised his hand, and it was true. It was maimed. There was no trigger finger.

"My beech trees outside Lyon. Every one!"

"My driving privileges."

"My husband."

It was amusing how this had slipped in there, and they chuckled.

"My memory."

They howled at this one.

"It's true. Can't remember . . . get everything mixed up!"

"You never know when the last time for anything might come!"

"Now we're cooking," one of the Pauls cried.

My breast . . . my potency . . . my beloved Skippy.

Time began to tear through there. Inside, their lives were passing as though in a single night. They longed for a nice Teeny-Tiny, you know, of the GIVE ME MY BONE! sort. For a spectral bridegroom or a brain on a stick, even a vampire or a cannibal. Anything but this deathly entertainment, these dreadful drinks, these hideous old gentlemen whom they were feeling more and more indebted and attached to. These Pauls, urging them on to even greater and more fearful acts of admission to loss. The time passing. The blackness pressing against the greasy windows. And the morning that had always come, delayed.

The Country

I ATTEND A MEETING CALLED COME AND SEE! THE GROUP GATHers weekly at the Episcopal church in one of the many, many rooms available there but in the way these things are it's wide open to everyone—atheists, Buddhists, addicts, depressives, everyone. The discussion that evening concerned the old reliable: Why Are We Here? And one woman, Jeanette it was, offered that she never knew what her purpose was until recently. She discovered her purpose was to be there with the dying in their final moments. Right there, in attendance. Strangers for the most part. No one she knew particularly well. She found that she loved this new role. It was wonderful, it was amazing to be present for that moment of transport. It was such an honor being there and she believed she provided reassurance. And she shared with us the story of this one old girl who was actively dying—that was her phrase, *actively dying*—and at one point the old girl looked at Jeanette and said, "Am I still here?" and when she was told yes, yes, she was, the dying woman said, "Darn."

"She was so cute," Jeanette said.

My fellow travelers in Come and See! listened to this with equanimity. Jeanette was as happy as I'd ever seen her—she doesn't come every week—and enthusiastic as she shared with us how positive and comforting it is to witness the final voyage. She's affiliated with the church somehow, she studied chaplaincy services or something, so she has a certain amount of access to these situations; that is, she's not doing this illegally or inappropriately or anything.

I sincerely cannot remember the circumstances that brought me to Come and See! for the first time and why I continue to attend. I seldom speak and never share. I sit erect but with my eyes downcast, focusing on a large paper clip that has rested in a groove between two tiles for months. Surely the chairs must be folded and stacked or rearranged for other functions and the floor swept or mopped on occasion, but the paper clip remains.

Beside me, Harold—he's sixty-three and the father of two-year-old triplets—says, "I believe we are here for the future, to build a better future," blandly cutting off any communal amplification of Jeanette's deathbed theme.

My eyes lowered, I stare at the paper clip. I dislike Harold. Triplets, for god's sake. One day I will no longer come here and listen to these wretched things.

After Come and See! there is a brief social period when packaged cheese and crackers and cheap wine are provided. There is always difficulty in opening the cheese packets. Someone always manages to spill wine.

Jeanette appears before me. After some consideration, I smile.

She says, "I'm sorry, I've forgotten your name."

"That was my best wintery smile," I say.

"Yes, it was quite good."

I hope she thinks I would be a challenge, an insurmountable challenge.

Poor Pearl limps up. She has multiple sclerosis or something similarly awful and she begins talking about being with a number of her cats over the years as they died and it is not something she would wish on her vilest enemy and how she never learns from this experience and how it never becomes beautiful.

I leave the ladies to thrash this one out and exit through the courtyard, which is being torn up for some reason of regeneration. Or perhaps they're just going to pave it over with commemorative bricks. Last year, Easter services were held in this courtyard because the sanctuary had been vandalized. Worshipers arrived for the sunrise service and found the sound system ripped out, flowers smashed, balloons filled with green paint exploded everywhere. Teenagers going through an initiation into some gang, probably. Several goats in some fellow's yard were beaten and harassed that morning as well, the same group most likely being responsible, although the authorities claim there are no gangs in our town. No one was ever charged. The church would forgive them, that's the way the church works, but the man who owns the goats is still upset. Perhaps the poor creatures were meant to be scapegoats in the biblical sense, cast into the wilderness of suffering with all the sins of the people upon their heads.

There is such evil in the world, so much evil. I believe Jeanette is evil, though maybe she's more like one of those medically intuitive dogs they're developing or exploiting. The dogs don't suffer from their knowledge. That is, empathy is beside the point here; they can just detect that illness is present in a body before, sometimes long before, more standardized inquiry and tests confirm it. In Jeanette's case, though some groundwork is undoubtedly required, she's honing her instinct of arrival, appearing just before another is about to enter the incomprehensible refuge. She'll be writing a book about her experiences next.

I leave the courtyard and commence my walk home. It's not particularly pleasant but there is no alternative route, or, rather, the alternatives are equally dispiriting. Highways are being straightened and widened everywhere, with the attendant uprooted trees and porta-toilets for the workmen.

I navigate my passage across the first monstrous intersection, where a sign announces the imminent arrival of a dessert parlor named Better Than Sex. I would like to move to the country but the boy refuses. Besides, "the country" exists only in our fantasies anymore. When I was a child, the country was where overly exuberant family pets often found themselves. One of our dogs, Tank, who liked to wander and eat clothes and the dirt in flowerpots, was dispatched to the country, where he would have more room to run and play and do his mischief under the purview of a tolerant farmer. When I returned from school that afternoon, Tank was settling into his new home. My parents' explanations and assurances became so elaborate that I knew something terrible was being withheld from me.

Above me, billboards advertise gun shows, mobile-telephone plans and law firms that specialize in drunk-driving cases. I looked into renting a billboard recently but my application was rejected.

THE GREATEST PROSPERITY COMES TO ITS END,
DISSOLVING INTO EMPTINESS; THE MIGHTIEST

EMPIRE IS OVERTAKEN BY STUPOR AMIDST
THE FLICKER OF ITS FESTIVAL LIGHTS

—Rabindranath Tagore

it would have said.

The billboard people told me they didn't know who Rabindranath Tagore was and could not verify anything he might have thought. He was certainly foreign and his sentiments insurrectionary. As well, what he was saying wasn't advertising anything. This night I see that space I tried to claim depicts black-and-white cows painting the words EAT MORE CHIKEN on the side of a barn.

I could far more easily drive to church and spare myself the discomfort of walking through this wasteland but I am in no hurry to reach home. I never know whom I will be coming home to, whether it will be mother, father, wife or son. Often it is just my son, my boy, and matters are quite as they should be, but since the end of school things have become more volatile. We live alone, you understand, the child and I. He's nine, and the changes in this decade have been unfathomable. Indeed, it's a different civilization now. My parents, with whom we were very close, died last year. My wife left in the spring. She just couldn't feel anything for us anymore, she said, and was only trying to salvage the bit of life she could.

Dusty pickups speed by, gun racks prominent. Gun racks in vehicles have surged in popularity. Even expensive sedans display cradled weapons, visible through lightly tinted windows. People know their names and capabilities like they used to know those of baseball players. Not my boy, though. He doesn't know these things. He knows other things. For example, we planted a few trees in the yard after his mother left, fruit trees, citrus. The tree that bears the fruit is not the tree that was planted. He knows that much, it goes without saying.

It's almost dark now as I turn down our street. It's garbage day tomorrow and my neighbors have rolled their vast receptacles to the curb. The bins are as tall as the boy and they contain god knows what, and over and over again.

The door is unlocked, the lights are on. "Hi, Daddy," Colson says. He's in the kitchen making sandwiches for supper. "Daddy," he says, "we have to eat soon because I want to go to bed." I'm not disappointed that he's himself tonight, though more and more, given the situation, that self seems imaginary. He likes to play the Diné prayer songs tape as we eat, particularly the "Happy Birthday, My Dear Child" track. The chants are unintelligible but then the words *Happy Birthday Happy Birthday to You* arise in this morose intonation and he never tires of it.

In the morning my wife is in the yard, cutting back the orange tree. We rush out and prevent her from doing more. Summer is not the time to prune anything of course and we just planted the trees, they haven't even adjusted to being in the soil yet with the freedom of their roots to wander. She dismisses our concerns but flings down the little saw, which I have never seen before, and leaves, though were you to ask if we actually saw her leave we would have to say no. The tree looks terrible and with small cries we gather up the broken buds and little branches. Still, it will survive. It has not been destroyed, we assure each other, at least not this day. There is no question of our planting a replacement. This would not be a useful lesson to learn.

Perhaps she is annoyed because, since her absence, Colson has seldom tried to invoke her except in the broadest terms. That is because, he explains, she is only gone from us, not from the world she still inhabits. I think her arrival this morning was a shock to him and I doubt she will visit us again.

I pick up the curved saw. It looks new but now blond crumbs of wood cling to its shiny serrated teeth.

"Should we keep this?" I ask Colson.

He frowns and shakes his head, then shrugs and returns to the house. He's through with her. I wonder if somehow I have caused this latest unpleasantness. I have never known how to talk about death or the loss of meaning or love. I seek but will never find, I think.

I toss the saw into the closest container at the very moment I hear the trash truck moving imperiously down the street. It's garbage day. Garbage day! The neighborhood prepares for it with joy. Some wish it would arrive more than once a week.

Later I bring up the possibility of moving. We could have an orchard and bike trails and dig a pond for swimming. We could have horses. "You can pick up horses these days for a song," I say.

"A song?" the boy says. "What kind of song?"

But I can't think of any. I gaze at him foolishly.

"Like the Diné prayer songs," he suggests.

"Yes, but we don't even have to pray for horses. We can just get them."

Immediately I realize I have spoken infelicitously, without grace. He doesn't say anything right away but then he says, "You have to be here to prepare for not being here."

The voice is familiar to me because it is my mother's voice, though I find it less familiar than it once was. She's been in a grave for over a year now, my father with her. They'd been working at an animal sanctuary in their retirement and were returning home from a long day of caring for a variety of beasts. They had borrowed my car, as they were getting new tires for their own. I had planned to drive them home that night but the arrangement had been altered for some reason. We still don't know exactly what happened. A moment's inattention, possibly.

The sanctuary that was so important to them was controversial, as the animals were not native to this region, though the natives hardly enjoy grateful regard here, being considered either pests or game. It has since closed, the animals removed to what are referred to as other facilities, where some of them can still be visited. In fact, Colson and I went out to see one of the elephants my father was particularly fond of. There were two in the original preserve—Carol and Lucy—but they were separated, which seemed to me a dreadful decision. We visited Carol, who is an hour closer. She has some disease of the trunk that makes it difficult for her to eat, but someone was obviously still taking care of her. It wasn't a good visit, not at all. We felt bad that we had come. Knowing what we now know would break my parents' hearts, I think, but when Colson talks on their behalf they do not speak of elephants, those extraordinary beings. They do not speak of extraordinary matters. Colson does not bring them back to perform feats of omniscience or magicians' tricks. I don't know why he brings them back. I tried to prevent him at first. I appealed to his reasonableness, though in truth he is not particularly reasonable. I threatened him with psychiatric counseling, hours of irrelevant questions and quizzes. I told him his performances were futile and cruel. I teased him and even insulted him, saying that if he considered himself gifted or precocious he was sadly mistaken. Nothing availed.

When he enters these phases I become exhausted. Sometimes, I admit, I flee. He doesn't seem to need me to fulfill his conversations with the dead, if indeed they are conversations. They seem more like inhabitations. And they're harmless enough, if disorienting, though this morning's remark disturbs me, perhaps because his mother, my wife, had just made her unnecessary appearance. Really, why would she return only to hack wordlessly at our little tree? It seems so unlikely.

"Sorry?" I say.

"We are here to prepare for not being here," he says in my mother's soft, rather stroke-fuddled voice.

It's as though he is answering the very question posed at Come and See! I took him there once. Sometimes someone brings a child or grandchild, it's not unheard of. He listened attentively. No one expected him to contribute and everyone found him adorable. "Don't ever take me into that stupid room again," he later instructed me.

He may be right that it is a stupid room and that of all the great rooms he might or will enter, attentively and with expectation, it will on conclusion be the stupidest.

I study Colson. My dear boy is skinny and needs a haircut. He rubs his eyes the way my mother did. Don't rub your eyes so! we'd all exclaim. But I say nothing.

Colson says, "Then you're in the other here, where the funny thing is no one realizes you've arrived."

He sits down heavily at the kitchen table. "Would you like a cup of tea," I ask.

"That would be nice," he says in my mother's voice of wonderment.

But I can't find the tea. We haven't had tea in the house since they died. We'd keep it on hand just for them when they visited.

"I'll go out and get some right now," I say.

But he says not to bother. He says, "Just sit with me, talk with me."

I sit opposite my boy. I notice that the clock on the stove reads 9:47 and the stovetop is dusty, as though no one has cooked on it for a long time. I vow that I will cook a hot, nourishing and comforting dinner tonight. And I do, and we talk quietly then as well, though nothing of import is being decided or even said.

I find it easier to be with my father when Colson brings him. Though he always seemed rather inscrutable to me he now doesn't sadden me so. He would not accept an offer of tea that he suspected was unlikely to be provided. He was able to confer with the animals in a way my mother couldn't, and felt that great advances would soon be made in appreciating and comprehending animal consciousness, though these advancements would coincide with the dramatic worldwide decline of our nonhuman brothers and sisters. Once, I'm ashamed to say, I maudlinly brought up the Tank of my childhood, and my father said he had been shot by a sheriff's deputy who thought he was a stray, and that the man had also shot a woman's horse in winter, making the same claim, and that he had been reprimanded but neither fined nor fired. Yes. And that they had lied to me, my mother and father. It was Colson who told me this in my father's voice, Colson, who had never known Tank or felt his "happy fur," as I called it as a child. Bad, happy Tank. He ate his dinner from my mother's Bundt pan. It slowed him down some, having to work around the pan. He always ate his food too fast.

But this was the only time a disclosure occurred, and I am more cautious now in conversation. I find I want neither the past nor the future illuminated. But my discomfort is growing that my boy will find access to other people, people we do not know, like the woman the next town over who died in a fire of her own setting, or even one of Jeanette's unfortunate customers. That I will come home one evening and that Colson will be not himself but a stranger whose death means little to me and that even so we will talk quietly and inconsequentially and with puzzled desperation.

The week passes. Colson has a tutor in mathematics for the summer who is oblivious to the situation and I have the office I'm obliged to occupy. Colson wants to be an engineer or an architect but he has difficulty with concepts of scale and measurability. The tutor claims he's progressing nicely but Colson never talks about these hours, only stubbornly reiterates his desire to create soaring nonutilitarian spaces.

At the end of the week I return to Come and See! My passage through the construction zone is much the same. I suppose change will appear to come all at once. Suddenly there will be a smooth six-lane road with additional turning lanes and sidewalks with high baffle walls concealing a remaining landscape soon to be converted to housing. The walls will be decorated with abstract designs or sometimes the stylized images of birds. I've seen it before. Everyone's seen it before.

Jeanette is the only one there. I feel immediately uncomfortable and settle quickly into my customary chair. There is the paper clip, as annoying and meaningless a presence as ever.

"There's a flu going around," she says.

"The flu?" I say. "Everyone has the flu?"

"Or they're afraid of contracting the flu," she says. "The hospital is even restricting visitors. You haven't heard about the flu?"

"Only in the most general terms," I say. "I didn't think there was an epidemic."

"Pandemic, possibly a pandemic. We should all be in our homes, trying not to panic."

We wait but no one shows up. There's a large window in the room that looks out over the parking lot, but the lot is empty and continues to be empty. The sky is doing that strange thing it does, brightening fiercely before dark.

"Why don't we begin anyway?" she says. "'For where two are gathered in my name . . .' and so on. Or is it three?"

"Why would it be three?" I say. "I don't think it's three."

"You're right," she says.

She has a round pale face and small hands. Nothing about her is attractive, though she is agreeable, certainly, or trying to be.

"I'm not dying," I say. God only knows what possessed me.

"Of course not!" she exclaims, her round face growing pink. "Goodness!"

But then she says, "On Wednesday, Wednesday I think it was, it was certainly not Thursday, I was in this woman's room where the smell of flowers was overwhelming. You could hardly breathe and I knew her friends meant well, but I offered to remove the arrangements, there were more than a dozen of them, I'm surprised there wasn't some policy restricting their number, and she said, 'I'm not dying,' and then she died."

"You never know," I say.

"I hope they let me back soon."

"Why wouldn't they?"

"Thank you," she says quietly.

"I meant to say why would they?"

She stands up but then sits down again. "No," she says, "I'm not leaving."

"It's disgusting what you're doing, you're like the thief's accomplice," I say. "No one can be certain about these things."

Suddenly she appears not nervous or accommodating in the least.

We do not speak further, just sit there staring at each other until the sexton arrives and insists it's time to lock the place up.

At home, Colson is watching a television special on our dying oceans.

"Please turn that off," I say.

"Grandma wanted to watch it."

He has made popcorn and poured it into a large blue bowl that is utterly unfamiliar to me. It's a beautiful bowl of popcorn.

"You have another bowl like that?" I ask. "I want to make myself a drink."

He laughs like my wife might have when she still loved me, but then returns to watching the television.

"This is tragic," he says. "Can anything be done?"

"So much can be done," I say. "But everything would have to be different."

"Well," he sighs, "now Grandma and Poppa know. She wanted to watch it."

"Have you heard anything about a flu," I ask. "Does anyone you know have the flu?"

"Grandma died of the flu."

"No. They died in a car accident. You know that."

"Sometimes they get mixed up," he says.

Colson's the age I was when I was told about the country. Ten years later I'd be married. I married too young and unwisely, for sure.

"Do they sometimes tell you stories you don't believe?"

"Daddy," he says with no inflection, so I don't know what he means.

We finish the popcorn. He did a good job. Every kernel was popped. I take the bowl to the sink and rinse it out carefully, then take a clean dish towel from a drawer and dry it. It really is an extraordinarily lovely bowl. I don't know where to put it because I don't know where it came from.

A few days later my father is back. He was a handsome man with handsome thick gray hair.

"Son," he says, "I don't know what to tell you."

"It's all right," I say.

"No, it's not all right. I wish I knew what to tell you."

"Colson, honey," I say. "Stop."

"That's no way to have an understanding," he says. "Your mother and I just wish it were otherwise."

"Me too," I say.

"We wish we could help but there's so much they haven't figured out. You'd think by now, but they haven't."

"Who's they," I ask reluctantly.

But Colson doesn't seem to have heard me. He runs his fingers through his shaggy hair, which looks damp and hot. My boy has always run hot. I wonder if he's bathing and brushing his teeth. My poor boy, I think, my poor dear boy. Someone should remind him.

The following afternoon when Colson is with his tutor, who, I think, is deceiving both of us, though to all appearances he is a forthright and sincere young man, I drive almost one hundred miles to see Lucy, the other elephant. She is being sponsored by two brothers who maintain the county's graveyards, some sort of perpetual care operation, though to be responsible for an elephant is quite another matter, I would think. The brothers are extremely private and shun publicity. It was only after great effort that I learned anything about them at all or the actual whereabouts of Lucy. Someone—though neither of the brothers, a friend of the brothers is how I imagine him—agreed to show me around the grounds that she now occupies, but I find that once I reach the gate I cannot continue.

I turn back, ashamed, and more estranged from my situation than ever.

When I return home the tutor has left and Colson is putting his drawings in order, cataloging them by some method unknown to me. When my mother and father were taken from us so abruptly I knew that Colson was terribly bereaved. Still, he did not want my father's safari hat or his water-bottle holster. He did not want his watch or his magnetic travel backgammon. Nor did he want my mother's collection of ink pens, which I suggested would be ideal for his drawings.

He wanted no mementos. Instead he went directly to communication channels that are impossible to establish.

"Where were you, Daddy," Colson asks.

"Why, at work," I say quickly.

Surely I am back at my usual time. I seldom lie, indeed I cannot even remember the circumstances of my last falsehood. Why would he ask such a question? I kiss him and go into the kitchen to make myself a drink but then remember that I have stopped drinking.

"A lady came by today but I told her I didn't know where you were."

"What did she look like," I ask, and of course he describes Jeanette to a T.

I am so weary I can hardly lift my hand to my head. I must make dinner for us but I think the simplest omelet is beyond my capabilities now. I suggest that we go out but he says he has already eaten with the tutor. They had tacos made and sold from a truck painted with flowers and sat at a picnic table chained to a linden tree. I have no idea what he's talking about. My rage at Jeanette is almost blinding and I gaze at him without seeing as he orders and then reorders his papers, some of which seem to be marked with only a single line. I feel staggeringly innocent. That is the unlikely word that comes to me. Colson puts away his papers and smiles, a smile so radiant that I close my eyes without at all wanting to, and then rather gently somehow it is day again and I am striding through the bustling wasteland to Come and See! The reflection concerns Gregory of Nyssa. He is a popular subject but I am forever having difficulty in recalling what I already know about him. Something about the Really Real and its ultimate importance to us, though the Really Real is inaccessible to our understanding. Food for thought indeed, and over and over again.

When the meeting concludes and we are dismissed I practically hurl myself on Jeanette, who has uncharacteristically contributed nothing to the conversation this night.

"Don't ever come to my house again," I say.

"Was I really there, then? I thought I had the wrong place. Was that your son? A fine little boy. He can certainly keep a secret, can't he."

"I'll call the police," I say.

"Goodness," she laughs. "The police."

It sounded absurd, I have to agree.

"I was concerned about you," she says. "You haven't been here for a while. You've been avoiding us."

"Don't ever again . . ." I say.

"A delightful little boy," she continues. "But you mustn't burden him with secrets."

". . . come to my house." I couldn't be more insistent.

"Actually," she says, "no one would fault you if you stopped attending. How many times must we endure someone making a hash of Gregory of Nyssa? People are so tenacious when they should be free. Free!"

I begin to speak but find I have no need to speak. The room is more familiar to me than I would care to admit. Who was it whose last breath didn't bring him home?

Or am I the first?

The Mother Cell

S HE HAD BEEN LIVING THERE FOR A FEW MONTHS WHEN AN
acquaintance said, "I think you should meet this person. She's new.
She lives over by the conservation easement, the one with the moths."
She, too, was the mother of a murderer, that was the connection, but
Emily and this Leslie didn't hit it off particularly well, though they were
both fiercely nonjudgmental, of course. But then another mother, well
into her twilight years but unaccompanied by caregivers, moved down
less than three months later, around the Fourth of July, the time of
pie and fireworks and bunting-draped baby carriages. It was as though
some mysterious word had gotten out. These things happen, like when
highly allergic people, practically allergic to life itself, all gravitate to
some mountain in Arizona, or when a bayside town in Maine becomes
the locus for lipstick lesbians overnight. Penny arrived next, followed
by a few more mothers in quick succession until the influx stopped.

Nobody had to tell them outright that they had better be model
citizens. When a bear mauled a young couple out at the state park, the
mothers worried that the incident might be perceived as their inad-
vertent doing for weren't black bears shy as a rule? And this was an
extremely aggressive bear and small, hardly more than a cub, but determined and deliberate.

One mother, Francine, thought a hunter had shot the bear with a
hallucinogen prior to the attack, just for fun, to see what would happen.
"It must get boring for them to just shoot something and have it die,"
Francine said. "Someone shot it with a mind-altering drug."

"Most everything around here has been shot out for years now,"
another mother said. "Where did this bear even come from?"

"Exactly," Francine said.

The eldest mother had the sugar and was so arthritic she had
long enjoyed the awe of X-ray technicians. She was half blind too

and described herself as dumb as a box of nails, but she knew how to keep on living. Whereas Penny, who wasn't even forty—she'd had Edward when she was sixteen—died of lung cancer without having ever smoked a cigarette, even in the worst of times.

It was Penny's death that brought them together, though they weren't about to take up the task of writing to her boy in prison. Penny had liked to say there was a part in each of us that had never sinned and that was the part of Edward she addressed when she wrote to him. But as the eldest mother pointed out, that was the same part that was never born and will never die. It was thus irrelevant. Better to address a plate with a covered bridge printed on it.

They still thought of themselves as being seven in number even though without Penny it was six. In general they believed that the dead remained around, fulfilling all but the most technical requirements of residency on earth, yet relieved of the banality of daily suffering. In this respect, they could argue, though they never did, that their children's victims weren't as bad off as commonly assumed.

Fathers didn't flock like this, they agreed. Leslie had stuck it out with a father the longest. Their boy, Gordon, had done something terrible, just terrible. And he had been one of those kids who had never caused a bit of trouble. This was scarcely believable given what happened but there was the record, their boy, Gordon's record, or rather the lack of it. Leslie said that after the trial, the outcome of which was never in doubt, she and the father tended more and more to behave as though they were performing before an audience. Not a sold-out house, to be sure, but a respectable enough number in attendance to ensure that the show wouldn't close for a while. When the lights dimmed and they were alone, except for the *audience*, the spectators and listeners, it became all choked poise and memory pieces between them, with the occasional brilliant burst of anger and loathing.

"It essentially became vanity," Leslie said.

The eldest mother said, "But what can you expect from men? They're like a virus with a penchant for the heart. They got a special affinity for attacking the heart. You can recover, sure, but the damage is done."

The fathers, it turned out, had all gone back to work. To a man they had returned to their places of employment. And they were doing all right. I'm doing, they'd say, when asked. Some had remarried. One had had his impulsive vasectomy reversed.

Barbara's daughter had been dubbed the End of the Dream murderer by the media, for that was what the girl said in the course of her serial rampage.

"It's only her who knows if she said it," Barbara argued. "Her saying she said it doesn't make it so. She was always that kind of kid, saying all kinds of crap and expecting you to believe her."

"Was she Buddhist," Leslie asked.

"Jesus no," Barbara said. "She didn't even do yoga. She didn't do nothing until she did."

"You can be a murderer without being a liar," the eldest mother said.

None of the mothers had pets. The children had all had pets of one kind or another and homes had to be found for them. There were hundreds of people out there who keenly wanted murderers' pets and by their very ambition and craving were utterly inappropriate as adopters. Sometimes these pets' stories ended badly too.

"It takes sixty-three days to make a dog," the eldest mother said. "Two hundred and seventy days to make a human being, give or take a few."

The mothers were atypical in that each had brought forth only one child. In their day, two had been the norm. Now three was the new two, whereas one was the old zero.

"People had more interesting thoughts before mass inoculations," Barbara maintained. "More generous and less damaging thoughts."

"Who knows what's in all the inoculations they give the little babies," Francine said. "Oh, they tell you, but still you don't know. How could you?"

"Minds used to move like rivers but they don't want our minds moving like that," Emily said. "They want to channelize our thinking, and some people can't tolerate their minds being dammed. They noticed it right away, whereas others never do, and they can't tolerate it."

"Damned," Leslie murmured.

"Exactly," Francine said.

Francine's boy had claimed that the family he'd slaughtered would have killed hundreds of people if they'd been left to prosper.

"You mean because they were into making pharmaceuticals or beer?" Barbara asked.

"I'm not defending him, but it could very well have been true."

"Genuine thinking is rare," the eldest mother said.

"I saw a sculpture of the river god once," Leslie said. "It was the most frightening work of art I've ever witnessed. Someone blew it up, I heard. It was just too frightening."

Emily looked at the bottle she was drinking water from. "How can it be pure if it's enhanced?" she said to no one in particular.

Pam then commenced to tell a story about gods. It was rendered fairly incoherent in her telling but it concerned a group of lost Greek sailors on a fishing boat who happened upon a desolate island where they found an old man in a hut attended by a bedraggled, almost featherless though immense bird and a large old hairless goat whose nipples were nonetheless rosy and whose udders were full of milk.

Yuck, thought Emily.

"It turns out," said Pam, "to make a long story short, that the decrepit old man was Jupiter, whose reign as supreme ruler of the universe was long past. The goat was his old nurse, Amalthea, who had once suckled him, and the bird was the fearsome eagle who once carried in its claws the god's devastating thunderbolts. When Jupiter heard from the sailors that any temples that remained were in ruins and then realized that all he remembered had disappeared, he began to sob and the eagle screamed and the old goat bleated, all in the most terrible anguish. The sailors were so frightened that they fled back to their boat. Among the crew was a learned Russian professor of philosophy, and he was the one who told them the old guy was Jupiter and—"

"There just happened to be a learned Russian professor of philosophy on this fishing boat?" Emily said.

"That's a melancholy story," Leslie said. "I'm not sure why."

"Birds are sad," Francine said. "Remember when Penny was here and she tried to establish a sanctuary for unwanted parrots and the town shut her down? They said there was no permitting process for such a thing. Penny said those birds cried when they were taken off her property. They knew. They knew their last chance had come and gone."

The mothers were silent.

Then Barbara said, "Well, I don't know why you told that story about the old god, but the nice thing about it was that he wasn't alone at the end."

"What about the one we got now," Emily asked.

"The one what?"

"The god we got now. Do you think somebody in the future will be telling a story about finding him exiled to some desolate island and crying when he learns that everything he had fashioned and understood has vanished and that he is subject to the same miserable destiny as any created thing?"

"Probably," someone finally said.

"I feel uneasy even thinking about the river god," Leslie said. "But it's gone now, I've heard, blown up. They're not even calling it an act of vandalism."

"If we lived in Palestine," Pam said, "and my boy had done there what he'd done here, the Israeli people would have blown up my home." She imagined herself being allowed to take from it whatever she could carry, though, but maybe not.

One of the mothers said that was called collective punishment.

"They might as well have blown up my home," Barbara said. "I've never had one. I butterfly around and always have."

She was living in a motel out on the highway that was next to a burned-out gas station and a knife outlet. The management of the motel was doing its part for the environment by changing the sheets and towels only after repeated requests, a notion picked up from the pieties of the better chains. Barbara was getting by with a debit card she'd found behind the bed. It was in the original paper sleeve with the PIN written on it. Some poor devil with shaky handwriting was out in the world not realizing his account was being discreetly drained.

The eldest mother made every effort to flex her arthritic hands and modestly succeeded. She couldn't lift a finger to save herself even if that was all it took, which it never was. She felt the darkness closing in without exactly seeing it. This was not unusual. Life was like a mirror that didn't know what it was reflecting. For the mirror, reflections didn't even exist. Whenever she saw a mirror where she didn't expect it, she thought: Poor old woman, how sad she looks.

"I had just said to the waitress that what I'd like was a nice cup of coffee," one of the mothers was remembering, "when the police came in. I had to go with them and tell them what I knew. Of course I knew nothing. He had never presented his dark plan to me. I sometimes feel he committed that crime in another state of existence."

"We don't live in the same time as our children, if that's what you mean," Pam ventured graciously.

"But here we are," Leslie said. "It doesn't seem right, does it, and what are we supposed to do now? What shall we do?"

Bathed in tender moonlight, everything looked lethal, the weeds in their beds, the bottled water, the ladder on its side, the painted nails of the mothers' feet in sandals.

"Have any of you performed community service," Emily asked, and then blushed at their silence. Clearly what had been done by the off-spring of those in the garden was beyond the salve of community service.

"When I first got here," one of the mothers said, "I would take electric bills out of people's mailboxes and pay them."

"Did anyone ever make themselves available for comment," Barbara asked. "I instinctively knew not to make myself available. And they respect that. Even the persistent ones give up after a while."

"I retained a spokesperson but it was a big mistake," Pam said. "Did anyone come up with an extenuating circumstance in the sentencing phase?"

The mothers shook their heads.

"Well," Francine said, "Allen called 911 when his girlfriend cut off her fingers and toes, though admittedly anyone would have sought emergency assistance. But it certainly might have affected him, seeing his girlfriend of only a few months cut off her fingers and toes."

"What did she think they were?" Emily wondered. "That she'd want to get rid of them."

"Did you say minutes," Barbara asked. "That's like—"

"Months," Francine told her. "A girlfriend of a few months."

"I thought you said he was a sociopath."

"He was a sociopath, a harmless sociopath at the time. He didn't care for society or crowds. He didn't like traffic, bars, sitting on planes. Then he found a girlfriend. I had great hopes for her but it turned out she was nuttier than he was."

"In her fashion," Emily said.

"One human family," the eldest mother said. "That's what we are. That's what we've got to remember. This is Thyself. It should always be spoken of any creature to keep us in mind of the similarity of their inmost being with ours."

"This is Thyself," Pam repeated. She made fists of her hands and struck her breasts softly.

Emily thought of the several minutes she had spent yesterday looking out her window at the neighbor's cat taking a dump. It didn't cover up its deposit after it finished, just shook itself and walked away. It was a large white cat with a shining red sore on its head. The neighbor said she was allowing the matter of the sore to run its course. The cat still had a good appetite.

"I live beside a woman who lost a boy in the war, and she lords it over me something awful," Leslie said. "She's a police dispatcher, and when I smile at her in greeting she hisses at me, actually hisses. She planted a cherry tree, I guess for the boy, and it got the gall. It's a few years old now and it's got this enormous gall. I know it must be breaking her heart. I want to tell her that some galls can be beneficial. They return nitrogen to the soil, which is good. Or in other ways they can be beneficial to man."

"You know a lot, Leslie," Pam said, "but I don't think this would give that woman any peace, coming from you."

"It would be suicide to speak like that," one of the mothers said.

"We must behave here as though we didn't exist," the eldest mother said.

"Didn't exist?" said Barbara. "But we do."

"What I like about our group is that it isn't a support group," Francine said. "I couldn't handle a support group. I would consider it suspect in the extreme."

They all agreed that any kind of support group for the mothers of celebrity killers would be in poor taste.

"Ours is a delicate situation," the eldest mother said. She requested that someone, it didn't matter who, light the candles.

Leslie said, "My first thought in the morning and my last thought at night is: We are going to be asked to leave."

"I've still got the Popsicle-stick box he made as a kid," Francine said. "I keep the kitchen sponge in it."

"That can't be sanitary," Emily noted.

"I threw away the handprint. You know how they make plaster-of-paris casts of little kids' hands for Mother's Day in kindergarten and mount them on blocks of wood?"

"That would be worth something on eBay," Barbara said. "People are such creeps."

"What have we been discussing tonight, actually," Leslie asked. "If I had to guess, I'd say we've been talking about God."

"That's a stretch," Barbara said.

"I'd say that saying that is making a pretty safe bet," Francine said. "It's sort of vague. Not to hurt your feelings, Leslie."

"OK," Leslie said.

"It's like each time we meet, you think we should have a subject or something. It's not as though we're going down a stairwell, one step at a time, putting what's happened behind us, one step at a time."

"OK, OK," Leslie said.

The candles would not light as the cups they were in had filled with the rainwater of days past. "We should be going anyway," one of the mothers said. Candles always discomfited this one. Vigils, sex, dinner, prayer . . . they had too many uses.

"I wish I had dropped him as an infant out of his snuggle sack on the rocks," Barbara said loudly.

Emily had heard her voice this absolutely useless sentiment before. It was always a sure sign that the evening was winding down.

"We've settled nothing," the eldest mother said. "We cannot make amends for the sins of our children. We gave birth to mayhem and therefore history. Oh, ladies, oh, my friends, we have resolved nothing and the earth is no more beautiful."

She struggled to her feet and was helped inside. Her old knees creaked like doors. She always liked to end these evenings on an uncompromising note. Of course it was all just whistling in the dark, but sometimes she would conclude by saying that despite their clumsy grief and all the lost and puzzling years that still lay ahead of them, the earth was no less beautiful.

Craving

T HEY WERE IN A BAR FAR FROM HOME WHEN SHE REALIZED HE was falling to pieces. That's what she'd thought: Why, he's falling to pieces. The place was called Gary's.

"Honey," he said. He took the napkin from his lap and dipped it in his gin. He leaned toward her and started wiping her face, gently at first but then harder. "Oh, honey," he said in alarm. His tie rested in his Mignon Gary as he was pressed forward. He was overweight and pale but his hair was dark and he wore elegant two-toned shoes. Before this, he had whispered something unintelligible to her. No one watched them. Sweat ran down his face. His drink toppled over and fell on them both.

She was wearing a green dress and the next day she left it behind in the hotel along with the clothes he had been wearing, the tan suit and the tie and the two-toned shoes. The clothes had let them down. The following night they were in a different hotel. It was near the coast and their room had a balcony from which they could see the distant ocean. They knew how to drink. They sought out the slippery places that tempted one to have a drink. Every place was a slippery place.

Denise and Steadman watched the moon rising. Denise played the game she did with herself. She transferred all her own convulsive, compulsive associations to Steadman. She gave them all to him. This was not as difficult as it might once have been because all her thoughts concerned Steadman anyway. Though her mind became smooth and flat and borderless, she wasn't thinking anything so she never felt lost. It was quiet until a deeper silence began to unfold, but she was still all right. Then the silence became like a giant hand mutely offered. When she sensed the giant hand, she got up quickly. That giant hand was always too much for her. She went into the other room and made more drinks. They took suites whenever possible. The gin seemed to need a room of its own. She came back out to the balcony.

"Let's drink this and go get something to eat," she said.

They found themselves in the dining room of the hotel. It was claustrophobic and the service was poor. They sat on a cracked red leather banquette under a mirror. On a shelf between them and the mirror was a pair of limp rubber gloves. Denise didn't bring them to Steadman's attention. She reasoned that they had been left behind by some maintenance person. They gazed at a table of seven who were telling loud stories about traffic accidents they had witnessed. They seemed to be trying to top one another.

"The French have spectacular wrecks," a man said.

"I love that Jaws of Life thing," a woman said. "Have you ever seen that thing?" She had streaked blond hair and a heavily freckled bosom.

"I saw an incredible Mexican bus crash once," a small man said. But his remark was immediately dismissed by the group.

"A Mexican wreck? There's nothing extraordinary about a Mexican wreck . . ."

"It's true. The landscape's such a void that there's not the same effect . . ."

Steadman and Denise listened attentively. Denise didn't have a car-crash story and if she ever did she wouldn't tell it, she decided.

The waitress told them the previous couple at their booth had given her a five-dollar tip but had torn the bill in half, forcing on her the ignominy of taping it back together. She said she despised people, present company excepted, and told them not to order the veal. If they ordered the veal, she told them, she would not serve it, which would be cause for her dismissal but she didn't care.

They decided to have another couple of drinks, and return to their room.

The room was not welcoming. It had seen too many people come and go. It was wearying to be constantly reminded that time passes and everything with it, purposelessly.

Denise watched Steadman place himself on the bed. He lay on his back. The room surrounded them. For a while, Denise lay on the bed too, thinking. Where had it gone, it had gone someplace. The way they were. Then she went into the other room, where the writing table and television set were. Their new traveling bags were there, big soft black ones. She turned off the lights, feeling a little dizzy. She wrung her hands. They should go someplace, she thought. There was tomorrow, something had to be done with it. She reviewed the day's events. Her mind was like a raven, picking over gravel with its oily, luminous feathers. She could almost hear it as it hopped across the small stones but she couldn't quite, thank God. Then she heard someone passing by in the corridor, laughing. A thin breeze entered the room and she thought of the distant water as they had seen it from the balcony, folded like a package between two enormous buildings. She looked at their bags, heaped in a corner. Night was a bad time. Night would simply give her no rest. Steadman was quiet now but he might get up soon and they would have their conversation. It was a mess, they were in an awful mess. He didn't know how much longer he could stand this and so on and so on ... Her eyes ached and her throat was dry, she hated this room. It, it just didn't like them. She could hear it saying, Well, there's a pathetic pair, how did they ever find each other? She'd like to set fire to the room. Or beat it up. She could hit, no question. There was someone passing in the hall again, laughing, the fools. The room stared at her lidlessly. Perhaps they could leave tonight. They would go down—Denise and Steadman, Steadman and Denise—past the night clerk trying to read a book—*10,000 Dreams Interpreted*. She remembered what the book looked like: red and falling apart. They had done this before, left in the night when the moon was setting and the sun rising. To get out while the moon was setting, that's exactly what she wanted. She lay down on the floor. The room was not letting them breathe the way they had to; it was scandalous that they'd been given this room instead of another. Listening to Steadman breathe, she tried to breathe. She wished it were June. It was June once and they were somewhere and a mockingbird sang from midnight to daybreak, or so it seemed, imitating other birds, and Steadman had made a list of all the birds he recognized in the mockingbird's song. He learned things and then remembered them, that's just how he was.

Denise crept across the carpet toward Steadman's bed and held on to it. His face was turned toward her, his eyes open, looking at her. That was Steadman, he knew everything but he didn't share. He made her feel like a little animal sometimes, one with little animal emotions and breathing little animal devotions. She would ask him for the list very quietly, very nicely, the little piece of paper with the names of the birds, where was it, he was always putting it someplace and she had already gone through their bags, their beautiful traveling bags, ready for the larger stage.

"Steadman," she said reasonably.

But how could he hear her? This annoying room was listening to every word she uttered. And what did it know? It couldn't know anything. It couldn't climb from the basement into a life of spiritual sunshine like she was capable of doing, not that she could claim she had. The individual in the hall howled with laughter at this. There were several of them out there now, a whole gang, the ones from the dinner party, probably, the spectacular-wrecks people, just shrieking.

At once Denise realized that the gang was herself and it was morning. Her hands hurt terribly. They were as pink as though they'd been boiled. She'd hurt them somehow. Actually, they were broken. Incredible.

She stared at them in the car on the drive to the hospital. Those hands weren't going to do anything more for Denise for a while.

The doctor in the emergency room wrapped them up, the left first, then the right, indifferently. Even so, some things fascinated him.

"We've got a kid on the third floor," he said. "He was born with all the bones in his head broken. Now there's a problem. Are you aware that our heads are getting smaller? Our skulls are smaller than those of our brothers in the Paleolithic period. Do you know why? I'll tell you why. Society's the answer. Society has reduced our awareness skills. Personal and direct contact with the natural world requires a continual awareness, but now we just don't have it. We're aware of dick-all."

Denise looked at her hands covered in the casts. They were like little dead creatures safely concealed in snow-covered burrows. Ugly dishes don't break, she thought. But they had.

"Try to stay alert, miss," the doctor said, playfully slapping her now utterly exempt hands.

Then they were driving slowly away from the coast through small towns. "I'm tired, Denise," Steadman was saying. "I'm really tired."

"Yes, yes," Denise said. She was thinking of all the nice things she would do for this man she loved.

"I think we should stay somewhere until your hands are better," he said. "Rent a house. Get some rest."

"I agree, I agree. No more hotels. We'll get a house for a while." She was crazy about him, everything was going to be fine.

He turned off the road at a sign that said CAFE REALITY and into a parking lot. Actually, it said CAPE REALTY. Denise laughed. "And we'll stop drinking," she said. "We'll just stop."

"Sure," Steadman said.

"I don't want to see a lot of places, though," Denise said. "I don't want to choose."

She sat in the car. She had ruined that room back there. Embarrassing, she thought. But the room had fought back. It made one think, really.

Steadman returned to the car and put several photographs of a house on her lap. It had a porch in front and a pool in back and was surrounded by a tall, whitewashed wall.

"I'm going to use this month wisely," Denise assured him.

"Good," Steadman said.

The important thing was to stop drinking. If she could get twenty-four hours away from last night, she could start stopping. Maybe they could get rid of all the glasses in the house. Glasses were always calling to you. Maybe this house wouldn't have any. Their drinking had brought them here. Denise was determined to learn something, to leave this place refreshed. She yawned nervously. Steadman's forehead was beaded with sweat, the back of his jacket was dark with sweat as he lifted their bags from the trunk.

In one of the rooms, a young woman was sweeping the floor. "I'm the cleaning woman," she said. "Are you renting this place? I'll be through in a minute." She wore shorts and red high-top sneakers. "I'll put on a shirt," she said. "I didn't know anyone was coming. I always sweep without a shirt." With her was a small dog with black saucery eyes, thick ears and double dewclaws.

"What is that," Denise asked. It was one of the strangest dogs she had ever seen.

"Everyone asks that," the girl said. "It's a Lundehund. It's used for hunting puffins in Norway."

"But what's it doing here?"

"He comes with me while I clean. You'll probably ask next how I ended up with a dog like this. I can't remember the ins and outs of it. I started off wanting a Welsh corgi, the ones you always see in pictures of the queen, greeting her on her return from somewhere or bidding her farewell as she departs. I'm not English, of course. I've never been to England. The Lake District, the Cotswolds, the white cliffs of Dover . . . you couldn't prove any of them by me. I was born in this town and I've never been anywhere else. But I make sure that everything I have comes from other places, though I try to avoid China. This shirt comes from Nepal, and my perfume's from Paris. I realize it's wrong to subject caged civet cats to daily genital scrapings just to make perfume, but it was a present. My sneakers were put together in Brazil and you're probably about to say that Brazilian laborers make only pennies an hour, but I did purchase them secondhand. See the little stones in these earrings? They come from Arizona. Navajoland."

She had put on a shirt and was buttoning it as she spoke.

Denise wasn't going to allow the cleaning woman to unnerve her. Her hands throbbed and itched. She had to drink a lot of water, lots and lots of water.

"You shouldn't be here, should you," she said to the Lundehund. "You should be scrambling up and down rocky crevices, carrying birds' eggs in your teeth."

It was disgusting and sad, Denise thought, but a great many things were. One's talents should be used.

The woman and the grotesque dog were clearly fresh catastrophes. She was trying to begin and then these catastrophes appeared immediately. Though it wasn't what you thought that was important, but how you acted. Or was it the other way around?

Denise took leave of them and went into a narrow monochromatic room that overlooked the pool. There were empty bookcases over a single bed and numerous indentations in the hardwood floor as though a woman wearing high heels in need of repair had moved back and forth across it, again and again. Her own shoes, too, were run-down. She kicked them off. She sighed, and later it seemed the water in the pool was darker and the shadows were different. Her hair smelled of gin, and her skin. There was someone in the pool, a man, but he left quickly when she got up. It was just the liquor leaving, she thought.

She could understand that. The doors in the house were sliding ones she could move with her foot. Her hands bobbed in the casts beside her as she walked. Steadman was where she had last seen him but he was sitting down. The cleaning woman was holding him in her arms and he was weeping loudly.

"I just saw your husband," Denise said. "He was swimming in the pool. No one should be using the pool now that we're here, should they? We've rented this place, after all. And we don't need a cleaning woman either. This place is clean enough. We'll keep it clean."

"I don't have a husband," the cleaning woman said. "You have a husband." Her shirt was off again, she just couldn't seem to keep that shirt on. She had been combing Steadman's hair back with her fingers. His tears had dried and he looked like a boy, washed and fresh.

While Denise was musing on this, the Lundehund rose softly up against her side and began chewing on the casts.

"Get down," the cleaning woman scolded him. "That's a naughty boy."

"You should allow dogs their pleasures," Denise said. "They don't live long." She had intended this remark to make the woman sad, but apparently everyone realized the truth of it. It had no effect because it was something that was already known.

"You're in terrible shape," the cleaning woman said. "Both of you. Let me come a few hours each day. I'll make the meals and keep things tidy. Drink, drank, drunk, no more. That was there but now you're here. This is the subjunctive here. Look," she said, "it's going to be all right."

It's like when a person dies and someone says it's going to be all right, Denise thought. So stupid! This woman wanted to be Steadman's mistress, she could tell. She'd been pressing her lips against his temple and laying her long breasts against his chest. But she could only be the mistress of some delusion, Denise thought triumphantly. The woman gathered up her things, the Lundehund's nails clicked across the floor, the door closed and they were gone.

Denise looked at Steadman. She was crazy about him. Though it wasn't easy, this house. It was small and hot in the dark. They hadn't had a drink in hours. She looked at Steadman's watch: sixteen hours, exactly. Maybe they shouldn't try to get better here. That was the problem with houses. They belonged to other people, even if those people were far away, but a hotel room didn't belong to anybody. Maybe they should just get back in the car. This was the law, the *doctrine*, of maybe. She believed in this, and in her love for Steadman, and these were her beliefs.

She smiled at him.

"Denise," he said. "Please."

She was standing in the dark and he was still sitting. She wanted a drink badly. She closed her eyes and swallowed. You are what you drink, she thought, but here they were nothing, they were nowhere. Maybe she should say farewell to love, she thought. It gives you more balance. She should have considered this long ago. She stared at Steadman in the dark.

At last he said, "Groceries."

She had been thinking about the state they were in. They executed people in this state for certain things, but before they could do it the person had to realize what the results, the significance, of execution would be. That was the law. So of course you pretended you didn't realize. As long as you could do that they had to leave you alone.

"So," Steadman said. "What do you want?"

She felt a little Februaryish, as she always did in that forlorn, short, spiky month.

"Let's not get groceries now," she said. Groceries meant more than food. They implied duration. She didn't want that here. "There's nothing to drink here. It's fantastic, isn't it? Let's lie down. Would you hold me? I can't hold you."

She raised her hands, moving them up and down in their white casts. She remembered a bar they'd been in. Was it Gary's? There were framed hunting and fishing pictures on the walls. A woman was holding two snow geese by their necks. She held them high, in gloved hands, close to her head, as though they were earrings.

"Where are you going," Denise asked.

"I'm not going anywhere," Steadman said. He ran his hands across his face.

"You're not going to get a drink, are you?"

"No," Steadman said. "I am not."

Denise wandered back into the bedroom again. The man had returned to the pool and was swimming with powerful strokes. She heard herself speaking to him, asking him to leave. "Be reasonable," she said. "We're here now. You can't be here now that we are." She said this and that, choosing her words carefully, shouting from inside the house. The man pulled himself out and stood, dripping. Then he crouched and she was afraid of this, she had worried that something like this would happen, that he would begin to dismantle the pool somehow, that he would begin by pulling at the big submerged light at the deep end, rotating it, twisting it out. Water was spilling and buckling everywhere and the light was trailing its cord behind it, like a huge white eye on its long stalk.

Denise couldn't stay here a moment longer. She was trembling, she had to get out. They would get in the car, she and Steadman, they would drive away and never come back. They loved driving in the dark and drinking, mixing cocktails in paper cups, driving around. They had done it a lot. They would mix up some drinks and go out and tease cars. That's what they called it, Steadman and Denise. They'd tailgate them, pounce on them out of nowhere. Crazy stuff.

"Steadman!" she called. He knew what she wanted, he knew what they would do, that this had been a mistake. He opened the door to their car, and she smelled the lovely gin. It was in a glass from before, wedged between the seats.

They drove down the street, picking up speed. They passed a house with a wrought-iron sign hanging from a post. The design was of a wrought-iron palm tree and the wrought-iron waves of a sea. Below it, where the custom lettering was supposed to be, it said YOUR NAME. Delightful! Denise thought. They had ordered it just the way it had been advertised.

"God, that was funny," she said. People could be so funny.

"It really was," Steadman said.

They were driving fast now. They were so much alike, they were just alike, Denise thought. "Roll my window down, please," she said.

Steadman reached across her and did.

"Oh, thank you," she said. Warm, humid, lovely air passed across her face. "Go faster."

He did. She giggled.

"Slow down," she said, "speed up. That road there."

Steadman did, he did.

They had left the town behind. "Turn the lights off, maybe," she said.

They rocketed down the road in the dark. Before them was nothing, but behind them a car was gaining.

She turned and saw the two wild lights moving closer. They're going to tease us, she thought. "Faster," she said.

But the car, weaving, was almost upon them and then, with a roar, was beside them. It was all outside them now.

"There it is, Steadman," Denise said. It all just hung there for an instant before the car swerved around them and turned in inches beyond their front bumper. Then, whatever was driving it slammed on the brakes.